THE ORB OF EVIL

Birds of all feather raced past, squawked, and fled to and fro in more panic than even an approaching storm would have produced. Far away, a circle of blackness crawled across the countryside at the pace of a man walking.

This wonder was huge, a hundred cubits in diameter, a moving half-orb which crawled back and forth in a jagged path. It was dark against the bright daylight, utterly black, a piece of night into which Sir Palador could not even begin to see.

And it was evil. The Knight of Pallas felt a tremor go through him as instinct told him just how vile the thing was. Even as he watched, a sparrow screeched, fluttered, and then dropped past the window. It hit the paving below, dead as a stone. Another bird fell farther away.

By Dennis McCarty
Published by Ballantine Books:

FLIGHT TO THLASSA MEY
WARRIORS OF THLASSA MEY
LORDS OF THLASSA MEY
ACROSS THE THLASSA MEY

ACROSS THE THLASSA MEY

Dennis McCarty

A Del Rey Book

BALLANTINE BOOKS • NEW YORK

The author would like to dedicate this volume to his father, Paul Dwight McCarty, who taught him that even Murphy's Law cannot stand up to a truly persistent man.

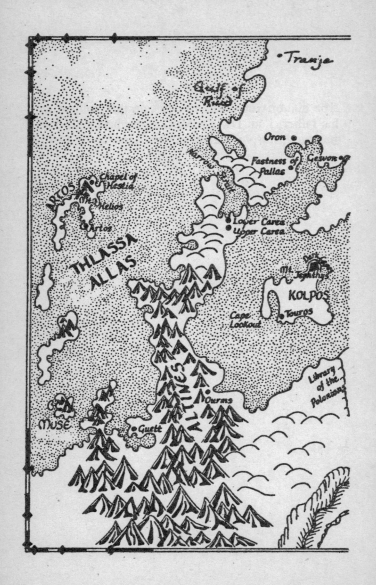

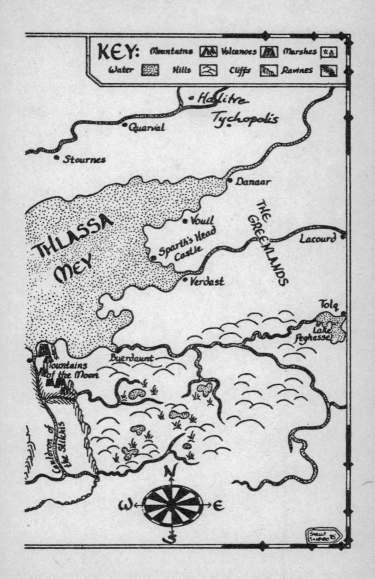

KEY: Mountains 🅰 Volcanoes 🅰 Marshes 🅰
Water 🅰 Hills 🅰 Cliffs 🅰 Ravines 🅰

• Halitre

Tychopolis

• Quarval

• Stournes

• Danaar

THLASSA MEY

• Vouil

Sparth's Head Castle

THE GREENLANDS

Lacourd

• Verdast

Tole

the Lake Pyghesse

Mountains of the Moon

Buerdaunt

Cauldron of the Silichis

N
W   E
S

Chapter One:
Velocipod

FLIN THE BRIGAND ran his fingers along the huge warhorse's rippling neck. "So here's my pet," he said with a shiny grin. "You brought him up soundly, Putney, I'll hand you that." He stepped back and admired the beast. "By Tyche's dice, I'd swear he's a fathom across the rump."

"Same as my woman," Putney replied with a smile of his own. "And twice as handsome." He was an experienced hostler; he had kept his stable in the city of Stournes for thirty years. "I'll say you true, Sir. I told myself you were crazy as a hazed hen when you first crowed about buying the finest destrier colt ever to pull a tussock. But he's growed into the finest *I've* ever seen. Though why you wanted him brung up here in Stournes is more than I can guess."

"I've my reasons," Flin said with a wink. "I didn't want other knights to get a look at him; they'd never dare joust against me."

"I don't doubt it. He's as fast as he is big, and smarter than either. If you hold up *your* end, there's no man can beat the two of you."

Flin rubbed the horse's broad nose and whispered a loving word into one flicking ear. The beast bobbed its head, then nuzzled the front of his doublet for the apple he had hid there. "Oho, so it's a bribe you want? Here you go." He tossed the apple to the animal, which jerked its head and caught the fruit on the fly. Spittle and apple seeds dribbled from one side of its mouth as it chewed happily. "You're a fine one," Flin said with a laugh. "After Princess Bessina, you're the great love of my life, do you know that?'' He laughed even louder when the horse tossed its head up and down as if it were nodding.

"I didn't want a soul to know about him," Flin said to Putney. "That's why I kept him under wraps. The year's first tournament starts a few days from now in Tranje and I'm going to win enough armor and trap to founder a galley. That's my plan at least. If folks know I've got him, they won't let me lay a single bet."

The older man laughed. "You're a regular conniver, aren't you? Well, I've oated him and curried him—myself, mind you—and watched you train him through a year. It's sad I'll be to see him go. What a beauty." He stood back and shook his head. "What yer Bessina must think; she must be swearin' you've got a mistress in Stournes."

"I have," Flin said with a smirk. "Is that what you are, Velocipod? Are you my mistress? Oh-oh. Better not make him mad—he's too big for that."

"You've spent more gold on him than any sane man ever did on any mistress. I hope it's worth it to you."

"It will be, though I have to tell you, tournaments are bland sport for an animal like him." He cocked his head. "What we need is a good war; that would put the glow on all our cheeks."

Putney spat. "Nay, nay, don't say such things. You never know when the gods are listening."

"They don't listen to me," Flin said. "They'd have red faces if they ever did. No, I'm not worried. We've had twenty years of Palamon the Peacemaker. Twenty quiet years—and a knight's business has turned mighty soft and boring."

"Us commons bless him for it, Sir."

Flin winked at the older man. "Don't be so selfish. By Tyche's dice, a fellow needs excitement. This peace is dull as a cloth merchant's mind." He took Velocipod's lead line and walked toward the stable door. The horse clopped after him, so large it had to duck its head as it followed him out of the building. "But a man has to live with disappointment, I suppose." Flin leaned his head toward the older man. "I'll get by. A tournament here, chase a few bandits there. It's not much, but it keeps me from going completely stale."

"I warrant there's not much that would make *you* go stale, Sir Flin." Putney followed Flin into the street. "But tell me now, will you be bringin' this horse back here? We'll all be missing him."

Flin vaulted onto his palfrey, the light horse he rode for

travel. A warhorse was ridden only in combat, after all. "I'll bring him back at the end of the season, old fellow. That is, if I don't have to build a castle around him to keep him from getting either filled full of arrows or stolen. His name will be on a lot of lips before the fortnight's out, I know that."

"Farewell, Sir Flin. I'll look for the day."

"Farewell, Putney." Flin adjusted himself in his saddle, grasped Velocipod's lead rope in his right hand, then rode down the street to join his squire. He let that young man lead the packhorse, as he always did, but Flin himself led the big warhorse as the two of them rode out of Stournes. Passersby gawked at the huge beast, and children ran through the dust behind the animal. That made Flin's smile even broader; he would have a lot of fun, a lot of laughs, at the expense of many rich knights. He would have to do it fast, though, before word got out about his new mount.

They headed toward Tranje, the fief ruled by Arcite the Balladeer, King Palamon's brother-in-law. The tournament honored the twentieth wedding anniversary of Arcite and Berengeria, the king's sister. Flin grinned to himself. If all went well, he would be the one who would hold a celebration.

The road wound northwest. It was a long road but quiet and well traveled, with pretty little inns found every few leagues along its course. The two men stopped at one that evening. Their sleeping arrangements were unique; Flin spent many talents on a lavish dinner and many more so his squire could sleep in the finest lodgings, but he himself spent the night in the stable. He slept alone in the straw, next to his warhorse.

They rode for a couple of days; Flin took care not to tire his four-footed prize. The country's trees stood in broad copses and had just crowned themselves with the luscious green of spring's first full growth. Villages dotted the countryside between the forests, and the peasants worked the fields along the roadside, nurturing crops which poked their first green shoots out of the ground to taste the warm, moist air.

On the third day, clouds moved in from the west and the breeze turned cooler. As the sun settled toward the horizon, the darkening puffs covered it and produced an early twilight. The two travelers had just passed a village and their horses began to labor as the road took them into the range of hills south of Tranje itself. "Looks like we could get wet," Flin said. "What do you say, Pafney? Should we turn back or should we try to make the Firedrake's Lady tonight?"

The Firedrake's Lady was a sumptuous inn which stood by itself at the summit of this range of hills. A former rider from Flin's old Red Company had built it years ago and named it for his wife, whom he always claimed came from noble stock. Flin's young companion licked his lips at the mention of the place. "I've waited for our night there since we first set out. A pair of leagues will bring us to it; even if the rains should come, I do not think we'll melt."

Flin laughed. "That's my boy. I knew I had some good reason to pick you for my squire. On to the Firedrake's Lady, then."

The road narrowed ahead of them; in one place it became a track wide enough for only one rider at a time to pass down a gully between two knolls. Flin drew his sword as they neared this spot; years before, it had been known as a prime ambush place. As he entered the narrow way, he glanced back to make sure his squire also took care.

Their shadows slid beneath the lowering clouds and the wind crooned between the hills, picking up the sound of the horse's hooves and carrying it off to distant hollows. Flin reached the end of the narrow way, then heard a shout: "Now."

Something heavy landed on him from behind, knocked the sword from his hand, and drove him from the saddle. He fell to earth with a grunt, flipped over, and shot a fist at his assailant. He managed to strike the fellow's jaw and he saw the eyes glaze, but two more men leaped on him and grappled him back to the ground. The first one came to, then the three of them pinned the squirming knight and tied his hands.

"By Typhon's spear, we've got a couple of beauties this time," one shouted. "This one is made of money by the look of him."

Flin only grinned at them. "Miracle of miracles. You're outlaws, aren't you?"

The robbers stared back at him while two more hauled the squire toward the group. "Of course we're outlaws. What did you think we were, choirboys?"

"I could kiss you, fellow," Flin cried. "I thought your kind was extinct in these parts."

"You're crazy."

"By the gods, I was about to become crazy, all right, from boredom. But you've saved me. Velocipod," he shouted. "Hither."

With his lead rope flying behind him, the huge courser

bowled into the outlaws and knocked them sprawling. Men scattered before the gnashing teeth and flailing hooves; they heaved away from Flin, who rolled over and worked at his bindings. "Velocipod," he shouted again. "Hence."

The horse reared and charged into the men who held the squire. The horse sent them sprawling, too; the young noble stared about as he found himself standing alone beside the great animal. Flin managed to free his hands at the same time. He spotted his sword glinting in the shadow of a bush, leaped toward it, and snatched it up a heartbeat ahead of one of the outlaws. He rolled to his feet, wheeled around the man, and clamped a powerful forearm about the dirty neck. "Hold, sirrah," he shouted. "Or I'll run you through."

At the same time, Pafney wheeled and grabbed another of the rascals. A third lay in the dust, his head caved in by Velocipod's hooves. The rest stared at one another, then took off down the road. The man in Flin's grip struggled to join them until the tip of Flin's longsword tickled his ribs. He went slack and said in a piteous voice, "Please, my Lord, I'm only a poor wretch trying to scrape a living for my family. Please don't kill me."

"Kill you?" Flin said. "I ought to thank you. Excitement's hard to find these days. You fellows are miserable robbers but you gave me a little sport."

Pafney's captive looked at Flin in dumb amazement. "You're not going to lay us out for trying to rob you?"

"What do you think, Pafney?"

The younger man shrugged. "I'm only your attendant, Sir. I'll leave the say to you."

Flin laughed. "I suppose we should turn the two of them in to be hanged, at least, and try to ride their friends down in the bargain." He turned to one captive. "What are your names?"

"I'm Alan," the older man said. "He's Magyar."

"Well, Alan and Magyar, should I see the two of you in irons? I really haven't the heart."

"You haven't?"

Flin turned the man loose, then dug into his purse and flipped a golden talent at each of the would-be outlaws. "No, I haven't. You've given me exercise and a chance to find if Velocipod's training was worthwhile." He shrugged. "I've no grudge if you haven't. But it looks as if we've done for your friend, here." He walked across the road and gazed down at the man the warhorse had kicked.

The outlaw called Magyar stared at the fallen man and his face grew even more somber. "He's dead," he murmured.

"I'm afraid that's so," Flin said. "You've chosen a rugged career, friend. We'll help you bury him, then we'll be on our way."

The rest of the outlaws must have received enough fright for one afternoon; they did not come back. Together, the two nobles and their two captives dug a hole for the man who had been killed. "You know," Flin said at one point, "I'm a bit of a brigand myself—of a higher grade than you, of course. Leuval was my father's name, bless his memory. He led the Red Company and I rode with them for years."

The two men looked at him, more impressed and surprised than ever. "Is that so?" Magyar said. "If we'd of known that, we would never of tried you."

"It's true," Flin said. "Though it's been so long, I don't know any of that band anymore. I wouldn't even be able to find their headquarters, now."

"They're still about, I think. In smaller numbers than twenty years ago, though. I used to know a few of them."

Flin nodded. "A pleasant lot they were."

"Faugh," Alan said. "Brigandage is a lousy way to make a living these days. Everything's too organized. It's enough to make you turn respectable."

"Oh, don't do that," Pafney said with a smile.

"I mean it," the outlaw went on. "Constables, patrols, guardsmen—everyone hounds us these days. We've sunk so low, we're even at the mercy of the people we're supposed to rob. The only place men like us can be safe now is east of here, around Hautre. And that land's become so deserted, robbers are the only ones who live there. No one to rob."

"Even at that, I'm setting off for there after this long day," Magyar said as he leaned on his spade. "This is humiliating."

Flin had to laugh. "I'm almost sorry I didn't just let you lads take my money," he said. "But cheer up. I'll see that it's not a complete loss for you. This burying is a nasty job; after we're done, you can walk behind my horse and I'll treat you to roast and pottage at the Firedrake's Lady."

The tournament in Tranje turned into a glorious affair and every bit the success Flin had known it would be. From the days of his youth, he had loved to teach tricks to animals, and he had trained Velocipod with all the skill of his forty-odd years. The huge horse gave him the advantage over all other knights; it could sidestep the cubit needed to make a lance miss, would turn the few degrees Flin needed to get the perfect angle of attack. In mêlée, it so intimidated other horses that Flin was still mounted at the end of the fray. Gasps rose from watching crowds, then turned into brave cheers. Flin drank in the applause as if it were fine wine.

Huzzahs thundered as he rode to the royal stand to receive laurels of victory. Princess Bessina, his unmatchable wife, eyed him with a hungry smile as Princess Berengeria, Countess of Tranje, presented him his prize.

"I honor you, O mighty Flin," she said with cool dignity. "You have a triumph here which will anoint the tongues of minstrels for a thousand years." Flin decided that was a lovely speech, considering that her husband, Arcite, had been among the riders Flin had unhorsed.

"Indeed," the voice came of Aelia, Queen of Carea. "You've shown us mighty feats this day." She settled the royal award, a huge medallion on a gold chain, about Flin's neck.

He bowed and kissed the older woman's hand. "Thank you, Queen," he said. "I'm only sorry King Palamon couldn't be here to see this. It's been a perfect day already, but that would have made it even finer."

Sunlight danced off the salt-and-pepper of Aelia's hair. "He sends regrets, but when the Oracle at Euelpis sends a summons, no man—even though he be a king—may put her off."

They all turned then, faced the crowd and bathed in applause. But Flin kept his eyes on Aelia. "I understand that—even though I'm just a plain fellow. Maybe I should have gone with him—he might have great adventure."

"Impossible," Berengeria said.

The queen nodded. "Indeed, it is. The person summoned by the Oracle should never share that honor. Only one may travel to her temple at a time."

"Ah, well," Flin said. "He'll come back from his quest and then we can give him a big hug, all of us together."

With that, he drew Bessina to him and kissed her on the mouth, which made the crowd cheer louder than ever. Bessina was his wife, his woman, his beauty. No female on any shore of the Thlassa Mey could match her. Two dozen years of marriage and three children had not changed her, except to sharpen her features an iota and hone her skills in the ways of Aphrodite. At this moment, with the crowd's voice in his ears and his wife clasped tight to his side, Flin felt as happy as any man could be.

He and his squire spent the rest of the afternoon gathering up armor, wagers, and prizes he had won from his victims. It was pure pleasure; they gossiped, renewed old friendships, and enjoyed themselves as if they were children at a picnic. Since this was the year's first big tournament, every knight had much news to trade. In the peaceful years of King Palamon's reign, the lands about the Thlassa Mey had become almost as family.

Courts exchanged their heirs to serve as pages, squires, and handmaidens in every friendly house. Of Flin's own three children, only one remained at home. The dashing knight had a daughter in Queen Aelia's train and his elder son worked in the household of Count Geoffrey of the Montaigne, in the southern reaches of the Carean peninsula. It was the same with the children of Arcite and Berengeria and with all noble families. So it was that such tournaments as these became huge family reunions and social gatherings, as well as competitions.

"Your son's a chip off you, you heartless rogue," Count Geoffrey said as he turned his part of the wager over to Flin. "I quake to ponder what will follow when he comes of age and joins you in the lists."

Flin smiled. "It'll be good sport, I know that. He might carry my steel off the field or I might carry his, but if we laugh when we remember it all, who cares?"

"Those are noble thoughts," Count Geoffrey said. But he did not smile as he handed his shield and breastplate to Pafney and the young man laid them on the stack behind Flin. "But come, Sir; you have won a pile of plate to fit a regiment. I would pay you well to give mine back to me before we meet again. The next event is only one short fortnight from this moment." He spoke of the season's second tournament, which would be the annual pageant held in honor of the Knights of Pallas.

Flin laughed. "What, don't the armorers and blacksmiths need work, too? I have special plans for this armor—all of it."

"Unless you plan an army of your own, I cannot guess it."

"You'll see." Flin laughed again, but only on the inside. It tickled him to see the other man's surprise and dismay. Of course, Flin's refusal was just part of his jolly plan. It would take half a ship's hold to transport to Oron the gear he had won, but that was what he would do. Carts would haul it the rest of the way to the Fastness of Pallas. On the eve of the tournament there, he would give all his winnings back to his victims so he could win the goods all over again. He eyed Count Geoffrey and had to slap his knee as he pictured the look the man would have when Flin brought the joke full circle.

It would be an expensive joke, not to mention a great deal of work, but it would keep tongues buzzing for a while. Flin was still collecting the fruits of his victory as the sun's golden chariot rode low in the western sky. At last, a page from Count Arcite's palace arrived and handed him a note which bore Bessina's seal.

While Pafney watched, Flin tore open the missive and read his wife's message. "Oh-oh," he said. "I forgot—we're late for the banquet. My lovebird wants me to know she's already left."

"By all the gods," Pafney said. "She'll make it hot for you when you arrive at last. You'd best be on your way to bathe and change your clothing."

Flin looked at the younger man. Pafney was tall and comely, a fine-looking fellow who would soon earn his own knighthood. But he worried too much. "We can't go yet," Flin said. "First, we've got to get all this stuff stored. We can't just leave it lying about, after all. My lady will get over it if I don't eat Arcite's beef. Besides, I walked through the hall last night and we wouldn't get to sit together anyway. They've got all the men seated on the floor and all the women have to sit in the balcony and look down on them. Whoever laid down *that* rule must have had rocks for glands."

"It is an ancient Tranjian custom at such feasts," Pafney said.

"Custom or no, it's not to my taste. We'll get there soon enough."

A stableboy brought a wineskin and Flin took a draught. He passed the skin to Pafney and the three of them drank while they carried the goods into a room that could be locked. It was a mighty haul, with a king's ransom in gold to be added to it over the next few days. Darkness had all but covered the land by the time they finished. Flin sent his squire on his way, then strolled from Count Arcite's stables toward the main wing of the palace.

Under Arcite and Berengeria, Tranje had become the most stately city about the Thlassa Mey. Its temples shone; the finest architecture and stone graced each one. The long peace had let the count build his palace outside the castle which defended the city. It, too, was the most lovely anywhere. Though Tranje's funds were more limited than those of Carea, Buerdaunt, or some other lands, the palace was roomier and more lovely than any in the civilized world. That went well with Arcite's role as the most elegant noble in any kingdom.

Torchlight shone across the courtyard in front of the banquet hall, a looming structure which formed the palace's south wing. Flin walked from the stable, crossed the courtyard, then passed through a beam of light which shot from a doorway. He took a look at himself: dirt and sweat glistened all over him and the straw and dust from the stable covered his clothing. He smiled to think of haughty Princess Berengeria and her elegant husband. If he stepped into their banquet looking like this, neither of them would ever speak to him again.

"Sir Flin," a voice came. "You're well late for the feast. They've gone on without you."

He saw a knot of guardsmen in the shadows beside the doorway. "Ah, there you are. Oh, they can have the party to themselves if they want; I had more fun where I was. Don't I know you?"

"Right enough, Sir. I rode with you many a year ago."

Flin peered more closely at the man, then nodded. "Many a year. I remember you; Enar, wasn't that your name?" He smiled when the man nodded. "What have you fellows got there?"

"A skin of Gueltic wine. Odus of Guelt gave the count a couple of tuns for the occasion, so we benefit thereby—at least so long as we're quiet about it. Festive occasion and all that. Care for a pull?"

"Don't mind if I do." Flin took the heavy skin from the man and helped himself to a long swallow. It was good wine. The free province of Guelt lay southwest of the Carean peninsula and was known for the quality of its vineyards. "You're right; I've had a good day. I don't need any feast to end it." He nudged the man with his elbow. "Truth to tell, I'm just as happy out here with you fellows and your wine."

"We're glad to have you, Sir. But that wife of yours, won't she be miffed over the whole thing?"

Flin shrugged and watched the other men pass the wineskin.

"Who knows? We've had differences over the years but we always manage to get things straightened out between us." He sighed happily. "You know, I had no idea who she was when I first met her. I had no more idea she was a noble's daughter than a worm would know a hummingbird drinks dew. Chose her for her looks and her spunk, and never regretted it."

"That's the way it ought to be," Enar said. "I remember her. Not a woman could touch her for looks in her day."

"In her day? Go on, fellow, it's still her day."

"No insult intended, Sir. But you know how it is, you can't stop Father Time. Of course, she's held him off better than most."

Flin laughed. "You don't know as much as you think—she's fought the old rascal to a dead standstill. I wouldn't trade her for a harem, and that's the truth."

"I vow it is." Enar winked. "I've heard tell you still take the occasional sample elsewhere, just to make sure."

All five men laughed, then Flin thought of something. "Do you know, I've not lost a bet since I rode into this city? I'll make one more wager, just to make it an even score. You see, I know what you don't know—I know what goes under Bessina's gown, and that's why I never look at another woman. Now I wager that she stands so far above any other maiden in that hall tonight, I can find her by no more than the thinness of her ankles—they outstrip any others."

"Go on. No one can recognize a woman just by her ankles."

Flin smiled and thought on the heap of equipment he had won that day. "A suit of armor for each of you says you're wrong."

"She's got scars, then," Enar said with a laugh. "You'll know her by the scars."

"By Pallas herself, who guards truth the way a hen guards chicks, it'll be by the slimness of her ankles."

"What?" another guard said. "You can't just get all the ladies in that hall to cover their faces and lift their dresses, now can you?"

"No, I can't do that." Flin thought for a moment, then slipped past the guards and peeked through the door. Laughter, music, and people filled the grand hall. The babble of it all leaped out the door at him, the bright light all but dazzled him, the aroma from all the food was enough to make a man drool. He stepped away. "Let's go up to the balcony," he said.

Enar laughed. "How? Our station's down here."

"Get someone to trade with you, or take your place."

Enar put his head together with one of the others, then they both grinned at Flin. The other man left at a trot. "We'll see," Enar said.

A moment later, the other guard came back with three men. "They'll take the rest of our watch if you'll pay them. I'll stand with them to make a fourth."

"The officer knows?"

"The officer knows. But tell me all that happens."

"It's as good as done, then." Flin flipped a gold piece to each new guard, then he and the three relieved men climbed the wide stairs to a long upper vestibule and the balcony where the women dined. Again, Flin tiptoed to a doorway and peeped in. A long table stood at the balcony's edge; the women ate where they could look down at their menfolk in the chamber below. They talked and laughed. Servants passed among them, clearing away old courses and setting new ones.

"I have it," Flin said. "You get me under that tablecloth. All I'll be able to see is their feet and ankles, but I'll just ease their dresses up enough to pick out my Bessina. It'll be as easy as if she had purple toes."

"How'll you prove you knew her?" one guard challenged. "I doubt any of the women'll appreciate the joke. Are you going to have one stand up and take a bow?"

"Wait, wait," Enar said. He reached inside his doublet and produced a garter. "This is a keepsake from a lass I know— she's a merry wench and she'll go along with a jest. You just have to slip this onto the ankle you pick."

"How'll we know if he gets the right one?" another guard asked.

"Easy," Enar said. "My lady is chambermaid in the guests' wing. If a strange garter shows up in this palace, she'll know about it."

Flin laughed. "It won't have to go that far. My Bessina will show it to you herself, once she knows how it got there. I daresay, it's a noble plan. Now, to cases. I've wagered a suit of armor for each of your men. What will you wager in return?"

The three men started to babble but Flin stopped them. "Wait, wait, don't all talk at once. I have it. When I win, you all have to carry placards for the next week. One will say, 'The Wisest—Flin.' Another will say, 'The Loveliest—Bessina.' If any person questions you about it, you have to tell them the whole tale."

"We can't do that," Enar said. "That'd be humiliating."

"Yes we can," another guard said. "It'll be worth it."

"Then swear," Flin said.

They all swore an oath on the wager, then one of the guards stepped to the doorway. "She's on the other side of the hall," he said. "You'll have to go in on that side—and that's the boundary of the advice you'll get from me." He and the others chortled.

They made their way back down the stairs, then up to the vestibule on the other side of the hall. They jabbered like schoolboys as they went. "Now we have to get you under the table," Enar said.

"There's an answer to that, too," Flin said. "Look there." Behind them, a bevy of servants made their way in from the kitchens, laden with platters full of dessert.

Chapter Two:
Flin's Wager

"I SWEAR TO you, I'll have him hung up by the heels and tickled with a rod—at least I ought to do it." Princess Bessina glared about as she spoke to Berengeria. Her eyes flashed toward the hall's main floor, toward the dapper men who ate at the long banquet table, shouted at servants, and sent messages or mouthed words of love to the women seated above.

Princess Berengeria smiled a very small smile. "I could not blame you. Still, this ancient custom of my husband's land would keep him from your side in any case."

"At least I'd have him then beneath my eyes." Bessina finished the last course of her meal, then sighed. "Ah, Flin," she said, mostly to herself. "Your ways will drive me distracted."

"And that's because he is a brigand," Berengeria whispered to Aelia, who sat on the other side of her. "Ah, they trouble me, the two of them. They've looks and dashing ways and Flin has all the courage of a wolverine. But he will never be an honest man."

"Be patient," the queen said. "For he is the staunchest of your brother's friends."

"Of course—my brother gave him all the lands and titles which he now enjoys."

"Such wealth is not the reason. Flin has no more use for that than fish for fur. He is a warrior by inclination. Even your Arcite, though brave and strong, cannot cross lances with him and remain upon his horse."

Nor can he match the rogue in taverns or boudoirs across

the land, Berengeria thought to herself, but she did not say it. She glanced toward the doorway, for servants brought in the dessert course. She had taken only a bite of each dish from the lavish meal, yet she knew she had already overeaten. She eyed Bessina and felt a tingle of jealousy. The younger woman had just finished her fourth decade, yet she still had a figure fit for a fresh bride. She ate like a stallion and had borne three children, yet nothing fazed her beauty. That was not a thing to hold against her, of course, yet, in a way, it was. Berengeria's mouth curled as she watched the steward himself lay a pair of rich pastries before Bessina.

Singers entered behind the servants and set their pipes and strings onto a jolly ditty. They drowned out the music and laughter from the hall below. Then Berengeria saw Aelia look up. "What was that?" the queen exclaimed.

"What?"

"I thought I felt a movement."

Berengeria eyed the older woman; she did not have a notion of what Aelia was talking about. Then the countess, too, felt something touch her on the foot. "I felt it also," she said, and drew the foot back.

She jerked again. Fingers touched her ankle, a hand reached its way under her gown and curled about the calf of her leg. Yet she could look down and see her Arcite clearly, sitting with a knot of nobles. She tried to pull away from the hand, but the grip was too strong. A second hand fumbled with her slipper, pulled it off, and slid along her foot, up her ankle. Berengeria forced herself to stay icily calm. "Call a guardsman," she whispered to the queen.

Aelia caught the steward's attention, then sent him hurrying from the room. Meanwhile, the blood drained from Berengeria's face; someone unknown and hidden was rubbing her leg. She pushed her seat back and tried to stand, but lost her balance and fell with a cry. Silence spread down the balcony like a stain; women stared at her, mouths fell open. She struck at the tablecloth and the man behind it. "Unhand me, villain. Who are you and what mean your touches?"

Her hand collided with something solid and a male voice said, "Ouch." The hand left her ankle and she scrambled away from the table just as four soldiers clattered into the room. They surrounded the spot and one snatched away the long tablecloth. Dishes flew, women screamed, and the four men pulled out the lean figure of Flin himself.

"You," Berengeria said, her mouth drawn into a grim line. "By all the gods, what prank is this? To be assaulted in my husband's hall, before these noble guests . . ." Anger, insult, indignation nearly strangled her. "You'd better have a good excuse for me, or else swift punishment shall fall upon you." Her eyes stared daggers at him. "Ah, you ruffian."

Flin smiled stupidly up at her. It was plain that he had oiled himself with wine to the point of saturation. "Woman," he said drunkenly. "How dare you keep my wife's ankles under your gown?"

"What? Are you mad?"

"O, Flin," Bessina cried. "What means this prank? You have disgraced yourself and me besides."

The guards hauled the dashing knight to his feet just in time for him to look face-to-face at Count Arcite himself, who had rushed up from the hall's main floor. "Besides that, I seem to have lost my bet," Flin mumbled.

"What bet?"

"It's a long story. You don't need to know."

A dark, bearded man came up beside Arcite. He was Odus of Guelt, who had traveled far to attend this banquet. In fact, as a gift to his host, he had supplied the wine which had laid Flin so low. Now he threw back his head and laughed. He wore a turban with a flowing train of white silk; the fine cloth shook with his mirth. "Oh, this is rich. It was a bet, a prank. Forgive me, all you gentle hosts, but I must laugh. What jolly people you must be, to have such pranksters in your midst."

"It doesn't make me jolly," Bessina said. She looked even more angry than Berengeria, caught between fury and tears. "You wicked, wicked Flin. I do not know the meaning of your prank; perhaps I do not want to know. Still, I'll not speak to you until you have explained it all, and to my satisfaction."

"Bessina, love," Flin said. "I was doing it for you."

"You say you have no laughter for this man?" Berengeria cried at her niece. "Then what of me? My body is reserved unto my husband; never in my life would I allow a man beside Arcite to take the freedom with his touch that this rough Flin has taken." She turned on the drunken knight. "For my part, I have no need for explanations, Flin. I want you from this court before the dawn rolls 'round—in fact, before another hour of sand can patter through the glass."

"But Berengeria, he is a guest," Arcite said.

"A guest who could not trouble his fair self to come and

eat in his assigned place, but who humiliates his wife, his hostess, and yourself by turning this event into a circus. If you love me, you will give me your support."

"That's not a matter to be argued, wife." Arcite's face reddened. "My love for you is full and sacred." He paused. "But still, this Flin's a guest—and known to all as brave and gallant."

"Never, for no knight is gallant who would so mishandle any woman for the sake of some lewd prank."

Arcite stared into his wife's flushing face. "In all our married life," he finally said, "I have not seen you angered thus." He paused, thought, then turned toward Flin. "While there may be no malice in your heart, Sir Flin, I find that I must banish you from Tranje. Your wife and children may remain as long as they desire. But you must go."

"That's funny," Flin said as guards hustled him off the balcony. "It wasn't supposed to work out like this. Wait," he shouted from the doorway. "At least I have to give your guards their suits of armor."

"Ah, Flin," Bessina cried as he vanished around a corner. "How could you do this to us?"

"What madness," Berengeria said. She swallowed, forced down her anger, and touched her niece on a bare arm. "What's done is done. It was a foolish prank and I suppose I should not bear a grudge. Your Flin will suffer his humiliation when he wakes tomorrow morn—along with an expanded head, from all the spirits which he poured into himself. His punishment shall then be finished—I'll relent. Forgive me for my loss of temper." She took another breath. "I'll not discuss the matter more."

"You took no action I would not have taken in your place," Bessina replied softly. "Ah, Flin, I'll strangle you when next we meet."

Berengeria turned to Arcite. "My husband, I shall now retire into my chambers. By the gods, this evening's been quite enough for me."

"As you think best," Arcite replied.

"But hold," Odus of Guelt said. His teeth shone white through his dark beard and he eyed Tranje's countess. "My Lady, this is still a night for revelry, for celebration of the coming season. You must stay, visitors might look upon you and enjoy your company. Why, that will salve your feelings more than such an early journey to your chambers."

"Nay," Berengeria replied. "I thank you for your interest in my welfare but I've had sufficient; it's been a tiring day." She smiled a dry smile. "I give orders that these revels rattle on. I'm sure the laughter will bloom better in my absence."

Arcite placed gentle hands on her shoulders and kissed her forehead. "Indeed, my darling. We have many guests and they shall all be entertained. Please rest you well. I'll come to you when our last feaster has imbibed and sung and eaten to his fill."

"I trow the sun will rise before that happens," Berengeria said. She kissed her husband back, then she and her attendants moved from the hall.

Disappointment filled Odus of Guelt's face as he looked after her. "Alas, that such a lovely ornament must leave us over such a trifle."

Arcite smiled. Guelt was an isolated land and the customs there were different from those in Tranje, especially the Tranje ruled by Arcite the Balladeer. "My wife is not an ornament, my friend; she does what's called for by propriety. When morrow comes, you'll find her pleasant and as gracious as she was before all this."

"Um," Odus of Guelt said. He clasped his arms behind his back and gazed about the hall.

"And what of you, Bessina?" Arcite asked. "I tell you that your husband's larking does not faze our love for you; please stay with us, enjoy the rest of your repast."

Bessina shook her head. "I cannot," she said. "I know not what to do. Flin's nature has embarrassed me before, but this drains all the revelry from me as if it were the color from a rotting apple."

"Oh, pshaw. It's not as serious as that. The law demands that he remain outside these lands for some small space of time. But we—but I, at least—do still admire and love him. Any fool can see no malice lay in what has passed."

Bessina pursed her lips. "I'm sure that's so. But still, I shall retire, the same as Berengeria."

"And I," Queen Aelia said. "This evening proves too strenuous by half."

"What's this?" Odus of Guelt cried in dismay. "Catastrophe, I say. The loveliest depart."

Aelia eyed him. "I've threescore years and more behind me, Count. I doubt my loss will dispossess your glands of stimulation." She turned toward Arcite and inclined her head toward him. "Good evening, Sir. I'll to my chamber and my labors, now, for I have much to do with Palamon, my husband, off in distant lands."

She and Bessina moved toward the doorway while Odus of Guelt looked more distressed than ever. "Oh, sad affair. I'll miss them all, these daughters of Carea's court."

Arcite gazed at him. "I fear that by your look you really do regret their leaving. That will stiffen my resolve; I shall commit an act I'd not intended. By the way of nurturing the spirits of the house, I'll give you all a song." Women heard him and clapped; the applause spread through the two-tiered hall. Arcite turned to his squire. "Go, lad, and fetch my lute. I'll meet you then below, where I'll perform a melody or two."

Odus of Guelt put on a happy face and followed the Count of Tranje to the hall's lower level. Arcite was known across the Thlassa Mey for his melodies, but to hear him sing was a rare treat, even in his own hall. The prospect quickly put spirit back into the guests who remained. As for Odus of Guelt, that worthy listened to the gifted count absently—itself an accomplishment—and glanced nervously about the hall through the rest of the evening.

It was past the middle of night by the time the feasting and singing ended and the last guests rose to leave or slumped forward with faces in platters. Odus stood at last, sighed, and walked toward the courtyard. "Ah, sir," he heard a voice behind him. "Did you not gain enjoyment from our revels?"

He turned, saw Arcite, and forced himself to put on a smile. "Alas, my friend, it has not been the same since your sweet lady left this hall."

"I see," Arcite replied. "Do not let little quarrels trouble you. Gay Flin has vexed her oftentimes before—I think he does it for amusement. Carean women, and especially the women educated in the Temple, pride themselves on their propriety. She may anger quickly but her temper fades with equal speed. In scant two days, 'twill be as if it never happened."

"She'll stay that long in chambers?"

Arcite shrugged, almost laughed. "Possibly. But not from Flin's odd prank. She's tough as nails, my Berengeria, but we have sons within Carea's court; they visit only once or twice each year. She now has opportunity to lavish her attention on them with no rivals. I am sure she'll do so till the day they both depart."

"Ah." Odus of Guelt nodded as if he understood everything. "But the queen? Will she remain in quarters, too?"

"It's possible," Arcite replied. "With Palamon away, her duties press her. Now, like Berengeria, she's given ceremony all the time she wishes. Daily labors nip at her. Well may she deal with them throughout the rest of this long festival."

"You'll see her, though?"

"Oh, certainly. My wife and she have ties which go back many years."

"A fascinating family," Odus of Guelt said as they walked across the courtyard under a star-strewn sky. "Your women work as hard as men, it seems. I must reflect on these events."

The two nobles parted. Odus of Guelt walked toward the sprawling guest wing of the palace while Arcite walked toward Berengeria's chambers. But on the cobblestones outside the guest wing, Odus of Guelt stroked his beard as he found a litter and a string of pack mules waiting to be loaded. Servants hustled about, tying the packs into place. "What's this?" the visiting noble asked.

"The princess wants her goods all gathered," one man said. "She leaves tonight."

"The countess?"

"No, no. Princess Bessina. Her husband's been banished for a year because of a prank and now she's going to meet him."

"I see," Odus of Guelt said. He stood and watched the busy men for a moment, then Bessina herself appeared from a doorway in her traveling wrap. "Good evening," he said to her with a smile. "I see you're leaving us."

"Indeed I am," she replied. She was no longer a young woman; still, she was one of the most striking women he had ever met. Her hair still flowed from her scalp, an auburn river which did not show a strand of gray. In the light from her servant's torches, her eyes shone a deep and dazzling green.

"I rue the accident which drives you from this place."

"Oh, Flin," she said with a sigh. "He's a child in many ways; his antics drive me to distraction. Sometimes, I know not whether I should hug him or should impale him on a spear. But still, my place is at his side; I'll journey homeward, there to wait his coming." She looked up at the older man. "You know, his prank was for my sake. I hear it had to do with betting on the comeliest of ankles." She blushed. "On some such thing, at any rate. Oh, Flin, I'll kill you this time."

Odus of Guelt laughed. "You are an understanding wife. I

still am sorry—I shall miss the company of you and your most merry husband. Me thinks I would enjoy his friendship.'' He stood for a moment, as if in thought, then he looked down at her. ''But would you take a gift before you go?''

''Of course.''

''Then come up to my quarters.''

She peered up at him. ''I'll not do that. One impropriety upon this night's enough.''

He laughed again. ''Oh, only to a common storage chamber. All my men will be there. No foul gossip will arise, I promise you. Please come, and I will let you choose the gift for you and your mercurial husband.''

She hesitated, eyed the servants who loaded the mules, then said, ''Well, I suppose so.''

He beamed and ushered her through an archway, along a corridor, and up a flight of stone steps. ''Our quarters aren't far apart,'' he said as they climbed to the wing's upper floor and a guard in Gueltic uniform greeted them. ''If things had gone more smoothly, who can know? We might have formed a hearty friendship. Would you like some wine?'' he asked as they passed into a chamber and another pair of his men joined them.

''No thank you,'' she replied.

They passed through that chamber and entered another, which overlooked the courtyard. A few more men came from some nearby room and watched him as he waved an arm at the strange objects stacked high against one wall. ''So there you are; are they not beautiful? Select one and I promise that it shall be yours.''

Bessina looked at the things. ''Little horses, knit from worsted!'' she said in surprise. ''Why, I have never seen the like. What workmanship, what craft.'' She moved closer to the toys, each one the size of a large dog or a small pony. ''The colors are so delicate, and I can trace the saddles, ears, each tiny hoof, as if they were alive.'' She looked back at Odus of Guelt. ''But why so many, and for what are they so large?''

He smiled as if he would burst into laughter. ''Indeed, they are immense for stuffed toys, are they not? The numbers, Lady, are so everyone who has desire for one shall be indulged. The size is necessary, that they might support the weight which shall be placed upon them.''

Bessina stared at him. '' ''The weight which shall be placed upon them?' What, have they business other than their beauty?"

"Oh, indeed, they have." He wheeled away from her and shouted at his housecarls. "You men, stop up her mouth and bind her hands. Move quickly, now—she must not be allowed to scream."

Men pounced on Bessina. She writhed against their hold but they threw her on the floor like a sack of potatoes, forced a gag into her mouth, then rolled her onto her stomach so they could tie her hands behind her. Her eyes bulged in fury; she grimaced most of all at the grinning, turban-topped noble who commanded them. But her glare did her no more good than rosewater sprinkled on her enemies.

They hoisted her to their shoulders and hauled her to the knit ponies. "You never chose one," Odus of Guelt said sadly. "That's too bad—but I shall pick one for you. Hurry, men, and place her there upon the dark one. Then grab you one apiece, for we must fly before her husband can return to give her aid, or any other person can suspect."

The housecarls pulled one of the knit ponies from the pile, stood it up, and strapped her across its back as if it were a real horse. The worsted body did not sag, the thin legs did not buckle. Bessina's eyes fastened on Odus of Guelt as he took the largest toy for himself and let his housecarls divide the rest among them. "One man unlatch the windows," he ordered.

A man followed that order. The chill night air poured in, Odus of Guelt pulled a folded piece of paper from his turban. He opened it, read a singsong chant which ended with the word "Selevay." Bessina felt her knit pony grow warm. She thought she would spew forth her supper and choke on her gag and her own vomit as the thing trembled, shook, then rose from the floor. She managed to control her twitching stomach, but just barely, as she stared about the room. The other toys, two dozen of them, did the same. Each held a man seated securely upon its knit saddle.

The housecarl who had pulled open the windows jumped onto the last knit pony and the lot of them shot forward, streaked through the window and over the courtyard. The cobbled space was dark and empty. No one looked up as the strange company flitted toward the south, splitting the darkness like a flight of fairies.

Chapter Three:
The Oracle

THE MORNING AFTER Odus of Guelt spirited Bessina out of Tranje, Carea's King Palamon rose early, drank a cup of wine, and left the galley which had carried him to the island of Euelpis. He took with him no weapons, only a jar of wine and a skin filled with blood from a white doe. These items he would use as sacrifices when the time came.

He walked alone toward the mountains at the north end of the island. The sun came up, the day grew warm, sweat dampened his white hair and trickled down his face, but he wiped it away with a cloth and kept on. These mountains, tallest on this land which lay two islands south of Artos, held a temple. The great Oracle had summoned Palamon to speak to her.

Noon came and went as he climbed the trail, the afternoon sun beat down, and at last he came to a grove of towering oak trees. A cluster of marble buildings stood at the center of the grove. Hunger gnawed at the tall monarch by this time, thirst clutched his throat. But he would satisfy neither craving until nightfall. He had spoken with the Oracle once before and he knew the rituals by heart.

He prayed and cleansed himself at the fountain, then priests approached and he let them slide a postulant's robe about his shoulders. They blessed him. Then he picked up the jar of wine and skin of deer blood and they led him into a cleared space behind the temple. Stately oaks stood about a circle of lawn, in the center of which stood a simple altar of marble. He knelt there and closed his eyes while the priests retired.

"My gentle Palamon," he heard a voice say. "The years

have passed for both of us. The snows of age have sprinkled over us; the changing season comes, when we shall leave this world and be replaced by younger wights.''

He looked over his shoulder. Behind him stood a woman: thin, white-skinned, with hair that fell from her head in black-and-white ringlets. She looked younger than he, but not much younger. She laughed as she gazed back at him. ''How shock lights up your eyes.'' She spread her hands. ''Now, am I such a prodigy?''

He groped for words. ''I'd not expected this.'' He lifted the two containers he had brought. ''I have not even spread the blood and wine I brought for sacrifice.''

''No need for them now. You spread them long ago, the last time you sought words and wisdom here.''

''I full remember. 'Twas long ago—and I was not permitted even one small glance at you.''

She favored him with a smile that was at once feminine, motherly, and divine. ''Then look upon me now, and know the Fates are not yet done with you. Great work's at hand, great fears, great threats—and that is why my messengers have summoned you.''

Palamon looked back at her. ''Does it involve my Berethane?''

''Your son?''

Palamon turned his eyes away but remained kneeling. ''My son, indeed, my Berethane. Dark magic caught him up long years ago, and mighty Pallas summoned him to her. She saved him from an evil man's enchantment but her price was great—for twenty years, he has been lost to both his parents. Now I seek him out.''

Again, the Oracle smiled. ''I know the tale, good Palamon.''

''I'm sure you do,'' Palamon said quietly. She was, after all, the Oracle.

''The goddess saved the little boy from wicked magic—but she drew him from this world to do it. She gave promise that he would be returned to you.''

''In twenty years, she said. Those years have drained away.'' He hesitated. ''I'd hoped . . .''

''You hoped my summons dealt with that alone.''

''And does it?'' He gazed up at her. ''I am old; the years devour me without remorse, implacable as any maggot tunneling within a wound. How many years are left to me? I cannot know—my death could come upon this day, this hour. And yet my heir remains concealed from me. Will I have time to train him for the tasks he'll face when he assumes the crown?''

"Every father worries thus, from king to country shepherd.''

"That does not ease my anguish.''

"Nor should it,'' she said. She turned and strolled off a few steps. "But he and all things in this world are still the same. The future of your son is tied in with the festering evil which we must discuss.''

"My Berethane and deadly evil? Oracle, I've fought too many times already in my life—I'm old. I beg to live my fading years in quiet and with my son restored to me.'' He sighed. "But what's the nature of the evil?''

She pursed her lips. "I don't know yet; I only sense its presence. Some great force beyond my vision teases me, disdains to show itself. So far. But heed me well, King Palamon. Momentous times are coming.'' She paused, then eyed him with an air of command—a mortal woman who could command even a king. "Now spread your substances about us both, so I might beg the Fates to yield their unknown truths to me.''

Palamon fumbled with the skin of doe's blood and glanced up at the holy woman before he sprinkled the clotted liquid in a circle about the two of them. She eyed him with a slight smile. He finished, then advanced to the altar and raised the jar of wine. He felt her eyes upon him as he began to pray.

The Oracle said nothing, offered no chant, no invocation to the gods while he went through his part of the ritual. She stood still as stone beside the altar, clenched her eyelids, spread her hands as if she would absorb the sun's rays across the full expanse of her body.

Palamon lowered the wine jar and began to splash its contents over the altar itself. But before he could spill much, the jar turned hot between his hands. The dead marble of the altar started at him, shook like a building in the grip of an earthquake. The wine steamed and boiled, then the jar shattered. Shards cut Palamon's face and hands. The ring of doe's blood burst into flame with a loud snap and he staggered toward the center of the circle.

The Oracle stood as if turned to stone. The altar, twice a man's weight of marble, shattered like a jar struck by a hammer. The blast blinded Palamon and threw him to the ground. When he scrambled to his hands and knees, he found the Oracle lying on her back, eyes still shut, arms still outstretched, as if she were a fallen monument. He tried to drag her away from the smoke and flames.

Her lips moved and stopped him. "The peace which reigns across the Thlassa Mey is but illusion," she murmured. "Velvet skin above a deep infection. Soon the darkness comes; it shall arise from salty water; it shall seek a foothold on the land, supported by man's little evils."

"What of Berethane?" Palamon begged.

"An artifact of mighty power must be used against the darkness. The *Tome of Winds*, long missing, must be lifted from its hiding place."

"Am I to find it, then? I grow too old. Six decades and a portion lie upon my brow. O gods, cannot some younger man assume this quest? Is this the price which I must pay before my child will be restored to me?"

The Oracle's face sagged, the lines about her eyes and the corners of her mouth deepened. She said, "Along a river's course, a league or two above a coastal city, where the running water bends as would a sapling bowed to snare a rabbit, stands a hut beneath two towering beeches. There you shall begin."

Palamon took a deep breath. "If Pallas and her holy brethren will it," he finally said. "I don the mantle of your quest." He clenched his fingers, then turned his face to the heavens. "O, mighty gods, if you will have it so, I'll seek the place and find the artifact." He went silent as he saw the Oracle move. Her head rolled to one side and a soft snore escaped her lips.

When he touched her on the shoulder, she stirred. Her eyes opened, she stared up at him. "By all the gods," she said softly. "In all my sainted life, I never have been overcome so fully. That dark force which threatens us must be enough to consternate the gods themselves." She sat up and shook her head as if she had received a hard blow.

"Do you remember all your vision?"

"I recall the sense of what I uttered."

"The *Tome of Winds*," Palamon said. "I've never heard of it."

"It is a volume filled with formulae so powerful, the gods themselves concealed it. It exists in legend only, now; it vanished generations in the past. In tales alone it's lived since long before the Empire Grand spread o'er the Thlassa Mey."

"And that's the quest which I must undertake," Palamon

said. "I hope and pray it leads me to my son."

"The images are jumbled," she said. "I saw a land cut by a river."

"That much you mentioned."

She brushed a strand of hair from her face. "Youth stands by to help you—I divine a plain and sensitive young man who lives beside that river. He has sight for things which others cannot see. If he accompanies you, then be assured your quest will end successfully."

"And he will lead me to my Berethane?"

"Perhaps." She shrugged. "I cannot say. The images are mixed." She reached her hand to him and he helped her climb to her feet. Then she smoothed her gown and gazed up at him. "The plain described, the river's bend—are you familiar with those places?"

"I will have to ponder them," he said. "I've traveled many lands and might have passed the site in bygone years. I'll flog my memory."

"I've faith in any man the gods select," she said. "But I grow tired. When you depart, please send a priest to me and tell him to bring wine. Goodbye." With that, she turned from him and walked into the trees.

Palamon watched her, then hurried from the clearing himself. Two priests greeted him with surprised looks, for the Oracle always made her guests wait to see her. He passed her order on, made a large donation to the temple, and returned to his galley.

Nobles met him as he neared the shore, which was a good thing. The forces which had swept through the clearing and his own fasting had weakened him; he had to smile to himself as his men helped him the last half a league to his ship. The gods, who had designed and created the first human body, seemed to retain little regard for their own invention when they selected an old man as their agent. What was their intent, he wondered? What could he offer that a younger man could not?

Evening came by the time they reached the vessel. The commander gave the order to set sail and Palamon went below to break his fast in his stateroom. Once he had eaten and rested, he called his officers to him and ordered them to bring maps and their memories. They met until the wee hours as Palamon poured over charts of all the seaports and inland waterways of the Thlassa Mey.

He prayed for inspiration daily as the galley sailed north,

along the Carean peninsula. As they neared the mouth of the Narrow Strait, they sighted another ship, a gaudy vessel which made its way south under full sail. Besides that, three banks of oars rose and fell, rose and fell, as if operated by the same giant machine. "A noble sight," Palamon said to his galley's commander. "Not one of man's creations can compare to such a vessel under way at sea."

"You'd make a seaman, Sire," the commander said. "A ship's a glorious sight, a fleet's e'en better. That one's making haste, though." He pursed his lips.

"She is," Palamon agreed. "What flag is that?"

"The flag of Guelt," the commander replied. "Unless I miss my guess, that ship's the transport of the count himself, for they have few such galleys and I know of only one that size."

"The count's own barge," Palamon mused. "That's strange. He was supposed to be among the guests at Tranje."

"He must have left before the feasting ended," the commander ventured.

"Perhaps emergency demands his presence in his homeland," Palamon said. "All the same, give orders that we greet him with a signal."

"Done already," the commander replied with a smile. Even as they spoke, Palamon looked up and saw the line of signal flags which fluttered up the vessel's signal mast.

But the Gueltic galley must have been in a great rush indeed, for they did not respond to the Carean message. They altered course to clear Palamon's ship by a wide margin and the rowers labored even harder until the vessel disappeared below the curve of the horizon. That puzzled Palamon but he did not question such haste as his own ship prepared to make its way through the Narrow Strait and into the Thlassa Mey.

Chapter Four:
The Barbray

THE COURBEE WAS a broad, sleepy stream which wound out of the northern Greenlands in a series of slow curves. On the outer edges of its bends, the current cut hollows under the bank, forming overhangs and caves where fish and turtles hid. On inside curves, sand and silt settled into low beaches where trees, brush, and sometimes even houses, grew.

A half league from one such curve, posts jutted from the dark waters in a line which slanted off downstream, vanished, then angled back upstream on the far side. The two lines of posts formed a sort of funnel into the middle of the river. During the day, barges and galleys passed between many such lines en route to and from the city of Stournes. At night, vessels did not come, so at sunset, fishermen stretched long nets to close off the funnels and turn them into traps for unwary fish.

A young man named Reale waded from post to post with a ball of twine strapped to his belt. The netting had to be repaired each afternoon and today was his turn. He stopped at each post and retied the mesh where it had come loose. He mended tears and broken strands while he fought to keep his balance in the sluggish current, black mud squeezing between his bare toes.

Reale would rather have been anything but a fisherman. He hated the drudgery of the trade. Already, his father and brother unrolled their long net on the sand. Soon, the three of them would stretch it across the river and tie it into place. He hated the stink of that net, the stink of the fish he had to clean. He hated the debris he had to pick from the net, the floating garbage and dead animals. A few times, he had even found a bloated human corpse tangled in the mesh. Each time, his father had cut the horrid sight loose and it had slid downstream with disgusting grace.

Reale did not know how his father could take such an event in stride. For his own part, Reale knew he would have at least dragged the thing ashore and buried it; maybe even sent a message to the village church. But his father had never bothered. Curses, a flick of a knife blade, a kick, and the unknown victim would roll over in the murky water and bob away.

Any life but a fisherman's, Reale told himself. He would not spend all his days sucking half a living from the Courbee's murky waters. He sometimes saw the local baron's housecarls ride by. He thought about them; he was a broad-shouldered lad, strong and able. He knew he was fit for such a life. Once, in a nearby village, he had watched twelve knights gallop past on huge horses. Gleaming armor had shielded men and animals—their clatter had filled the air. They swept along amid clouds of summer dust but that could not hide their rich trappings and banners.

Such men stood as far above Reale as he stood above the fish which made his living. But Reale knew in his heart he would not always be a lowly net mender. He would rise. Some special destiny awaited him, even while the water chilled him and the mud licked his toes.

Reale's older brother stepped into the water and dragged the long net into place. He passed Reale as the younger man made his last repair. "Hurry," their father shouted. "You have to get the weir closed before the tide turns and the duckfish swim back to the estuary. Sunset and high tide at the same time; good night for business, lads. Hurry, hurry."

The old man unrolled the net on the shore and the elder son, Hars, strained his way across the river with it. "We know, we know," Hars cried.

"Then do it," the old man shouted back. "We haven't much time, I can tell by the current."

"We're hurrying," Hars grumbled. For his part, Reale also took hold of the net and started into deeper water. It was a heavy thing, long and baglike, and they had to struggle like men in purgatory to get it lashed into place. The water flowed dark and treacherous and they had to hurry to finish before dark.

"Careful," the old man shouted. "The current's starting to change. Don't get sucked under."

The words had hardly left the old man's lips when Hars screamed. "Oh. Oh, I'm stung." To Reale's shock, the tall youth let go of his end of the net and flailed against the water. He stumbled, grabbed for netting or post, missed all, and drifted downstream. "Help me," he cried. "Help me, help me."

"By all the gods," Reale's father cried. "There can't be rays this far upstream."

Hars screamed again, thrashed like a wildman. Reale lashed the net fast to the nearest post and struck out after his stricken brother. He thought he would catch up; then he saw a huge shadow roll at the water's surface and something huge and cold brushed against him. It towed his brother. "That's what it is," Reale shouted. "It's a barbray, a monster one."

Reale's father staggered into the water. "It can't be," he said, his voice so low it barely carried to Reale's ears. Then the old man wheeled toward a figure Reale had not noticed before, lifted his arms, and shouted, "You there. How can you watch and not help? Are you a man? Do you fear the gods? You have to help my boy."

With the splash and confusion of his brother's struggle, Reale had no idea how long the stranger had watched. He was simply there on the bank, like a tree which had stood for a century but had never been noticed till now. He looked dark against the evening sky, tall, broad-shouldered. He sat astride a powerful horse and led an even larger one. Reale was sure the fading light glinted off armor.

But Reale had no time to observe such things. He made a last lunge for Hars, caught a shoulder, and hauled Hars' dark head to the surface. The stricken man coughed, gagged, spit water, and they both swept ever farther downstream. "It's no use," Reale shouted. "The barb's still in his leg. I can't hold him."

The mounted warrior spurred his horse across the sand and sent spray flying as animal and rider plunged into the river. "Grab hold of something," the stranger shouted. "My poor horse can't swim as fast as you are drifting."

Reale lashed out with his free hand and managed to latch on to one end of the net where it still trailed downstream. His stricken brother screamed in agony and fear as man and creature struggled to possess him; Reale felt as if his fingers would snap or his arms rip out of their sockets. "Hurry," he cried. "I can't hold on."

The stranger reached them and yanked a longsword from its hanger. "I can't see where to strike," he shouted.

"Straight down," Reale screamed. "The barb is in his left leg; it's a good cubit long."

The stranger leaned from his mount and stabbed where Reale had told him; the water sizzled as the blade cleaved downward. The tip struck something and a dark shape thrashed toward the surface, lifted Reale's stricken brother behind it. Heavy jaws broke water and gnashed at the knight, who stabbed again with his sword. This time the blade pierced the flat head and the creature tore into a frenzy of motion, rolled and cartwheeled in the water, tore its victim from Reale's grip.

A sinuous tail surged into view and showed a series of long, white bones with razor tips barbed like fish hooks. The stranger slashed at the tail, sheared it away, and Hars floated free. The barbray surged out of sight beneath the waves. "Grab my horse's tail," the knight shouted. "We have to reach the shore."

The stricken man cried out, but could not hold on as the horse turned toward the bank. The poor fellow could only whimper with pain and shock. Reale had to grasp him, then hold fast while the horse towed both of them to shore. Reale's father had lit a lantern by then, which was a good thing. By the time they reached the sand, it was too dark to see.

The two young men floundered out of the water and Hars fell into the sand. As the old man ran up, the lamplight showed the snaky tail still attached by two of the long, white barbs which stuck out of it. "The pain, the pain," Hars cried. "I wish I could die."

"Nay, nay," the strange knight shouted as he climbed down from his horse. "You mustn't say such things." He grimaced as he took a closer look at the barbs and the blood which surged from the two wounds. "But still I cannot blame you. Are these fish's weapons poisonous?"

"No," Reale's father said. "The barbray strikes, then holds with its barbs till you die, or maybe it turns on its tail and bites you to death. It doesn't need poison." He wrung his hands. "But I've never heard of one attacking a man. Or feeding this far upstream."

"This one was huge," Reale said. "I think Hars stepped on it."

"No doubt," the knight said as he eyed Reale. "But tell me, lad, how was it that you saw where I should aim my blade beneath the water? Twixt the twilight and the murk, no man could see the deadly fish which held your brother fast."

Reale stopped short. He had seen the barbray's ugly bulk, had seen its spurs in Hars' leg as clearly as if the muddy water had been glass. "I don't know," he finally said. "I only told you what I saw."

"Ah. So you did." The knight smiled slowly. He was an old man, old as Reale's father—which surprised the youth. One would never have guessed the fellow's age by watching him in action. His hair and moustache gleamed white in the lantern's light, his body looked lean and vigorous despite his age, and gray eyes shone from beneath a finely creased brow. His blood was as noble as any in the world; Reale suddenly knew that. But the man gazed on Reale with the eye of a favorite uncle before he turned back to wounded Hars.

"He will survive and flourish if we cut these spurs out of his flesh," the knight said. "We'll have to disinfect his wounds before we bind them, though."

"We're just poor fishermen," Reale's father said. "We don't have any way to clean a wound like that."

The knight drew a razor-keen dagger from his waist. "I've quested long enough to carry all the goods I need," he said. "I have a vial of salve which will make pure the wound and aid its healing. Come now, we've no choice—you both must hold him down." Reale and his father grasped Hars' limbs while the knight cut the two barbs out of the tortured flesh. Hars revived in the middle of the operation, struggled, then passed out again.

Hars' blood washed into the sand as the knight cleaned the wounds, poured in the salve from his saddlebags, then bound the leg with bandages he also carried. "We have to get him to a resting place," the man said as he finished the operation. "Have you a dwelling?"

"Of course we do," Reale's father said. "It's a half a league east of here." Reale had to stare at him. He looked sick with worry. He had always been a hard man, a sharp man, but the injury to his son seemed to have taken the strength from him.

"Then lay this wounded man across my horse and I will walk with you."

Reale's father looked at him as if he were crazy. "But you're a nobleman. Why do you care what happens to my son?"

The knight smiled. "You asked for my assistance. Do you not remember? And besides, a life's a life. A human soul's a soul. I have a son myself, you see, a boy who disappeared some twenty years ago. How can I know I do not help my own lad, or a boy who's known to him?"

"I don't know about that," Reale's father replied. "Hars is mine as far as I know. So is Reale, here, his younger brother." He looked back at the knight, held the lantern higher, and a suspicious look swept over his face. "And I know you, too. I remember you from twenty-five years ago."

The knight smiled a little smile as they brought Hars around and helped him onto the palfrey. "You do?"

"Don't you remember me?"

"I've seen a raft of faces in the years since first I learned my heritage and journeyed to Carea."

"You ought to remember mine. My name is Phatyr; you engaged my ship on her final voyage."

Now it was the noble's turn to stare. He looked Reale's father over, then said, "Hair turned white and snowy stubble of a beard, but still the eyes are hard, the face is firm and square. It's possible."

"Is *this* possible?" Reale's father said. He rolled up the full sleeves of his peasant tunic and displayed the scars on his arms. Reale had seen those jagged marks often but had no idea where they had come from. "The evil wizard's lightning struck our mast and blew splinters all over. You should remember that."

"I must believe you, then," the tall noble whispered. "Tell me how this came to be, and how you find yourself a fisherman."

While they walked the distance to the fishermen's hut, Reale's father told the noble all that had passed after the two of them had fought the evil wizard Alyubol at the island of Krupos' dark capes. The story was all a new epic to Reale. His father's vessel, the *Proteus*, had been shattered by storm and lightning; Reale's father and a couple of his men had hid among the stones of the cape, then had struck south along the shore line the morning after the last fighting. A pirate ship had put in at the cove where the shattered *Proteus* lay, Phatyr and his men had stowed away. But they had been found and sold as slaves to a Buerdic galley which happened to put in at the same watering place as the pirates.

The war between Buerdaunt and Carea had carried the old

man all across the Thlassa Mey. He finally gained his freedom after his ship was captured by a Carean flotilla. He had landed near the city of Gesvon, where he had settled down, married, and reared his two sons. He had had enough of adventure. "Now I'm a fisherman," he said. "We scrape a living by drying duckfish and carp and hauling them to market in Stournes or Gesvon. It's not a noble life but it's free of risk." He looked up at Hars. "At least I thought it was." He turned back to the old horseman. "I understand you've become a mighty man, now, King Palamon of Carea. But all I know is that whenever you get near me, things go wrong."

Now it was Reale's turn to be shocked. His mouth fell open and he stared from one man to the other. His father knew a king! And of all kings, Palamon the Peacemaker! Reale's father had never been one to hide his past—or so Reale had thought—but this was something no one could have suspected.

As for Palamon, he started to smile but did not. Phatyr's last words had been no joke. "Indeed," the tall monarch said at last. "Our charter of your vessel brought you perils no man e'er could have forseen. But you were paid in gold for all the risks you took."

Phatyr pursed his dried lips and looked straight ahead. "You never paid the balance of the sum."

"You never brought us to our destination."

Reale tried to follow the conversation, but understood none of it. "Father," he asked, "do you mean to say you know this man?"

"From many years gone by," Palamon answered. "Your father was a dashing figure then, with many hands to man the swiftest ship on all the Thlassa Mey."

"Those days are past," Phatyr said. "Now I'm just a wrinkled old toad. But you never paid the balance, I'll tell you that."

"I'll deal with you again," Palamon said. "If you will let me stay this night beneath your roof, I'll make it worth your while."

Phatyr eyed Palamon and his mouth curled. "You're the king," he said at last. "You wouldn't like my hut."

"It's better than a night upon the ground. Come, man, I saved your son."

Phatyr looked up at Hars, who swayed in the saddle as they made their way. At last he agreed. When they reached Reale's house, they made arrangements with Reale's mother to give

Palamon sleeping space on the floor next to the fire. For the first time, Reale felt ashamed of his home. It was just a wattle-and-daub hut. No furniture, just a thatched roof—nothing compared to a castle's splendor, or even with the comforts a good inn could offer. But while Reale kept silent and his father acted as dour as ever he had in his life, Reale's mother gave the tall monarch a pleasant reception and tried to make him the best of everything—as royalty and hospitality demanded. In the morning, she even made the king a breakfast of fish boiled in milk she bought from a nearby peasant holding.

For Reale's part, he slept little during the night. How could a young man sleep, after all, when royalty breathed beneath the same roof? Hars' accident, which had brought them close to tragedy, had instead ushered in the greatest night of Reale's life. This was the answer to all his prayers, Reale knew it. Mere fortune could never have brought the king to pass the night in this house.

Reale's eyes followed Palamon's every move. To the youth's surprise, the tall monarch acted quite as much at home in a fisherman's hut as in any castle or palace. He gratefully received his breakfast from Reale's mother and devoured it with as much gusto as if he had not eaten for days. He flattered her on her cooking and held his wooden bowl between weathered hands as he stepped to the door and gazed out at the new day.

Something caught his eye. He glanced up at the towering beech trees which stood one on each side of the hut, then out at the Courbee, where it curved like a sapling bent into a trap, and he stopped chewing. He swallowed, pursed his lips, then almost smiled. "I've come to it already," he finally said.

No one answered until Reale said, "Say what?"

Palamon's head jerked about and the two of them stared at one another. "And you as well," the tall monarch said.

"I don't understand."

Palamon did smile then. "No reason that you should—it's just what someone told me not too long ago. The Oracle told me that this hut's where I begin my quest."

"A quest?"

"To find the *Tome of Winds*." Palamon smiled as if he had made a joke.

Phatyr heard and came closer. "What's a *Tome of Winds*?"

"An artifact," Palamon said simply. "An object I must locate."

"You really are on a quest, aren't you?" Reale asked. "A real quest."

"Perhaps you'd call it that," Palamon replied. "It's just a little matter."

"Not so little," Reale said. "You must have a reason for going after it. And when you looked outside just now, you saw something important, didn't you? You recognized something."

"Don't talk to the king that way," Phatyr said. He turned to the tall monarch. "I apologize for my son, your Majesty. He doesn't know any better, being of low stock, far from your station. We're all too low for you. Now morning's here and I'm sure you have to be on your way. We've held you here long enough."

"No, no," Palamon said. "The lad is right—a prophecy described this scene for me. But why, I wonder? What could you folk know about the *Tome of Winds*?"

The old man grumbled to himself. "I have no idea," he finally replied.

"Don't you be discourteous either," Reale's mother said. "You're no better than your son."

"If the Oracle sent him here, we must know something or have something that's important," Reale said.

"Don't interrupt," Phatyr snapped.

But Reale could not remain silent. "He's the king, Father, only a finger's length below the gods themselves. They sent him here for a reason."

Phatyr's expression became more bitter by the moment. "Kneel to him, then. Grovel on your belly. But keep your mouth shut."

Palamon ignored the old man's words and addressed the younger man instead. "A king's a mortal, just as you, lad. But the gods themselves have sent me here, as you remark, for reasons of their own. Perhaps there's information here that can be gained no other place."

Reale stared back at him. "What about Crossback? He's supposed to know everything."

"Hush," Reale's mother said.

As for Phatyr, his expression faded. "How do you know Crossback?"

"You told Mother you worked for him."

"Never. You never heard it from me." The old man wheeled on the woman. "What did you tell this boy? You're always telling him too much."

"I never said a thing." Reale's mother looked as surprised as anyone.

Hars had awakened by this time. He propped himself up on one elbow. "Who's Crossback? I never heard of him."

"No one ever hears of Crossback," Phatyr answered bitterly. "Don't ask questions."

"May *I* ask questions?" Palamon said. "I see a glimmer here."

Phatyr looked up at the tall monarch, then finally said, "How should I know what's going on?"

"No matter. But you know." The Carean king looked down on the fisherman and Reale watched them both, wondering how many knights the great man commanded, how many guardsmen he could summon at will.

"Crossback's a businessman in Stournes," Phatyr finally said.

Palamon's expression dried into a mask. "And what's his business? Tell me now, old Phatyr, tell the truth. My eyes and ears detect an undercurrent—not in river waters, either. You've a good location for some types of 'business,' haven't you? A boat sails by, a fisherman stands on the bank and throws aboard a package given him by someone from the city. No guard sees it, no night watch observes the matter. But a bag of coin's thrown back, you take a few and pass the bulk unto your master—what's his name? Yes, Crossback. When I met you, you were smuggling for good profit. Your misfortune has reduced your enterprise but I misdoubt you've ended it entirely. Tell me true, now, am I close?"

The woman looked at the old man but Phatyr's aged eyes did not flinch from Palamon's. "You can't prove a thing."

"I've no desire to prove a thing. By all the gods, I only need my questions answered. Crossback, whom you mentioned, who is he?"

"I've never seen the man," Phatyr said.

"He's very mysterious," Reale said. "Sometimes you hear his name spoken when people don't know anyone's listening."

"We only learned about him by accident," Phatyr said quickly. "But I think all the pickpockets and housebreakers and pimps along the Courbee work for him. A lot of them have never heard his name, though."

"That's enough," Reale's mother said. "Do you want to ruin us?"

Reale turned toward her. "But the king's searching for

something, Mother, and he came to us.'' A thought nudged him. ''And I want to go with him on his quest.''

All eyes fell on Reale; both his parents looked stunned. ''That's stupid,'' Phatyr finally said. ''We need you here, especially with Hars hurt.'' The old man turned to Palamon. ''The last time I dealt with you, I came to the worst misfortune that ever hit me. Now you show up again and by the next morning, I've got one son crippled and another who wants to leave me. You're bad luck for me, I tell you. Why don't you just go away and leave us alone?''

Palamon hardly listened. To Reale's surprise and pleasure, *he* became the object of the king's questions. ''Do you think you could guide me to the person you've described?''

Reale shrugged. ''I don't know. I might be able to.''

''We need you here,'' Phatyr said again.

Palamon wheeled toward the old man. ''For what? For dredging up this river's stinking fish and passing contraband to shadowed ships. Is that the way your son should pass his days?''

''A man has to live.''

''He does not need to limit life for your sake. Let the lad go out and take a risk, perhaps to gain a dream thereby. I like him well from what I've seen of him, and I would take him with me as a guide, at least until we've passed the gates of Stournes.'' He fumbled at his belt for his coin purse. ''You say your dealings with me cost you dearly many years gone by, and that you need your son at home? Here, then.'' He dug into the pouch and handed Reale's father a handful of Carean talents. ''That should be enough to pay you for the troubles of your past, at least as much as coin can pay for pain. And here's another, for the services of this fair lad.''

Coins heaped over Phatyr's cupped hands and some slid onto the floor. The old man stared at the fortune. ''You really must be the king,'' Reale's mother said.

''Please, Father,'' Reale said. ''I'll help him find this Crossback and we'll find his *Tome of Winds*. Crossback will know where it is. I'll make my fortune, don't you see? I'll be able to help you in your old age, more than I ever could as a fisherman.''

Palamon nodded his agreement. ''If your son guides me well and serves me as my squire, I'll open up for him a future brighter than the one which you claim fate denied you. But if you keep him from this opportunity, then you've no right to speak a scornful word of any man. Now give your answer, does he come or does he not?''

Phatyr looked up at the Carean king. There must have been over a hundred talents in the pile of coins, money enough to buy a house in the city, to move and leave petty adventures behind forever. ''I didn't expect this,'' he said. Then he added, ''Of course he can go.''

Reale hugged the old man and coins scattered across the floor. ''Thank you, Father. I'll make you proud of me.''

Reale's mother had some words to say—the lad could not ride with the king until he had bathed and put on his best jerkin and breeches, however plain they might still be. The sun climbed into the sky another thirty degrees before the lad at last followed Palamon outside. Together, they oated the tall monarch's horses. Before the sun's golden chariot climbed another jot, they started toward Stournes and the shadowy figure known as Crossback.

Chapter Five: Crossback

REALE WALKED BESIDE Palamon's riding horse until the two of them reached the first village between Phatyr's hut and the city of Stournes. There, Palamon had enough gold left to purchase the young man a decent horse, along with a used saddle and bridle. Since it came only from a small village, the equipment was not nearly as fine as the tall monarch's gear, but Reale managed to climb up and ride with as much pride as the finest knight on the banks of the Thlassa Mey.

"I can't help liking you," Palamon said as they rode along. "You have your father's look, but there is something more to you."

"Thanks," Reale said, for lack of a better answer.

"How long have you lived upon that river's bank?"

"As long as I can remember," Reale answered.

"You never went to school or studied your religion, I suppose."

Reale shook his head. "No."

"And yet you saw the barbray there beneath the murky water and you knew of a mysterious man named Crossback." Palamon's voice sounded far away. "Curious." Then he turned a smile on the younger man and clapped him on the shoulder. "You have all the charm of youth, at any rate. I'm pleased to ride with you."

Reale had never been as far as Stournes in his life. It turned out to be a thriving city. Palamon said it was not as large as Buerdaunt or either of the Careas, but it was a wonderland all the same, as far as Reale was concerned. Twenty years of

peace had brought thriving trade to the villages about the city
and much of that trade funneled itself through the city's ware-
houses and docks. For all its bends and shallows, the Courbee
was navigable to this point, and many shipmasters preferred
to sail the extra leagues upstream from Gesvon for the sake of
lower prices at the waterfront. Besides that trade, barges carried
goods between the smaller city and the larger.

Wine was the region's most prized product. In the vineyards
about Stournes, it was said that the sun caressed each individual
grape, presented it with a personal token of love each day before
he passed the rim of the world. Palamon told Reale that the
image of a curling grapevine decorated the local count's crest
and rows of barrels lined the waterfront.

They rode toward the oldest part of the town, the river
district. Palamon took the lead; he told Reale he had spent time
in Stournes, though it had been dozens of years earlier. "I'll
find the river district," the tall monarch said. "It is old and
rough, most fitting as a lair for him we seek. But you will have
to guide me on from there, the same as you directed my sword
into the barbray."

"I'll try," Reale murmured. Then he grew more confident.
"I've never been in Stournes," he said. "But my father used
to talk about a place called the Pilot Fish. Maybe we should
start there."

" 'Twas such a place when I resided here," Palamon said.
"An old saloon e'en then, a hangout for the loafers and the
lowlifes who infest this district. Very well, on to the Pilot
Fish."

The street led them downhill and along a stone wall. Soon
they found themselves riding along the river itself. Quays jutted
into the murmuring waters; barges or riverboats lay at some of
them. Reale could barely stand the stink of this place—it
smelled even worse than the Courbee's muddy bottoms at low
water. Debris rotted in backwaters or eddies and added to the
fumes which rose from the open sewer on the inland side of
the street.

After a bit, they came to the place Reale had named, the
Pilot Fish. Their arrival was well timed. The sun had set and
rough-looking characters came wandering out of the dusk.
Some looked like honest sailors and longshoremen, others had
the looks of beggars, vagabonds, and thieves.

Reale reined his horse in at the tavern door but Palamon
laid a hand on the young man's shoulder. "Let's go away from

here and lodge our horses. Then, I'll don a cloak to shade my armor, for I feel conspicuous, dressed as I am."

Palamon took the time to show Reale the complexities of care for three horses and the youth wondered at the mass of equipment the tall monarch possessed. He whistled as Carea's king drew forth his two-handed sword and concealed it as well as he could beneath a heavy blanket. He would carry it as a parcel but Reale could still see the long handle. "What a sword," the young man said. "To me, that's what it means to be a knight."

Palamon smiled grimly. "I know not what it means—I never have. The *Spada Korrigaine*'s a gift which I've found useful many times." He studied Reale. "You think there's glory to be had in steel?"

"I'm not sure what you mean. But I don't want to be a fisherman for the rest of my life, I know that. I've seen you and I saw a company of knights ride through a village once. I wouldn't mind being like them."

"Brave lad," Palamon said. But Reale could not guess whether the tall monarch was serious or just making fun of him. Then the Carean king unbuckled his own longsword. "If you want metal, strap this to your waist—and may it bring you all the pleasure you expect."

They left the stable and walked back to the Pilot Fish tavern, which they found infested by every sort of character. They bought some ale, milled about, eavesdropped. But in all the talk which buzzed through the place, they never once caught the name of Crossback. Palamon strained to see each man in the crowd at once, then he ducked his head and said to Reale, "What sort of man would know your Crossback?"

"I think my father once spoke to a big fellow with a bunch back. I've never watched any of his dealings myself."

"The search could be a long one."

"I'll shorten it." Before Palamon could stop him, Reale shouldered his way to the counter and caught the bartender's attention. "Have you ever heard the name Crossback? I've heard of the man but I don't have any way to find him."

Reale turned but the expression on Palamon's face told him he had made a mistake. The innkeeper stared at him, too, and other men stopped speaking to listen. "I never heard the name," one man answered in a gruff voice.

If he had never heard the name, why did the fellow stare

so? Reale wondered. But the young man did not compound his earlier mistake by saying it out loud.

The innkeeper snorted at the young man. "I never before saw such stupidity on two legs. You don't just walk into a place and ask a question like that."

Deep voices murmured and bearded chins rose and fell. Two rough-looking fellows headed for the door, while another pushed his way through the crowd toward Reale. But Palamon reached the young fisherman first, laid an arm around his shoulder, and drew him toward the far side of the room. "Let's go and talk," he said with a smile. "I fear the water here may grow too hot for swimmers such as this."

"I just wanted to stir things up a little, make something happen."

"I have no doubt that you succeeded. But we might not want to stay and watch the flames from your experiment." Palamon edged Reale toward the street door but the shabby-looking man caught them before they reached it. He was thin and grimy, a slouching weasel of a man. His breath smelled of ale and raw onions. "What's your business with Crossback?"

By now, Reale knew better than to give a straight answer. He shrugged and shook his head. "No business. I just heard the name once, that's all."

"Indeed," Palamon added. "And we have urgent business elsewhere."

"Hold on, old man," the rough said. "I don't think you'd mention the name and not care about the owner." He pushed Reale away with one hand and shot Palamon an evil smile. "What is it you want?"

Palamon eyed the fellow and handed to Reale the bundle which held the *Spada Korrigaine*. "We only want to leave."

The man saw the sword's hilt and edged away from Palamon, but his smile never wavered. "Take a warning," he said. "That's a dangerous name to bandy about."

Palamon did not answer. The two of them made it out the door and the tall monarch let out a breath as the cool night air kissed their faces. "I know not who this Crossback is," he said as they hurried uphill toward the stable. "But plainly,'tis a name to conjure with. I do feel curious for speech with him."

"I'll let you ask the questions, then," Reale replied. "I think I went about it the wrong way."

Palamon shrugged. "You tried a shortcut and we shall not

know its outcome till we've lingered for a while within this city. But we'll try a different way for now, I warrant you.''

But before they could talk longer, they turned a corner to find a half dozen shadowy forms waiting for them in the darkness. ''You're the ones from the Pilot Fish, ain't you?'' one of them said.

''And if we are, it's no concern of yours,'' Palamon replied in as smooth a voice as Reale had ever heard. ''If all of you are rugged as your looks, then you must know we have the means to counter any violence by you. We wish to spill no blood, but we will not be threatened.''

None of the toughs spoke, but a couple more men joined them. Palamon untied the outer covering of the *Spada Korrigaine* but did not pull it all the way off. He and Reale turned away from the street.

The men did not attempt to follow. Still, Palamon moved the cloth enough to unwrap the great sword. ''I grow too old for frolics such as this,'' he whispered. ''The longsword on your belt—it's time for you to take it in your hand. If we're accosted more, our only hope will lie in violence. But don't leap into fighting till I give the signal.''

Reale turned the gleaming blade in the dim light. ''I've used knives, but I've never even held a sword.''

''And you said you desired to be a knight.'' The tall monarch's smile was like a mask. ''We'll hope this does not mark your introduction to the craft.''

They backed along that dark street, then turned into another alley in an attempt to outflank the troop, to get back on the street which led to the stable. But a door opened, light poured into the darkness, and Reale found himself face to chest with a huge man, a giant two feet taller than himself. The giant looked strong as an ape beneath his ragged cloak. ''Who wants Crossback?'' a deep voice demanded.

''No one I know,'' Palamon replied. ''Therefore, you've no need to block our way.''

The man laughed and eyed the two of them. He turned in the light and Reale saw that he was a hunchback; his deformity was so huge his clothing bulged as if it had another head under it. From his looming height, he scowled at them. ''You caused a stir with your questions, though you say you don't want to meet the great man. Quite a stir. Maybe you have questions you don't want me and my friends to hear.''

Reale heard something; he glanced back and saw the gang

of toughs turn the corner behind him. Palamon saw them, too. "Not every question is intended for all ears," the tall monarch said.

The huge man laughed. "That's true, all right. We don't want our private affairs bandied about for everyone to hear, do we? What ho, Alan," he called to one of the men behind Palamon and Reale. "These gentlemen don't have anyone following them, do they?"

"No one that we've seen," one ruffian called back. "But they're not very humble. The old one even threatened us."

"He did? By all the gods, that's treasonous."

Palamon smiled a grim smile. "I rather did the opposite," he said. "For I entreated them to help prevent a combat which might spill unnecessary blood."

"Whose blood?" the hunchback asked with a snicker. "Yours or ours?"

"I've no desire for either," Palamon replied.

"You're cocky for a little man." Steel sighed against leather and the hunchback lifted a huge longsword into the doorway's light. "I like to fight cocky strangers," he said. "How would you like to fight me?"

"You see my meaning?" Palamon muttered to Reale. "Do not attack before I give the word." Then to the hunchback he said, "I have no urge to fight. I do not step upon unnecessary bugs; it soils my shoes and leaves revolting sights for those who follow me."

"You're the funny one, aren't you? Now listen to my joke." He pointed his sword at Palamon. "No man speaks to Crossback or even talks about him without my knowing and my sayso. That includes you, stranger."

"Who are you to pose such grave conditions?"

"My name be Alpus and I be the great man's brother."

"I see. Then Alpus, we have needs to speak with your respected brother, to gain information crucial to our cause."

Alpus laughed again. "It all comes down to the same thing, doesn't it? You did want to see him. How much will you pay for what you want?"

"That, Sir, depends on what it's worth to us."

Alpus cocked his head as if listening for something. Then he lowered his sword and leaned on the weapon as if it were a walking stick. "You sound like a man of condition. Pretty rare to see your kind scurrying around these alleys. Take off your cloak."

Palamon pursed his lips, then did as the hunchback demanded. Reale heard murmurs from the men behind him as the tall monarch exposed his glittering chain mail. Alpus roared with laughter. "You see? You see? He shows his knighthood. Good, that means you'll have good coin. Fifty talents for whatever it is you want to know, paid in advance."

"A goodly sum," Palamon said. "Quite high, I trow."

"Not too high. That chain suit shows you've got it, or that you can get it."

"I have it. Let us meet your brother, then."

Alpus shook his head. "Not likely. I take care of all business. I'll carry your question to him, then I'll carry his reply to you." He put away his longsword and Palamon signaled Reale to do the same. The younger man slid his weapon back into its hanger with relief.

"Nay, nay," the tall monarch said. "I'll not discuss this matter while an audience listens." He gestured toward Alpus' rough friends. "And I'll not send messages. I'll speak directly to your brother, not to you."

"Don't talk to me that way. I could have your arms torn off if I wanted."

"Perhaps, but retribution would be quick. As you have shown, I am a nobleman, a power in my own land. Harm one hair upon my head and retribution follows just as surely as the sun climbs from the sea each morning."

"How do I know that's true?" The hunchback once more stood as if he were listening for something.

"You cannot know. That's part and parcel of your risk."

"Ha-ha-ha. You're a bold one, that's all I have to say. Very well, then." Alpus waved at his henchmen. "Go ahead, you don't have to worry about me. This 'nobleman' isn't going to do anything drastic—and if he does, I can handle him and his boy."

The cadre of toughs broke up like a shoal of fish; every man went his own dark way. "Now, where shall we confer with your 'great man?' " Palamon asked.

"Right here's good enough."

" 'Tis not. I'll not conduct affairs as delicate as mine within a greasy alley. Find a better place."

Alpus shrugged. "That's right enough. Follow me." He pushed by Palamon. They followed; both of them eyed his huge hump with fascination while he led them to a place near the river. Wine casks lay in stacks as high as a building. "We're close to his headquarters. But before I take you that far, there's one more condition you have to meet.''

''And what is that?''

The beard split to show a broad grin as the hunchback drew his sword once more. ''You'll have to fight me. No one gets to see Crossback unless he fights me first. Most men back down at a challenge like that—are you one of them?''

''Indeed not,'' Palamon replied, taking his own longsword back from Reale. ''But still, I hate such strife. I've grown too old for foolishness; besides, when I have killed you, you will not be fit to guide me to your place of business.''

Alpus' laughter echoed along the street. ''Kill me? You're the one who's in danger. Don't worry, though—first blood is all I ask. Once that flows, we'll ease up. Are you game?''

''If you insist.'' Palamon held his cloak draped across his arm.

''Then let's have . . .'' Before Alpus could even get the line out, Palamon whipped the end of the cloak toward the hunchback. The tying cords twisted about the huge man's legs, Palamon pulled, and the giant's feet slipped from beneath him. He toppled to the paving with a loud cry.

Before Alpus could recover, Palamon leaped past him, caught his cape on the big man's swordblade, and jerked the weapon free. ''How now, you ruffian,'' the tall monarch cried with heaving breath. ''If you would vie until the first blood flows, then choose the place from which you'd lose it: arm, or leg or hand or face or neck. I did not come to play child's games with you, but to request your brother's information. I will gladly pay. I therefore ask these games to end.''

Palamon backed away and allowed Alpus to rise. The hunchback glared, pulled himself together, then brushed himself off with a surprising show of dignity. ''All right, all right. I have to allow you got the best of me that time. Not many men can do that. Come into my brother's headquarters.''

''I thank you.''

Alpus stepped to the largest wine cask, a huge tun which lay over on one side. To Reale's surprise, the hunchback picked up his sword and knocked in the end of the cask with the hilt, then clambered into the opening. ''Follow me,'' he ordered. ''Crawl in feet first; it makes it easier to keep an eye on you.''

Palamon crawled in, then Reale, and they crawled on hands and knees, rear ends foremost, till they emerged in a damp grotto dark as the inside of a whale's belly. Reale heard a click and saw the flicker as Alpus used a flint and steel to light a lantern. The place turned out to be the size of Reale's hut; moisture glistened on the walls and the bright eyes of rats gleamed from niches between the stones. A brick wall had been built along one side, probably to hold out water from the river, but it did not do a very good job. The mortar had turned rotten from dampness and age and crumbled out in many places.

In the center of the chamber stood tables and benches, surrounded by chests, bureaus, barrels, and an open space for a fire. At one side of the cave stood a cot with a rumpled cloak at one end. "So this is where he lives," Palamon said. "He must be fortified against the cold and damp to bear with such a place."

"It's not bad once you've built a fire and taken the chill off." Alpus lifted a couple of sticks from the woodpile, along with a handful of shavings, and did just that. Reale dreaded the thought of this place filled with blinding smoke. But as the fire burst into life, he was surprised to see that the smoke escaped quite neatly through a grate above.

"A neat arrangement," Palamon observed.

"It gets us by, my brother and me."

"You both live here?"

Alpus grinned. "We do."

"And do you both sleep in that single bed?" Palamon pointed toward the cot at the end of the chamber.

"You might say we do."

"Hmm. Where is Crossback now?"

"He's here."

Palamon and Reale looked about but could see no one. Reale could picture the shadowed master hiding in one of the grotto's chests or barrels; if so, he was smaller than Alpus. "If he is here," Palamon said, "I'd speak to him."

"Give me the money first. Fifty talents in advance, whether he gives you any information you can use or not."

Palamon sighed and turned to Reale. "Tell me what you know," he whispered to the younger man. "The *Tome of Winds*—how sure are you this prince of thugs might know its whereabouts?"

Reale marveled that a king would ask him such a question. "I don't know," he whispered back. "But if he doesn't know, I'll bet he knows someone who does."

Palamon studied the younger man, then reached into his purse and turned back to Alpus. "Then here's your gold. Now bring your legendary brother from the corner where he's hid.''

Alpus jangled the coins together and laughed. "Oh, he's not really hiding.''

"No, I'm right here,'' came a tinny voice from behind the hunchback. Reale blinked in amazement; he saw no one there.

Alpus laughed uproariously, then turned away from the two men, sat down at the table, and threw off his cape. Reale felt his mouth open as he beheld a neatly dressed little man, a tiny dwarf, seated between the big man's shoulders. The young man stepped closer and saw that the dwarf and the hunchback actually were attached; the dwarf grew from the broad back. Alpus was no hunchback. The hump was Crossback himself, neatly concealed by a cape.

Palamon seemed just as bemused. "How many men have seen this prodigy?'' he finally asked.

The dwarf lifted his wizened face and smiled a pinched smile. He was every way the opposite of his host-brother. Where Alpus was huge, he was tiny; where Alpus was broad and hairy, he was narrow and hairless. He was bald as an egg, had thin, almost transparent eyebrows, and barely enough stringy whiskers on his chin to form a limp goatee. "You're lucky,'' he said in a merry voice. "Not ten people have looked at me in my whole life. But I know most of the men in this district.''

"How?''

"By voice. Next time you meet with Alpus, I'll know you the first time you open your mouth. Alpus is my body—I'm little and helpless. But I can hear and I can live by my wits.''

"He remembers everything,'' Alpus said with a laugh that jounced the freakish dwarf who grew from his shoulders. "He knows everything there is to know about every deal going within twenty leagues of here.''

"Quit that laughing,'' Crossback snapped. "It's damnable that laughing—shakes me about like some brat's toy.''

Alpus managed to restrain himself and Crossback's smile returned. "My ears are very keen,'' the freakish dwarf said. "I heard all you whispered a moment ago. And yes, I can help you find your *Tome of Winds*, though why you'd want to is a matter only the gods can guess.''

"You can?'' Reale cried. He wheeled toward Palamon. "I told you he could. I didn't know anything about him but still I knew he was the man we had to ask.''

"Your guess was sound,'' Palamon said with a faint smile.

Then he eyed Crossback again. "What is the *Tome of Winds*, exactly?"

"You funny fellow. You mean you're after it and you don't even know what it is?"

"That seems to be the case."

"Hmm. Takes all kinds, doesn't it? Very well, it's a book."

"I assumed that much," Palamon said.

"Very good." Crossback laughed a mirthless laugh. "It dates from a time even before the Great Empire. Big. Brass cover. No one knows just what it can do, but it's supposed to contain chants and rituals the gods themselves use." He eyed Palamon keenly. "I've heard that just to read it is death, unless you're in direct communion."

"What's that?" Reale asked.

"Direct communication with a god," Palamon answered. "I have to say you're knowledgeable," he said to Crossback. "Then, tell me where this volume might be found."

"I have some ideas on the subject."

"I'll hear them."

"Not quite yet," Crossback said with a little laugh of his own. "You have to remember, information is my business."

"I've paid you fifty talents."

"Oh, that's plenty of money. But before I help you, you have to trade me information for information. After all, I have to get it somewhere; there's a limit to what I can pick up in my own dealings. You have to give me facts as useful to me as my information is to you."

"I've no idea what might interest you and what might not," Palamon replied. Reale listened and it dawned on him how this isolated little freak could know so much. Doubtless, he squeezed every client for news this same way. His brain, like a library, stored all he heard from criminals, priests, sailors, nobles, peasants.

"Just start talking," the dwarf said to the tall monarch. "I'll stop you when I've heard enough."

"That could take much time."

Crossback smiled merrily. "You can leave this instant if you want."

Palamon chuckled and seated himself next to Alpus. "You are a master of your trade, my friend. I'll tell you what I may." While the fire burned low and had to be replenished several times, the tall monarch told Crossback of the Carean court's intrigues. Reale felt bored and sleepy before long but Crossback's attention never wavered, his wizened little smile never dimmed. At last he allowed the tall monarch to lapse into silence. "That's enough. Now for the young one. Tell me all you know, lad."

Palamon glared at the little freak. "Must he give testimony also? How long must this take?"

"As long as I want it to take. You don't think we let him down here for nothing, do you?"

Palamon sighed and signaled Reale, who began to talk. But Crossback had no patience with the younger man; he stopped him after only a moment. "That's enough," he said. "I've heard that already." He turned a piercing eye on Palamon. "Are you ready to listen?"

"I am."

"To my mind, there are three possibilities. First, you could try the Library of the Polonians."

"You know of them?" Palamon asked, surprised.

"I do, and of old Reovalis. He passed on—let me think—about fifteen years ago. I understand the place is a shrine, now."

"Indeed, that's so."

"Myself, I doubt the *Tome of Winds* would be there. But you might find scrolls or accounts that would throw light on it. You'd have to do that research; I can't read, myself."

"That could take months," Palamon said.

"Don't get excited, there are two other possibilities. First, Count Hextin of Parvu, south of here. He collects all sorts of items."

"I know of him," Palamon said.

Crossback's smile showed narrow teeth. "I bet you don't know about the secret chamber in his donjon, where he stores shelves and chests full of forbidden volumes, odd trinkets. Curious man; he's going to get himself into trouble someday."

"That does not seem to worry you."

"Should it?"

"I would think you'd be discreet."

Crossback shrugged. "I am discreet. I know who you are, mighty King of Carean—I'd be a fool if I didn't. I'm sure you have bigger fish to catch than Hextin. You're out to find your long lost son, aren't you?"

Reale watched in bewilderment as Palamon inclined his white head and issued the dwarf a respectful smile. "Your logic is impeccable. Say on."

"The last likely place is the temple of Typhon in Quarval. A workman from there once told me how he'd helped widen a secret crypt in the sub-sub-basement of that temple. In return for hard labor, the priests apparently ordered all the masons and carpenters to be tracked down and slain. This fellow was a pitiful little man with a lot of fear in his voice."

"With good reason," Alpus said with a chuckle. "He had a lot of fear in his face, too. I talked to him, Crossback only listened in. At any rate, we managed to get him onto a ship. As far as I know, he's doing just fine on the island of Artos."

"Muse," Crossback said. "He slipped off Artos."

"Oh," Alpus said. "I forgot."

"You took considerable interest in him, then?" Palamon said.

Crossback shrugged his tiny shoulders. "He was interesting, his news was interesting. That counts for a lot. Now your time here is finished, I'm afraid."

Palamon stood. "I see. Then I shall send my messengers to Parvu and unto dour Typhon's priests as well. The *Tome of Winds* will fall into my hands before the end of summer."

"I hope so," Crossback said with a smile. "And much good may it do you."

Chapter Six:
The Red Company

THE DAY AFTER Odus of Guelt snatched Bessina from the palace at Tranje, Pafney brought the tale to Sir Flin, along with the dashing knight's horse and some supplies. They talked in a corner of the inn where the disgraced noble had gone after being ejected from the banquet. For once in his life, Flin was taken aback. "What are you telling me, lad?"

"She's gone. She disappeared along with Guelt's Count Odus and his men."

Flin rubbed his red eyes and stared at the younger man. "I didn't think she'd be that mad, even if I did lose the bet."

Pafney shrugged. "It seems she was, although the news is puzzling. Her attendants told me they packed all her goods and bedding onto mules. But then she left those items sitting, and the attendants, too."

Flin looked more open-mouthed than ever. "She left with Odus, then?"

"They say she spoke with him a moment, then accompanied him to parts unknown. They tell me they expected her return on any moment, but she did not come. When dawn broke, it was learned they both had gone, along with all his men, with precious little left behind."

Flin cradled his head in his hands. "I must have been even drunker than I thought. Nothing could make her run away with that persimmon. It's unbelievable—I swear to you, Pafney, I'll never take another drop as long as I live. I'll live on water, if only she'll forgive me."

"Yes, Sir." Pafney eyed his master but didn't say more than that.

Flin sat in misery and humiliation, then rubbed his eyes once more and looked up at the younger man. "You know, something's fishy about all this."

"Indeed, my Lord."

"Don't 'my Lord' me; I'm really serious. Bessina couldn't run away from me—that's an impossibility. Can the flower run away from the bee? Does the moth fly away from the flame? No. I tell you, there's more to this than meets the eye. That cursed Odus has kidnapped my wife, stolen her out of the palace under everyone's noses."

Pafney hesitated. "Do you really think so?"

"I don't think it, I know it." Flin leaned his elbows on the table and pressed his fingertips against his temples. "Oh, my head! Never again, I'll tell you that. Never again. And now I have to ride off and rescue my wife—what a time for a headache." A thought came to him. "Did you bring my armor?"

"I bore your personal equipment from the palace. All the armor you acquired in tournament still lies in storage; no way could I bring it here."

"And Velocipod? Did you bring him?"

Pafney nodded. "He waits for you outside."

Flin stood, took his purse loose from his belt, and studied the contents. "No great fortune, but enough," he announced. "It'll start us on our way and with a little luck, our wits will see us through. Oh, my head! But lead me outside and we'll get started on this adventure." His face brightened. "You know, maybe I ought to thank old Odus. At least this will make for some excitement."

Flin gathered his things, then the two men mounted their horses and draggled out of the city. As they rode south, Flin devised a plan. Odus of Guelt must have taken Bessina back to his own fief; it would be the safest refuge for him. Guelt lay far away, was isolated on three sides by mountains and on the fourth by water, and the Gueltic count ruled with an iron hand.

"I wonder," Flin said as they rode along. "Getting into Guelt is going to be a tough order, isn't it?"

"*Is* going to be?" The squire glanced at his master. "You've decided, then?"

"Of course I have." Flin scratched his chin. "But I need a few helpers."

"You cannot ask Queen Aelia or the Count of Tranje for troops."

Flin laughed. "Hardly. But I've a pretty good idea where I can find some men. We'll ride to the Greenlands and we'll hunt up my father's old band, the Red Company. I think they've still got a castle somewhere over there." He wrinkled his mouth up. "He's long dead, bless his soul, but they'll remember me. They're fighters, those lads; they'll jump at a chance for adventure in a place like Guelt."

"You're sure?" Pafney said.

"Of course I'm sure."

"Then onward to the Greenlands."

It took days for them to cross the endless hills and rivers which lay between Tranje and the River Fleuve, which marked the northern border of the Greenlands. Even in the domain of the brigands, the long peace had had its effect. The land lay quiet. The Red Company and their rival bands of freebooters had dwindled and had become complacent; many had given up raiding, had suffered lord, peasant, and clergy to live unmolested with the payment of a tithe.

Many leagues above the city of Danaar, the Fleuve flowed its lazy way through a gentle valley, which had once been the fief of some rich baron. A tumbledown old castle overlooked the smooth waters; the place had fallen to the Red Company many years before and had served as their headquarters ever since. Flin and his squire rode down the valley toward the old castle's jagged outline.

Though it was the middle of the afternoon, and any good sentry had to see them coming, no trumpets blared their arrival, no squires or outriders met them as they approached. A rough fellow in a leather jerkin looked down from the top of the wall and shouted, "Who be ye, strangers?"

"Flin, Leuval's son," the knight shouted back. "And my squire. I rode with this company a couple dozen years ago."

"I don't remember ye, but I remember old Leuval; he was our Lord High Commander many a year. He's dead, you know."

"I know. But I have other business here."

The man laughed. "I hope ye're not come to bag us all and turn us in to the proper authorities. It'll take more than a pair of you to do that."

Flin laughed back. "No, that's not what I'm here for. Who's your new boss?"

"Lord High Commander, you mean? We have to call him by his proper title now."

"Whatever he's called, I have a proposition for him."

The man atop the wall laughed again and Flin heard him say something to the fellow behind him. "A proposition for Pikefast," he said. "All right, Leuval's son, what's your proposition?"

"I'd rather give it to Pikefast myself."

"Ye would, would ye?" Another conversation took place at the top of the wall, then the man said, "Very well, but we shan't be responsible for your backside once you pass in. Pikefast's got a way with strangers."

The man yelled something down to the courtyard below and the rusty iron portcullis creaked upward. As it rose, Flin put heels to his horse and rode into the outlaw fortress. He smiled at Pafney as he heard the cry go ahead of him: "A visitor for Pikefast, a visitor for Pikefast."

A pair of lads who looked like hostlers ran up and led the two through the castle's inner ward to a stable, which was one of the few buildings in the compound in good repair. An old groom reached up and grabbed Flin by the hand. "Ah, Flin, my boy. It's been many a year since you last came to visit your old friend. Most of the old company's dead or retired, you know."

Flin returned the handshake, then leaped from his steed to throw his arms about the old man's shoulders. "I know it, Virgus, but I knew for certain you'd be here. You're too tough and gnarly an old stump to wither in less than a couple of centuries."

"Oh, I don't know about that," the groom said with a smile. "I get a little more worn out every year." Then he turned and admired Velocipod. "That's a fine piece of horseflesh," he said.

"That he is," Flin replied. "It'll probably take me a lifetime to pay for him, but he's the finest warhorse this side of the sun." He nudged Pafney. "He's the second love of my life, as this lad will tell you."

"Yes, that he is." Pafney smiled back.

Virgus touched the horse on one cheek. "I've kept the Red Company's coursers for four dozen years if it's a day," he said. "He's the finest I've ever seen. You know, Flin, lad, I kept horses for you in your youth and for your father and for others after that. Those were glory days; we were more than just rent collectors then. We took what we wanted and we lived like kings. This new boss, this Lord High Commander, as he's started calling himself, he's not the man your father was, though he'd tear my tongue out if he caught me saying it.''

"No one's the man my father was," Flin said with a laugh.

"Pikefast thinks he's ten times more high-falutin'." Virgus spat. "He thinks he's some Lord High Admiral, some baron, high and mighty, waiting to dine with the king, instead of one of the Red Company. He lives on tithes from the lands around here instead of riding the way we used to. Faugh, it's a pitiful world." He looked up at Flin and squinted slyly. "But now you've come back, a man who really does have the king's eye. You'd better watch out for yourself, that's all I can say."

"Don't worry," Flin said. "I won't have any trouble."

"I wish we'd get into a war," Virgus said dreamily. "I'd ride out and join with one side or the other in a minute, rather than stay with this band of pale-livered dogs. Between the two of us, that's what a lot of the others would do, too."

"Then be of good cheer," Flin said. "That's what I'm here for."

Virgus' eyes took on a gleam. "Really? Name the time, name the place. I'll come."

Flin laughed. "I suppose I'll have to talk to his 'Lordship' first. I have to observe all the niceties. And don't you think you're too old to ride off on an adventure like this?"

"Too old? You little whoreson. You knave. Are you less of a man than when you were at twenty-five? Nay, I'll bet not. You're craftier, you're more steady in the saddle; if not, you're a nincompoop and I have no time for you." He pointed toward the forge and the rack of tools that hung along one stable wall. "You call me too old again and I'll take a mallet to you; I'll stretch you out on that floor like a fathom of tired hemp."

"All right, all right." Flin laughed again. "You've made your point."

"Then whatever it is, I'm in?"

"You're in, you're in," Flin said. "I can see my life's at risk otherwise."

"You'd better believe it."

Just then, a skinny man in armor and a crimson tunic strode into the stable. "The Lord High Commander has learned of your visit, Sir Flin. He will meet with you at his convenience, if you will be so good as to follow me."

"That's Melvo," Virgus said. "He's one of the Lord High Admiral's little captains."

"Watch your mouth," Melvo said to the old man. Then he turned back to Flin and said, "Please accompany me."

The man was such a walking parody of the marshal of some lord's great hall that Flin had to press down a smile. He glanced back at Virgus, who shot him an "I told you so" look. "All right," the knight said. "Let's go."

The gawky fellow led Flin and Pafney from the stable into the castle's main keep. He took them to a little chamber which was lavishly appointed, though in terrible taste, and told them to wait. The two of them cooled their heels for what seemed forever. The room became stuffy and hot, Flin grew impatient, Pafney paced back and forth and looked at his master every now and again as if wondering whether they had been imprisoned.

Finally, Melvo came back and led them to a larger room, decorated in no better taste. The walls stood festooned with weapons, mementoes, silver and gold cups and plates, candlesticks hung on chains, and all other manner bric-a-brac. At the far end of the room stood an ironwood desk piled high with parchments, scrolls, receipts, inkstands, pens, and blotters.

Behind the desk sat a man a little older than Flin. He had a round face, no beard, and his hair was dark and shaggy, with large patches of gray—the gray patches had a yellowish tint. One look told Flin the man had recently tried to dye his hair, but the tint had washed out. Once more, the knight barely kept back a smile.

"So you're the great Sir Flin," the man said. "My name is Pikefast; I'm Lord High Commander of the Red Company, as you probably know. Pardon the confusion in my office, but I'm sure you know how much paperwork it takes to manage such a large estate as this one."

Flin shrugged. His own estate in Carea was managed by the warden he had hired for the purpose, and by Bessina when she was not off being kidnapped. But he doubted this Pikefast had any desire to hear that.

"Do I remember you?" Pikefast asked as he shook Flin's hand. "I seem to remember a skinny, dark-haired lad who ran at old Leuval's heels sometimes."

"It might have been me," Flin replied. "That's so long ago I don't like to remember."

Pikefast laughed. "Yes, yes, that's true. The years go by, don't they? Leuval was a great man but he belonged to a differ-

ent age. I'm afraid the old ways of doing things don't hold anymore. I've had to change many things, streamline the Red
Company, as it were. But what brings you to Castle Fording?''

"I need men for an operation.''

"Oh? How so?''

"I have a quarrel with Count Odus of Guelt.''

Pikefast pursed his lips and led Flin toward the door. "A
quarrel, eh? But you have the Carean king's ear and I'm sure
you know other counts and barons, too.''

Flin shrugged again. "This quarrel doesn't involve them.''

"It doesn't involve me, either.''

"You might say I had a difference of opinion with the
countess of Tranje, who's also the king's sister. Besides, he's
off on his own mission and I don't want to bother him. If you're
worrying about whether I'll pay you, I guarantee spoils enough
for all.''

"Think nothing of that. Men of honor can always trust one
another; I have no worries on that score.'' A servant walked
into the chamber, bowed, then walked out, and Pikefast gestured after him. "But come, let's have dinner. We eat well
here, I'll warrant you.'' He called the servant back. "Geoffrey,
tell Sir Flin what items are on today's bill of fare.''

The servant bowed again and spoke like a trained parrot.
"Since this is a feast day, your Lordship, the bulk of the
company will be present. The first remove comprises larded
boar's head and a pottage made of leeks, bread, and blood.
We will also enjoy beef, mutton, pork, goose, and wild rabbit.

"The second remove will comprise duck, pheasant, and
chicken stuffed with egg yolks and dried currants, a pottage of
parboiled birds—thrushes, sparrows, starlings, magpies,
rooks, and jackdaws—and tarts made from capons and hens
beaten in a mortar.

"The last remove will include rabbits, hares, teals, wood-
cocks, snipe, and a pie made of ground pork, cheese, sugar,
and pepper.''

The servant glowed with pride as he recited the complex
menu and Flin noticed that Pikefast glowed just as much on
watching Flin's reaction. "There, now,'' the Lord High Commander said as the monologue ended. "Is that not fare fit for
any noble—or even a king?''

"I drool just to hear it,'' Flin replied.

A bevy of servants marched down the corridor and broke
into the conversation. The leader knelt and held a bowl of water

in front of Pikefast. Pikefast washed his hands in the bowl and dried them on a towel presented by a second servant. "These are my yeomen," Pikefast said to Flin as he pointed out each of the line of servants. "They serve at the head table, though I have others to serve at the other tables. Yeoman of the ewer, yeoman of the chamber, yeoman of the cutlery, yeoman of the cellar, of the buttery, of the pantry, the carver, my cupbearer, and my personal sayer, who tastes my food before I dine." He looked at Flin. "As a courtesy, I'll have him taste yours, as well."

"Oh, thanks," Flin said.

"Don't mention it. You see, the old days of brigandage and raiding had to end; now we live as refined a life as any of your friends at the Carean court."

"I'm surprised your men don't revolt, what with all the servants cutting into their share of the booty."

Pikefast smiled a superior smile. "Times have changed, times have changed. It's not your father's day anymore."

"I can see that." They walked into the hall and Flin looked at the men who roistered at the tables below the dais. They certainly sounded and drank like the Red Company of old, but their numbers were dreadfully thinned. He saw barely two-thirds as many as had ridden with the Red Company of old, and many of these were old men now, past forty. The company he had known had been mostly young rogues.

They sang lusty songs, drank wine from deep pitchers, and laughed at their own coarse jokes. Occasionally one would flick a dagger at one of the rats which scurried through the deep straw strewn across the floor. Flin shrugged. Their numbers had dwindled and they had grown older, but they still looked like stout men who would welcome an adventure.

Pikefast sent Pafney to eat with the men on the lower floor, but he kept Flin beside him on the dais. The men went more or less quiet as their leader walked to his place. They waited for him to sit, then started in all over again at their songs and horseplay. Another pause followed as an almoner offered a prayer. Then servants brought the food in and the meal began in earnest.

Flin could feel the older man's eye on him with each bite he took. The food was decently prepared, though, so that did not bother him. He ate lightly and, when the meal had ended, he asked Pikefast for permission to speak to the hall.

"Certainly," Pikefast answered. He stood, drew his dagger, and rapped the side of his silver goblet. The hall went silent and he said, "Our noble guest, Sir Flin, would like to speak to you."

"Then let's hear it for Flin," one man shouted, and laughter ringed the hall. Pikefast scowled, though the laughter did not bother Flin himself. The knight stood and spread his hands to restore order.

"Old friends," he cried. "I've ridden with you and shared your danger. I've shared the bread of your table many years past and again today. Now I need you to listen. I need armed men, independent men who answer to no noble."

"For what purpose?" one man cried.

"I want revenge against Odus, Count of Guelt. He wronged me and he's got to pay."

"What was his crime?" another man asked, but was drowned out by cries of "Who cares what he did?"

Flin answered anyway. "He kidnapped my wife, my Bessina."

"How do you know she didn't just run away with him? If she did, just kill her."

Flin smiled. "Nay, nay, friends. I know her as well as the handle of my sword, as well as I know myself. She would never leave me of her free will."

More cries filled the hall: "That's what every husband says" and "Guelt's too far away and too strong to go a'raiding." Flin had to wait for the clamor to die down before he could speak again.

Pikefast broke in. "Sir Flin, when I allowed you to speak, I had no idea you were going to put such a proposal. Do not seek to sway my men, for I am their Lord High Commander and you do me wrong thereby. Any such question must be put to me."

Flin turned on the older man. "But the Red Company always decides its course by a majority vote."

"Maybe in your father's time, but not now. Hold your peace."

Flin stared at the man. "I offered a bonny venture. We'll have to use our wits, I grant, but there's good booty to be had. All you have to do is lay low Count Odus' citadel."

Pikefast shook his head. "I told you, I am the Lord High Commander. I don't care how things were done in your father's day."

Uproar filled the hall; men shouted, pounded the tables, and threw food. Cups and trenchers clattered off the walls and servants ran for cover until Flin finally made himself heard over the confusion. "Then I claim the ancient right of the free companies. I challenge your leadership."

Pikefast stared. "How? I am elected by my peers and appointed by the gods. You can't walk into a hall and challenge the lord thereof."

"Oh, yes I can," Flin cried. "You say you're a lord? Then I challenge you to knightly combat, the two of us with horse and lance outside this hall right now."

Pikefast looked as if he had turned into a building about to cave in. He stared at the company of men, then at Flin, and finally said to the knight, "No, I'll not face you."

"Then you're no lord in your heart—and these men are free to do whatever they want."

"Ask them, then. They won't go with you. Times have changed, times have changed." A smile crept across the older man's face. "If you insist, I will answer your challenge, too—but in my own way."

Flin brightened. "You'll meet me on the field? When I win, you'll have to let your men ride with me."

Pikefast glanced across the hall, where a few men chanted, "Answer him, answer him." The cry rose and spread through the long chamber. Finally, he nodded. "I'll not meet you myself but you can fight my champion. If he wins, he will receive your horse, your trap, and all your equipment. If you win, you have only to pledge some sort of surety and you can have however many men will go with you."

Flin beamed. "Let's have at it," he said.

Pikefast looked out over the hall. "Who will be my champion?" Many men had roared for action; now they went silent. Only a few remained standing. Pikefast looked them over, then called, "Sheldorr, you are appointed to serve. Approach us."

A huge fellow walked toward the dais. He looked like a walking mountain and was one of the younger men in the hall. He had a square, ruddy face, no neck at all, and arms that looked as big around as Flin's thighs. "Here I come," he roared. "I'll fight him, just for the excitement."

Flin looked at the huge man and had a hard time holding on to his smile. The fellow was so big he did not look as if he would even need a horse. "The gods and Velocipod be with me now," the knight murmured to himself. "Bessina, you're going to get me into trouble some day."

Chapter Seven:
A Friendly Joust

WHILE PIKEFAST LOOKED on, the human titan named Sheldorr strode the length of the hall and stood before the dais, so tall his face rose almost level with Flin's even though the dais stood half a cubit higher than the hall's floor. The man's arms bulged as if they could shove a sword's blade through a tree trunk. "I've heard of you, Sir Flin," Sheldorr said. "I'll enjoy breaking a lance with you."

Flin smiled back. "You're a solid fellow, aren't you? So much the better, though; you'll make a fine target." He turned to Pikefast. "Where are your lists?"

"The two of you can meet in the bailey," Pikefast said. He turned and swept out of the chamber, followed by the long line of his servants.

Sheldorr tapped Flin on the shoulder and said, "Follow me," upon which he and Flin joined the crowd and moved toward the hall's main door. They made their way to the yard the Lord High Commander had named. Flin could see the place was not really a listing ground, but rather an enclosure between old stone walls. It was barely long enough for two horses to charge one another and wide enough for unhorsed warriors to duel.

He found his squire in the crowd and sent him to the stables, to bring Velocipod and Flin's armor. Sheldorr spoke with the knight for a moment before he also gathered up a couple of young men and walked to his quarters.

Approving murmurs rose as Squire led Velocipod back through the crowd. The magnificent beast stood a hand higher than other warhorses and his intelligence and spirit showed with every step. Pafney also led their packhorse; when he stopped, he pulled down a large package which held Velocipod's caparisons. "I wager we must gird this animal within this rowdy place," the young man said unhappily. "We've no pavilion and no quarters are assigned to us."

"We'll see about that," Flin said. "You give me my armor and take these two back to the stables. Virgus will caparison Velocipod or I'll be very surprised. As to my own armor, I'll be buggered before I'll suit up in front of a mob like this. Where's Pikefast?" he yelled. "Where's the boss?"

Flin looked around and finally saw the Lord High Commander of the Red Company, standing on a landing which overlooked the bailey. "Where are my quarters?" he yelled up at the man. "Doesn't this castle have a place for visiting knights? And a man to help me put on my armor. It's the accepted thing to quarter emissaries, isn't it?"

Pikefast's mouth twisted and he turned to one of the servants behind him. "Find him rooms." The man hurried down to Flin, led him to a chamber, and the knight soon returned in fine form. Burnished plate covered his arms and legs, from his articulated gauntlets to his pointed sallerets. The coat of arms embroidered onto his tunic was of his own design, for his father had worn the colors of the Red Company. The crest featured a cock, rampant, standing atop a snake, nowed, proper.

Sheldorr appeared in his armor, leading his warhorse, wearing the same kind of red tunic Flin's father had once worn. Then Pafney appeared, leading Velocipod, who outsized Sheldorr's warhorse by the same proportion that huge man outsized Flin.

Sheldorr looked enviously at the mount. "A good animal," he said, his voice tinny from inside his basinet.

"I think so," Flin replied. He swung up and into his saddle, grasped Velocipod's reins, and gently nudged the horse's flanks. He edged close to the big man. "But let's take a look at one another's lances."

Sheldorr's laugh sounded as if it came from the bottom of a well. "What's the matter, don't you trust me?"

"Of course I trust you. I just don't trust your boss." He took the lance Pafney handed him and passed it to his opponent. "This is the kind of shaft I use."

"Nice," Sheldorr said as he looked the weapon over. "You like good gear, don't you?" He passed it back to Flin, then handed over one of his own lances. The shaft did not show the quality of the weapons Flin used but it was as huge as its owner. It was a cubit longer than Flin's lance and heavy in proportion.

He had half expected to see at the tip of it the heart-shaped lance head used in battle. Such a spearpoint would have been deadly had it struck home; it was the reason he had asked for the exchange. Instead, he smiled to look on a coronel, the standard, three-pointed head used for jousting. Such a tip would catch armor, would hurl a man from the saddle and bruise him, but would not kill. "Good," Flin said. "You're an honest man."

"It's a coronel, same as yours. What did you expect?"

"Who knows? Are you ready?"

"I'm always ready."

Flin cantered toward one end of the bailey while men scattered to give him room. His specially smithed armor fitted him into the saddle perfectly, as secure as a babe in a cradle. He gripped the animal with his legs the way a magnet grips a nail. This was the way life was meant to be lived.

He swung his lance tip down and adjusted the ring behind the grip, fastened it to the ring on his saddle. The Red Company's champion rode his own horse to the other end of the bailey and did the same. The two men eyed one another, then charged. Velocipod's body surged beneath Flin; the knight's lance tip shot toward his opponent. The weapon struck with bone-jarring impact and shattered like matchwood.

Sheldorr's lance tip missed and barely glanced off Flin's shoulder. The two men circled their horses, Flin took another lance from Pafney, and they charged again. This time, Flin's lance was once more on the mark and so was his opponent's. But while Flin's weapon shattered a second time, Sheldorr's coronel caught the knight square on his breastplate, and hurled him from his snug saddle like a sack of flour. The world whirled about him, the ground struck the breath from him, and he found himself clambering to his feet while the watching men cheered their lungs out.

Flin's head twirled but he threw himself out of the way as Sheldorr charged again, then whistled for Velocipod. All his life, Flin had had a rare knack for training animals—and Velocipod was a horse of rare intelligence. At Flin's signal, the animal threw itself against Sheldorr and his mount, teeth gnashing, hooves flailing, like a black lightning bolt. The smaller animal whinnied in panic, then stumbled and went down. Sheldorr had to leap from the saddle to keep from being pinned.

The big man struck the ground in a heap while his horse rolled on its back, a flailing mass of legs which rolled upright and scrambled away, its bardings clattering. Before Sheldorr could do the same, Flin was upon him, sword drawn. He caught Sheldorr's helmet visor and jerked the man upright. "Do you yield?" Flin shouted as he brandished his weapon before Sheldorr's astonished eyes.

"Wait, no fair," Sheldorr cried. "I was supposed to fight you, not your horse."

"A knight and his horse are one, just like a man and wife. Fight one, you fight both. Do you yield?"

The huge warrior yelled and twisted, but he was helpless in Flin's grasp and had no choice. Though the men who lined the bailey, Pikefast most of all, swore and shouted catcalls, the big man could only yield.

Flin let him go and helped him to his feet, which was a considerable effort. Then he turned toward the Lord High Commander. "Now you have to keep your end of the bargain," he shouted toward the balcony. "Your men will go with me to fight Odus of Guelt."

Pikefast hesitated. "I'll have to think on it."

"No thinking to be done. Your champion fell and we both know what that means."

"He didn't fall to you," Pikefast shouted. "Your horse beat him, not you. And your horse wasn't a party to the challenge."

"A knight and his horse are the same," Flin said again, but men clustered about him and shouted him down. They spouted oaths and cries in support of their leader.

To Flin's surprise, Sheldorr himself appeared at his side and held up his brawny arms for a chance to speak. "Hold on a breath," he cried. "I'll grant this fellow used a nasty trick to knock me out of the saddle. But I'll also warrant his horse didn't learn that trick by itself. He beat me, I'll admit it. And as far as I'm concerned, he did it fair and square. If we both fought afoot, maybe he'd get the better of it and maybe I would, but I say it doesn't matter. I say this fight is the most excitement I've had in the last year, for all that it didn't last very long." He laid his gauntlet-covered hand on Flin's mailed shoulder. "In my mind, this fellow promises excitement and booty— and I'm for riding with him."

The huge warrior's speech took the bowels out of the protest.

Then Virgus, the old man from the stables, forced his way through the crowd. "I agree with Sheldorr," the old man shouted. "I'm older than oak roots, worn out, creaking, full of winds. But I'm game for the venture, if none of you are. Why, we haven't lived as fighting men should live these last five years. We've lived as fat franklins, and I'm dead against it. I'll tie my banner onto Flin's staff, if he'll have me."

The crowd's air changed. Men eyed one another, then at the two men who stood by Flin. Many nodded. Pikefast plainly saw that the day swayed against him and he said, "That's well and good, but times change. This company has to refine itself and live as a company should, on lands we've already won."

"On lands we hold for you, you mean," came a voice from the crowd. "You're the one who gets to live like a great lord."

Pikefast pursed his lips. "All right, then. Am I to understand some of you want to go with this man?"

A dozen voices shouted the affirmative. Flin looked about; that dozen was still only a fraction of the company. Then Sheldorr glowered about and shouted, "How many?" his eyes darting such sparks that another dozen raised their fists.

Flin looked back up at Pikefast; the man was plainly struggling to keep his hold on the situation. "Who stands with me?" the Lord High Commander cried from his balcony. And when no more men raised their hands than had shouted in Flin's support, he seemed more worried than ever. "The bulk stands undecided," he shouted hastily. "Very well, Sir Flin, you may take whoever will go with you and you may attack Odus of Guelt. But I require a ransom for the men who will be killed or maimed in your hire."

"There'll be booty enough to pay the mark," Flin shouted.

"So say you. But how are we to trust you?"

"What's your ransom?"

"That horse you're so proud of."

Flin's mouth fell open and he stared up at the balcony. "You can't be serious. Me give up Velocipod? After all the hours I put in on him? I'd sooner give up my own wife."

"If you take him with you, that's exactly what you will be doing."

Flin glanced about, sifted the faces of the men who surrounded him. One of them nodded and said, "It's a fair price." The others nodded, too.

"But he's the nicest thing I own," Flin shouted.

"It's not too much," Sheldorr said. "And if we bring down

the booty you promise, you can ransom him back.'' He looked about at his henchmen. ''I'll stand with you and so will any man who wants to call me a friend.''

Flin stared about, frowned, put his hands on his hips. While he stared, Sheldorr lifted his face to the balcony and shouted, ''If the horse stays with you, can all our men ride with Sir Flin?''

Pikefast swore to himself. Finally, he nodded.

''And if we bring back the right booty, will you ransom the horse back for a share?''

''Nay. The animal belongs to me.''

''Wait, wait,'' another man shouted. ''Only one man can ride any horse at a time—and that'll be you, won't it? I say we take the booty, if there be any, and spread it between us, rather than one animal for you.''

Pikefast glowered but he could see the way of things. ''You men are not loyal,'' he sputtered.

''We elected you and set you in your place;'' Sheldorr shouted back. ''And you've forgotten it. I say we decide our destiny; we set out with Sir Flin first thing in the morning. It's a vote, just the way we used to do.''

''And the horse is the ransom?'' Pikefast shouted.

Flin's mouth ground itself into a line. Finally, he answered, ''Yes.''

Cheers filled the bailey, though some men still refused to join the expedition. Flin watched sadly as the great horse was led off to Pikestaff's section of the stable. ''Don't you worry,'' Virgus whispered. ''He'll be waiting here if ye return—the Lord High Admiral would rather shove a leek up his nose than take part in any real fighting. He's not the man we thought we elected boss, I'll warrant you that much.''

And so it was that Flin purchased the aid of the Red Company, or at least of about fifty warriors who joined him. He made himself general of the expedition while Sheldorr and Virgus became his captains. They agreed to spend the rest of the day preparing and to set out in the morning at first light.

Flin and Pafney took turns that night, standing watch inside the door to their sleeping chamber. Neither of them trusted Pikefast and their suspicions were borne out toward morning when the door inched open and a candlelit face appeared. Melvo's eyes locked with Flin's, he blanched, stammered, then said, ''The Lord High Commander asked that I look in on you. He feared you might not sleep well.''

"I daresay I don't sleep as well as he'd like," Flin said with a smile. Then Melvo's face pulled back and the door slipped shut once more.

They set out the following morning, all fifty of them. It was a smaller force than Flin would have liked, but it would have to do. They foraged as they went, headed southeast toward the Thlassa Mey, where they would split up. Some would ride horses to Danaar, some would ride to the smaller city of Vouill. Separately, they would book passage to the city of Ourms, so as not to arouse suspicions about where such a body of men might be heading.

Flin and Pafney rode with the Vouill group, while Sheldorr and Virgus led the other men to Danaar. It took two days to reach the coast. The sun glided behind the hills and dusk fell, but Flin's party rode on in hopes of reaching the port and spending the night there.

They followed the shore line for leagues as the glow faded on one side of them and a pale half moon rose on the other. Silver light played off the sea; the breakers stretched away and away. Combers dashed against the sand a fathom from the horses' hooves. Flin glanced across the moonlit sea and said, "By Tyche's dice, what in Hades' name can *that* be?"

Many eyes followed Flin's gaze; the waters frothed themselves into a dome a couple hundred cubits out from the shore. On the occasions when he had been coaxed into bathing as a youth, he had sometimes taken the wet washing cloth, folded it into a sackful of air, and held it under the surface of the washing pan. When he had squeezed the air out of the cloth, the soapy surface of the water had rolled and bubbled exactly as these waters. But this was a thousand times greater than that, and it kept on, like a volcano erupting.

The men reined in and stared at the prodigy. It moved toward the shore at a steady pace and teased their ears with a steaming sound, ominous as any rumble of any marching army. "I wonder what it is," Pafney breathed.

"I don't have any idea," Flin replied. "But I don't want to stay and find out." He set spurs to his horse and the other men did the same; they galloped along the sands as hard as their mounts could run, then thundered up a path to the top of the bluff beyond the beach. Here the riding was harder; shadows lurked everywhere to make their horses stumble. But at least they had gained a safe margin from whatever it was that approached the beach.

They reined their horses again and saw the waters actually leap now, hash themselves into froth and spume that hissed into the air like white sparks. Then the seas recoiled from the center of the disturbance and Flin saw an unearthly sphere of darkness, blackness blacker than the darkest night. It rolled toward the shore. The surface looked fuzzy, like the soft smear of stars which looked down from the clear sky. But at the center of the blur, the blackness was complete and unfathomable.

"By all the mighty gods," Pafney said in wonder. " 'Tis such a sight as I have never witnessed. I believe it is a portent of some evil."

"Who knows?" Flin replied. "We have other rats to skin."

"But see how it advances up the shore, and how that darkness swarms upon the beach as if it were a living, growing thing. I fear it, milord."

"Ow," Flin said. He and some of the other men swatted at a flight of biting flies that came from nowhere. "These bugs aren't necessary. Let's get out of here—but wait, I think I see a man in the middle of all that blackness."

Pafney brushed off an insect as he peered down at the object, which now advanced along the beach. "I cannot tell, milord," he said. "Your eyes are keener than my own, or else you are mistaken."

"Who cares?" another man said, adding a slap at a fly and an oath for good measure. "These flies are more than I can stand."

"Let's ride, then," Flin said. "I don't love scratching bites more than any other man." So the company took out along the edge of the bluff and rode toward Vouill as quickly as they could go in the darkness.

Chapter Eight:
The Pale King's Hireling

VILLAGES DOTTED THE countryside about Buerdaunt, ranging in size from a couple of peasant hovels built a few cubits apart to settlements of a couple dozen buildings and others of a hundred or more. Some had names, some did not. All of the larger ones boasted an inn and at least one alehouse to quench the thirst of travelers, freemen, and the tradesmen who might ply their businesses nearby.

The village of Loth lay four leagues up the Priscus river from the great city, astride the road which led from Buerdaunt to Tolq. The alehouse there was known to the townspeople as the Red Boar, though no signboard announced that name to the public. Rather, the first owner of the place had been a huge, red-bearded man, jovial and of a warm temper. The name had been given in his honor and had remained even after he had died and the place had passed to his son.

It was normally a quiet place but on Sabbath evenings a rougher crowd came in—due to the fact that respectable men would be at home with their families. Vagabonds, soldiers, and the rougher hired men and craftsmen gave no heed to things higher than their own bellies and their own glands.

On this night, a dozen men sat about the place, mostly young fellows: a pair of cavalrymen, a traveler, and a half dozen apprentices who worked for the town's tradesmen. The only two older men sat by themselves. They came from the largest of the local estates, Count Guntram of Bosc's fief, which lay south of the river. The younger man, who was about forty-five, operated Count Guntram's mill. The other, named

Diomedes, was the count's reeve, the overseer of his lands. He was nearing fifty.

"I don't care what you say," Diomedes muttered as he glanced over his shoulder at the apprentices who joked merrily at their own table. "Times aren't what they used to be. I was a powerful man once, did you know that? I had the ear of nobility—and high nobility, too. I could have any woman I wanted, I wore the finest clothes. Now I can't even afford a cup of wine when I want it." To punctuate his remark, he spat into the rushes which covered the dirt floor. Then he quaffed another gulp of bitter ale.

"It's true, it's true," Stul the miller replied. "The young ones are just a brainless lot now. They don't know how to run things." He nudged Diomedes in the side and whispered, "Look at that collection of snot-noses there. Is there one of them who'll amount to anything, I wonder?"

Diomedes smiled, scratched his brown-and-white beard, then shook his head. "It's a mighty strange world," he said with a belch. "When I was their age, I was in his Majesty's employ and I was on my way up. I'll tell you this: if I hadn't run into the worst kind of luck after the last war ended, I'd be a rich man by now. I'd have lands of my own." He smiled again, showed his teeth. "I'd be able to swim in a vat of purple wine every night and I'd spend the day deflowering all my peasants' daughters."

"And a fine life it would be," Stul agreed with a laugh.

"I wouldn't think one of you old graybeards would have enough manhood left to deflower a goat," came a voice from the apprentices' table, followed by a storm of laughter.

Stul grew red in the face and whirled toward the younger men. "Who said that?"

The apprentices' table went silent, then one of the young men said, "Wasn't any of us. Must have been night spirits."

Stul turned back toward Diomedes, who also glared at the youths. "Young fools," the miller said in a low voice. "Why, you and I have seen more than they've ever dreamed of." Another gale of laughter from that table caused him to jerk his head about again. "I wonder what foolishness that was," he muttered as he turned back to his drink.

"I don't know," Diomedes said. "A young man is just like a young crow. All mouth and arse—and nothing in between."

The laughter at the table stopped as if a blanket had been thrown over it. One of the apprentices stood and spoke to

Diomedes through curling lips. "What did you just say?"

"Who, me?" Diomedes replied innocently. "I didn't say a thing. Must have been the night spirits."

A couple of the apprentices chortled, but not the one who stood. "I think you said it, you old graybeard. I think you'd better take it back."

A chuckle rose from Diomedes' throat, a low rumble which sounded like a table being slid across a rough floor. "Now what do you plan to do about it if I don't take it back?"

"Maybe we ought to step outside and settle it—that is, if you think you can walk that far."

Diomedes eased off his stool, turned toward the young man, and yawned. "No," he said sleepily. "I don't want to step outside. I want to settle it right in here." With a lightning motion that belied his tone and the gray in his beard, he seized the startled youth by the scruff of the neck and sent him hurtling headfirst into the counter where the alehouse's startled host stood. The lad struck the barrier, released a gasp, and crumpled.

The other five apprentices threw over their table and charged in a rage, while Stul and Diomedes met the charge using stools as weapons. The two soldiers leaped up and tried to break up the riot but Diomedes snatched the halberd from one of them, broke the shank over the man's head, and beat back his opponents with the piece left to him.

Oaths, screams, and the crash of splintering furniture filled the place; the host ran into the street, screaming at the top of his lungs. "Murder, murder in the alehouse. Riot, riot, alas and wey'awey."

His shouts brought no help and had no effect on the carnage within. The second soldier went down with his head split open, Stul went down, but Diomedes still remained upright, grinning, sweat flying as he fought the three apprentices who were left.

Suddenly, trumpet notes shredded the air, pierced the eardrums, and halted the combatants in the midst of their strife. The alehouse door crashed open and two men in chain mail forced their way in, followed by a column of others. They kicked broken furniture out of the way, jerked men to their feet, and dragged the wounded aside. Diomedes himself helped Stul to his feet.

"You've done a noble raft of damage," one of the warriors said. "Is this the kind of recreation you prefer on Sabbath eves?"

"They started it," one of the apprentices shouted as he flung a finger at Diomedes.

But the officer shoved him away. "Silence. You have not a right to speak until I say so."

The lad glared at the officer and wiped straggled hair from his forehead. Then trumpets outside sounded again and a noble figure entered the alehouse, escorted by two towering knights in full armor. Despite the knights' height and breadth of shoulder, the figure between them drew all eyes to himself. He was a tiny man, scarcely over five feet tall, and so bound up in a purple traveling cloak that the shape of his body could hardly be seen. He was old, with long hair so white and thin it was almost transparent. The pink pupils of his eyes took in the setting in a glance. His expression was a hard one as those eyes came to rest on Diomedes.

"The king," Diomedes breathed. Even he was overawed by the man's presence and he sank to one knee.

Indeed, it was Buerdaunt's king, Lothar the Pale, traveling this Sabbath night on some unknown errand. He glanced about the room once more and then said to the officer in a low, hard voice, "Clear this place."

The king's guardsmen pounced on apprentice and soldier alike, wounded or not, shoved men through the door and into the muddy street outside. Diomedes did not wait to be collared. He moved toward the entrance by himself until the king's voice stopped him. "Not you. You shall remain before me."

Diomedes nodded and dropped to his knee once more. In a moment, the place was clear; Stul, the soldiers, and the apprentices had departed and the guards had even hurled several pieces of broken furniture through the door after them. Diomedes remained kneeling while the guardsmen shoved tables and stools back against walls to clear a large space in the middle of the room, then filed out. An instant later, three of them came back in, struggling beneath the weight of a large chair, which they placed before the counter. That done, they filed out again.

Lothar the Pale never took his eyes off Diomedes as he mounted the towering chair and eased himself into the seat: "Are you that Diomedes who was *aide-de-camp* unto the constable some twenty years ago?"

Diomedes nodded. "I am."

"Ah." The king nodded, then dismissed his two knights

with a gesture. "Leave us," he said to them. "I will speak alone with this man Diomedes."

The two knights departed and left Diomedes alone with Lothar the Pale. Diomedes remained speechless but the king paid him no attention; the pale monarch restlessly glanced about the room. Finally, the king pointed toward one of the stools which lay against the wall. "You need not kneel forever; grasp a seat and place yourself upon it."

Diomedes did as he was told, though sitting on the stool alone before those pink and deadly eyes made him feel more ridiculous and exposed than ever. Finally, he managed to say, "What does your Majesty want with me?"

Lothar the Pale's expression did not change. "I have important work for such a man as you," he finally said.

Diomedes stared up at the wrinkled face. In spite of the fact that Diomedes was much the larger man, the king's traveling throne put his head at a point at least four cubits above the floor. Diomedes unclasped his hands. "I'm proud. Whatever you ask me to do, I'll do." A thought came to him. "Will I be doing this on my own, or will I be paid for it?"

The shadow of a smile flicked onto Lothar the Pale's face. "You shall be reimbursed—and well. In years gone by, your master spoke of you in glowing terms. He said you were a man ideal for tasks which called for violence and discretion. Was that true?"

Diomedes nodded.

"The act which I demand is dangerous and taxing—but is crucial to my policies."

Diomedes' confidence grew. "Danger doesn't bother me; gold pays for danger."

Lothar the Pale reached inside his cloak, drew forth a heavy leather bag, and cast it toward the larger man. It landed with a loud clank. Diomedes knew it contained gold, a lot of gold. He did not bother to pick it up. The king was a godlike force; he would pay what he wanted to pay. "What do you want me to do?" Diomedes asked.

Lothar the Pale studied him. "You know of Palamon, Carea's king?"

"I have dealt with him," Diomedes replied with a vicious shake of the head. "I had him in my hands and at my mercy, but he wriggled through my fingers. Pity, too, for Count Ursid might be here today if things had gone differently. Yes, by Tyche's nipples, the Carean king's a sly one. But that was years ago; I wager he's old by now, if he still even lives.''

"Oh, he lives,'' Lothar the Pale said. "His nation still bestrides the Narrow Strait and chokes our commerce as the python grips the goat. They shall devour Buerdaunt unless we do with them for once and all. I've bided time for twenty years; now I am ready for my stroke. I've laid the ink to treaties and gained allies against them. I have spread a web of plots to bring tall Palamon away from refuge and to lay him at our feet. The Count of Guelt has wrested a Carean high noblewoman from her land. Carea's armies will pursue the count while I strike at their unprotected backs. I'll sweep the Thlassa Mey and clean it of their tribe.''

"It sounds to me like you know what you're doing,'' Diomedes said.

"I'll not leave life before Carea falls,'' Lothar the Pale replied. He paused. "But now for your assignment. Palamon still lives.'' He pursed his lips, glanced about the room again as if to be certain no one could hear him, then went on. "You must take care to finish him—he slithers from all perils.'' His eyes fell on Diomedes. "As you well know.''

"He slipped through my fingers once, that's the truth,'' Diomedes said. "But that was because I was being too careful. If I had it to do over again, I'd lay him out the first chance I got. That would take care of luck and Fortune and Tyche and all the rest.''

"That's right,'' Lothar said with the least curl to his lip. "And that is what I wish of you. My spies inform me Palamon has left his court to meet the Oracle at Euelpis. Follow him; find out his whereabouts, and kill him any way you can.''

A smile crept across Diomedes' face. "I can kill him any way I want to?''

Lothar the Pale returned a slow nod.

Diomedes dragged his fingers through his beard. "It might not be easy. I'll need transportation, money for weapons and information. It'll be a big project.''

Lothar pointed toward the pouch which still lay between Diomedes' feet. "There's gold for all your needs. When you have done the deed and have his head, return to me in Pomfract Castle. I will double what's within that pouch and add a knighthood, at the least.''

Diomedes grinned. "I'll show my gratitude in the way I do the deed.''

"That's well. Now you may go, and call my knights to me as you depart."

Diomedes did as he was told. When he walked from the village of Loth, he was nearly laughing to himself. His years of dearth had ended; only King Palamon's life stood between him and all the riches he had dreamed of.

Chapter Nine:
Sir Pallador's Challenge

IF CHIVALRY RULED the lands about the Thlassa Mey, that chivalry kept its throne at the Fastness of Pallas. The world's staunchest knights held that sprawling structure, high on its coastal cliff. They lived, breathed, and died the ideals of their order—with chivalry highest among those ideals.

The Fastness of Pallas stood under the rule of no land, no king. Its high crag stood fast against salty sea winds and upheld virtue, honor, and purity before all lands. Noble youths flocked from every city to seek a place among the order's ranks. Many applied, few gained admission.

The Fastness was known to take in orphans and a few such children grew up to join the order. Others, young nobles, became apprentice squires—tercelets, they were called. But the most honorable way to gain admission was by skill at arms. Despite the remote location, the windy steppes which stretched away from the Fastness witnessed many a noble skirmish. Each spring, the Knights of Pallas hosted a tournament for youths below the age of sixteen. Young men could test their new skills at horse, at lance, at mace and morning star against the order's squires. If an outsider could win that tournament, he could enter the hallowed company.

Years ago, a young man named Pallador Lorfelin had left his noble family and had journeyed to the Youth Tournament, where he had swept the other young men before him. He had passed all other tests and had become squire to one of the noblest knights, a man called Sir Phebos. Sir Phebos later became Grand Master of the order. Pallador Lorfelin, now Sir

Pallador, was a full-fledged knight. This spring, he looked forward to the tournament which would take place in the grand old man's honor.

This tournament took place less than a fortnight after the tournament which Sir Flin had won in Tranje. Many knights had fought in the first tournament, then traveled from Tranje to set up their pavilions across the high plains west of the Fastness. All good men wanted to test their strength against the Knights of Pallas.

Sir Flin had vanished, which disappointed Sir Pallador. The young knight had heard of Sir Flin's dazzling feats at Tranje and had waited for this tournament in hopes of testing himself against the great warrior. But as the day neared, he searched in vain for Sir Flin's colors among the flags and pennants that danced beside the tilting grounds.

People jammed the remote location when the great day came. Nobles brought large parties and folk from nearby estates traveled on horses, on wagons, in litters, and in sedan chairs to watch the spectacle. Newly built scaffolds stood on either side of the field; even so, men and women overflowed the grandstands and thronged all the grounds.

Sir Pallador hardly noticed the crowd, however. He did not care about the crowd, though he always did his best. He fought for the honor of Pallas and to test his own skills, not for glory. At least he told himself that.

The sun rode into the sky and the hour neared. He walked to the Fastness' grand chapel to pray. He threw himself on his knees before the altar and placed his sword on the stand built to receive it; the relic in the weapon's handle would augment the power of his prayer. He did not beg the Holy Maiden for glory when he prayed; he only asked that neither he nor those who strove against him would suffer injury. When he finished, he rose, slid the sword back into its scabbard, and walked back to his quarters.

Sir Pallador had a squire of his own by this time. That young man helped him put on his armor for the tournament. Sir Pallador would not wear the order's armor and colors for this meet. They were reserved for the Holy Maiden's service; they were never worn for such events as these. Instead, he donned dark, burnished plate.

Dozens of Knights of Pallas strode beside him when he walked from the Fastness' gates. They led huge warhorses, curried and caparisoned for the event. They made a glorious procession which wound its way to the tilting grounds and met the cheers of the assembled throng.

They mounted and formed a line which rode in parade along one sideline, then wheeled as one and faced the other side of the field. An even greater number of knights from the outside world waited, renowned warriors gathered from all the lands about the Thlassa Mey. At a signal from Sir Phebos on the grandstand, the two companies threw themselves toward one another in a mock battle of harrowing proportions.

Despite the numbers involved, the mêlée's outcome was practically a foregone conclusion. The Knights of Pallas' ranks swelled with the most renowned men of many lands, and they fought as a well-ordered body. Many powerful knights challenged them but they did not fight as a unit. The Knights of Pallas hardly ever lost an event like this. Still, the fighting was hot. Sir Pallador thundered toward the opposing line, struck a challenging knight from the saddle, and then settled to the grueling work of wielding his mace. Lust for the fray filled him. His heart swelled and sweat rained down the inside his armor. Might the gods help him—he really did enjoy this combat.

The fighting raged through the morning and into the afternoon, with defeated knights forced to the sideline and out of the competition. By the time it ended, the challenging company had been swept away; Sir Pallador and two of his fellow knights were the last men holding the field. That had made for a close competition, though. Spectators cheered themselves hoarse as the three victorious men mounted to the Grand Master's box to receive their victory laurels.

Sir Phebos presented the victory garlands to Sir Paulus first, then to Sir Pharadyne, and finally to Sir Pallador, youngest and tallest of the three. "Ah, friend," the Grand Master said. The sunlight danced off the fine wrinkles which cased his eyes, for he could be a merry fellow when he wanted. "You've grown in strength until you have the awe of men who must oppose you. You are strong and straight and stout. In truth, I say, you are a lantern waiting to be lit."

"I thank you, Master," Sir Pallador said. He and his two comrades turned to receive the accolades of the crowd. He was a young man, his hair sprouted in sandy curls which cascaded across his scalp in a rich flood. To his embarrassment, he knew playful maidens would make much of him. All three knights would be honored and feted through many pavilions and camps tonight; it would be a long evening and they would be hard pressed to keep their vows. And a day of single combat would follow on the morrow.

As they stood, Sir Phebos placed himself next to Sir Pallador. "Come see me after evening prayers," the Grand Master said.

"Beg pardon?"

"See me. I must have a talk with you." Then the older man turned away.

Sir Pallador frowned as Sir Phebos returned to his place. The younger knight marked the exchange, then focused his attention on the rest of the day's events. He would learn his Master's desire when it was time.

Nobles and old friends descended on him to pound his back, congratulate him, and beg him to attend banquets. Such was the price of victory. But he soon slipped away from all the fuss and made his way back to his quarters, where his squire hauled the steaming plates of armor from his back.

He bathed himself and dressed in a light tunic, tights, round-toed shoes and a soft cap. He then made as many appearances as seemed prudent. He took care not to linger too long, nor to imbibe too much. The day passed, evening prayers came and went, and he finally made his way to the Grand Masters' quarters, a suite in the tower above the Fastness' chapel.

He rapped the heavy door and whistled to himself while he gazed up at the massive groinings and vaults above his head. Many floors lay above this one; the tower rose toward the heavens the way the souls of men sought the gods. But the tower was stone and each floor had to be massive enough to support all that rested above.

A young page swung the door open and Sir Pallador walked into Sir Phebos' office. It was a spartan place; hardly any furnishings stood in the huge chamber other than a statue of the Holy Maiden in the center of the room and a heavy desk against one wall. Charts lay on the desk and Sir Phebos studied them with intent eyes.

The older man lifted his eyes and looked the young knight up and down as if measuring him both outside and inside. "How proud I am of you, Sir Pallador," he said. "Although you still are young, your prowess is unmatched among us. You're a flaming prodigy within our ranks."

"I thank you, Sir."

The Grand Master took two cups of wine from the page. He handed one to Sir Pallador. "You'll gain the high rewards your strength and courage merit,'' He went on. ''Do you know Sir Paral is retiring at the end of summer?''

''I did not know that.'' The younger knight sipped his wine.

''I've prayed and fasted many nights, and kept a weary vigil in the vaults below the chapel. For Sir Paral's post grows vacant with his leaving, and field master is a crucial post—I have to choose a proper man to fill it.''

''Surely, Sir, not I . . .''

''Yes, you.''

Sir Pallador stared at the older man. ''Why, I am twenty years too young for such advancement. Others will resent it, and with cause, for I've not earned the right.''

Sir Phebos smiled, threw himself into the seat behind the desk, and sipped his wine. ''You'll earn it; have no fear on that account. I tell you, things are clear to me as water flowing from a spring. You're chosen by the goddess and myself. I knew your father and your mother. You have mighty promise. You are born to lead brave men the way the swiftest stallion's born to run. It disappointed me your parents did not sponsor you into our ranks and I was pleased as any mouse in grain when you appeared and won the Tournament of Youth ten years ago.''

Sir Phebos finished his drink, then explained his thoughts. He would nominate Sir Pallador for field master even though the post had been reserved for much older knights. Sir Pallador's prowess and ability qualified him for the post. Still, Sir Phebos agreed that resentment could follow—and would have to be forestalled. Though Sir Pallador protested the honor, the inner man felt deeply touched. Whatever he might say to the contrary, it tickled his pride to hear the older knight's praise.

As for the solution, Sir Phebos knew what he would do. Sir Pallador had to complete a quest which would earn him the post before the eyes of all. It had to be done alone, an assignment no other man would want, and which no other man would be able to complete.

The older knight fastened his eyes on the younger. ''Some twenty years ago,'' he said, ''when old Buerdaunt made war against Carea, Prince Ursid besieged the city known as Hautre. He broke its walls, destroyed its commerce, hauled away a train of hostages. Proud Ulfin, baron of the city, died soon afterward—and few were left to mourn him. That poor town has ne'er recovered. Silent ruins stand and mark its passing in the hills beyond the Greenlands.''

''What must I do?'' Sir Pallador asked.

"The land has been deserted for so long, it's come to be a haven for the worst of thieves and brigands. Now no traveler dares set foot within ten leagues of Hautre for fear of murder, robbery, extortion. We cannot allow such brigandage—therefore, the robbers must be rooted out like gophers in a garden."

"And am I the agent you have chosen? Why not send a company of our brave knights?"

"I can't. For complex reasons, politics between the rival lands, the lords around this long-deserted place prefer the situation not be changed. Thus, you alone must travel unto Hautre and scrub away the stains of brigandage."

Sir Pallador pursed his lips. "A daunting challenge."

"I'll not force you to accept the charge. But if you will not go, I must withdraw the post I've offered you."

"Pooh-pooh," Sir Pallador said. "No knight turns down a challenge—you know that. You know my honor forces me to take the gauntlet up. If it's the Maiden's will, then I accept."

"The task's a dangerous one."

"You knew that when you offered it to me."

Sir Phebos clapped Sir Pallador on the back and the thing was done. He summoned pages and squires, ordered horses saddled and provisions loaded. Before dawn came, Sir Pallador cast away the tournament's glory and rode from the Fastness of Pallas. He passed through the camps while knights and nobles rose for the new day; he left them behind and turned his mount toward the deserted city of Hautre.

He made a lonely camp that night in the steppes north of Oron but enough inns dotted the land that he was able to sleep most nights in a bed. He forded the Courbee River north of Stournes, made his way northeast, and finally reached the last holdings south of deserted Hautre.

Now that evening was upon him and the dangerous land lay ahead, he took out the chain mail of his order. He clucked to his horse and rode toward a puff of green willows which showed the course of a small stream. It would hide him from prying eyes while he put on his armor.

Birds twittered and the stream murmured between its banks as he swung off his palfrey and tethered it and his packhorse to a skinny birch in the center of the thicket. He laid his chain mail out on the ground, then took out his gauntlets, upper and lower cannon plates for his arms, and greaves for his calves. He tied his caped basinet to the pommel of his warhorse's saddle. He would not don the sweltering helmet until he had to.

As he began to dress, he heard a sound behind him, wheeled, and saw five bearded men who carried clubs and knives. They grinned and advanced toward him, slapping their weapons against fist or thigh.

Sir Pallador held no weapon, only his hauberk, so he hurled that into their faces. The mail struck and entangled a pair of the men but the others cursed and charged him. He snatched his longsword from its scabbard, met the first of them, and ran the man through. The fellow screamed and went down but the other two fell on the lone knight, rained blows on his head and shoulders. He fended them off, parried blows, struck one club from its owner's hand. The third brigand turned to flee.

But the first two had scuttled free of the mail by this time. One hurled his dagger. The blade struck Sir Pallador's gambeson, the quilted padding he wore beneath his armor, and buried itself in his chest. The knight cried out, clenched his teeth, snatched the weapon from the wound, and threw it down. "You miserable curs," he shouted. "Is that the very best that you can do?"

The men stared at him, he brandished his longsword, and they fled. He forced a laugh as he watched them go, but he did not pursue them. Instead, he fell to his knees and gripped his bloodsoaked gambeson. He pulled out his own dagger and slit the material; the wound was deep. A dribble of blood about the opening frothed with each breath he took.

In spite of pain and weakness, he managed to climb onto his palfrey. It would be death to ride far with such a wound, he knew, but quicker death if he did not reach help. He kept one hand pressed to his chest as he rode back up the trail. "O, mighty Pallas," he whispered. "Please be with me now."

Darkness fell quickly; soon, he could hardly see. He spied a light down the little stream's course. The light must have been a very bright one, because he was able to see it clearly, even though it seemed a long way off.

Tightness gripped his chest like a huge hand, his breath grew short, he felt his mind clog from his body's weariness, with unearthly thoughts in the darkness. But he could not give in to his shock and fatigue; he had to push on. The land turned liquid, his horse stopped, and his reins fell from limp fingers. He sighed, swayed, and toppled from the saddle like a bag of grain.

Chapter Ten:
The Cottage

WHEN SIR PALLADOR woke up, he found himself lying on the ground beneath a grove of tall trees. It was broad daylight. He felt weak, not to mention dizzy as a top. His muscles ached all over but at least he was able to raise himself to one elbow and look about.

To his amazement, he found he had almost made it to the light he had seen the night before. A little stone cottage stood beneath the swaying trees. It looked tidy and clean as a new chalice, with a tile roof and a chimney which breathed a wisp of smoke. A garden lay around it and Sir Pallador could see a large, bald-headed man hoeing weeds.

The Knight of Pallas raised himself farther and tried to shout, but the effort sent agony through his chest. He could only make a sort of cough. The man kept at his labors. Sir Pallador tried to inch his way toward the garden; buzzing filled his ears and turned into a roar. Before he even realized it, darkness swept over him again.

When he awoke the next time, he found himself lying on a straw mattress. A thin man about his own age was leaning over him. "Very serious," he heard the fellow mutter to himself. "I am amazed he even lived the night."

"Who are you?" Sir Pallador tried to croak, but the young man stopped him.

"No words until I've put on salve and bandaged up your wound," the other said. "Your life's wind ebbs from you with every breath—the use of speech will hasten your demise." He eyed the young Knight of Pallas. "I have removed your underclothes; they shall be cleaned. I hope you do not think me too discourteous."

Sir Pallador shook his head and the fellow went on. "I am not practiced at the healing arts. E'en so, I have a salve which will maintain your life, although I fear you'll never wield a sword again. But still, a quiet life is better than no life at all, is it not, Son?"

Sir Pallador groaned and closed his eyes. Would it be better to live as half a man than to die? He doubted it. "O, holy Pallas," he breathed.

"Don't speak, I tell you." Sir Pallador could feel the fellow working on his chest; the wound felt less tormented as deft fingers rubbed in the ointment. "I heard you speak the goddess' name, my friend. So might you be a Knight of Pallas, one of that most noble order?"

Sir Pallador started to speak until fingers laid themselves across his lips. Then he simply nodded. To his surprise, the nod brought a grin and a laugh from his host. "Come now," the fellow cried. "If you are one of them, then heal yourself. I know the goddess gives to you the power. Lay on hands and heal your wound; it has not reached the heart."

The young warrior lay back and smiled a rueful smile. Yes, it was true, a Knight of Pallas possessed the power to heal wounds—the wounds of others. He had even performed the sacred function once himself. But never had he heard of a knight healing his own injury. Besides, the act required the full strength of a strong man—and Sir Pallador's strength was gone. Sir Pallador shook his head and smiled a wan smile. That was a forlorn hope, indeed.

But his host responded as if the young knight had actually explained each objection. "I know the meaning of that smile," he said. "You doubt my wisdom. I've some knowledge of such things myself; I've insight into many matters. Trust me, lay your hands upon my wrists while I place mine upon your wounded body. Speak your prayer, though only in your mind. The Maiden still shall hear you, and she will respond. I'll act as mirror for her powers."

Fire lay in the young man's eyes. Sir Pallador saw it to be a fire either of madness or of divine wisdom; the two could be very close. The young knight clenched his hands about the other's wrists and shut his eyes. He prayed. He never moved his lips; even so, weakness surged through him and he nearly blacked out again. He almost lost his grip as sweat streamed from his body.

He gasped as the young man leaned forward and placed slender hands across the wound. Force lanced from the long fingers; it was neither painful nor pleasant, but so strong that it overwhelmed the senses. Warmth and strength flooded Sir Pallador's body. Full breath flowed into his chest for the first time since he had felt the brigand's knife pierce him. He all but wept at the sweetness of the sensation; he clenched his teeth, opened his eyes, and asked, "How?"

"My name is Peristeras; I believe you are the reason I exist."

"The reason you exist?"

Peristeras smiled. "Have you not heard of me?"

Sir Pallador shook his head. "No matter," Peristeras said. "Just rest for now. The Maiden's holy strength performs within you. Sleep. And when you have awakened, I'll explain."

Peristeras finished bandaging Sir Pallador, then left the bedside and climbed down through a trapdoor in the chamber's floor. The young knight watched in wonder; he doubted he would ever sleep, so full of turmoil was his mind. But he lay back and fell into a deep, healing slumber before he knew it.

When he awoke, not a ray of light survived in his low chamber; the windows at either end showed that night had long since fallen. He could not hear a sound. Then the trapdoor creaked open and swarthy arms appeared, holding a lantern.

A tall man, broad and bald, climbed up. He wore a dark robe like a monk's garment. Sir Pallador recognized him as the man he had seen in the garden. "Good evening," the young knight said, but the man did not reply.

Rather, the fellow stepped away from the trapdoor and Peristeras himself climbed through. "I see you are awake," Peristeras said. "Will you take supper with us?"

"Yes, indeed." Sir Pallador sat up in the bed, then it occurred to him that he was naked. "My clothing—do you have it?"

"I kept what I could clean," Peristeras said. "The other bloody rags have been destroyed. I have replacements." He issued a series of complex hand signals to the bald man, who hung the lantern from a rafter and climbed down. When he returned, he carried the leather pack which held Sir Pallador's armor.

The servant placed the bundle before Sir Pallador. "You

men are prodigies," the young knight breathed. "What magic did you use to find this?"

"My servant, Omo, fetched it," Peristeras said. "And two of your horses, too."

"The Fates have brought me here," Sir Pallador breathed. "The gods intended us to meet."

"You are perceptive," Peristeras said as the young knight donned the new, quilted gambeson which lay at the top of the package. When he had finished, the two men helped him climb down the ladder, where they came to a dining room and a table laid with a hearty meal.

Peristeras and Sir Pallador seated themselves. "I thank you for your hospitality," Sir Pallador said as he tasted the first food to pass his lips in a day. "My final breath would be long passed away without your aid."

"The Maiden and a bandit's blade produced this meeting," Peristeras said. "Every being is a minion of the Fates."

"Bandits," Sir Pallador said. "Indeed, the brigands which infest this land—Sir Phebos sent me here to rid the world of them."

"I know that," Peristeras said with a smile. He looked up from his platter. "Do not look so astounded, for I know your parents and Sir Phebos, too." He pointed toward the sideboard, where sat a small crucible, flame-blackened as if it had just come from a hot fire. "There lies the thing which told me. I'll not bore you with particulars. I know your mission, know how 'tis you gained your wound. I know the thing which you must do to gain success in your endeavor."

"By Pallas' holy breath," Sir Pallador said. "Who are you? Are you saint or are you devil?"

"I am a vassal of the Fates, the same as you. I live my life, attain a wrinkled age, then die and pass through life's full course again. Why, I've lived out as many lifetimes as you've lived of years. Sometimes I know my rôle, sometimes I only do as I see fit. But always do I serve the gods. Now would you know the act you must perform before you can expect success?"

Silence filled the chamber, gripped it as tightly as a fist gripping a dagger. Finally, Sir Pallador said, "I would, indeed."

"First," Peristeras said. "Await the coming of your charger, which has run away, but which will gallop back into this copse of trees in moments. Once it's come, then gather your three horses and ride north, along this stream until you reach its source. There, you will find a narrow pass between two granite walls. Foul bandits will have snared two women. They will threaten them with knives and truncheons. At that moment, you will know the thing that you must do.''

"No doubt I shall," Sir Pallador murmured. He studied his host. "You say my nut-brown charger shall return unto this place?"

Peristeras nodded.

"When shall it?" Sir Pallador asked. "And my other animals, how fare they now?"

"They fare within a lean-to stable on the south side of my cottage. They are yours when you may need them. Omo trailed the horse you rode in hopes of catching it, but could not. But he did discover your two others, tethered to a bush with blood and clothing and the other signs of struggle all laid out. He brought your goods back here; the other things he buried.''

"Thank you," Sir Pallador said. "Perhaps the gods will grant me some way to reward you in the future.''

Peristeras waved a hand. "Perform the deeds the gods have laid on you and you shall pay us hundredfold for all we've done." As he spoke, hoofbeats sounded outside and the whinny of a horse interrupted him.

Peristeras issued hand signals to his deaf servant. The fellow fetched a lantern, stepped outside, then returned and made a long series of gestures in front of the mystical host. "He says your charger's come," Peristeras said. "He was reluctant to approach it, for the fear that it would flee again.''

Sir Pallador shot out the cottage's door. Omo followed him and by the lantern's light, the young knight saw his horse, heavily sweated and nervous, but still with saddle and bridle in good order. He walked to it and caught the reins, then soothed it and gentled it as he led it to the little stable. He pulled off its harness, watered it, oated it, and brushed it down before he felt weak and returned to his host.

Peristeras had not even stood all that while. "Complete your dinner now," he said matter-of-factly. "If I perceive correctly, you will leave ere brother sun's first rays caress these hills.''

"I shall.''

"I have a gift for you. In case I stay abed past dawn, do not depart before I pass it on to you.''

Sir Pallador nodded. He finished eating, they spoke awhile, then he clambered back up the ladder to the cottage's low loft. He spent a restless night but rose in the morning, dressed, prayed, then climbed down and asked the servant for water so he could bathe.

Omo brought water and a breakfast, then Peristeras entered with a small object in one hand. He tossed it up, caught it, turned it over and over between his fingers while the young knight washed himself. Peristeras handed the thing to his guest with an inscrutable smile. "A trinket for the nonce," he said. "Perhaps you'll find it useful—at some time or other."

"What's its purpose?" Sir Pallador asked.

Peristeras only smiled. "Who knows? But you should use it well enough—you'll learn things from it ere you're done." The mystical young man clapped his guest on one shoulder. "But fare you well. I know that as you pass through life, you'll give the gods the credit they deserve." Then they ate and he sent Sir Pallador on his way. Midmorning found the young knight in full armor and astride his warhorse, penetrating the wilds near Hautre.

Peristeras' instructions lay engraved in Sir Pallador's mind as he followed the stream's sparkling course into a range of lush hills. He scanned the slopes and the greenery, but he spied neither hide nor hair of the two women Peristeras had described. He rode on. Then he heard a shout and a clang, muffled as if they had come from a distance.

He slid his basinet over his ears and laced it in place. Then he spurred his horse toward the sound. The canyon grew narrow but the trail was plain and the noise of the skirmish grew louder.

The stream bent back on itself and produced a little amphitheater. The trail led up a chink in the cliff. In the bottom of the wide place, several men fought like demons; even as Sir Pallador came on the scene, the last of the defenders went down and the victorious ones tore into the packsaddles of their supply horses. The sight made the young knight smile grimly. These were the same men who had left him bleeding in the dust two days ago.

"I serve the Holy Maiden," he cried. "Yield or die." He slammed his visor shut with a clang and spurred his courser into a charge. This was no noble joust; it was an extermination of men little better than insects. He threw his lance to the ground and drew his longsword, with its gleaming blade and artifact set into the handle.

Nearly a dozen brigands turned on him but that meant nothing to a man who rode for the Maiden. He scattered the band like chickens; one swung a truncheon and pain lanced up the

young knight's leg, but he struck back with his sword and the
fellow's head rolled in the dust.

Another grabbed the horse's tail and tried to vault up behind
Sir Pallador, but the young knight jerked the reins, set his feet
in his stirrups, and the animal wheeled as abruptly as a trout
in a pool. The sword's blade flicked once more and served that
foeman as it had the first.

The rest saw the way of things and scattered like so many
cockroaches before a lantern. Sir Pallador galloped down on a
pair of them and bowled them over, but they rolled to their
feet and disappeared into the brush. He did not pursue them;
there was no honor in striking down beaten men from behind.

But his heart sank as he saw he had arrived too late. The
brigands had killed the travelers to the last man. He dismounted
and searched through the bodies, but found no women. That
put him into a quandary. He eyed the brush on all sides, then
doffed his basinet and prepared to complete his duty. Whether
this skirmish brought him nearer his goal or not, he would give
thanks to Pallas and provide burial for those who had fallen.
Then he would see.

He drew his longsword, set the tip into a patch of soft earth,
then knelt and began to pray. But before he had uttered three
words, he heard a cry behind him: "Help us, help us."

He shot to his feet, snatched up the sword, and wheeled
toward the sound. He saw nothing save rocks, heavy brush,
and the stream which babbled through this ravine. Then the
call came again, "Help us, help us."

He walked toward the sound, then broke into a run as finally
he did see its source. The stream had carved a deep overhang
into the rock wall. All but hidden in that shadow, he saw two
female faces. The women must have fled to that pocket when
the bandits struck their packtrain; no one would have noticed
them if they had not shouted.

Floodwaters had filled the hollow with brush. A snag had
tangled the older woman's traveling robe without mercy. Now
the snag had broken loose and threatened to pull her under.
She struggled and tore at her clothing while a younger woman
fought to keep both their heads above water.

Sir Pallador threw himself into the pool, armor and all. He
had found two women, had he not? The young knight felt sure
he was still on the path chosen for him by the Fates. The two
anxious faces gazed down at him as he splashed toward them.

Chapter Eleven:
Two Ladies

SIR PALLADOR MADE his way across the pool and used his longsword to chop the older woman free of the snag. He and the younger woman helped her to safe ground, where she threw herself onto the grass and caught her breath. "I thank you, gallant Knight," she said. "A welcome sight you are, as beautiful as dry land to a drowning person—which I almost was. The gods directed you to save us, by my troth."

Sir Pallador smiled a little smile. "Those words are truer than you may suspect, my Lady. I'll not ponder any god's intent—I only give my thanks that you are safe. Alas, however, for the others of your party. They have all been slain."

"I see that's so." The older woman turned her head away, her face fell, and she shut her large eyes.

Sir Pallador did not know how to treat a distraught woman, so he changed the subject. "What are your names? Whereto are you bound?"

"My name is Alcyone," the woman replied. "This is my daughter, Krisamee. We traveled from a holding in the Greenlands. There, my husband was a knight. Upon his death, my daughter and myself desired to travel to the town of Hautre, where I first saw the light of day."

Krisamee had knelt beside her mother. Now she lifted her head. "But speak correctly, Mother," she said. "It was you alone who wished to make this trek." She looked up at Sir Pallador. "She's very headstrong, Mother is."

Sir Pallador gazed at both women. Both were striking, each in her own way. Both were ladies, for all their wet clothing.

That only accented the curve and flow of their bodies, added luster to their charms. Lady Alcyone was forty or perhaps forty-five years old, prim, attractive. Krisamee was a young beauty, thin as a whisper, with sandy hair that cascaded about her shoulders in a torrent of color. And tall. Sir Pallador stood taller than most men, yet she could look him almost eye-to-eye.

Krisamee's gaze was too direct for him, too unsettling. He turned back to the older woman. "You journey unto Hautre?" he asked. "That is madness; danger waits for you with every step. You've barely sampled from the ills which might befall you."

Lady Alcyone sat up and looked sadly at the fallen bodies and the pack mules which stood patiently beside their dead masters. "That's plainly so," she said quietly. "But I must see my parents one more time before I die."

"Ah," Sir Pallador said. "I spoke in haste."

"When I was but a budding maid," she went on. "I found myself made captive by the Buerdic army. That came when they sacked our city. Prince Ursid, their general, took me and many others as his hostages." She shook her head. "'Twas twenty years ago. He was a stunning man, the Buerdic prince, as brave and strong as any lion. And for all that he had overthrown the city of my birth, I fell in love with him the moment I first saw him. But I was a hostage and no more—he never noticed me." She turned her eyes on the young knight. "Sir, have you ever been dismembered from your parents?"

"My parents both passed on when I was still a child," Sir Pallador said.

"That's sad indeed, dear youth. My heart goes out to you. Perhaps you'll understand me when I tell you how it was, though. Prince Ursid's victorious soldiers tore me from my mother even though we clung to one another just the way the peach clings to its stone. They trussed me up in irons and hauled me off, and never did I see my loved ones more."

Sir Pallador could only listen as she went on. "They never ransomed me, but sold me to the highest bidder. He was one of Prince Ursid's stout knights. For twenty years, I made for him as loyal and as true a wife as I knew how to be." She raised her hands, then dropped them. "So it is—the Fates deal you a blow but you must carry on as best you can. The man has passed away—can I not see once more the land and people whom I left behind? Can I not show my daughter where I sprouted, even though that act may bear a danger? Will the gods not show the way, as they have done by bringing you to us?''

Sir Pallador hesitated. "No words can paint the way your story touches me," he finally said. "And yet I sense in you no wave of bitterness, no sour resentment of the blows you've suffered. As I told you, both my parents have been dead and gone for many years; perhaps that helps me comprehend your state." He chose his words carefully. "But still I tell you that this land has lain here empty far too long. Is it not possible your parents have departed long, long since?''

Lady Alcyone shook her head. "No, that is not a possibility. They ne'er would flee their land, as long as breath remained within them. They will be in Hautre still when we arrive e'en if it meant their deaths. Then I must take my daughter to their graves, where we shall pay our last respects.''

Sir Pallador eyed the woman for a moment, but her daughter pulled his gaze to her the way velvet pulls lint. What woman could survive a life as Prince Ursid's hostage, could speak so matter-of-factly of a forced marriage? What manner daughter would she produce? Who was he to say them nay? "I'll go with you to Hautre, Ladies. If it can be done, I'll see the both of you into the place, then back again.''

A shadow of a smile flicked across Lady Alcyone's face and he saw the smile mirrored on the face of her daughter. "That's well," she said.

He eyed the two of them, then felt himself blush. "Indeed." He cleared his throat. "And we must give a decent burial to all who fell this day. I'll see to that; there's no need for the two of you to help me.''

"Our hands are not of glass," Lady Alcyone said. "I've looked on death before and both of us will gladly help the knight who took us out of danger.''

"Must we bury those who would have killed us?" Krisamee asked.

Sir Pallador could hardly take his eyes off the tall beauty as he answered. "It is not for us to judge," he said. "We'll give them decent burial—if they're to be condemned, it is a choice the gods must make, and not ourselves.''

"Ah, bravely answered, charming Knight," Lady Alcyone said. She favored him with a smile kinder than her last one.

Krisamee also smiled at him, though he felt unsure what lay behind her dancing features. "Yes, bravely answered," she agreed.

The sun settled behind the ravine's rim long before they finished the nasty task. They decided to camp in that place, since it was well sheltered. Sir Pallador brought up his extra horses and helped the two women take care of their own animals and set up their tent. Once they had lit candles and disappeared within their shelter, he laid a blanket roll out on the ground.

He leaned against a rock, surveyed the darkening sky and shadows which spread across the stones, then his eyes fell on the women's tent. Their candle cast its light on every side of the shelter; the glow threw their shadows perfectly on the heavy fabric. As they prepared for sleep, he could see their outlines perfectly as they slid on their shifts. The men who had handled their packtrain could not have been without guilt if they had let the two women perform thus every night without telling them. "My Ladies," he cried softly. "Every candle throws a shadow." He heard a sound from the tent and the candle went out.

He maintained a watch through the hours of darkness, using the ancient discipline of the Knights of Pallas to ward off sleep in case the brigands should return. When he spied the first pale light above the eastern hills, he rose. He walked to the tent and shook the flap until he heard a voice. "What is it?"

"Morning has arrived, Ladies."

"Very well. Could you please be so kind as to construct a fire? A little cauldron lies beside the tent; if it is filled with water, I will boil a porridge for our breakfast."

Sir Pallador found the cauldron and carried it down to the stream to fill it with water. Then he found a good place between several rocks, gathered kindling, made a fire. He found a tripod and by the time he set it up, Lady Alcyone came from the tent, wiping her hands on a cloth.

"Well done," she said. "I did not relish carrying water up for cooking; now I'll gladly make your breakfast." She took a bag from one of the packs and busied herself about the cauldron, then smiled once more as Sir Pallador watched her. "My husband never was too handy in the kitchen," she said. "It is pleasant to be helped so well."

"All Pallas' Knights must learn to tend a fire and cook a broth," he said. "It keeps us humble."

"And yet a proud and haughty order," she replied. "My late husband could have learned a thing, then, couldn't he? But bless his soul, he's gone—and he presented me with such a lovely daughter. It's not within my heart to hate him."

"Some women would."

She nodded. "Perhaps. But hate is such a small thing. Any heart which can be filled by that is undernourished and lamentable. I'll opt for love." She smiled up at him. "May my heart always feast on that, instead of petty hate."

"You are a saint in spirit," Sir Pallador said. "But I must be alone a scrap of time. I shall return before my breakfast's done." He left her and made his way along the stream until he found a place where there was room to kneel. There, he leaned his sword against a broad log, knelt, and began his morning prayer to the goddess Pallas.

He followed his formal supplication with a plea for the strength and wisdom he would need to carry out his quest, as well as the goddess' support in escorting the two women to and from their destination. He gave thanks for his meeting with mysterious Peristeras and pledged all his strength to continued service to the Maiden. Even when his parents had been alive, he had longed to wear the Holy Maiden's colors. For him, this morning, as every morning, was a dream come true.

Refreshed and filled with ardor for this day's labors, he stood. He wiped the dirt from his knees and slid his sword back into its scabbard. As he turned, he saw to his surprise that Krisamee watched him.

She smiled at his expression. "I know I never should have watched," she said. "I hope and pray 'twas not a sacrilege, but when I saw you thus, I could not tear my eyes away."

He glanced about uncomfortably. "I cannot say if it was sin or no," he finally said.

"Please, be not angry with me."

He shrugged. "No, I shall not be angry."

She turned her head to one side and studied him with a strange expression. "I feel I've witnessed something special— very special. I am honored to have seen it."

"I thank you," he said. But the subject still made him uncomfortable. "But what brought you to this lonely place?"

"I came to wash myself," she replied. Then, as though remembering her errand for the first time, she turned from him and knelt by the babbling waters to perform that function, mouthing words between applications of the cold liquid. "But I forgot all that when I saw you."

"I see," he said—though he was not sure he did. "A wash is my intention, too, for it is said a dirty man can never hope to win the goddess' heart. I bathe myself each morning after prayers." Her head turned and she favored him with another smile. He looked back at her, somewhat stupidly, he thought. "Of course, when one is in the field, one cannot bathe as fully as one can in one's own quarters." He paused. "Excuse me, I will step beyond yon thicket and remove my hauberk."

Her smile never dimmed. "It's not my office to excuse you or to grant permission," she said. "Perform the function as you trust most wise."

He stared at her, then stepped away. Once enough foliage separated them for it to be seemly, he unbuckled his belt, removed his hauberk, and washed himself as well as one could in a bandit-ridden wilderness.

"How did you come to be a Knight of Pallas?" He heard Krisamee's voice downstream from him.

"My sire, a knight named Ardan, and my mother, named Alanna, both expired while I was very young. I reached the age of ten and five, and left my home. I rode up to the Fastness of gray Pallas to compete for full admission." He shook the water out of his hair and smiled. "Now I'm here."

"Ah," she replied thoughtfully. Her voice was higher in pitch than a man's; there was a music to it, a beckoning quality that no man's voice could ever duplicate. He mused on that while he dried himself and put his clothing back on.

" 'Tis said you Knights of Pallas must forebear from drink and love and every sort of vanity," she asked. "Is that the truth?"

"It is," he replied. "Our lone attachment is unto the Queen of Heaven, Holy Pallas. Appetite—of any sort—is but a trap for us."

"And love's forbidden, too? That would be hard."

"All earthly love's forbidden," he replied. "Love of things divine must satisfy us—for to trade true love for one yet higher is no sacrifice." Then, under his voice, he added the words, "Till now." It was a bad joke, a stupid remark, and he was sorry for it as soon as he had made it.

They made their way back toward the campsite but they had to cross the stream to get there. A log lay across the rapid waters, a different crossing than Sir Pallador had used when he had gone to pray. He made his way across while she followed. As he reached the end and stepped off, the shift in weight caused the tree trunk to roll. Krisamee's feet slipped and she fell with a cry. He wheeled more quickly than a cat, threw an arm about her, and hauled her onto solid ground.

Her bosom heaved with the moment. They stood for the space of a hundred heartbeats and Sir Pallador did not remove his arm from her waist. Her gown was as soft as an eider's breast, her breath full of a delicate and fleshly scent, her eyes alight with the very stuff of life.

No words passed between them. She rested her hands on his shoulders; then, to his own complete surprise, he found himself kissing her. He had never kissed a woman before, never even touched a female. Her lips felt soft, warm, moist beneath his and the nearness of her flesh was a treasure that begged him to harvest it.

The kiss ended, their lips moved apart, he stared in wonder. His mouth opened, but he could not speak as she stared back at him. "I'm sorry," she said. "Was that proper?"

"No, 'twas not."

"'Twas no more than one small kiss. You look as if you'd seen the gate to Hades yawning to receive you."

"I did," he said. Then he stepped back. "Excuse me, I must go." He turned from her and stumbled into the brushy thickets which grew all along the stream's length. His blood ran hot and cold with shame. He had lost control; temptation had seized him and he had made a fool of himself. Worse, another human being had seen him in his weakness. She had seen him. The thought sent chills down his spine. He broke through a tangled wall of brush, found an open space, and threw himself down. There, he prayed for the second time that morning.

> "O, gentle Pallas, What possesses me?
> What awful force impels such movement in
> The flesh I called my own? The call of sin
> Compels me ruthlessly, tears my eyes from thee.
> I pledged myself to thee eternally,
> An oath that's all but silenced by the din
> Of my own pulse. Can my faith be so thin
> That one fair maiden's glance tears it from me?
> Forgive my weakness, goddess. Hear my cry.
> Release my body from indentureship
> To passion's call and lust's lewd mastery. Pry
> Me from the breathless and compelling grip
> Of my own loins. The open chasm's nigh—
> Please catch me by the fingers ere I slip."

Chapter Twelve:
Diomedes' Quest

DIOMEDES LOOKED FORWARD to serving Lothar the Pale, but one daunting problem faced him: where was Palamon? The Carean monarch had left his capital city. According to reports, the tall king had spoken with the Oracle at Euelpis, then had disappeared somewhere near the mouth of the Courbee River. No one seemed to know where he was now or what he was after.

Even so, Diomedes did not fret. A hard task at high pay was much to be preferred, after all, over the simple task of living on a reeve's wage. He would find the tall monarch before Lothar's gold ran out. Even if he did not, he would have good sport as long as that money lasted.

Time was of the essence. He left the Buerdic king, bought a handsome stallion, and hired himself a pair of rough henchmen. Then the three of them set off for the city of Stournes, the city nearest the twisted river's mouth.

They rode hard and slept little. No adventure overtook them and they arrived in only a few days; then they began their search in earnest. Diomedes knew his plan, even before they rode through the city's gate. "We have to buy new clothes and position ourselves," he said. "Carea keeps an embassy here, atop a hill in the noble section of town. If anyone on earth knows where their king is, it'll be those diplomats. All we have to do is get a grip on one of them."

His partners nodded. The three of them found a clothier and replaced their rough garb with the raiment a trio of wealthy merchants or even minor nobles might wear. Then they went to the Carean embassy, a suite of rooms in a large house near the Baron of Stournes' castle. They watched and waited for events.

For two full days, they took turns in front of the place. They did not hope to see the Carean king himself but they did hope for some hint of his purpose or his whereabouts. But the watch was fruitless. The diplomats in Stournes plainly had little to do; only a few people entered or left the embassy and the staff itself numbered only two or three men.

On the afternoon of the second day, Diomedes walked to a nearby hostel and bought a lunch for the three of them. When he brought the food back, they crept into a dark alley, tore at their meal, and considered their next strategy.

They were not even through chewing their provender when Diomedes heard a sound and looked up. A young man had entered the alleyway behind the three of them and Diomedes recognized him as one of the Carean embassy's staff. The youth walked along the alley with a shock of letters in his hands and his head down; he apparently did not even notice the three men who lurked in the shadows.

"The gods provide," Diomedes said in a guttural voice. The young man looked up but before he could shy away from the three men, Diomedes dropped his lunch, grabbed the youth by one richly covered arm, and forced him against a wall with a dagger to his throat. "Don't yell," the assassin growled. "Just tell us what you're doing here." Before the young man could reply, he snarled to his henchmen, "Pick up those letters."

"By all the gods," the young man cried.

Diomedes clamped a heavy hand over his mouth and caged the rest of his words. "Don't yell again, or it'll be your last song," he said. Then he lifted his hand. "What are you doing?"

"You don't want me," the young man said. "I have no money; I am but a young and worthless scribe within the embassy."

"I don't want your gold," Diomedes said sweetly. "I only want information." He turned to his henchmen, who had gathered the young man's papers. "Roche and Aigu, present yourselves to this fellow."

The two henchmen bowed and smiled like choirboys at the young man, though his bulging eyes showed that he was affected more by their cruel features than by their manners. "I have no information, either,'' he squeaked. ''I am but a scribe, an underling. The papers are no more than the routine dispatches I deliver to the waterfront each month, for transport to our homeland.''

Diomedes tightened his grip. ''It's not my homeland.''

''No, please. I meant no insult.''

''Where do you hail from, lad? From here, or do you come from the Carean mainland?''

''I was born in the Montaigne, a province which bestrides the long peninsula.''

Diomedes smiled. ''You're from the heart of the Carean territories, then. You know what your king looks like?''

''Indeed. His portrait hangs outside the chamber where I labor at my duties.''

Diomedes' mind raced. The lad was nothing; he knew even less than he thought he did. If he had seen Palamon inside the embassy, he would certainly have marked it. But what if the tall monarch had visited the place in disguise? It would not have mattered—whatever they did to this youth, he would not be able to give them information he did not himself possess. The assassin glanced at the sealed papers Roche and Aigu held, then relaxed his grip on the young man's neck. He might still get something out of this. ''You seem to be a loyal man.''

The youth took a breath. ''I am. What will you do with me?''

''Why, not a thing, except give you some advice. Do you know who I am?''

The scribe straightened his collar and shook his head. ''No.''

''I'm Argas, of your king's secret service.''

''I've never heard of you.''

Diomedes smiled. ''That's good, you're not supposed to. Now listen to me, your king is in Stournes right this moment.''

''King Pal . . .'' The young man was unable to finish the exclamation as Diomedes slapped his palm back across the young mouth.

''No one is supposed to know,'' the assassin said. ''Not even the ambassador himself.''

''Then why tell me?''

''I do it only in passing—you've shown your mettle. But you are to tell no one, do you understand?''

The young man straightened his clothes and appeared impressed that he had been entrusted with such a secret. "I understand."

"Because of the king's secret mission to this land, we have to take a very close look at this embassy. The ambassador himself may be replaced."

The young man's eyes bulged. "Indeed?"

"Not a word about it," Diomedes said. He threatened to shut the scribe's mouth again, but the youth stepped back. "Security is the problem—not enough care being taken to protect state secrets. Look at you, for instance, carrying your dispatches in the open. Why, any low thief could get them from you. You should have them in a pouch and they should be hidden from the public eye. Even the master of the ship which takes them to Carea shouldn't know what he carries. There's no excuse for it—I can tell you, heads will roll when I make my report."

The scribe lowered his eyes. "I'm sorry, Sir. I did not realize . . ."

"It's not your fault, I know," Diomedes said gently. "How can we expect you to be careful when your master doesn't tell you? Still and all, it's serious."

The scribe reached for the papers. "I'll get them down there straightaway."

Diomedes pushed him away. "No you won't. You've done enough for one day. We'll take care of them—at least we can hope to get them to their transport safe and sound if we do it."

"What will I do? My master will administer a thrashing to me if he finds I gave the letters to another."

"You'll tell him nothing. It won't do for him to know he's being investigated. Which ship do these go to?"

"The *Xanthus*. It's the one Carean vessel in the harbor at this time."

"And the master will have the diplomatic pouch, I suppose."

"He will."

"And there's a password."

" 'Liaison.' "

"Good." Diomedes smiled with satisfaction. "We'll deliver them and your master will never know the difference— and we'll all know it was done properly. Where had you planned to go afterward?"

The scribe eyed the three older men in embarrassment. "It

will be awhile before I am expected back. I'd planned . . ." he hesitated.

"You'd better tell us if you want to stay out of trouble."

"On the days I run this errand I return by way of a small inn, the Cormorant. I meet a maiden there and we eat lunch."

Diomedes laughed. "Young men are the same everywhere, aren't they? All right, here's a coin." He flipped a golden talent into the astonished youth's hands. "Tell your maid her lunch was bought today by the king's treasury."

The scribe gazed at the piece in joyful disbelief. It probably represented three weeks' wages for such an underling as him. "I thank you," he said at last. "No words express my gratitude."

"Be more careful," Diomedes said smugly. "That's the kind of thanks the king wants. You are young but you show promise. But you must learn to be more careful. Now away with you."

"Thank you, thank you," the younger man said, and hurried away from the three assassins. As soon as he was gone, Diomedes pounced on the dispatches and tore the first group from Roche's hands.

"Hurry," he said. "We have to get these open and have a look at them." In less time than it took for him to say it, his dagger had flicked to the first message, expertly sliced open the seal, and he was reading it. "Nothing here," he muttered. "Who wants to know whether Carea is favored or unfavored in wine exports?"

His eyes crossed Roche's face. "Oh," he said with a smile. "You want me to answer the great question—how do we dare hand unsealed dispatches to the master of a Carean ship? Fetch a little tinder and I'll show you."

Roche and Aigu handed every message to him. He continued to slit them open and read them as the two henchmen moved along the alley and gathered up rags, bits of wood, other rubbish which might burn. Diomedes opened the things all the while, but found nothing he could use. The two men finally laid the debris at his feet and he looked up.

"It's easy to cover your tracks if you have the right branches," he said with a smile. "Watch this."

He took out his fire case, removed his flint and steel and a bit of the charred linen he carried for tinder. Once he had built a little flame, he heated his dagger blade and used that to warm the wax on the first message's seal just enough to melt it back together without hurting the seal itself. "There," he said as he handed the resealed message back to a grinning Aigu. "When I worked for Prince Ursid, I used to do that all the time with his messages. It's easy when you practice—a body will never notice unless he takes the time to look extra close. No shipmaster will know the difference and by the time these reach the Carean ministry, we'll be long gone."

He read the rest of the messages while the two henchmen labored nimbly to reseal them the way he had showed them. "I've got something," he finally said. "Listen to this: 'The king, whose mission still lies undisclosed, was verified to be in Stournes upon the seventh instant. Passed into a place known as the Pilot Fish, and had with him a younger man of unknown origin. He did not reappear; have lost all trace. Will send report when more is known.' And then he puts his signature."

He turned the note over in his mind, then said, "Seal up the rest and we'll get them down to the dock. At least we have a clue, now, a starting place." His mouth worked as he slit the last dispatch open, but he only glanced at it and did not see anything more of value. "Keep your daggers sharp, men," he said as they gathered up the papers and hurried toward the docks. "The Pilot Fish—that should be easy enough to find. The Carean king's tall and he stands out in a crowd—someone will have seen him. I tell you, my dagger can almost taste his blood."

Chapter Thirteen:
The Pilot Fish

DIOMEDES AND HIS men found the Pilot Fish tavern near the waterfront. They searched long and hard and asked the district's denizens many whispered questions. But they made no further progress. No one, it seemed, had seen the Carean king.

"This is ridiculous," Diomedes snarled as he and the two henchmen finally relaxed at one of the tables in the Pilot Fish. "The man was here, I know he was here. But no one for half a league about has seen him." He shook his head. "Something fishy's going on, by Tyche's nipples. When I read that dispatch, I thought sure we were on our way. Now I'm not so sure." He shook his head again.

The three sipped their ale silently. Then Diomedes looked up to see a man standing beside his table. The fellow was as scroungy a parcel as the assassin had ever looked on, from the dirty toes which poked out through the ends of his boots, to the piece of fishnet which served as his tunic, to the flaming carbuncle which graced the end of his nose, a little to one side. Diomedes eyed him. "What do you want?"

"I hear yer lookin fer a man," the fellow said in a singsong voice.

"I might be," Diomedes replied. "What's it to you?"

"Give me a coin." The creature held out his hand.

Diomedes studied the hand for an instant, then he looked back up at its owner. If the man was not a complete idiot, he was close to it. And he stank to boot. But Diomedes finally grunted, reached to his purse, and produced a small, silver coin, which he laid into the filthy palm.

Black-nailed fingers closed around the coin and the creature smiled. "Crossback," he said through rotting teeth. Then he hurried for the door.

Diomedes decided it was not worth the trouble to catch him and beat more information out of him. "Crossback," he whispered to himself as the grotesque figure disappeared out the building's front entrance. "What's a Crossback, I wonder?"

He looked about the ragged inn; it was late and hardly anyone was in the place. The innkeeper stood behind the counter and puttered about with the rag. A couple of dockworkers drank ale at a corner table, and two more rough-looking characters sat at a table next to the door. A third leaned on that table with both hands. Diomedes turned in his seat and looked them all over. Would any of them know who or what a Crossback was?

He took a long drink, then stood and strode to the counter. He stopped in front of the innkeeper, laid a coin on the hardwood, and said, "I'm in a fix."

"We all have problems," the innkeeper said with a smile. "More ale?"

"Ale won't help. What does 'Crossback' mean to you?"

The man stared at the assassin, then looked away. "Don't you know?"

"Should I?"

The innkeeper shrugged. "Maybe not."

"What does it mean to you?"

"Nothing."

"Don't give me that." Diomedes pulled out his dagger and let it fall to the countertop with a clatter. "I offered you money but I'm not a patient man. I can give you edged steel just as easy—and disappear before anyone can do a thing about it."

The innkeeper stared and started to back away, but Diomedes shot out a hand and grabbed the front of his jerkin. "Why pick on me?" the innkeeper whined. "Why not bother someone else?"

"Because you know the answer." Silence filled the place; Diomedes could feel all eyes on the two of them. But he did not let go. "Tell me what it means."

"Everyone knows. And it's not 'it.' It's 'he.'"

"A person?"

The innkeeper nodded.

"Who is he?"

"It's not healthy to talk about him."

Diomedes smiled and let go. "I see. Does he smuggle, or deal in women, or what?"

The fellow who had leaned on the table next to the door straightened and hurried out. "Now you've done it," the inn-keeper said. Before Diomedes could catch him again, he backed into another room. The other two men at the table near the door rose softly and followed their friend. "Well, well," Diomedes said absently. "At least something's going on, now."

Roche and Aigu looked about uneasily as a large, bearded man strolled into the place, advanced to the table occupied by the two dockworkers, and jerked his thumb toward the entrance. "Git," he said in a deep voice.

"What for?" one of the laborers answered. But the other tugged him on the shoulder and the two of them rose. With the heavyset newcomer behind them, they laid some money on the counter and walked toward the street outside. Diomedes noticed that the heavy man behind them picked the coins up and handed them back to the two men with a few softly spoken words. "Whoever this Crossback is, he seems to have a world of pull," he mused.

Diomedes returned to his table. He and his henchmen sat for a long time while the tavern remained as silent as a peat bog at night. No one passed on the street outside, no one came in, no one asked the three men about paying for their food. Even Diomedes began to feel nervous.

At last a hulking hunchback strolled into the room. He stopped, put his hands on his hips, and looked about. When his eyes came to rest on the three men, a slow smile lit his features. "Diomedes of Buerdaunt," he said in a rumbling voice. "If I'd known it was you, I'd have come sooner."

Diomedes looked at him with mild surprise. "You know me, then?"

The hunchback looked huge; he was the tallest man Diomedes had ever seen—and broad in proportion. The hood which covered his pate nearly brushed the rafters overhead. He walked toward their table with supreme confidence that whatever he wanted to happen *would* happen. "I know you, yes," he said. "I was in your prince's army for a few weeks." He shrugged. "There wasn't any room for advancement, so I left."

"You deserted?"

"Not quite. I joined of my own free will, me and my brother

both. We learned a few things and saw you ride by with the constable more than once. But it was no way to make a living. The point is, no·one asked us to join and no one asked us to leave. The slate was even all across.''

Diomedes studied the man. Whether this giant had deserted Prince Ursid's army or been mustered out with honors did not matter in the slightest. All that mattered was that Diomedes locate the Carean king. ''Do you know of Crossback?'' he asked.

The towering hunchback winked. ''I know all about him. But what's that worth to you?''

''It's worth new minted gold if your information's good.''

''Much gold?''

''That depends on how good the information is.''

The hunchback shook his ogre's head and laughed. ''No, no, no, no, no,'' he said in the softest possible voice. ''Let me explain things to you. Stournes belongs to Crossback and me. It's our fief, our holding, our castle, our palace. Little people—even ones who ride with princes—don't come around and tell how the thing will be done.''

Diomedes grew warm at the hunchback's manner but he forced a smile. ''All right, then. How will it be done?''

The hunchback eyed the three men. ''You wear pretty clothes,'' he said at last. ''I don't know whether you're rich or poor but Crossback can help any man. How much money do you have?''

''Enough.''

The hunchback nodded. ''I'd expect that. If you were bright enough to ride with the constable, you're bright enough to drive a tough bargain. Very well, then, ten talents and Crossback will tell you what you want to know.''

''Ten talents,'' Diomedes exclaimed. ''That's pretty steep when I haven't even asked the question, yet.''

''That's a detail. Ask, then, and I'll take the question to Crossback.''

''I want to see Crossback myself.''

The hunchback shook his head. ''No one does that.''

Diomedes scowled. ''How about the Carean king? Did he get to speak to Crossback?''

The hunchback's face became a mask. ''What Carean king?''

''King Palamon.'' Diomedes saw the reaction to that name, then laughed. ''Didn't you know it when Carea's king passed through your 'fief'? Your Crossback's information must not be as good as you say it is, certainly not worth ten talents.''

The hunchback smiled broadly then reached back and took the time to draw a pair of chairs from another table. He placed the two chairs side-by-side and they creaked as he seated himself. ''Well, well. We're not asking about the weather, are we? You want to know about the king—that raises the price.''

''Money doesn't matter.'' Diomedes leaned toward the bigger man. ''Can you tell us where he is?''

''It'll cost you.''

''I'll pay it. I may have to send for the money.''

''You'll get no answer till you've paid your gold.''

He started to rise but Diomedes caught his wrist. ''I don't want you out of my sight; I want to see Crossback myself. How do I know you won't go straight to the authorities?''

The hulking man flung Diomedes' hand away like a gnat, then stood. The least trace of anger flicked onto his features. ''That's not a very smart question for a fellow who's supposed to be intelligent. Crossback and I don't get along with the authorities.'' The smile crawled back onto his face and split his heavy beard. ''You know what? I've let you off too easy. I usually tell a man he can see Crossback if he can draw first blood from me in a fair fight. Do you think you can do that? By the gods, I'll face you right here, in the Pilot Fish—if you can lay a whisker of steel on me, I might just let you speak to the Great Man.''

Diomedes smiled back at him. This inn in this sleazy city was the hunchback's territory; he had emptied the place at will and would doubtless conduct his business as long as he wished without being disturbed. ''I'm in the enemy's camp, it seems,'' Diomedes said. ''That excites me. If you want to have it out, I'm eager.''

Their eyes met. ''Have your men clear a space,'' the hunchback finally said. ''We'll get some exercise.''

Diomedes rose and brushed against him as the four men turned toward the center of the chamber. But as they touched, Diomedes whisked a long dagger from its sheath; quick as a viper's tongue, he buried the weapon in the hunchback's side. He felt the blade slide off bone and penetrate deep. He shivered with glee as his victim released a hiss of pain.

''Treachery,'' the hunchback groaned. ''You'll die for this, and your men with you.'' He staggered; before he could get his sword from its hanger, the Buerdic assassin had yanked the dagger from its blood-weeping burrow and used it to carve a new one. The huge man groaned from this second wound and sank to one knee. Two crimson rivers pulsed down his side.

Roche and Aigu each grabbed a huge arm. Though they were strong men, the hunchback jerked them to and fro till the blood from his wound spattered everywhere. They managed to control him after a moment, though. Diomedes held his dripping blade before the hunchback's pain-wracked face. "You fool," the assassin said with a sneer. "To think you could get the better of me. Where's Crossback?"

"You'll die for this. Umm, it hurts; I'll kill you myself. A dozen men wait outside this building."

"Where's Crossback?" Diomedes insisted, but received no decipherable answer. Then a strange voice gargled something and movement brought his eye to the dirty cape the hunchback wore. He swept it aside and to his amazement, saw the dwarf who grew from the broad back. "By Typhon's spear," Diomedes breathed. "What in the world are you?"

"Never mind that," the pinched dwarf said in a desperate voice. "You've got to get help for him. He'll bleed to death." Even then, the huge man's struggles against Roche and Aigu grew weaker.

"Yes, he will," Diomedes said with his sweetest smile. "He'll die and you'll die with him, it seems to me. You'd better tell him to quit fighting or he'll die even sooner."

"Be reasonable."

"Who are you?" Diomedes held his knife to the freak's throat. "You'd better tell me, or you'll die before he does."

"I'm Crossback, I'm Crossback. Quit struggling, Alpus; I'm starting to feel a little weak, myself."

Diomedes threw back his head and laughed as the hunchback went slack and the dwarf glanced about, wild-eyed with terror. "So that's the game," the assassin said. "I can't see you but you listen to me all the while. That's just fine, but you'll not live out the night unless you answer my question. Where's Palamon?"

Crossback's eyes flicked from Diomedes to Diomedes' dagger, to the two leering henchmen. "He's looking for the *Tome of Winds*."

"What in Hades' name is that?"

"It's an artifact. Very rare. By all the gods, you have to get us to help. We'll die."

"I might do that, but not until I get what I want. Where's Palamon headed; where can I find him?"

Fear crowded the half-man's eyes. "Count Hextin's court," he said. "That was one of the places I said he might find it. But I don't think he'll find it there even if he tries, because Hextin isn't smart enough to know what it is even if he has it. He'd let it go, for sure."

Diomedes pressed the dagger's blade against the little throat. "You're not telling me anything," he said. "Talk. Talk plain. It won't help any for you to play for time."

"All right, all right. The temple of Typhon in Quarval, I'm almost sure they'll have it, and they'll hang on to it if they do. He'll have the fiend's own time talking them out of it because they're such an unpleasant lot."

"Did you tell him to go to either one place or the other?"

"Never. I only gave him what I've given you. More than that, I can't say."

"A likely story." Diomedes sneered. "You know more than you're saying, I'd stake my life on it."

"No, no," Crossback answered. "I swear I don't."

"Tell it all." Diomedes snarled. He gave the little head a wrench with his free hand. "I want to know where he is right now." But he was interrupted by a sound from outside the building; someone moved along the wooden walkway in front of the place. "That's enough," he said. "Let's get out of here."

He released Crossback's head and leaped to his feet, along with his two henchmen. Hulking Alpus was too weak to support himself by this time; he slumped over as the two men let him go. "Wait," Crossback screamed. "What about me?"

"Take care of yourself," Diomedes said over his shoulder. He and his henchmen hurled themselves toward the counter at one end of the room. Like three stags, they vaulted the wooden barrier and tore through the backroom of the Pilot Fish, rebounding off heavy barrels and knocking over furniture. They heard a crash at the other end of the building and Diomedes knew the dockside vermin had found their wounded master. Then he broke through the inn's rear door to find that more men blocked off the rear of the building.

The three assassins scrambled into the alley and into a half dozen thugs. "What?" one cried in surprise; then the battle was on. Diomedes buried his dagger in the gut of one man before the fellow could yank his sword out; Roche knocked over another, but then they both heard a scream from Aigu, who was rearmost of the three. Two men had grabbed him by the arms and a third leered as he drew the edge of his sword across the assassin's throat.

"Leave him," Diomedes yelled to Roche. "He's done for anyway." He bowled over another man and the two of them thundered toward the open street.

Chapter Fourteen:
Priests of Typhon

SOUTH OF STOURNES, a towering dome of granite lifted its head above the Courbee's forested banks. Palamon and Reale rode their steeds toward that pale mound of rock, for it was the last hope the tall monarch had of laying his hands on the *Tome of Winds*.

They had paid a visit to Count Hextin of Parvu and the errand had produced no result. The count was a vain man. He recognized Palamon and took delight in showing the tall monarch every artifact and curiosity which graced his towering castle, but he had never heard of the mystical volume. He was proud of the mementos he did possess; therefore, Palamon doubted the treasure might lie concealed in that place.

Palamon's face formed a tight frown and Reale gazed at him thoughtfully. "You're full of troubles, by the look of you," the younger man finally said. "You haven't said three words running since we reached this road, you just frown like an old judge."

Palamon turned his eyes toward Phatyr's son. The darkness of the lad's black hair was a striking contrast to his own snowy locks, the tall monarch knew, not to mention the pure white of his full moustache. But the young man was quiet and thoughtful, a good traveling partner. The tall monarch's mouth formed the beginnings of a smile. "Ah, me. I grow too old for questing. Lad, the Oracle herself was frighted when the blood began to blaze and then the vase burst. Troubles come to plague our lands—and I am but a fading relic to fulfill my mission. Battles lurk beyond our gaze—that makes me weary."

"Who'll fight them, these battles you speak of?"

Palamon's smile deepened but no joy lay in it. "Who knows? A prophecy asks full as many questions as it answers, lad. But by my troth, when time for struggle comes, 'tis like the two of us will find ourselves deep in the thick of things."

"I don't know whether to be tickled or scared. I guess it'll help me become a knight, though."

"Without a doubt."

"Will we win?"

"My faith prescribes my answer: yes."

Reale frowned. "I hope you're right."

"I, too."

They rode a long time before Reale spoke again. "More troubles you than just what you have told me. Is it not so?"

Palamon glanced at him. "Indeed," he finally said. "We must accost the temple of the priests of Typhon, most inscrutable of the twelve divinities." As he spoke, he headed his mount's nose into the timber. "Come, let us turn aside a moment."

Reale followed him to the shadowed forest. The young man watched while the tall monarch dismounted and stripped away his outer clothing. Reale had to admire the coat of glossy chain mail which shimmered in the shadows. "You wear noble armor," he said.

"A token of a holy covenant," Palamon said as he folded his outer clothing and tucked it into his pack.

Reale could hardly tear his eyes from the unearthly shimmer of links which themselves seemed to be living beings united in a marvelous oneness. Then his wonder turned into a little smile as he watched his master remove the leather casing from the huge, two-handed sword. "My Lord," Reale said softly. "I warrant you could thrill my ears with many a story of wars and wonders if you only wanted to."

Palamon shook his head. " 'Tis likely I would bore you, Phatyr's son. A bard I'm not. But I have lived a life of dedication to the gods, especially to Pallas, ruler of the bravest warriors—and of man's immortal soul. These priests of Typhon are a sullen lot, as well befits their deity. I'll have my colors showing ere I speak to them."

"Your chain mail is like a badge of honor."

"I claim no honors, but it is a symbol of the Maiden's favor. I will not conceal it from them. Let us hurry; I would have this duty finished."

Palamon shoved his *Spada Korrigaine* into a scabbard which hung from his saddle. He rested one hand on the gleaming pommel as the two of them rode back onto the road toward Typhon's temple. The stronghold stood atop the granite dome like a mountain in its own right, a man-made mountain. It was built from huge blocks, a brooding pile which towered heavenward. Rooks and magpies wheeled about its pinnacles, high above the Courbee's sluggish waters.

Palamon and Reale rode slowly and eyed the place. They arrived at a large stone building, a kind of sentry post a couple of hundred cubits downhill from the main structure. Two brown-robed monks darted from the building and blocked their way. The two carried cudgels and looked unfriendly. "Ye be upon the road to mighty Typhon's abbey," one monk shouted. "Stop and state your business."

"I seek an audience before your abbot," Palamon replied.

The two sentries looked at one another. "Why would any Knight of Pallas seek our order?" one finally asked.

"I journey here because the Oracle at Euelpis prompts me to. Now tell me, is the abbot well and able to converse with me?"

"He's well, praise Typhon," one priest answered. "But whether he has time to speak to you's another question."

"Why don't you tell them who you are?" Reale asked Palamon in a whisper. But the tall monarch merely made a face and shook his head.

One sentry said, "Our sanctuary is not open to all men who happen to approach it. Ride up to the outer gate, say Kal has let you pass that far, and state your mission to the day-priest. If he lets you, you may give all thanks unto the mighty god, and pass within."

Palamon frowned, but he nodded and let fall a polite word of thanks. The two sentry monks moved back into their building.

"Why didn't you tell them you were King of Carea?" Reale asked as they rode on.

" 'Twould not have made a difference," Palamon replied. "No name or title awes them, but for Typhon's. He holds all their thoughts to him."

Reale studied the tall monarch, then glanced back toward the sentry post. "I don't know much about the gods," he finally said. "But it doesn't seem right to me that they should worship one of the twelve so much that they ignore all the others."

Palamon half smiled but he did not reply. When they arrived at the abbey's main gate, they found the place more of a citadel than an abbey. Whether or not the god Typhon might defend it, an army would have been hard-pressed to gain entry by force.

Palamon's interview with the priests at the main gate went no better than his exchange with the sentries. This time, the man in charge demanded a large donation. The gold would help the priests conduct their holy work, he said, though he gave no explanation of how the funds would be used, or even whether the coins would pass any farther than his own pockets. He merely said, "Typhon be praised," as Palamon handed him a handful of talents. Then they ushered the two men through the gate.

They reached a large inner building and were ushered into a dark chamber with lavish hangings on the walls. They waited for more time than Reale could guess. At last a door opened at the far end and two men entered. One was a young fellow who carried torches. The other was an old, old man, thin, balding, with cheeks and forehead so full of wrinkles that his face looked like a wadded piece of parchment. That face was the only part of him that showed; robes of rich silk hid the rest. They shimmered in the torchlight.

He fixed his glittering eyes on Palamon, smiled, and extended an arm so that a withered hand appeared from the folds of clothing, as if by magic. The tall monarch bent and placed his lips softly against the huge ruby ring which adorned one finger. As the tall monarch straightened, the old man withdrew the hand and smiled up at him.

"So," he said in a voice cracked by age. "I know you by your reputation. You are Palamon, King of Carea."

"I am."

A corner of the man's mouth curled and he said, "Then welcome to you. I am Monus, abbot of this blessed stronghold. It is seldom that such royalty comes here. What business brings you?"

"I seek an artifact known as the *Tome of Winds*. My search has led me here."

Monus' eyes narrowed. "Why here?"

Palamon smiled. "The wisdoms all combined, of Oracles and criminals and counts. To tell you all the story of my search would be a tedious endeavor. Does the artifact lie here, within these walls?"

Monus leaned his head back, pursed his lips, and thought for a moment. At last his eye lit on the tall monarch's face once more. "Perhaps."

"You've heard of it?"

"I have."

Palamon straightened. "By all the hallowed gods, 'twould be a boon if you might grant the loan of it. You'd earn my gratitude and that of higher ones than I."

"Wait, wait," the abbot said with a little laugh. "I only said the thing was possible. I've no idea, really—vaults lie far below these corridors. They harbor treasures, prizes, mysteries, from generations long expired. No man has plumbed those depths within my lifetime. None shall go there now."

Reale's jaw dropped. "That's cruel," he said in his uncultured tones.

"Indeed, indeed," Palamon said. "I am a pious man; for all my life, I've honored all the twelve divinities. What right lets you deny the Oracle's true prophecy? I'd not allow a danger to confront you or your flock, if that is what you fear. Let me but search the labyrinths where your treasures lie, then seal the door behind me if it is your will."

Monus waved a wrinkled palm. "Save your pride, great King. Your plea is meaningless. Those halls stay closed, whatever you might say."

Palamon stared at him. "Do not deny my honorable request."

"Come, come. Your own words indicate you be not sure your artifact lies here. I'd never let you pierce this temple's secrets on mere speculation. On ten times the assurances you've given, I would never do it."

"But why?" Palamon cried.

"You grant small honor to *my* deity, exalted ruler." The man's face became hard. "How many temples have you dedicated to my patron, Typhon? Do they grace Carea's streets?"

"Or those of far Buerdaunt, or any other land?" Palamon replied. "Yours is a solitary order; you don't seek such dedications, that I know of. Why blame me for that?"

" 'Tis not so easy," the abbot countered. "For you should have given them without the asking. Your sweet god, your Pallas, had no need to beg such favors."

Palamon frowned and let one fist drop against his mailed thigh. "My life was dedicated to the Maiden e'en before I tasted meat. How can you punish any man for that?" His eyes flashed and he stood. "But well enough; I see your meaning and I see that I'll receive no hearing in this place. I'll take my leave, good sir; the twelve gods hear these words between us and they mark your doings quite as much as mine. The time will come when all men—warriors, even priests—must answer for their deeds."

"What all the gods may think's not my concern," the abbot replied. He also rose and signaled his novice to do the same. "I worship Typhon only. For the rest, I tell you they will thrive as well for anything I may or may not do. Farewell." With that, he walked from the dark chamber, leaving Palamon and Reale to stare at one another.

Both men glared after the temple's master, then a door at the other end of the chamber swung open and a half dozen priests armed with cudgels escorted the two of them from the abbey. Reale did not resist them; neither did Palamon.

As they reached the yard, the tall monarch laid his hand on the younger man's shoulder. "Our aims are thwarted here," he said. "Still, we cannot surrender hope. The gods will not allow one human's verdict to deflect the bolt they've hurled. We'll go from here; their light shall pierce the darkness which this abbot casts on us."

Monks brought their horses from the stables. Reale noted the animals had been fed, watered, and brushed. He also saw Palamon smile dryly as one of the hostlers handed the tall monarch a tab for the care. Carea's king tossed the man a talent, then he and Reale turned the animals' heads toward the gate. "Farewell, you monks of Typhon," Palamon said.

For all it tempted him, Reale did not allow himself to say or even think of a word. But as they started back down the trail, he whispered, "May the gods pay you well for your services."

"A double meaning," the tall monarch noted. "I allow you have a wit, young man. But strike blind rage from out your heart, for that is evil's tool. We'll find another way; we must, we shall."

"I could strangle the lot of them." The younger man looked at Palamon. "And for all your honorable phrases, you have to admit you'd like to do the same."

Palamon smiled as the two of them rode past the sentry building. "My heart is dark," the tall monarch said. "Ah, Maiden, please forgive me, for Reale is right."

Toward the base of the granite dome, they came to a burly

oak tree which rose from a cleft in the stone. It spread thick branches a hundred feet from the road, the only living thing across that expanse of gray. It stood perhaps thirty cubits high; they had not noticed it on their journey up the hill.

"Wait, now," Palamon said. "We have to tarry here, beneath these branches. I would contemplate this prodigy."

They turned off the road and Palamon studied the fissure from which the tree sprouted; it was as if the force of the plant's growing had split the stone itself. "What are we going to do here?" Reale asked.

"I do not know," Palamon said softly. "Old age has made me easy to confuse; sometimes it seems a head with whitened hairs does not contain as clear a thought as one with dark adornments. Yet I know the oak tree is a special growth, held sacred by the gods. Stout Typhon's priests—do they speak for the god himself? And if they do, is his stand honored by his heavenly brethren? Lad, too many questions addle me. What can I do but ponder this awhile and lift my voice unto the beings who perplex me. Do a favor: take your horse and stand away from here."

Reale flipped his reins and rode toward the river's edge while Palamon dismounted, unsheathed his two-handed sword, and studied the tree. Reale did not watch while several moments passed. Was the old king praying? Then the youth heard a clatter as if someone had thrown a handful of pebbles against the side of a house. Palamon shouted, "Catch them, lad. Catch all of them; they are the key to our success."

Reale turned in his saddle and was amazed to spy a multitude of acorns clattering toward him across the granite hillside. They bounded down the slanting surface like a horde of mice, so many of them he could hardly think to dismount. "Hurry," Palamon's voice came. "Gather every one." To Reale's surprise, the tall monarch bounded across the granite himself, snatching up acorns and dumping them into his gathered cloak with amazing agility for one who showed so much white hair.

Reale leaped to the ground and did the same, though there were so many of the things, two men could hardly pick them all up. It was crazy. Acorns were a nut of the autumn; this had to be last year's crop, retained by the tree just long enough to fall while Palamon prayed. For all Reale's efforts, a few acorns rolled past before he could grab them. They tumbled down the stone and plunked into the river.

It almost made Reale laugh to see them but the laughter

froze in his throat as he saw Palamon's stare. "I tried, but missed those few," the younger man said lamely.

"Go get them," Palamon shouted. "Hurry, give me yours and snatch those others." The tall monarch gathered the younger man's acorns into the folds of his own cloak, then tied the broad garment into a bag and fastened it to his saddle. The younger man scuttled along the rocks and tried to retrieve those which floated just out of reach. He leaped over the stone like a clumsy hound, skinned his knees and knuckles, passed them, then splashed into the water to gather them in.

He managed to lay his hands on all but three before he stepped into an underwater hole and plunged beneath the surface. He had been so intent that he retained his grip despite the murky waters which filled his eyes and nose. He thrashed about like a drowning man, which he very nearly was before he managed to clamber back out onto the dry stone.

Palamon had passed him by this time and still kept pace with the three uncollected acorns. At this point, the granite rose ever more steeply at the river's edge, until it formed a sheer cliff some three hundred cubits high, at the apex of which stood Typhon's abbey. For though the rock slanted gradually enough to be climbed on the land side, it formed the shape of a dome cut in half; that side formed a sheer cliff.

Progress along the base of the cliff became difficult; Reale saw Palamon vanish behind a couple of boulders, then reached them to see the tall monarch making his way through ankle-deep water.

The two of them plunged into the cliff's shadow. The rock shelved off steeply at the water's edge and Reale had a tough time keeping his feet. He caught up with Palamon just as the tall monarch snatched up the last three acorns with a cry.

He turned and said, "At last we have them. Grant forgiveness, lad; I know this seems a piece of foolishness. Yet not one thing takes place without a reason; why do acorns fall at springtime's peak?"

Reale gazed up at the older man, who in turn studied the three acorns in his hand. Long, thin, with one tapered end and one rounded end in its pithy cap; there could be no doubt as to what they were. Then Reale noticed something over the older man's shoulder.

"My Lord," he said. "Behind you—I see an opening."

Palamon followed the line of the younger man's finger. A fissure a couple of cubits high in the solid granite lay amid a cluster of boulders at the water's edge, huge stones which apparently had fallen from the cliff above. They concealed it so well that its existence never would have been suspected from above, or by a traveler on the river's surface.

It was not very big, hardly large enough for a man to squeeze through. Even so, Reale could see Palamon's face light up. "So this is what the oak tree led us to," the tall monarch said. He clenched the last three acorns in his fist and held them aloft. "O, mighty Pallas, I give fervent thanks. With your most blessed face before me, I shall delve into this opening and seek whatever lies within its depths."

Chapter Fifteen:
Beneath the Rock

THE OPENING LAY at the water's edge; each ripple from the river splashed down the incline until the bottom of the cleft shone slimy and green with moss before it disappeared into blackness. A musty odor rose from the hole, the smell of a damp vault.

Palamon looked from the hole to Reale's face, then back again. "So here's the avenue. One does not turn away when the almighty gods present a sign."

"Your prayer brought all this about?" Reale asked doubtfully.

The tall monarch almost laughed. "Perhaps, perhaps not. I am not so foolish as to think the gods wait upon my beck and call." He became more thoughtful. "But acorns from a summer's tree—I'll harken to a special melody if it should hint at answers. Wait a bit. I'll to my horse and fetch my weapon down, then we shall start."

"I'm anxious to go."

Palamon clapped Reale on the shoulder. "Ah, doughty lad. Now wait." The tall monarch vanished along the base of the cliff, then returned with his sword, his *Spada Korrigaine*. "I left the horses in the oak tree's shade," the tall monarch said. "Perhaps they will remain when we return, perhaps they'll not—that is adventure's risk. Are you still game?"

"As much as ever," Reale replied.

Palamon stepped past the younger man and squeezed through the cleft with surprising agility. Reale waited till the tall monarch cleared the opening, then he lowered himself,

123

caught his breath at the stinking tightness of the space, wriggled past the snug spot, and found himself standing in the slick mud of a more-or-less level floor. He had expected the space to be dark save the feeble light from above, but he was surprised to see that Palamon had just put flint to steel and lit a wax candle. The wick gave off a smoky light. "A slight precaution," the tall monarch said. "It's not a lantern, yet will serve."

Palamon tapped the hilt of Reale's longsword. "Draw forth your blade," he said. "But may the gods prevent your needing it." He lifted his *Spada Korrigaine* and the two of them moved along the smelly tunnel.

Water flowed down the passage as if it were a creek bed. The way twisted and turned; in places it was so narrow they could barely squeeze through. Reale's mouth curled in distaste as he felt the grime that sloughed all over his jerkin and his breeches. He had waded the Courbee's mud all his life; he had romped through the swampy fields which bordered that river. But there was something stomach-turning about the mud and grime in this mole's hole beneath Typhon's rock. Worse, their path took them ever farther beneath the river itself.

The watery tunnel led down a long way, then steeply upward. Palamon had lit a second candle by the time they came to a stagnant pool which all but blocked their way. Palamon waded into the pool as if it were nothing more than a few more cubits of empty passage. "Your fortitude impresses me," Reale said quietly. "Some would say you look too old to wade this kind of water."

"I'm far too ancient e'en to enter such a place as this," the tall monarch said. " 'Tis said the gods watch out for crazy men; if that's the case, I've every right to think I'm special to them. Keep stout heart, my lad; this passage could get worse."

The tall monarch's voice bounded off the rock, flat and dead one instant, loud as a bell the next. Soft liquid sounds marked his progress until only his head and the candle remained above the black ripples. Reale followed him in. The water was colder than ice in Hades; it chilled the young man's calves to the bone, then his thighs, his hips, his belly and chest. Current plucked at him, tried to pull him under so that the pool seemed almost alive. He shivered as if to pop his teeth from his gums, almost lost his balance, and put out a hand to steady himself.

But he felt nothing; his hand found emptiness. He toppled, his head plunged below the freezing surface, and his weightless feet lifted from the stone beneath him. Panic seized him; he thrashed about to right himself, then found that he had floated into some watery hollow. He could find no air; each place he reached showed his grasping fingers only water and cold stone.

The air in his lungs turned putrid, the icy waters fought their way up his nostrils like evil fingers. He writhed like a madman against the fear and the liquid which clutched him. He scrambled through water and muck, stumbled onto the uneven floor, fell to his hands and knees, nearly lost the sword Palamon had given him. Finally, he regained control over himself and stood in the dizzying darkness, dripping, trying to decide his next act. Things were not as bad as they seemed. He had become separated from the tall monarch, that was all; he had only to retrace his steps, back through the underground pool, and the candle's glimmer would draw him to his leader once more. He hoped.

He felt his way back. To his dismay, he sloshed along the wet tunnel only a few steps before he came up against a wall of rock, a dead end. He bumped his head against it, recoiled and landed on the seat of his breeches, then shook the cobwebs from his brain. He had bloodied his nose. In the blackness, nothing was the way it seemed.

Fear rose inside him once more but he kept it under control this time. There must be many passages in this place; the bowels of the mountain must be honeycombed with tunnels. He rose and made his way back again, feeling more carefully this time. But though he did not notice where the tunnel branched, the floor suddenly canted upward and he found himself in a dry passage. Hoping against hope, he kept on. Perhaps he had passed this dry spot once and had simply ignored it in his haste. But the way kept up and up until he had to admit to himself that he had taken yet another wrong turn.

He released a groan, the hope went out of him, he slumped to his knees. "By all the gods," he whispered to himself. "What sort of place have I found?"

The soft words echoed and echoed as if repeated by a column of dwarves. Then he heard a whispered reply, as if it came from over his shoulder. "Reale? Where have you gotten to?"

Reale's head jerked up; the voice was Palamon's. "I'm here," the younger man shouted back. "Where are you?" The echo rolled away again, mocking him. "Are you? Are you? Are you?" Nothing followed them but a sigh like snakes hissing.

He rolled onto his haunches and laid his face into his hands.

"Palamon," he called, more quietly this time. But the name rolled away from him, "amon, amon, amon," and no reply followed.

He had lost track of his longsword. He scrabbled about frantically, then sighed with relief when his hand bumped the steel blade. It was clammy and covered by mud. To be trapped in such a place was bad enough; at least he had his weapon with him.

He clambered back to his feet and went on, bracing his hands against the sides of the passage so he would not stumble on the uneven floor. Then the wall on his left turned away in a manner it never had before and he found himself in what must have been a larger space.

"Ah, here you are," a soft voice said behind him, and a hand laid itself on his shoulder. He turned in relief and reached forth to greet Palamon, but his fingers found roughness, a scaly mass of sores and dry flesh. The hand brushed his face; scaly, caked by filth, cold as the wet stone.

He cried out and swung his longsword; steel met substance, dug in, but no sound came from the foe. Ragged fingernails scoured his cheek. He hissed in horror, then swung again. He did not hear any sound which might mean a body falling, but the hand did not touch him anymore. He winced with pain as he knelt in the blackness and lifted his own fingers to his face. The wounds were deep and long, he felt blood dribble down his neck.

A bone-chilling hiss came from behind him, like a gasp from Hades itself. He wheeled but no shape altered the blackness. He felt as if he were being digested by unreality. Something cold and slimy flicked out of the darkness and curled about his forearm; he almost lost hold of his sword. Icy calm gripped him as he moved the sword to his left hand and aimed a stroke at the darkness. The blade met something solid, severed it, and the slimy thing dropped to the cavern floor with a splat.

He did not feel for it; instead, he struck again. His blade rebounded off bare stone, pain shot through his fingers, and his ears rang with the sound. Before he could recover, something came out of the darkness behind him and struck the back of his head.

His sword dropped from his fingers, he tumbled to the stone floor dazed, but managed to roll to one side. A baffled grunt told him he had eluded one more attacker. He tried to scramble to his feet, but came against something soft and smooth in the blackness. Another blow sent him sprawling. This time a second blow caught him, filled his head with blinding lights. The flash lit up the entire cavern. It was a huge place. The roof loomed out of sight above him. Jewels lay scattered across the floor; chests and barrels stood with their lids askew. But most important, as Reale lost consciousness, were the three dark-robed judges who glared at him as he sank to the floor.

He did not quit fighting back, even though he had lost his senses. He rolled back and forth, kicked his legs, flailed his arms, bit, scratched, shrieked out against the men who held him to the floor. At least he thought he did. But when a hand touched him on the shoulder, he found himself waking up as if from a trance, and his limbs were as stiff and still as dunnage.

He thrashed one arm, to smash whatever thing might be accosting him this time, but a hand seized his wrist and clamped it in a vicelike grip. He almost cried out, then the shout died on his lips as he spied Palamon's shadowy face. The tall monarch's candle still reflected itself in his gleaming eyes.

Reale could hardly speak. He finally caught his breath and said, "You're strong for an old man."

"I thank you, lad. It's served me once or twice."

"Where am I? I was seized by awful things."

"I see no signs of struggle."

Reale coughed as he remembered the unearthly assault. "A wraith clawed my face and men attacked me . . ."

Palamon smiled grimly and shook his head. "Perhaps, perhaps not. When a mind as young and active as your own leaps on a new experience, it can become as agitated as a bug upon a stove."

Reale thought about that, then sat up. "How did you find me?"

"This rock is laced by caves and galleries. I heard your splashing exit from my side and could not follow you. Though with my feet I probed the pool, the opening eluded me." Palamon smiled again. "This place is most unusual. Some forces work here which no scholar could explain."

"Then maybe I did fight something."

"You say a specter clawed your face? Reach up and feel it."

Reale did so. To his amazement, no fearsome weals met his touch. He dropped his hand, relieved but embarrassed.

"At any rate," Palamon went on, "I heard you cry out once, then once again. They say that if you listen to an echo, then the final sound will tell the way to travel if you'd reach the source. And so I did, though not without some difficulty." He stood, lifted the candle, and Reale saw the mystical boundary to this cavern. A wall reached from floor to ceiling, featureless, flat, and black as slate.

The younger man stared at it. "What's that?" he whispered.

"The source of your discomfort, I would say," Palamon answered. "Someone has conjured up this barricade as surely as the merchant bricks a cellar from invading rats."

Reale reached forth to touch the wall. Before Palamon could stop him, he had placed his fingers against, then into, the cold substance. A little galaxy of stars flared about his fingertips, eddied, and tingled against his bemused flesh. Then he felt a sudden jolt and found himself hurled through the air, thrown against the wall on the far side of the cavern. He cried out and struggled to his feet before Palamon could reach him.

"Are you all right?" the tall monarch cried.

Reale groaned and rubbed himself. "I think so," he answered.

"I blame myself for this," Palamon said as he put a protective arm about the young man's shoulder. "A mystical defense like this reacts to different minds in different ways. You are a sensitive young man. I think the magic filled your mind with visions. But a touch brings more direct response."

"I may have touched it earlier," Reale said. "I surely thought someone had beaten me."

Palamon only grunted as he studied the wall in the weak light. It blocked the cavern off completely; nothing pierced it. "A mystical creation," the tall monarch finally said. He stroked his white moustache. "For a purpose, by my faith. By Pallas' great, gray eyes, is there no piercing it?" He stood back and stared at the barrier. "I own a mystic sword, a weapon forged by the great, exalted gods. Yet magic weapon against a magic barrier . . ." He shook his head. "The opposition of the forces would be great, so great a mortal's flesh might not withstand them."

"But the wall's not hard," Reale said in wonder. "My fingers went right into it before it threw me back."

"Indeed, indeed." Palamon's face brightened. "And I have mystic armor, filled with magic that's protective, not offensive." He made a fist. "It might be worth the risk."

The tall monarch edged toward the wall, studied it, then extended one arm. He drew down on the left sleeve of his hauberk and pulled back his hand until it did not show, then shoved the empty sleeve into the void before him. Reale leaped back as the dark surface exploded into silver, gold, and white sparks. The older man set his jaw and pushed the arm farther. "Warmer air upon the other side," he said simply.

The wall glowed as if Palamon had plucked down a piece of the night sky. Specks eddied about his arm, raced across the flat surface, collided with one another and rebounded back toward the source of the disturbance. The whole surface went blank as a judge's face when Palamon jerked his arm free. "Come, lad," he said to Reale. "Let us test your courage."

Reale advanced toward him. "Whatever you want me to do, I'll chance it," he said in what he hoped was a brave voice.

"Come now, you need not be as glum as that," Palamon replied. "But while I join my arms—thus . . ." and here he slipped his hands each into the sleeve of the other arm, so that the chain mail of his hauberk formed an arc with no flesh showing. "And interrupt this mystic curtain, you must put your head into the opening and see what lies upon the other side."

Reale swallowed. His guts fluttered at the thought but curiosity goaded him. He nodded. Palamon held two joined arms so as to interrupt the mystical curtain, and the barrier shuddered and burst into a greater display than ever.

Reale shoved his head and shoulders through and gasped at what saw. "By all the gods," he said. "It is a treasure house." He stepped the rest of the way through. "I see a pair of chests filled with treasures, and a stack of silver plate upon a mighty oaken table. It's the place I surveyed in my vision just before you wakened me."

"A treasure trove," Palamon said grimly. "I see it, too. We face a cult of treasure hoarders, these proud priests of Typhon. Does the god of strength gain glory by this cellar full of golden goods, I wonder? But no matter. Search, search for our quarry."

Reale studied the chamber. The floor and the rock overhead had been smoothed and evened to make it a proper room. A pair of torches flared on the wall and Reale saw two passages open off the place. Those torches and those passages worried him: the chamber looked as if it was visited often. "The *Tome of Winds*," he murmured. "What would it look like?"

"I've no idea; just that it's a book possessed of heavenly powers. Make your search, and quickly, for we must be gone from here before we welcome company."

"Yes, I'm sure you're right," Reale said. "But I don't see a thing that looks like a book." He peered at the items which lay on the table's long surface: tiaras of gold, a pewter wine pitcher, scepters, the tribute of the ages amassed the way a miser would gather coin. Reale could picture the abbot running his crooked fingers through the heaps, so he could grin and cackle. A little shudder ran down the young man's spine as his eyes fell on a cleared space on the table. There stood ghastly little statues—one looked like a man long dead, with clawlike hands and moldering flesh. Another had a serpent's head and tentacles for arms. They were the things he had fought before Palamon had found him, though he could not guess what art had made it happen. But nowhere did he spy anything the least bit like a book.

"Hurry, please." Palamon's voice reflected the strain of maintaining the opening through the mystic wall.

Reale studied the cavern's contents frantically and at last drew up the courage to open one of the chests. He sent a jeweled coronet rolling across the floor as he pulled items out of the way and burrowed to the bottom of the box, trying to locate anything which might look like a book.

"No, careful," Palamon admonished him. "Do not loot this place, or use the items we find here in any violent manner. They might be here rightfully or might have come through cunning and deceit—but they're not ours to plunder. We will only touch the artifact the gods sent me to claim."

"I'm trying to be careful," Reale said. "But I cannot see a thing. I would that you could leave your place and search with me."

"I'd have it so, myself," Palamon said. "But since I'm bound in my position, be my eyes. If you cannot espy some volume, seek the case which bears it. Or the cabinet which may conceal it."

Reale scratched his head and looked the cavern over once more. At the far end of the table, spaced evenly between two unlit candles, rested a wooden stand not unlike the podium which might hold some great holy book in some temple. But nothing rested there. He examined it more closely; it was a beautiful thing, made of ebony inlaid with white gold and laquered over with clear enamel, in the shape of a box with a delicately slanted top. He lifted; it was heavy, heavier than it ought to be, but he could find no latch, no hinge, no opening of any kind. "There might be something in this box," he said.

"But if there is, I don't see how it got in there, unless someone built the box around it."

"Bring it nearer; we'll examine it together."

Reale started to slide the heavy container off the table, then froze as he heard a sound from one of the passages. As his eyes met Palamon's, silent alarm sprang between them. Voices.

Reale rolled beneath the table and Palamon pulled back his arms. The mystic barrier's flashing swirls faded instantly. Reale still panted from excitement and strain when two robed men walked in, each bearing a rough oak cudgel. They were priests of Typhon.

They spoke in low voices and one laughed. Then the shadows beneath the table swayed as they replaced the torches about the chamber. For his part, Reale watched the lower halves of their bodies in dumb horror; they were the men who had beat him in his vision. This chamber put pictures into a man's mind, visions which were not without truth. Reale knew by instinct these two men would act as viciously as the ones in his vision if they ever found him.

"What's this?" one said suddenly. "This chest's been opened."

"Perhaps the abbot did it," the second priest replied. "He visits this lair often, to reflect upon the heaped mementoes of our order. It is said he memorized each item and all facts pertaining to it, from the name and origin down to the last, wee chip of diamond on the Scepter of Diandros there."

Reale fumed even as a thrill of fear teased his spine. The abbot had denied such knowledge; he had lied to the two of them in that dark room at the top of this granite dome. Palamon could take some relief from that; the younger man knew the unease the older felt at probing through a temple's properties. But at the same time, Reale had all he could do to keep still as one priest picked up the crown the youth had dropped. Where was Palamon now?

"This crown," the first man said. "A coronet from Artos, it is listed in the catalogs—'twas in that chest. Could any man have cast it to the floor?"

"No, something's wrong," the second priest said. "Quick, search the place."

The figures hurried about. A glowering face suddenly peered at Reale and he scuttled out from beneath the oak table. "There he is, the interloper," the priest shouted. He drew his club as he moved to cut Reale off. "Come, let us beat him to oblivion, then take his senseless form unto the abbot."

"Help me, Palamon," Reale cried. He had left his own longsword on the other side of the barrier. One knotty club whizzed by his head; he bolted into the owner and shoved the man into the mystic barrier. The dark wall exploded into sparks; the priest flew across the room with a cry of pain. He struck the floor five cubits away and curled into a heap.

Reale dodged about the oak table, eluded the second priest. He snatched a small object of treasure, a bracelet, and hurled it at his foe, but it missed, struck the magic barrier, and rebounded like a tennis ball from the court wall. The man gave a cry of anger and swung again; his club whacked the table over which Reale had leaned an instant earlier.

Then the dark barrier burst into all colors of the spectrum and Reale heard Palamon's voice. "Escape now, with your life; don't risk yourself a moment longer." The tall monarch held the magic curtain at bay once more.

"By Typhon's spear," the priest gasped. He bolted down one passage, left his partner groaning in the corner while Reale stared after him. "Come, reinforcements, help," the holy man shouted at the top of his lungs. "The artifacts are being rifled. Thieves and base magicians; by the gods, alas, we're being robbed."

"But stare no longer, lad," Palamon shouted. "Bring out the case you pondered earlier and let's be on our way. We cannot stand against these priests who know these grottoes' every twist and turn; I'll not be shedding blood beneath a temple, though the cause be righteous as the Maiden's love."

Reale did not lose an instant. While the remaining priest struggled to his feet, the young man picked up the ebony case and shoved it through the opening ahead of him. Then he joined Palamon. The tall monarch snatched up the candle he had carried and the two of them hurried through the mountain's dark guts, guided only by the weak glow.

Chapter Sixteen:
Priests and Assassins

SHOUTS CAUSED PALAMON and Reale to turn. "Come back, you vagabonds, you thieves and knaves," a voice thundered from the grottoes they had just left. "You shall receive just punishment for blasphemy and trespass."

Reale clutched the ebony box but Palamon wheeled and shot a glare back down the tunnel. "Just punishment for my foul blasphemy?" the older man whispered, half to himself. "For freeing from your greedy hands an item deeded me by immortal gods—and after your false abbot lied to me about it?" He stepped past Reale, handed the younger man the candle, and swung the two-handed sword against the rock overhead.

"We'll see who pays for sins and blasphemy." The magical blade buried itself in the granite above them; the stone shattered with such force that both men staggered back. Palamon swung again, then a last time; the passage behind them lay blocked as thoroughly as if it had been bricked shut.

"Come, lad," Palamon said. "We have to hurry, for we do not know what passages divert around this barrier."

Hurry they did, or at least as quickly as their feeble light allowed. Reale's load was a clumsy one and Palamon had to pause at each intersecting passage to make sure of his way. The white-haired monarch's memory was remarkable; he only took a wrong turn one time, and managed to correct his mistake after only a few paces.

"How do you do that?" the younger man asked.

"It comes from years of training, lad. And all before your birth."

"You must have been a mighty knight; I marvel at your skills and weaponry."

Palamon only laughed. Fresh air thrilled Reale's nostrils as they neared the outer entrance. "You flatter me, Reale," Palamon said as they emerged from the last tunnel. They must have been inside the mountain a long time, for the sun had set and a swath of stars lit up the sky.

"I've never seen a man like you."

"Perhaps you're lucky." Palamon closed the entrance to the tangled grottoes with a few blows from his sword. "But we must hurry; priests will issue from the guardhouse and the temple once they've found this avenue completely blocked. We'll have a merry chase tonight."

They ran back to their horses. "Will you teach me all the knightly arts?" Reale asked. "You've seen that I am brave, that I can take a risk as well as any man."

Palamon glanced over his shoulder at the younger man; starlight showed sadness in the weathered features. "Yes, you are young and brave and can be made to take a risk." His face turned forward, but he spoke on. "And you would learn to kill, or die, or maim with noble weapons. Ah, Reale, it is the world's cruel pattern, is it not? Yes, I will teach you—or I'll have it done."

Reale's heart felt light, though the load he carried grew heavier each instant. He could think of no words to grace this moment, so he simply said, "Thank you."

They had no time to tarry; they tied the box behind Palamon's saddle, then they started out. They rode hard to outdistance the clamor behind them, then slowed after a league. Much later, Palamon led Reale away from the road and along the hillside above a shadowed stream. Once they had gone a fair way, they stopped and the tall monarch dismounted.

"Give me a hand," he said. "We'll gather wood and build a fire, the better for the cooking of a meal, and see the prize we've gamed for. I believe these walls of brush will baffle prying eyes."

Reale gathered sticks in the darkness, working as much by feel as by sight. The two men built a tiny blaze in the shelter of a rock. By the feeble light, Palamon fetched the box and set it down. "There's something in it, that much I am sure of," the tall monarch said as he studied the odd-sided ebony case. "I heard an object bounce as we escaped those ranting priests."

"But do you know the way to open it?" Reale asked.

"I don't," Palamon said. Then he smiled at the younger man. "But let's find out." He knelt and turned the case over in front of him. His expression showed Reale that the tall monarch could find no answer to the riddle.

"You could just cut it open with your sword," Reale suggested.

"I could," Palamon agreed. "But that could damage all that lies within. No, better to detect a latch, if any there so be. I'm not the man to work such puzzles, though I've met a few who'd be into this case like ermines down a rathole. My poor, clumsy fingers have no hope. Here, see what you can find."

Reale took the box from him uncertainly. "I couldn't figure it out earlier," he said. "I don't see how I'd do any better now. But it's a cunning thing, isn't it? I mean, the way the edges fit together, all dovetailed the long way, as it seems to me. Wait." He felt his excitement grow as he felt a minute movement along one side. "This moves a little. When it does, look here—this other side is freed to move a little more. Why, it's a puzzle."

"So it is," Palamon cried, who quickly caught the younger man's meaning. "Now move the top, which lies at such an angle that—you've done it, lad. It is a simple puzzle, how it fits each piece into the others. You must move the first one, then the next, and that sets free the third. But only when you slide it toward the first, as you do now. By all the gods, I'd sit here many hours before my heavy hands would ever have discovered that."

Reale beamed with pride. It felt good to win the praise of this remarkable old man, who ruled a land and yet was as boon a partner and teacher as any grandfather. The young man's pleasure turned into awe as Palamon reached into the open case and withdrew what appeared to be a second case, a brass one, as thick through as a man's thigh and a cubit long. It was set all about with cunning engravings of snakes and trees and birds and vines. The entire brass case seemed to dance in the firelight.

Palamon held it up and read the fine engraving inscribed along the upper edge. " 'Bear reverence unto this mystic volume. We, the Priests of Nodens, dedicate unto the mighty gods our . . .' " He hesitated. " 'Our *Tome of Winds*.' Quite so. We've found it, lad—or you have found it, I should say." He smiled a warm smile, quite different from the grim smiles and wry smiles Reale had seen cross his face. "I have a son named

Berethane; I almost feel his breath upon my cheek." He glanced back at the younger man. "This search has been a long one; now we start upon a different journey."

A harsh laugh split the night; it made Reale's hair stand on end. He leaped to his feet and saw Palamon drop the *Tome of Winds* and snatch up his sword. "They can't have traced us here so quickly," the tall monarch whispered to Reale. "But mount your horse and we will be from here."

Reale stepped toward his mount but a night-black figure blocked him, brought down something heavy, and Reale's brain exploded into pain and bright lights. He heard Palamon shout, then heard another voice, and lost consciousness.

He recovered his senses in a couple of heartbeats and felt himself being dragged into the underbrush. He writhed in his assailant's grip until something that felt like a bowstring tightened about his throat. He leaped like a fish, but could not free himself.

The harsh voice came again, this time from a different side of the fire. "We've got your friend, tall man. Oh, put down that sword; I know you could kill me and ten of my men with it, but you've been too slow. That's it, drop it or we'll kill the lad."

Whatever happened next was drowned out by the roaring sound which filled Reale's ears. He lost control of his hands, he felt his eyes bulge. He heard more sounds, blacked out, then found himself wheezing for breath and nursing a throat which he knew would be black and blue by morning.

He coughed, gagged, and tried to rub his throat, only to find his hands tied. He saw Palamon still standing, with two men binding his arms. "I'm sorry, Sir," Reale said. "I let them get ahold of me."

"The same is true of me," Palamon replied with a grim smile. "So sure was I that we'd outdistanced all pursuit, and so intent on fathoming the puzzle of the wooden case, I did not stop to think there might be other enemies. The error is my own, far more than yours—with all my years, I should have taken greater care."

"Yes," a bearded man said with a smirk. "And it's going to cost you dear this time. Do you remember me?" The speaker was a stocky, rough-faced man perhaps ten years the tall monarch's junior.

"I do," Palamon replied. "The name is Diomedes, I believe; you once were lapdog to the constable of far Buerdaunt."

The stocky man yanked on the rope with which he bound Palamon. "Talk nice, now. Yes, I was high in Prince Ursid's favor—till you killed him."

"He chose his fate," the tall monarch replied. Reale had no idea what the two men were talking about.

But Diomedes only smiled the more as he finished binding the taller man's hands and arms. "Doesn't matter," he said. "You were foolish twice, you know that? I mean, you're going to die; we'll talk and then you'll die. The lad will die as well. You shouldn't have given up." He belched happily. "King Lothar will be happy at the news, though."

"To cast one's sword down may not constitute surrender," Palamon said. "I have faith the gods control this night and these events."

Diomedes laughed a guttural laugh. "If you escape, the boy dies." He gave the second man a signal and the fellow yanked Reale to his feet.

"Then we will both escape together," Palamon said. A sound caused Diomedes to glance away. Reale saw the tall monarch's eyes shift too, but he knew the older man's mind worked feverishly. "King Lothar?" Palamon said. "Well, it seems my nemesis still has a scheme or two. You say he wants me dead—he pays you, I suppose, to see the act completed."

"He does," Diomedes said with a smile. "He has big plans afoot, I hear, and he doesn't want you around to complicate them. That doesn't surprise you, does it?"

"Not really," Palamon said. "You're wise to kill me here and haul my head back to your master. I can see I frighten you."

"Don't worry about me." Diomedes sneered, then turned to his partner. "Hey, Roche, does this royal creature frighten you?"

The man called Roche laughed a dark laugh, grinned an evil grin, and drew his finger across his throat with an ugly sound. Palamon himself looked as if he might laugh to see the clumsy gesture.

"What are you so cheerful for?" Diomedes said. "You're the one he's talking about, you know."

"Yes, yes, I know. But no one's vain enough to stave off pride on noting such a charming wit. But we're upon a mission given by the gods themselves. Come, do your worst, and we will see the outcome of it all."

Diomedes muttered something to himself, drew his dagger,

and grasped the silky hair on the back of the older man's head. "All right, then, blast you. We'll do the deed right now and may your unseen gods do what they can to stop me."

Diomedes raised the dagger and Reale felt his teeth clinch as he watched. The assassin's arm reached full extension, the blade began its downward plunge, and the four men heard a shout nearby. "They're right ahead. Have at them, priests, for they be interlopers against our holy order. Slay them, slay them all."

Like a pack of hellhounds, two dozen robed men swarmed up the hill with clubs. They fell on the astounded killers; Palamon dropped from Diomedes' grip and rolled away with a quickness that belied his age. Before Diomedes could fight off the priests and stop him, the tall monarch yelled, "*Spada Korrigaine. Spada Korrigaine.*"

The blade cleaved through its leather scabbard and sliced the air toward its master. To Reale's astonishment, Palamon clutched the weapon in his bound hands and shouted toward him. "Come to me, Reale, that I might slash your cords."

Diomedes and Roche bore the brunt of the priests' assault because they had been the ones standing. But that was only an instant's purchase; the two killers could not long hold off so many. Reale scrambled toward Palamon and blinked at the deftness with which the tall monarch managed to slash his bonds. The youth pulled out his borrowed longsword, returned the favor, and the two of them joined the battle.

Priests of Typhon swarmed like rats over a quartet of hounds, but the outcome of the battle was decided the instant Palamon lifted his great weapon. He used only the flat of the blade but he brought it down so hard against one man's shoulder that the fellow screamed and collapsed. He bashed another in the ribs so hard the man dropped his own weapon and spun away, clutching his side. Reale was not as careful; he plunged his sword into his foeman and felt the weapon twist from his fingers. The fallen man screamed, vomited blood, and died. Reale snatched up a fallen club and battled on, afraid that he would receive a blade in the back any instant from his captors. But none came.

All at once, the attackers turned and fled. Palamon and Reale did not pursue them. Rather, the tall monarch wheeled to meet attack from behind but saw no more foes. "They've fled," he shouted to Reale. "They and Diomedes and his rough accomplice, all are routed. We both are free." Then he spun his sword in frustration. "But they have snatched our prize. Ah, curse them; if they only knew what tides now run, they'd press the *Tome of Winds* into my hands and beg me utilize it for the gods' intent. This comes of men who value their prestige above the gods' high will."

"Which way did they go?" Reale shouted. "We'll ride them down."

"No matter; I cannot." Only now did Reale notice how hard Palamon was breathing. The tall monarch hesitated, then went to one knee. "Six decades have I on my back. My body does not take to questing as it once could."

"Give me your sword and I'll ride after them," the younger man offered.

Palamon smiled, his chest heaved, he rose once more. "A gallant offer, one which is appreciated. You are young and brave, my friend, but wisdom must be found to temper courage or you'll never grow to be a white old man." He caught Reale's shoulder and shoved him toward his horse. The beast still stamped at the edge of the firelight. "But yet you have a point— you must ride off and leave me here. Use all your skill; avoid all action but ride north and west until you reach the city known as Tranje."

"Tranje? What's there?"

"My sister and her husband, Count Arcite." Palamon pulled a signet ring off the middle finger of his right hand. "Bear them this ring; by that they'll mark your message. Tell them Lothar rises in the south and evil times lift up their ragged heads. Two decades' peace is ended like a sleep and battle waits for all of us, although I know but half the enemy. Tell them to levy knights and archers and to send my words to Aelia, my proud queen. Quick, off with you; may all the gods protect you."

"What of you?" Reale asked as he clambered into his saddle.

Palamon smiled grimly and walked toward his own mount. "I'll keep my quest. But go, for you now hold the fate of nations."

"I'll go," Reale replied as he seated himself and watched the older man mount his own steed. "I'll go and I'll be true to your instructions. But take care, my master. May the gods be with you."

Palamon glanced at him. "And with you also. Typhon with the rest, for he is one of them. And let him hasten to his mortal priests and break them of their pride, for I shall follow them and once more claim the prize which, by the Oracle's own words, is mine by right." With that, the two men turned their horses, rode back along the course of the stream, and spurred their mounts in opposite directions.

Not far away, a grim Diomedes stopped his own steed and glanced at his sagging companion. "How bad is it?" he asked.

The only reply was a groan as Roche swayed in his saddle, then toppled and landed with a cry of pain. The accomplice had received telling blows in at least two places.

"That bad, eh?" Diomedes said. He cursed softly and swung from his own saddle. "And the Carean king's given us the slip again. Of all the foul luck; whoever those priests were, they were howling for blood. We're lucky we had our horses tied where we could get to them." He glanced down at the fallen man. "Well, I am, at least."

He drew his dagger and knelt over his partner, who stared up at him in horror, but was helpless against the thrust. "Sorry, pal," Diomedes said as he finished his task, wiped his blade clean in some weeds, and put it away once more. "But you're not much use to me in your shape. With the job I face now, I can't have anyone around who might tell a story." He smiled a little, cold smile. "It's a risk of the trade, isn't it? A risk we all live with."

He rose and walked to his horse. "For all I know, those priests might have done for the Carean king ahead of me, though he's a slippery one and I doubt it. If they have, I'll find the body. And if they haven't, I might have some good bait. He looked mighty interested in this brass box when we interrupted him." He reached into a pack and pulled out the *Tome of Winds*; unbeknownst to Palamon, it was Diomedes and not the priests of Typhon who had borne it away. He studied the object, then repacked it carefully, swung into his saddle, and leaned out to grasp the reins of dead Roche's horse. A spare mount was a good thing, after all. He rode into the darkness, whistling a careless tune.

Chapter Seventeen:
Krisamee

THE EVENING AFTER Palamon and Reale battled for their lives, a Knight of Pallas found himself waging a battle of his own some leagues to the northeast. Sir Pallador had watched the two ladies, Alcyone and Krisamee, all afternoon as they had ridden toward the abandoned city of Hautre. In spite of all, the young knight found himself swamped by thoughts which made him ashamed. He shuddered to think what Sir Phebos might say if he even suspected what emotions lay in Sir Pallador's mind.

Both women were striking in appearance and each held the eye in her own way. Lady Alcyone, the elder, possessed grace and dignity as she sat in her sidesaddle. Her daughter possessed those attributes, along with a beauty and vibrance which should have made Sir Pallador turn away his eyes. He tried often enough, but each time he did, those orbs of vision would only bide their time for a moment before coming to rest once more on a pearly cheek, a rounded shoulder, a gently sweeping back. Sir Pallador sighed and cursed himself silently. Why had the gods afflicted Knights of Pallas with the same base drives as other men? The honors he had gained, the honors aspired to, the honor and traditions of his order; what were they, and what was this force which had swept down upon him, that they weighed so heavily in the scales of his thought?

In the afternoon, the party crossed a small stream and rode onto a sloping meadow of the upper Greenlands. They spied Hautre's walls, pale and sunbaked ahead of them. No sign of life greeted them other than squirrels which scurried back into the meadow grass, rooks which wheeled above the silent walls, and two head of deer which flicked their tails and bounded away. As far as human life was concerned, the city was dead and deserted as if no man had ever lived there.

"So there it stands," Lady Alcyone said quietly. Sir Pallador glanced at her; she held her features downcast, her mouth in a straight line. "Two decades have swept past since I enjoyed those walls' embrace. A happy people lived there once. Now no man calls poor, shattered Hautre his home."

"Oh, Mother," Krisamee said. "Why have you brought us here? Let's ride away and leave this place, for only grief awaits us."

"Nay," the older woman said. "I said that I—that we—would journey here and lay old memories to rest." Her eyes swept the hills, then past the two young people as if they were not even there. She fastened her gaze on the city's walls again. "O bosom of my homeland, where within your pale and sun-baked girth can lie the resting place of my poor parents? Is it in the sanctuary I remember? Is it in some other place?"

"I know not, Madam," Sir Pallador said. "All the people fled when Hautre fell to Buerdic foes. Mayhap your parents do not even lie within these walls."

"They must," she cried. "I know the story better than you do." She lifted her arm toward a nearby grove of trees. "From there did proud Ursid ride forth with all his army in his final charge." Her arm swung toward a jagged gap in the city's wall and the rubble beyond the opening. "And there he breached our stout defense. 'Twas late; we heard the shout and clash of arms, foul bedlam reigned, by morning it was done. He took the town and wrested treasure chests and hostages and tithes, indemnities and ransoms from us. Ah, it's small wonder Hautre's reduced to just a shattered skeleton. He disemboweled her and left her to bleed out her populace and commerce till she died."

"Now, Mother," Krisamee said. "You have said a dozen times that you adored Ursid when you were young."

"And it was true. Ursid was mighty, noble, proud, and filled with fire . . ."

"And scarred, just like a melon cracked from overwatering." Krisamee eyed her mother, then Sir Pallador.

"Yes." Lady Alcyone nodded. "Ursid bore scars, reflections of his inner agony. For all that he was scarred and he destroyed my home, I looked on him and loved him from the moment I first saw him. I was young, a maiden not yet twenty years in age, but still I would have thrown myself before him, had I had the chance.''

She looked at Sir Pallador. ''You remember I told you, Sir, I became his hostage, I and other maidens from the town? To proud Buerdaunt they took me, there to suffer such indignities.'' She hesitated. ''The war soon ended and Ursid was killed. To make up for the ransom lost when both my parents died, the Buerdic king used my body as a bit of merchandise.'' She paused again. ''He sold me as a noble bride unto the highest bidder, sold me into marriage as you'd sell a horse or cow.''

Sir Pallador listened once again to the woman's tale in silence. For her part, Krisamee's eyes went soft for the woman who had borne her.

Alycone touched the younger woman on the shoulder. ''Ah, Krisamee, the man who bought me was a lowly soldier who had come to money by his good fortune in the war. And he was humble and without much grace, but good enough in his own way. He took me as his bride and by my noble blood became a knight. And he became your father. I will not defame him; he was kind enough to me and gave me you.'' She sat in silence for a while before the blows of the past made her speak again. ''But still, 'twas not the life that I was meant to live.''

''Ah, Lady,'' Sir Pallador said, moved. ''Now you say your parents lie within those walls.''

''I know it. They would not have left this place except in irons.''

''Then by my troth, I'll wield this sword for your protection just as long as you desire.'' He gazed at Lady Alycone, then at her lovely daughter. They rode in silence toward the dead city.

They passed the crumbling main gate, which had been torn from its frame and cast into the dirt. Sir Pallador could tell by marks on the stonework, damage to rusted iron hinges, and rotting timbers which lay in the long grass. Inside, weeds poked their rude way between the loose cobblestones. Caved-in roofs opened their yawning mouths to the sky, and rotting wagons and equipment told a mute story of the city's hasty abandonment. A city laid waste, a land made desolate. No wonder these regions had become a country of brigands.

''You show a lasting knowledge of these streets,'' he said to Lady Alycone. ''I wonder at the memories which rush at you.''

''Yes, there are many,'' she said. ''But now we come before the keep itself. Alas, how bleak it looks.''

The sides of the moat had caved in and what once had been

a protective ditch was now a dry, weed-filled hollow. That was just as well, however, for the drawbridge had long since rotted; only a few gray and scattered timbers remained. Glass had once filled the upper tower windows but the afternoon sun now showed the apertures as vacant holes, gaping wounds in a dead carcass.

Their horses hesitated before the moat at first, but Sir Pallador found a place to cross and guided his warhorse to the far side. Into the gatehouse he rode, his packhorse and his palfrey behind him. He stopped, then shouted a word of encouragement to the two women. They followed with care.

The place had once been called Keep Securete, but now it stood only as a vacant reflection of the past. "I wish to peek into the chapel first," Lady Alcyone said. "If memory serves, I'll find my parents' resting place within those hallowed walls."

Sir Pallador eyed her and wondered how she could be so sure, but when she and Krisamee dismounted before the keep, he hobbled the horses and followed the women into the abandoned pile. All the while he kept a lookout for any bandits who might infest this place.

Bandits had scoured the dead castle; Sir Pallador frowned at the way they had desecrated the chapel most of all. Gold inlay, tapestries, silver candlesticks, all had been hauled out, either by priests when they had left, or by looters afterward. Even the gold leaf from the loft had been scraped away and what once had been stained glass windows now lay in fragments upon the stones because looters had taken the lead from between the glass panes.

"Ah, me," Lady Alcyone said as they approached the barren altar. "By all the gods, this is a desolated shell in which to seek my past." She caught her breath. As they approached the altar, all three of them spied the sarcophagi which lay behind it.

The older woman rushed forward, the younger couple followed. "And here they lie," she cried. "I'd hoped they would, for I was with them when they chose this place for their eternal rest." Tears welled up and she sank to her knees before the cold containers. "Ah, Father, Mother, it is Alcyone; I've lived out half my life and more, but finally I've come to·visit you."

Sir Pallador stared at the woman, then at the simple brass plate which listed the occupant of each deathly container. Baron Ulfin and his Lady—so Lady Alcyone had been their daughter. No wonder she had cherished every hope she would be able to find her parents. And no wonder mysterious Peristeras had told him she was the key to reclaiming this land. Lady Alcyone was the last surviving heir to Hautre.

She sobbed out grief which had been pent up too long; Sir Pallador let out a breath as he understood. Then the older woman turned a weary eye toward him, toward her daughter. "But leave me here, you babies," she said in a pleading voice. "You have not the years or griefs behind your backs to comprehend my miseries. Go, love, my Krisamee, and you too, noble Knight. Desert me here; I'll come to you once I have spewed my tears across this heartless stone." She turned her attention back to her dead parents. The knight and the young woman retreated in confusion.

For his part, Sir Pallador hesitated as they reached the corridor outside the dead chapel. While Krisamee watched, he knelt and silently addressed a prayer of his own on behalf of the grieving mother. Since Krisamee could not hear his thoughts, he also included her. As he eyed his clasped hands, a movement caught his glance. Krisamee had knelt next to him and joined him in a prayer of her own.

Joy flowed through him, joy he could not describe. Their reverent whispers softened the silence, then they stood. Lady Alcyone was nowhere to be seen. "My mother is possessed, I think," Krisamee said. "I have not seen her this emotional in all my days."

"But torn away from all she knew and auctioned to the highest bidder—yet to speak kind words of him who did the deed." Sir Pallador shook his head. "You mother is a tender-hearted woman."

Krisamee smiled. "She is a devotee of love. My father called her a romantic fool."

"Not fool," Sir Pallador gazed into Krisamee's bewitching eyes. "Not fool. She persevered when life gave every cause for her to yield to bitterness and cruel despair. She carved a home, a life for you she loved, when any other would have said, ' 'Tis done,'tis hopeless.' No one could have blamed her had she died of grief, yet she survived and reared you up to be a beauty." He caught himself, then went on more quietly. "No, do not say 'fool.' Or, if she is a fool, it's of a sort that makes the world a better place for her enchanted breed of foolishness."

"Do not grow angry with me, Sir." Krisamee's eyes flashed.

"Ah, pardon me. Do not infer my anger; I have none. But

reverence." He smiled at her sheepishly. "I've reverence for your good mother."

"I would hope so. She's my mother—you've no need to lecture me. You've known her for a day or two." She sighed. "My mother dotes upon romance because it was denied her all her life. A fool could see it. I do not begrudge her that."

Sir Pallador stared at the young women; her eyes enchanted him as she spoke. When she finally smiled at him, her happiness infected him and forced him to smile back.

"I understand her grief," he said. "I lost my parents years ago—ah, what a moment it must be for her to gaze upon the graves of those who bore her, nurtured her with loving hands, and saw her torn away. This world affords us cruelty and kindness, sometimes both at once."

"Yes," Krisamee said. "Still, it's strange. She's walked beside me all my life and always been the rock on which I leaned. Now it is strange to see her in her grief."

Sir Pallador gazed at her but did not respond. Emotion was a puppeteer. Since Lady Alcyone still did not come from the chapel, the two of them strolled along the corridor and stopped at a lancet window which looked down on the castle's deserted inner ward. Sparrows wheeled and played before the tower walls and Krisamee smiled at them. A pair of the little birds darted through the window, wheeled in the stale air, and flew back out, quick as lightning.

Krisamee rested her fingertips on Sir Pallador's shoulder and laughed. "The little things. They play before us, frisk about in air, as if their bodies had no weight at all. Like spirits are they, or like tiny sprites . . ."

She never finished. Her touch sent a flame through the Knight of Pallas, set into motion forces which no man could hope to withstand. Before he could comprehend or halt himself, he had clasped her by the shoulders, pulled her to him, and covered her fair mouth with his own.

Her eyes opened in astonishment, then grew soft, fluttered shut, and her arms twined about his broad shoulders. For a breathless moment they stood in one another's embrace; then their lips pulled apart. Sir Pallador released her and staggered back.

"What have I done?" he whispered. "Ah, maid, I beg your pardon; I know not what moved me."

"Fear not, glorious Knight," she replied softly. "You are pierced by arrows from some lusty goddess." She blushed at her own words. "And what I say; I fear I've been possessed as well as you."

She reached forth and wrapped her two tapered hands around one of his broad ones. He raised his arms so that her hands were at his lips; he kissed one. "These fingers and this form I see before me," he said. "They are presents from the gods themselves. I cannot take my eyes from them, from flesh as soft as this without a speck or blemish, soft and smooth as angels' down. Your face is perfect as a field of flowers when seen far off, but so much beauty in so small a space."

"My face is not so fair," Krisamee replied.

" 'Tis fair, 'tis fair, so fair it is unspeakable. And yet it's but the cap of your perfection. Krisamee, your throat is soft as babe's breath to my callused fingers. Spring back, hand. Don't mar that perfect flesh with your rough touch. Those shoulders dainty, so your gown sweeps down in folds more delicate than powdered snow upon . . ." He shook his head. "Ah, Pallas save me, for I am undone."

They kissed again, more passionately than ever. Her mouth moved beneath his, her hands fluttered against his cheeks and the back of his neck. Her breath played sweet music against his face. The kiss lasted a long time. When it was over, Sir Pallador wheeled from her, lifted clenched fists, and cried, "What am I doing?" He gazed at his fingers, flexed them one by one. "These hands, which were my allies but a moment past, betray me now as if employed by one who hates me. Ah! My body's turned into some foreign blot, as if it were a particle of sucking river mud, which oozes toward you as if you were the mother stream. And you." He turned back toward her and pointed an astonished finger. "And you. How can it be, for one so frail, so mild and lovely, to possess despotic power over me? You are a trap." His voice grew weak. "You are a trap, and I your helpless prey."

"Not helpless, manly Knight. You who are so tall and powerful and broad of thigh and shoulder have no need to fear an object frail as me."

"I do, I do. You are both bait and snare, while I, weak mortal, have no strength to overcome."

She put her head a little to one side and her mouth formed the first tracings of a frown. "I'll not be angry with you, Pallador, but one thing must you ponder in the midst of all your lamentation. No trap springs unless the victim seeks the bait you now compare me to."

His mouth opened, then closed. He stared at her all over again. "It's true," he finally said. "The appetite for touching you is mine, the arms are mine which press you close to me. No, fair Krisamee, I beg forgiveness for my rash words; I did not mean them in a scornful way. The appetite is mine, the weakness mine." He turned toward the lancet window, befuddled and angry at himself, then leaped back as another cluster of the little sparrows shot through the opening, one darting after the others past the end of his nose. They startled him so badly he almost fell.

In spite of their exchange, Krisamee had to chuckle at the startled expression on his face as he jerked his head back. Laughter sputtered out, peals of laughter as sweet as bells on Olympus. He stared at the darting birds, stared at her, and then, in spite of all his wonder and horror at what he had done, he also had to laugh. What a sweet maiden she was, how musical her voice, how fair, how full of joy and innocent life. "Ah, me," he said when the moment had passed. "I swear those fowl afrighted me as much as my own conduct."

"More; I see it in your face," she replied, still smiling.

"Perhaps." He returned her smile, then reached forth and gathered her into his arms. He managed to keep from kissing her this time, though he wondered that he had the strength. He let her lay her head against his chest, then he rested his chin softly atop her tawny locks. "And yet, maid, think upon my grievous state. A Knight of Pallas must be chaste and pure, as free from sin as any monk or priest. How sore a task that is when every nerve within my body cries for your embrace."

"As mine cries out for you," she replied softly. "Good Pallador, do not believe yourself to be the only one who bears this passion's taint. I should forbid your kisses and push off your hands as they encircle me. But see just how our bodies fit to one another where we stand, and how I reach and press your hands e'en tighter, help you make for me a firmer nest within your bosom. Passion's what it is, and mine for you is full as powerful as yours for me."

"So," he said. "May the gods forgive me for my weakness, but it gladdens me to hear it."

They stood that way for a long time. Sir Pallador reveled in the warmth and softness of the maiden's form against his but that was not the only reason his arms remained in place as long as they did. With his hands locked about her, with the top of her head tucked fondly against his throat, he did not have to face the demon which urged him to plunder her body. His feelings brought raw shame to his face and he felt relief that she could not see it.

At last they broke apart; Krisamee gazed out the vacant window. "Poor Pallador," she said, then glanced back at him. "Two passions—yours and mine—and you have but a single honor to oppose them both." She studied him and stepped to the other side of the casing; that separated her from him by another cubit. "I shall aid you all I can to keep your vows, although the gods know I am loath to do it." She blushed another time; each blush made her lovelier than the last. "How awful I've become."

"Nay, nay," he said. He started to put a hand on her shoulder, then drew it back and let it fall limply to his side. One touch led to another; he had learned that much. "Do not say things you know to be untrue. You are not awful, nor unkind, and the temptation of your body is a force, a test from the exalted gods. Men must withstand such tests, or they become no better than the beasts which serve them."

"'Tis so," she said. "But ah, how strong the beast within becomes—were you not of the Knights of Pallas . . ." She lowered her voice and Sir Pallador knew she had embarrassed herself once more. "But so it is between us, poor, dear Knight."

"Yes, so it is. Our love must ne'er be consummated." He cleared his throat. "I will use the words—'our love.' My feelings deepen with each instant but we must refrain from touching flesh together."

"That is difficult."

"Then will you pray with me?"

She nodded. They knelt together before the lancet window. While the light washed over them, he addressed Pallas yet another time. He begged the goddess to cleanse the two of them, to aid them against the passions of the world.

They closed the prayer together, then stood and he smiled at her. "I love you," he said. But he did not move a muscle.

"I love you," she replied. "Now we must return to Mother, if she's finished with her grieving. Grief and love spring up within two dozen cubits. What a wondrous, baffling world."

Chapter Eighteen:
The Darkness

THEY HURRIED BACK toward the chapel. "You are the key," Sir Pallador said quickly. "You and your mother."

She glanced back at him; her features told him she had no idea what he was talking about. "The key to what?"

"The region," Sir Pallador said. They paused in front of the chapel door. "A . . . a wise man told me once to look for you if I would drive the bandits from these lands. If Baron Ulfin was your mother's father, that makes you the heir to Hautre, this tall keep, and all the lands about."

"A dead and blasted legacy, say I."

"Not if it's reclaimed and folk brought back to settle it. The brigands shall make way before returning throngs, while you and he you marry will be lords of all."

"I'll have no husband, save for you."

Sir Pallador caught himself, then said, "But Krisamee, though I may love you, I am fettered by my vows. I cannot marry."

Her eyes flashed. "Then I'll have no man. I shall devote myself to Hestia or to Artemis, but not to life with one I cannot love. For I can love but one man: you, Sir Pallador." She raised the back of one hand to her lips, then retreated into the chapel. Lady Alcyone stood within, before the crypts which held her parents. She had collected herself and now she turned as the young woman approached.

"Ah, Daughter," Lady Alcyone said. "I have spilled my grief upon the tomb of those who brought me forth, and now my business here is ended. Why then are you pale? 'Tis not your parents who lie cold within these ruins." She looked from the young woman to Sir Pallador, then back again. A new light kindled in her eyes and the Knight of Pallas feared what she had read in their faces.

"My Lady," he said hastily. "Is it not true that you are daughter of the baron? Are you not the heir to all this land?"

Lady Alcyone laughed. "So that is why the dire expressions. Yes, it can be said that I am heir to all this rubble." She turned away.

"But Lady," he went on. "You must claim your legacy."

"But how to claim it?" Krisamee broke in. "We are both but women, poor and all alone. Inform us how to claim this fief."

Lady Alcyone smiled. "Send out a summons to the troops my father left to me. Will they come wriggling from their graves to serve beneath my banner? Please, have mercy, for the question's long since moot."

"Perhaps," Sir Pallador said. "Perhaps not, for the world is strange and full of wonderment." He glanced at Krisamee, then turned toward the door. "Where shall we spend this night?"

Lady Alcyone pursed her lips as they walked from the chapel. "We should be gone from here, I know. We cannot say what band of ruffians may seek their refuge in this sad city. We're in danger. Still, I say, I cannot leave this instant; I cannot desert this friend, this old love after such a separation."

Sir Pallador smiled. "Yet can you say you do not dare to rule this place and see its populace returned?"

"Come, Knight. These walls and streets are full of memories, good memories. The people are all dead. Now leave it, Sir; it is not kind to jostle my poor heart with your impossibilities."

Sir Pallador cleared his throat. He would not trouble the woman, not so soon. He eyed her, then her wondrous daughter, then he pulled his eyes from both of them. He had no idea what to do.

They started down the decaying stone steps which led toward the tower's ground floor. Round, round and down they went, watching each treacherous step, passing windows which grew narrower with each level. Outside the tower, the sparrows cried and called as if newly disturbed and Sir Pallador could hear rooks call from the highest battlements. Then something outside caught his eye and he stopped to look through the slit in the stone that served as this level's window.

"What look you for, O noble Knight?" Krisamee asked.

"I do not know. I thought I glimpsed a thing . . ." he hesitated. "We must ascend a level. I can hardly see above the castle's wall from here."

He wheeled and retraced his steps. The two women hesitated, eyed one another, then followed. By the time they caught up with him, he was gazing through the same window at which he and Krisamee had kissed.

Birds of all feather raced past, squawked, and fled to and fro in more panic than even an approaching storm would have produced. Far away, a circle of blackness crawled across the countryside at the pace of a man walking. It looked like ball lightning or like the fire which sometimes glows at a ship's mast-top during a storm—with two exceptions. First, this wonder was huge, a hundred cubits in diameter, a moving half-orb which crawled to and fro in a jagged path. Second, it was dark against the bright daylight, black, a piece of night into which Sir Pallador could not even begin to see. And it was evil; the Knight of Pallas felt a tremor go through him as instinct told him just how vile the thing was. Even as he watched, a sparrow screeched, fluttered, then dropped past the window. It hit the paving below, dead as a stone. Another fell farther away.

"By all the gods," Lady Alcyone breathed. "What manner of fog is that, which blots the world with death and darkness?"

"I have no idea," Sir Pallador replied. "But I feel fear for it—as much as I feel fear for anything. Ah, Ladies, we must leave this place. I shall escort the two of you to safety, and then carry word of this to Pallas' Fastness. In my years of knighthood, never have I felt foul evil's presence more than now."

"But we have shelter here," Krisamee said. "Do we dare flee to open lands outside the city?"

"I do not know," Lady Alcyone replied.

"Nor I," Sir Pallador said. He shook his head; he dared not risk these two women, yet he could not leave them—and his instincts told him the sphere of darkness represented an evil so great that no human could ever hope to oppose it. "But we must warn the world." He leaned against the stones and rubbed his forehead.

He pondered, then looked at the two women. "I trow this evil orb's a stronger thing than armies, let alone deserted castles. I do not know what it is, but have no doubt it's deadly. Come away with me; if I should fall, then you must go without me and deliver word unto the Fastness."

"We would only slow you down," Lady Alcyone said. "Remember, I lived out my childhood in this castle; I know every corridor and hiding place. Ride out, Sir Knight, and take your warning. We will wait for you and study your dark orb. If it should come too near, we'll flee down to the deepest cellars, where we'll hide till your return."

Sir Pallador was not sure of her plan; he could not know what this evil orb might seek in this empty land. Then again, what would happen to the women if they tried to ride with him and the darkness intercepted the three of them? At last he nodded. "Agreed. But lead me to the place. Before I leave, I'll haul your full provisions down and leave them there for you."

Together, they went down to the lower levels of the donjon, which they found in a state of musty disrepair, full of deserted spider's webs and rotted furnishings. But it remained good enough for an emergency. With their help, the Knight of Pallas carried their supplies down from their horses and quickly put back into running order the cistern which had supplied the castle's water during siege.

At last, Sir Pallador had done all he could do. "I must leave now," he said. "The afternoon grows old; I must make haste and thus require the day's light for my journey."

"We will wait for you and mark the way the apparition goes," Lady Alcyone replied.

"Observe it but do not attempt to block its path in any way." He turned to Krisamee. "My palfrey's ready; I must ride." He gazed into her eyes, then looked at Lady Alcyone, who observed with a little smile. What could he say about the way he felt, the emptiness he would feel the instant they parted? What could he say even if the two of them had been alone? If they spoke of feelings, they embraced, so it was best that the older woman was there. He would leave without saying another word.

"Brave Knight," Krisamee said. "I know what's in your mind. My thoughts run parallel to yours, believe that. Now go safely, please, for my . . ." She glanced at her mother. "For our sakes, make no grand attempt to counter that fell force with your own strength. As Mother said, we'll wait for your return."

He reached for her hand, hesitated, then made a fist. "I shall return or perish in the effort." Then he turned from them, strode to the castle's vacant courtyard, and climbed onto his palfrey. He would bring his war horse on its lead rope, though he doubted there would be time to switch if an emergency came.

He waved at the two women as they climbed back into the tower. They stopped and waved back at him from an embrasure. Even with a distance between them, Krisamee's body called to his; he felt as if his own flesh could float to hers the way the bubbles drift upward as wine is poured. What a maiden she was, and how forbidden she was. But he put his mind to the matter at hand and spurred his mount toward a northern gate.

He rode in deathly silence; the birds and small mammals which had infested the city had vanished. No rooks or magpies called their desolate calls, no squirrels chattered, nothing moved. He heard himself release a cry of pain as a silent wasp stung him on the cheek. He slapped at the insect; the crushed body fell away but left behind searing pain. It made him clench his teeth. The wasp landed on his thigh; he flicked it off and noted that it had an odd, white head. A couple of miller moths fluttered past his face and he heard the buzzing of flies.

He hurried toward the northern wall. A small gate drooped from rusted hinges; it was riddled by wormholes and rot. He had to lower his head onto his horse's neck to squeeze beneath the lintel. He headed north to skirt the wandering darkness; he planned to turn back toward the west after he had reached one of the groves which dotted the countryside. He rode as fast as he dared without galling his animals; just as he entered the trees, he glimpsed once more the ball of darkness which moved slowly across the plain.

Lady Alcyone gazed at her daughter through great, dark eyes. "A charming and a gallant fellow," she said. "Mind you, Daughter, he has eyes for you."

"Oh, Mother." Krisamee laughed. "He's a Knight of Pallas. I mean less to him than does his horse or longsword."

"Every man has limbs of flesh, your gallant knight with all the rest." She sighed. "He'd be a wondrous match."

"Don't marry us quite yet." The younger woman smiled down at the elder and her eyes twinkled. "And yet he is a pleasant-hearted man—I'd not refuse him if he asked."

"I knew it. You have eyes for him as well."

"Indeed. But do not purchase bridal cloth for me, not yet."

Lady Alcyone smiled. "I'll not. But if he asks you, you would be a fool to say him nay. Full stranger things have happened. Live in hope." She gazed out at the blasphemous darkness south of them. It had moved about a league toward the west, but had drawn closer to the city as well. It loomed taller than a castle's tower. "I did not love your father," she said sadly.

"No. I knew that. But you were a virtuous wife."

The older woman went on as if there had been no interruption. "I felt love's pangs one time—for Prince Ursid."

"Indeed?" Krisamee looked at her mother. "But he destroyed your city and your parents' lives and hauled you off for sale unto the highest bidder."

"It's true as gospel. Love is strange; it has no logic. Seventeen short years I had behind me and Ursid was strongly built and handsome for the scars which lay upon him. And he came before us as our conqueror; oh, Daughter, I'd have done his will within the instant if he'd ever asked me." Then she smiled at the younger woman. "But alas, for nothing ever came of it, my unrequited passion. Hear me, though—don't ever fear to hope—if I can hope, then you can hope as well." She swatted at a biting fly which had landed on her neck.

"The blackness," Krisamee said softly. "It is moving toward the city."

The older woman felt a little thrill of fear and drove away another flying insect. The castle had fallen silent except for their own voices and the hum of bugs which seemed to fly out of every crack and chink in the stones about them. Flies of every description circled beneath the sun, from bloated, white-headed blowflies the size of a fingertip to little biters she could hardly see, but at which she found herself slapping constantly. "These flies are disagreeable," she said. "They thicken as that prodigy moves closer." She ducked a white-faced paper wasp which buzzed past with dangling legs. "It's like watching a tornado; will it pass a long way off or close upon the city? Who'd have guessed its course from its odd movements when we first laid eyes on it?"

Darkness like a shadow fell across the collapsed corner of the city's wall, as if a cloud had come across the sun. But no cloud marred the perfect sky and this darkness was more profound than any shadow. The air became opaque where the orb advanced, and Lady Alcyone grimaced to see flights of insects which whirled as if swept by a great wind in the sunlight between themselves and the apparition.

Krisamee batted blackflies, shook a moth from her hair, then snatched her scarf and threw it about her head. "We cannot stay here," Lady Alcyone cried. "Insects strike at us as if a devil's voice instructed them. Let's flee into the cellars; we'll not keep our senses in this place."

"Perhaps that's what the blackness is," Krisamee said. "A wandering sphere of insects. Some old wizard must have set them loose upon the world, to plague us to distraction."

They fled the tower, flew down the stone steps. A hail of white-faced flies, gnats, and wasps zoomed after them. Krisamee gaped in disgust, then screamed. However she tried to keep them off, the things tormented her, bit her, drove her mad.

Lady Alcyone also fought the swarms with every step. By some miracle, the two of them gained the ground floor and stumbled into the castle's great hall, where things were not so bad. They tore through the long chamber, along corridors, and at last found themselves near the donjons. They had to light candles. But though the way was dark and clammy, the mad flights had not yet reached this point.

As they scrambled into their refuge, Krisamee cried out again. Lady Alcyone slammed the door and whirled toward the younger woman, who tore at her scarf, tore at her hair. A black-and-white hornet crawled onto the back of the maiden's hand, stung, and flew. As Krisamee ripped the scarf loose, more appeared.

"My poor, poor child," the older woman cried. She rushed to her daughter, swatted one insect only to gasp in pain herself as it stung her. "They must have nestled in your hair before we reached the shelter of the hall. Oh, how you start to swell from all their stings."

"The pain, the pain," Krisamee cried. "And now they sting at you as well." Another sting lanced Lady Alcyone's forehead just as Krisamee brought her palm down on the place so hard it made the older woman's head ring like a tocsin bell. She felt moisture atop the pain and a striped body fell to the floor.

Krisamee's plight was awful. Lady Alcyone leaped to her traveling bags and brought forth shears with which she attacked the younger woman's hair, fought the vicious insects. More agony flowed from each movement, each sting. Lady Alcyone cut away great shocks of hair, pinched and tore at the little monsters imbedded next to the skin, sheared them into halves, smashed them, batted them to the floor. At last she had done; every hornet lay killed except for a couple which buzzed about the flickering candleflame. Krisamee had turned into a suffering heap crouched upon the floor; from her neck to the crown of her head, the bruised and swollen flesh throbbed like a raw heart.

"By all the gods," Krisamee said through a sob. "What manner evil drifts across this land?"

"I've no idea. Something both profound and terrible."

They held one another. Only their breathing broke the silence until they became aware of another sound, a hum from beyond the chamber's sealed door. Lady Alcyone shot to her feet, ran to the oak panel, and listened. The corridor outside droned as if a million blowflies waited. They popped disgustingly against doors and stone walls. Even as she watched, black bodies crawled through the space between wood and floor, then flew about the room. Ugly, greasy flies hummed balefully; they looked like flying grapes with white heads.

"Quickly," she cried. "Now we must caulk up the door." She snatched her shears, cut material from her own gown, and stuffed it into the gap. She crushed flies, shoved them away, worked as quickly as she could. Krisamee helped, though her movements were stiff because of her stings.

They finished caulking that space but smaller insects streamed through the keyhole. Another moment and some candle wax blocked that entry. They both sat and dabbed sweat from their features, then Lady Alcyone rummaged through her bags one last time, for salve to apply to her daughter.

Before she could finish, a shadow fell across the candlelit chamber. The gloom became as profound as if someone had thrown a hand over the flame. The flies which had made it into the room seemed every bit as amazed as the two humans; they stopped their buzzing flight, lit on the floor, and became motionless.

"The darkness," Krisamee whispered. "The unknown darkness is upon us. What can be the nature of it?"

"I can't guess. But while it's here, we shall not venture from this chamber, though a million of these insects come to join us."

No sooner were those words from her lips than a tremor passed through the building, as if something heavy had been set down atop it. The chamber shook again, they heard a groan, and the earth floor at the far end heaved itself up, groaned, split. A huge, triangular head rose out of the opening, gleaming eyes as big around as platters fixed on them. Pincer jaws clacked open as if in anticipation of fresh meat.

Krisamee screamed; Lady Alcyone did not. Both rushed toward the chamber's door as the huge insect hauled itself up—head, neck and a body the size of a small boat. It was a monstrous mantis with clawed forelegs covered by daggerlike spikes.

As the women hauled on the door, the stout oak bowed inward. The wood shattered and knocked them backward, toward the thing behind them. Through the opening came a second mantis, one even longer than the first. It scrabbled with thick legs and clawed at the masonry until it broke a hole large enough to crawl through.

Lady Alcyone gasped with pain as the first snatched her up. She kicked and struggled, but her efforts affected the creature not at all. It lifted her, the other lifted Krisamee. Green heads swiveled on long necks; the creatures observed their captives with glowing eyes, scythelike mandibles clacked, and smaller mouthparts scraped and clattered. Lady Alcyone held her breath, waiting for that horrid machinery to tear her flesh— but to her amazement, the creature lowered her and followed the other into the passage.

Lady Alcyone's head bobbed violently with her captor's gait; she strained her neck to watch her surroundings. The creatures were too large for the passages, so they knocked out walls, bowled over stonework with each step. The ceiling caved in as supports fell away. The older woman whispered a quick prayer that none of the falling debris would strike her or her daughter.

Pitch blackness lay everywhere, hung in every corner like a mist, like some living thing. But all along the walls and rubble-strewn floor, Lady Alcyone saw pinpricks of light, millions of bright specks which made the dark donjon look as if she were flying through the center of a starry galaxy. At first she had no idea where she could be, or whether she even remained in the dead city of Hautre, north of the Thlassa Mey. Then she remembered the insects. Like the huge mantids, the insects possessed eyes which glowed in the dark. The thought of all those crawling bodies above and around her brought a shudder.

They burst into the courtyard, into what should have been broad daylight, but the air remained an eerie twilight shade. The keep's walls and cobblestones glittered with bright eyes. She craned her head but she could see no edge to the shadow. The sun did not pierce this darkness; no light seeped in at any point. The twilight itself seemed to pacify the insect hordes, however. They lay everywhere, on everything.

The mantids hauled the two women toward the castle's great hall, toward the high doors which led into that chamber. Wood splintered as a monstrous head butted into it. Debris flew, both doors shivered back on their hinges, and the huge creatures carried Krisamee and Lady Alcyone into the vaulted space beyond.

Within stood a dazzling white object—what seemed to be a rod of light in the center of the hall. It seemed like a great, white beacon at first but it was a beacon which shed no light. It glowed, yet did nothing to illuminate any other object. As Lady Alcyone's eyes adjusted to the brightness, she made out features: a human face, a human body, arms, and legs. Her jaw dropped; she would have screamed if she could have caught her breath. She had seen those features twenty years earlier, when her home had fallen to Buerdaunt's armies. The ghastly scars across the bright face—that image lay scribed into her memory the way an epitaph is scribed into a monument. It was Prince Ursid.

"So you're what my pets heard beneath these dead floors," he said. His voice sounded like an echo from a black cave a thousand leagues away. "They have brought you to me in hopes I'll let them feed upon your flesh and blood. So I may. But for now, they will set you both down. I've not heard a human voice for decades. Speak before you die then, mortal woman."

"Ursid," Lady Alcyone breathed. The huge insect set her down but she felt so weak she could hardly stand. "The minstrels sang that you were perished."

He laughed with a sound like gales sweeping off a hundred storm tossed seas. "So I was, O foolish woman. I died from out of my mortal, fallible existence, to become naught but force. I am now the dread dark deities' best tool and toy—but first I'm their invincible weapon of vengeance."

"But how did you survive dark Kruptos' phantom journey to the world's end?"

Again, he laughed; a storm of light and darkness tore through the chamber. Phantom Ursid held up a clenched fist, uncurled glowing fingers, and revealed a blackened object. "This was once a flask," the echoing voice proclaimed. "But you see how it's melted by the force which rebuilt and then refined me. I survived that harsh remaking by holding fast within my grip a holy artifact I'd snatched from Palamon—a goddess' finger." Laughter came again. "It carried me through dark Kruptos' fell purgation. Now I have come back to wreak my vengeance upon all the world."

Chapter Nineteen:
The Caravan

FLIN SQUINTED, THEN crawled atop a rock and gazed down at the trail which crossed the Altines Mountains between Ourms and Guelt. It had been a rough journey for him and his men, ever since they had left the ships which had carried them across the Thlassa Mey. Now they were within a few leagues of Guelt. No one suspected they were even there; Flin would move against Odus and would snatch Bessina from the count's grip before the fellow could even guess what had happened.

"This is living," Virgus said through his gray beard. "It does me good to find out real men still walk the land. Now all we need is a battle. I'll stretch my limbs by bashing in a helmet, one or twain."

"We'd better find a helmet to bash first," Flin replied.

Sheldorr heaved his red-haired body up onto the rock behind them. "You can bet your bones that's the truth," he said. "So what's our plan when we reach Guelt, Boss Flin?"

"A telling question," Pafney said to his master. "How do we gain entrance to the keep? And once we reach your lady's side, what measures do we use to get her out?"

"Better than that," Sheldorr added. "How do we grab the booty and get *that* out?"

A few men laughed at that, but Flin only smiled. "It's a good question, friends. I have to tell you—I don't have the slightest idea. But don't worry—a plan will come." He gazed along the narrow road where it twisted down the face of the escarpment before them. "A plan will come," he said again, quietly.

160

"What's this?" Virgus said suddenly. "I'm ashamed of you men. I'm so old and creaky I've got wrinkles on my eyeballs, but I'm a better watch than the lot of you. Someone's coming."

"Why, so they are," Flin said. "A whole caravan, by the gods."

"A caravan?" Sheldorr sounded eager. "What are they carrying, I wonder? Gold? Jewels? Rich tapestries, silks; I'd settle for glass beads, just for the practice."

Flin eyed the string of mules keenly. Each animal had a pair of huge baskets lashed across its back, one on each side. They made their way up the steep trail briskly and lightly, and the baskets bobbed with each step. Only a half dozen men guarded the lot of them. "They don't carry a thing by the look of them," he said. "They couldn't walk so fast if they were loaded."

"Then what might be their destination?" Pafney asked, puzzled. "What prize could send them into these forsaken cliffs with empty baskets, Sir? No city lies among these peaks, no mine or valued crop."

"Puzzling, puzzling." Flin watched them until they had approached within a couple hundred cubits. "Virgus, Sheldorr, get the men all hidden. I don't want to touch this packtrain and I don't want them to know we're here."

The unwonted seriousness of their leader's tone sent the two brigands hustling. In a moment, they had shoved and cajoled all the men into clefts and chinks in the rocks. When the unsuspecting caravan passed below them, the guards had no idea they were watched by dozens of eyes.

"What a disappointment," Sheldorr said as the last mule passed out of sight. "Where could they be going?"

"Send a scout to follow them," Flin answered. "We'll camp here tonight and maybe he can find out something by morning." Sheldorr agreed, though Virgus was inclined to move down toward the city. They had found an excellent place to ambush Guelt's commerce but that would only make them successful thieves. It would not free Bessina from Count Odus' clutches.

They made camp and Flin put in a restless night. If Odus of Guelt had kidnapped Bessina, Flin could free her. He knew that as surely as he knew the sun would drive a gold chariot across the skies the next day. But she had been furious with Flin the night she had disappeared. For the first time in his life, doubts about a woman's love flickered in his mind. What if she had gone away willingly with the Gueltic noble? What madness—but would she have recovered from it by now?

When he finally slept, he felt himself shaken awake after what seemed only instants. He coughed, blinked, and looked up at his squire's face. Dawn was only beginning to break, just enough paleness in the eastern sky to outline the youth's head and shoulders. "What's happened?" Flin asked.

"The scout's returned, all out of breath from running, Sir. The caravan wound up a narrow trail till darkness came, then vanished into an enormous cave with Gueltic soldiers stationed all about. Till after dark our scout hid in the rocks. At mid of night, the mules emerged again, well-guarded and well-laden. He is sure he reached us well ahead of them, though he has suffered falls and bruises in his haste."

"Good," Flin said as he digested the report. "Good, good lad. Wrap up his cuts and scrapes and see to it he gets something to eat. Oh, and wake the men." He got up and moved to Virgus' sleeping place.

The old man was awake already, hurrying about, stirring the camp into readiness. Sheldorr still lay asleep, snoring so loudly his armor rattled. Flin shook him awake; the three put their heads together, then moved their men into place above the narrow trail.

Though the brigands kept quiet, they scurried about frantically, each man trying to choose a good point of ambush, dropping and retrieving weapons and equipment, running to one hiding place, finding it occupied, running to another. Flin watched the confusion and shook his head. Virgus was right; the Red Company had been fat and idle for too long.

A horseman appeared on the trail below, then another, and the brigands were still trying to hide themselves. The last few threw themselves down flat on the rocks above the trail; they managed to get out of sight in time and the mounted warriors rode toward the ambush without hesitation. Flin licked his lips and watched as the mules appeared, a hundred cubits behind the lead soldiers.

More soldiers rode beside the shipment itself, some twenty or so. They made a powerful escort; surely the huge baskets held something worthwhile, maybe even something Odus of Guelt would trade Flin's princess for. Mules, guards, muleteers, came into view one by one until the procession lay stretched out below the waiting force.

To Flin's surprise, many of the brigands shouted and threw themselves down the mountainside before he could give a signal. They made a ragged attack; some tripped and rolled into the road, to the amazement of the soldiers. Others fell upon their foes with gusto, hacked, slashed, hauled Gueltic warriors from their saddles, and knifed them with glee.

Flin stared in dismay at the chaos, then he and his squire leaped up and joined the charge. Flin threw himself onto one rider, knocked the man from the saddle, and finished him off with a single stroke while Pafney did the same with another. Though the brigands made a ragged force, they so surprised the Gueltic guardsmen that there was no chance for defense. Many fell. The rest saw how their attackers rained down from the cliffs, so they put spurs to their horses and galloped for their lives.

The muleteers also ran. Some tried to pull themselves onto the backs of their mules as the startled animals jounced along the trail. Packs and all broke away and baskets rolled in the gravel as the beasts escaped. For all its flaws, the attack had turned into a rout.

"Have at them," Flin cried. "Don't let a single one escape to tell tales. After the mules, after the men." Then he stopped as he saw Sheldorr kick at a broken basket in disgust. "What's your peeve, friend? We've won the day, though we can improve with practice."

"We've won nothing," Sheldorr shouted back. "Look what we've captured." He kicked the split basket again and white stuff bulged from the rip. "We risked our lives for a shipment of wool."

"Wool?" In the midst of the skirmish, with battle lust foaming in his veins, Flin stared at the stuff from the basket. "Wool? What are twenty soldiers doing riding guard on a shipment of wool?" Virgus, Pafney, and others had leaped onto abandoned horses and thundered off after the defeated band. Flin stared about, then raised his voice after them. "Virgus, Pafney, Cornus, Salio, and all you others. Let them go. There's nothing on these mules but wool."

Groans and growls rose from the men. They shouted their disgust and gathered in dismay as the defeated mule drivers scampered down the road. "You're lucky we don't nip the heads off the lot of you," Sheldorr shouted at a couple of hastily departing backs. "The nerve of you, carrying nothing but wool."

"It was a good fight all the same," old Virgus offered. "And Nodens knows, we needed the practice." But even he sounded disappointed beneath the surface.

"What a world," Flin said. "I don't understand it."

Pafney galloped back up the trail. He had been one of the first to seize a Gueltic horse and take off in pursuit of the beaten enemy, but now he reined in with a spray of gravel. "We'd best not stand about," he shouted as he leaped down. "A hundred Gueltic knights ride up this trail and fleeing soldiers tell them of our deeds. In moments, they'll try to punish us for our attack."

"Hoy day," Flin said. "Twenty guardsmen on a shipment of wool—and knights sent out to meet it. By Tyche's toenails, something's not right here."

"I'm game for any fair fight," Sheldorr said. "But we can't stand against mounted knights."

"Gueltic knights are lighter armed than the ones you see around the Greenlands," Virgus said. He hesitated. "By Nodens' shining wall, though, Sheldorr's right." Even as he spoke, brigands moved off the trail.

Flin rubbed his chin and eyed his companions. "You're both right, there's not room for argument. All the same, it's a mighty puzzle." He kicked at some of the loose wool and a few strands drifted up with the breeze. "But I tell you, I don't understand it; I smell something rotten in it all." He pulled the cover off one of the baskets. "Pafney, help me get the wool out of this thing."

"What shall I do with it?"

"Dump it over the edge of the cliff for all I care. But don't dump it all—I'll need enough to cover me."

"Cover you?" Sheldorr and Virgus both turned on him in surprise. "What on earth are you going to do?"

"I'm going to find out where all this stuff is going." Flin was already climbing into the empty basket as he spoke. "Something doesn't measure up, I tell you, when a train of wool baskets gets knights to protect it—even if the brickheads did show up late. Careful, Pafney, my boy. You don't want to shove that stuff in so thick I can't breathe." His voice became muffled even as the younger man worked.

"It's a pretty good thought," Virgus said. "I'm going to stow away, too."

"Then hurry," Flin said with the sound of a man talking through a blanket. "You don't have much time."

Virgus, Sheldorr, and Pafney all decided to accompany Flin in his harebrained gamble. While the rest of the brigands faded into the mountains, a few stayed behind to help their leaders conceal themselves, and to watch from above in case of discovery. Personally, Flin didn't see any sense in their lingering—if the stowaways were discovered, the whole band could do nothing against a company of knights—even Gueltic knights. But he knew they would not be discovered anyway, so he said nothing. He heard covers being slapped onto baskets, then retreating footsteps, then he waited in silence until horses approached.

"Here they are," a voice announced. "Looks like none of it's been lost."

"I warrant you should thank the gods for that," a deeper voice answered. "The count would have your head upon a pole if but a single basket had been filched. Now off your horse. I want you and your men to repack those spilt baskets and then load them up again."

Flin heard a man slide to the ground, then the first voice spoke plaintively, "It wasn't our fault a bunch of bandits decided to rob us right here. How was I to know they'd show up, after all? If you'd done your job and got to the cave in time, this never would have happened and we wouldn't be picking up the pieces now."

"Enough," the Gueltic knight's voice returned. "I do not need to hear your drabble." The man stopped speaking, but Flin could hear him as he counted. He sounded all the more impatient for the fact that the muleteer had turned the blame for the attack back onto him. "Forty," he said at last. "That is all, though now I see that one or two are split. You there," he shouted. "Take some cord and bind up all the damaged baskets. Quickly, now."

"Where shall we get some cloth for patching?" a voice asked.

"Malroy, Andert, sacrifice your capes to fasten in the bulging wool. Lord Odus will reward you for it, so I trow."

Flin felt himself jostled as someone lifted his basket. "Augh," a voice next to his ear said. "Typhon's arms, this basket's heavy."

"This one, too," came another voice. "I swear, the hermit mage has filled it up with iron rather than his secret wool."

"Most likely, it is overpacked," the knight's voice said.

"But stop your sniveling; work, not talk, is how the day is won."

Flin had to prick up his ears in spite of the fact that he was crammed into a wicker basket which had been turned onto its side and was being carted along by two men. He had no idea who the hermit mage was, but he had heard enough to justify his belief that this shipment of wool was special.

He almost gasped as his basket was lashed back into its harness. He did let out a sound a moment or two later when the mule started up, a grunt of surprise and discomfort at the rough pace the beast set. Luckily, though, the other mules and their tenders made too much noise to overhear him.

He kept quiet during the bouncy ride down the mountain and he listened for more about the secret of this precious wool. But he heard no hint. He felt about inside his basket, twisted the smelly fibers between finger and thumb, did everything short of tasting them, but he could find nothing about them which seemed out of the ordinary.

The trip seemed to take forever. His back hurt and his limbs grew stiff; he almost became sorry for his brainstorm. But he had to smile at the thought of how his cohorts in the three other baskets had to be cursing him by this time, especially overgrown Sheldorr. If they ever reached a safe place, Flin hoped he would be able to climb out of his basket before Sheldorr could clamber out of his. The hulking brigand would likely run him through.

Voices and clopping hooves broke in on his lazy thoughts. He heard a few distant words of greeting, then the clopping faded, though the whole process repeated itself soon after. Flin realized the caravan was meeting other travelers; soon, they would reach their destination.

His spirits lifted as the party passed some buildings, perhaps a gate. The stolid clopping of the mules' steps turned louder, too, as if they were walking on paving stones. He squirmed about in his basket, tried to lay his hand on the hilt of his sword. He would need a weapon if someone were to jerk the cover off his basket—but it was no use. His quarters cramped him so closely he could not even touch the hilt, let alone draw the weapon.

The mule stopped and he heard voices, though they were so low and far away he could not tell exactly where they were coming from. He felt himself lifted once more and swung about. He clenched his teeth as he was set down so hard it hurt. More waiting, more voices. He heard the speech and labored breathing of men working hard, heard things set down beside him. Finally, a strange vibration shook the basket. It perplexed him until he realized his basket and others had been loaded onto some kind of cart. The vibration was the turning of the wheels as workmen rolled him up some sort of ramp.

The rolling ceased, and he felt himself slant forward; then the tall basket toppled and rolled, and he landed with a thud. He hoped no one heard him, even as he nursed a bruised elbow. But there was no need to worry; the hubbub of rolling carts and baskets would have covered a screaming fit.

At last the tumult died down. The voices faded until Flin shoved on the basket's lid and peeked out. He saw little, no more than the shadows of other baskets which lay or stood beside his, and the bleak shades of the unlit chamber's ceiling. He pushed the cover a little farther, poked his head out—and found himself face-to-face with an astonished fellow who wore a turban and a Gueltic robe.

The man was too surprised to shout. He and Flin stared at one another, he swallowed, then he turned and bolted for the dark chamber's door. It took Flin an instant to scramble to his feet, but, just as the fellow dove for the latch, a huge hand shot from another basket and caught him by the robe. He wrenched himself free but fell; by the time he could writhe to his feet, Flin was upon him.

Flin clamped one hand over the man's mouth and wrestled him to the floor while Sheldorr climbed out from his own basket. The fellow struggled and writhed, but it was only the work of a moment to pin him to the floor, then to bind him with cords from the split baskets. At last he knew he was beaten and relaxed in Flin's grip.

As the two men finished securing the man, Virgus and Pafney also appeared, squirming out of their baskets like two new moths out of their cocoons. But they did not even get a chance to speak before something struck the double door in front of them. "Quick," Flin whispered. "Hide."

Like cockroaches scurrying from a counter when a lamp is lit, the four men threw themselves between the stacked baskets. Flin and Sheldorr took longest because they had to haul the prisoner with them, but it did not matter because they heard a deep voice say, "Curses. Now I cannot find the key. I don't suppose you have it."

"No, not I," a second voice said. "I'll wager Haklit carried it with him.'' The door boomed like a drum as the man pounded it. ''Haklit, are you in there?''

Flin clamped his arm around the prisoner's neck, yanked out his dagger, and pressed the tip against the man's flesh. ''I know we can't keep you from making a fuss,'' he whispered. ''But if you even try, I'm going to damage you.''

The man plainly did not want to be damaged. He nodded, but otherwise remained as still and quiet as a stone while the two men outside pounded and called his name a couple more times. Finally, one of them cursed, struck the door a last blow, and they left.

''We'd better flee from here,'' Pafney said. ''By all the sound of those two men, I'm sure they're coming back.''

''Good thinking,'' Flin said. He hauled Haklit to his feet and hustled the prisoner toward the door. ''Where's that key those two were talking about?''

Flin pulled his hand from the man's mouth long enough to get an answer. ''Belt pouch inside robe.'' He slipped his hand inside the streaming robe's open front, found a common leather pouch, and fumbled a key out of it.

''Here,'' Flin said as he tossed the heavy key to Virgus. ''Open it and get us out of here.'' Then he turned to Haklit again. ''Quickly, friend, where's a good place to hide? You'd better tell the truth because you're going to be in there with us.''

''Wardrobe next door,'' Haklit responded. ''Hardly anyone ever goes there.''

''No sooner said than done,'' Flin said. Virgus unlocked the doors, peeked out to make sure the coast was clear, then the five of them nipped out, down a shadowy corridor and through an unlocked door. ''That was good advice,'' Flin said as they settled themselves between crowded racks of clothing. ''You're a good man, Haklit. By the way, where are we?''

''You're in Guelt.''

''Ho-ho, it all worked, then.'' Flin beamed at the men around him, though he could hardly see them in the shadows.

''There's a window if you care to open it and look out.''

''Don't be tricky with me. If I look out, someone else looks in,'' Flin said. ''Why don't you like us, fellow? All we did was what we had to. We didn't want your friends to poke us full of holes.''

''We can just crack that window and get a peak,'' Sheldorr said.

"Might be interesting. I've never seen Guelt. All right, hold Haklit. I'm going to look."

"You do not have to sit on top of me," Haklit said angrily. "I'm smart enough to see your number and discern how futile it would be for me to fight you."

"Hmm." Flin found the window's shutters. "Keep an eye on him, anyway. You know, this thing is loose enough, I can almost see between the slats without even unlatching it." He put his eye to a narrow opening and whistled softly.

Below him lay a mysterious city, baking beneath the afternoon sun. Guelt. He had heard it was unlike any city on the Thlassa Mey—now he saw that was true. It was a beautiful city, a metropolis of minarets, onion-shaped domes which sent sunlight glancing in all directions. Lofty towers stood everywhere and the azure of the Thlassa Allas gleamed in the broad harbor. It was a broad, beautiful city, a whole different world from what he knew.

More interesting than that, he could look down from the building which held him and see towering stone walls, ramparts, and barbicons which held onagers and ballistae ready to fling fire and death at any attacker. It had all come out as well as he could have hoped. He was in the Citadel of Guelt, the palace from which Count Odus ruled.

Chapter Twenty:
In the Citadel

FLIN BEAMED. "WE'RE here," he said. "We're in. All we have to do now is get into the count's rooms, grab Bessina, and get out."

"That's the spirit," Virgus said. "I knew it was just what we needed when you first came along."

"Maybe," Sheldorr said. "But all those things Flin mentioned make for a fair-sized 'all.' Strikes me that we're in a pickle—how do you propose to get the woman out?"

"What's the matter with you?" Virgus said with half a sneer. "Nobody forced you to come along."

"Wait, wait," Pafney broke in. "I've an idea."

Flin beamed at the young man. "Brave lad," he said. "I knew the first time you rode with me that you were resourceful. So speak up; what's your plan?"

"We pretend to be entertainers from some other land. That will get us into the count's presence, and maybe we can talk to a servant or two and find out where Bessina is."

Flin put his head to one side. "That's a wondrous idea, but what kind of entertainers do you think we'll be?" He smiled at the other men. "I'd like to entertain Count Odus by showing him the color of his blood."

Sheldorr and Virgus laughed near-silent laughs, but Pafney stood his ground. "I have it all worked out. Sheldorr is a huge man, strongest of the whole Red Company. We'll dress him down and make him an exhibit."

"I like that plan," Sheldorr said.

"And since I am the youngest and unknown, and of a size

commensurate with this good man," here, Pafney gestured toward Haklit, "I will wear his clothing and portray the leader of the troupe. Since I can use goodly speech, I'll entertain with words while Sheldorr shows his strength."

"A good idea, I have to admit," Flin said. "I like it. But tell me, we have only clothing enough for one man. You've taken care of yourself and Sheldorr, but what about Virgus and me?"

The younger man smiled; much of Flin had rubbed off on him. A few moments later, as the four of them made their way down toward Count Odus of Guelt's banquet hall, Flin was not sure whether to laugh or not. Though he still thought the matter something of a joke, Virgus fairly bristled beneath the veil and shapeless woman's clothing they had pulled off the racks in the wardrobe they had just left. Flin's moustache, Virgus' beard, all their weapons lay concealed behind yards of billowing cloth. And Virgus' eyes sent sparks; as far as he was concerned, his dignity lay back in the wardrobe with naked, bound Haklit.

They fumbled through the halls until they managed to corner a gullible-looking servant. Flin held his veil in place and smiled as Pafney told a lie or two and then asked the way to Count Odus' banquet.

"What banquet?" the servant asked with a blank expression.

Pafney hesitated, then made Flin proud. "By all the gods, his Lordship surely sups tonight."

"He does, but in his chambers. He does not have guests upon this night, and surely not a banquet."

Pafney smiled sweetly. "Good man, his merest snack would make a banquet in the eyes of lesser folk. But take us to him, or at least give us directions to the proper chambers. We are sent to bring him mirth and ease his mind upon this evening."

Again, the man pierced the odd company with a quizzical look. Finally, he shrugged and led them along a series of corridors, through a huge kitchen where a staff of at least a dozen prepared a luscious meal, and into another wing of the huge building. Flin took the liberty of filching a turkey leg from a stewpot, but he did not dare eat it because no one could mistake his dark moustache if he dropped his veil to take a bite. At last he shrugged and passed the morsel to Sheldorr, who took it with a grin and chomped it greedily.

"What's he got?" the serving man demanded as his ears drew his eyes to Sheldorr's smacking lips.

"Methinks he chews a turkey leg," Pafney replied blandly.

"Where'd he get it? None of you have earned a bite until the count approves your act."

"Remember that we delve in magic deeds, as well as strength and dance. The appearance of a tidbit such as that is one advantage to the craft."

The serving man scowled, but apparently felt too unsure of himself to comment further. A few more steps took them all to a large suite of rooms, where he turned the four of them over to a lavishly dressed man. "Entertainers for his pleasure," he said.

The man nodded, plainly aware of who "he" was. The fellow must have been some sort of majordomo; he gave the four of them a cold look and said, "Come with me."

They followed him past a half dozen bare-chested guards and into a lavish chamber. Music sounded from the far side of a curtain but they did not pass through. Rather, they followed the man through another door and down a corridor to an empty waiting room. "Did Fahn select you?" the fellow asked.

Flin smiled to himself. Pafney had no idea who Fahn was and Flin knew it. But the young man simply shrugged and said, "Someone sent us, but I know not who he was."

"I see." The majordomo frowned. "Well, wait for me."

He stepped out. As soon as the curtain swayed back into place, Flin nearly fell over from silent laughter. "You're a better prankster than myself," he whispered to the younger man.

Pafney sagged and wiped sweat from his forehead. "I grow unsettled. Our position grows more sticky by the heartbeat."

"You can do it. We'll have my Bessina out of here by sundown."

"You still got my sword?" Sheldorr asked. He looked chilly, clad as he was in only a breechclout.

"I have it," Flin said. "And it's loose in the scabbard. You'll . . ." He broke into a falsetto giggle when the curtain stirred and the majordomo faced them.

"Your coming is a blunder of some sort; you're not expected. But come forth and give your best performance." He smiled crookedly. "Much good may it do you, for his Grace is in a horrid mood this night."

He swept the curtain back and revealed a chamber which

hurt the eye by the glitter of its lavish decoration. The floor tiles formed black and white marble squares; they had been polished so brightly both colors reflected the alabaster columns with their gold inlay. Rich hangings, tapestries of silk and cloth-of-gold, concealed the walls. A fountain large enough to bathe in splashed dark liquid from a carved whale's spout.

Flin liked the look of the place. Whatever he might think of Odus of Guelt, that noble certainly knew how to live. A huge, canopied bed stood on a raised dais and its curtains shimmered like angels' wings in the torchlight. A pair of couches framed it; between them lay a huge carpet strewn high with cushions. In the center of the pile of cushions, surrounded by luxury and a brace of women who fondled and caressed him, sat a hard-faced man—Odus of Guelt. But for all the splendor of the little hall, Flin's gaze flew to the couch at the far side of the huge bed. Another woman reclined there and propped her head on one arm as if bored beyond tears.

She wore the same silken robes the other women wore, sheer layers which concealed everything but her eyes. A guard stood behind her, his hands clasped on a huge scimitar, as if to frighten any person from approaching. But for all that, and for the distance between them, Flin knew, as surely as he knew his own name, that the woman was Bessina.

Pafney's voice brought him back to the moment. "My Lord and Ladies of the court of Guelt, I bring before you one who's dazzled eyes from Gesvon to Buerdaunt across the Thlassa Mey."

"You can say that again," Flin added helpfully in his best falsetto voice. All eyes drew to him in surprise, but especially the eyes of the woman on the couch.

"What is this?" one of the scimitar-bearing guards behind the couch said. "Is this act good enough for the mighty count?"

Odus of Guelt smiled a sneering smile, as if laughing at the lot of them. "It all amuses me," he said. "So let them finish."

Pafney cleared his throat and began again. "Observe the mighty arms and stunning thighs of this great, hulking man. He . . ."

The guard interrupted again. "My wife has bigger arms."

"Oh, yeah?" Sheldorr said in anger. "Well I'll bet your wife's lover has bigger arms yet, you lout."

The room burst into laughter. The guard's face went red, and he faded into silence for the moment. Pafney continued bravely by turning to a different guard. "Now might I have your javelin? Ah, thank you. See, my friends, how this most deadly weapon's shaft is made of steadfast iron. Stout it is, and weighted so that it can force its way through even the thickest shield. Now I will give this weapon to the great and thewy Sheldorr and he shall attempt to change its shape." He handed the javelin to Sheldorr.

"What are you talking about?" the hulking brigand asked.

"Bend it," Flin whispered.

Sheldorr looked at the javelin, perplexed. He finally grasped one end in each hand and strained. The muscles of his chest and arms really did ripple nicely and the javelin gave before his might. But it bent only a little, so he finally put it across his knee to bow it further, until it described an angle a little more than ninety degrees. "So there you are," Pafney shouted. "An exhibition of the strength of a most mighty mortal."

Odus of Guelt eyed his majordomo. "Really? I would hope for better."

The majordomo looked uncomfortable and the insolent guard took the exchange as a cue for more ribaldry. "Yes, you false exhibit," he cried. "I've seen a dozen men who could bend it further than you have, and faster too."

Sheldorr glared at him. "Oh, is that right?" In a sudden motion, he leaped onto the dais and brought the bent javelin down atop the guard's head. The man's helmet split into two pieces and clattered to the floor, the scimitar slipped from his hands, and he crumpled. "Bend that," Sheldorr snarled.

Odus of Guelt leaped to his feet but Pafney was too fast for him. The young man grabbed the count, shoved him to the floor, then snatched his saber and ran another guard through. Virgus locked himself into deadly combat with a third guard, though the folds of his woman's robe encumbered him. As for Flin, he threw his robe off entirely, tossed Sheldorr's sword to him, and leaped toward Bessina's couch. He swept the woman into his arms, tore her veil away, and covered her face with kisses.

"Ah Flin, my Flin," she cried as she returned his embrace. "You've come to take me from this place."

"And you still love me?" Flin said joyfully. "I was sure you would, but I'm glad to hear it all the same. Now we have to hurry; we can kiss more later." Another guard rushed Flin. The knight drew his sword against the man, but the fellow keeled over when Bessina rammed an elbow into his guts. "That's my Bessina," Flin shouted.

"Seize them," Odus of Guelt shrieked. "Do not let a single man escape."

Pafney lifted a concubine bodily and hurled her atop the corrupt ruler. So entangled was Odus by her weight and endless folds of clothing that the two of them formed a helpless, writhing mass on the floor.

Clashes of steel filled the chamber and more guards thundered at the doors. "Let's get out of here," Flin yelled, and pulled Bessina after him.

She pulled back. "No, not that way," she cried. "Come, my chamber's over here, and there are many passages." They all ran after her just as the main door burst open and furious Gueltic soldiers flooded the chamber. Flin, Bessina, Pafney, Sheldorr, and Virgus leaped and danced across Odus of Guelt's huge bed, which collapsed beneath their weight. As they escaped, the canopy's folds and curtains caught the soldiers and tangled them like fish in a net. The five pattered through yet another door and down a hallway.

"Where are you going?" Flin asked as they ran. "Have you found a way out of here?"

"My time has not been wasted," she shouted back. "I searched out the best escape, for I was sure you'd come. That's what I told that bearded pig called Odus." She ran to a window and threw open the shutters. "It took you long enough."

"What can I say? There were delays." Flin watched Bessina. She had thrown off the heavy folds of the Gueltic woman's robe and now wore only the sheerest undergarments. But that was the only way she could climb onto the window casing. "Are you sure you can make it up there?"

Bessina gasped and heaved herself upward. "It would help if some strong man could boost me. I must catch the stones which form this corner, then climb up and reach that shuttered window."

Flin stared out after her. He could see what she was trying to do; the palace of Odus' citadel was a sort of pagoda, level after level in a towering cascade. Their corner jutted out from the rest of the building. A floor above it, in a wall which ran at right angles, lay another window, tightly shuttered. "I'll join you," he said. "You men help the two of us." He climbed out. While Bessina steadied him, he lifted himself and whacked at the shutter's louvers with his sword. A few strokes tore enough slats away for him to reach in and catch the latch. He swung the barricade open.

He hauled Bessina after him and gave her a hug as she lit in the darkened chamber. "All right," he said. "Everybody else climb up before the soldiers get here."

Pafney and Sheldorr climbed through, but Virgus stopped at the window. "Climb up," Flin called. "We have to hurry." Already, Gueltic soldiers made the lower chamber ring by hammering on the locked door.

Virgus smiled a thin smile and shrugged as if in apology. He still wore the heavy robe which had so hampered him in his battle with the guard. "I'd like to," he said. "I just can't."

"What do you mean?" Flin clambered back down to the lower chamber. But as he reached the floor beside Virgus, the older man sank to one knee. Flin tried to grab him beneath the shoulders and lift him, but drew back one hand in surprise. It was covered with blood. "What happened?"

Virgus had turned pale as paper. "That last guard I killed," he said. "He was a little too quick; just one time, I jumped too late."

"Pafney," Flin cried. "Come and help me lift him; he's hurt."

"Too late," Virgus said. "Too late for an old man. Leave me, Sir Flin. You don't have time to carry me with you. It wouldn't help anyway."

As Pafney jumped down beside him, Flin caught the old man's head in one hand and lowered his sagging form. "I hate to see you go, old chum."

"Me, too." Virgus replied with a weak smile. "But I go happy, that's the main thing. Better than rotting away in some stable, watching strong men get fat and lazy."

"You're so certain death is imminent?" Pafney asked.

"I've seen it enough times. You'd better get along."

Flin peered into the old face and saw that the eyes were already beginning to go vacant. It was sad to watch a good man die, but he could not weep. It was also good to see a brave man die well. He leaned forward and planted a soft kiss on the old man's forehead. "Good-bye, old friend," he said.

The door groaned; a splinter flew off and skated across the floor. "Come on," Flin said to his squire. "He's right, it's time for us to go." They bounded to the window, climbed up one behind the other, and hauled themselves into the upper chamber.

"What's happened to your friend?" Bessina asked.

"He's dead."

"Ah." Her face fell. "A heavy thing that is, to see a friend meet death in serving one's own cause."

"Let's push on," Flin said. "Let's hurry, my beautiful guide. Where do we go next?"

Bessina caught her breath. "We have to pass through yonder door, into a vaulted chamber. We must bar that opening, then snatch some worsted ponies."

"Worsted ponies?" Flin wrinkled his brow.

"Count Odus is a crafty man—he owns the services of some resourceful mage and plans to do great harm to our fair land. He's signed a truce with Lothar."

"Lothar the Pale?" Flin stared at her. "Explain this to me one part at a time. Why did the old goat Odus kidnap you?"

Bessina jerked her head as they reached the door. "It's complex. Ere I tell, you have to bar these doors. And fast."

"Easily done." Flin's eyes lit on a trio of long banquet tables set against one wall. "Stack two tables across the door and tear down the third for bars," he ordered.

It was no sooner said than done. While Sheldorr slid the first table into place, Flin and Pafney pried the planking off the second with swords and daggers. It was careful work to raise the planks without breaking a blade, but they managed in time to set planks against the door while Sheldorr slid the last table into place behind the first.

As with all doorways within this citadel, loops had been set in the stone for door bars. It took only a moment to split the planks down small enough to go through the loops. Then the three men were off behind Bessina, into the next chamber.

"The Count of Guelt abducted me because he could not lay his hands on Berengeria," Bessina said.

"He's crazy," Flin replied. "You're a lot better looking."

"Thank you. That has nought to do with it. He signed a secret treaty with Buerdaunt. He'd start a war, for which I or Berengeria was the bait, then Lothar would attack an undefended land while Aelia and Arcite fought Odus."

Flin whistled and Pafney said, "A cunning plot. But what's to be the count's reward once Palamon has battered Guelt into the ground?"

"Pale Lothar knew that Palamon was on a quest," Bessina replied. "He calculates Queen Aelia could not reach this land and conquer it before the Buerdic armies struck. Already, Lothar marches to the Greenlands. He will fall upon Carea soon.

Oh, he's a plotter, Lothar is, and he has had two decades to concoct his scheme.''

She reached another set of doors, fumbled with the latch, then threw them open. The chamber beyond lay heaped almost to the roof beams with stuffed toys, knit ponies the size of large dogs. "But Odus has his schemes as well," she went on. "High in the mountains east of Guelt, some hidden mage enchants this lowly wool. From that, the Gueltic concubines knit these.''

Flin tried to pick one knit pony up, but found they were tied into long bundles. He whisked one of the binding cords in two with his sword and lifted a strange toy. "I knew it," he said with a grin. "We intercepted a caravan of the wool and I knew it was important, just from the way the soldiers talked about it.'' He tossed the knit pony to Pafney, who caught it with a puzzled look on his face. Then he eyed Bessina again. "But what in the world do they do?''

Bessina took the knit pony from the squire. To Flin's astonishment, she placed it on the floor, straddled it, grasped its knit reins, then whispered a word. "Selevay." It lifted her as delicately as a butterfly leaving a flower. "The magic's precious," she said. "Odus let me learn the secret, for he never dreamed you'd snatch me from his clutches.''

"Poor fool," Flin said with a laugh. "He never understood the odds against him. His plot's sinking like a frog full of pebbles.''

Bessina shook her head. "He has these mystic toys. His army shall strike with terror from the air.''

"That's serious," Flin agreed. "But he's going to have to strike fast to reach Carea before we do." He grabbed two of the loose toys and tossed them to his partners. As he took a third for himself, they heard pounding on the outer door.

"I have a better plan," Pafney said. "Each one of us must haul a bundle of these knitted ponies. That way, we can give a mystic mount to each man of our band.''

"You're a genius," Flin said. "We'll take four bundles. Bessina, which way leads out?''

"Up to the roof," Bessina said and pointed toward a narrow flight of stairs. "There's room for only one man at a time.''

They retied the bundles, tethering the knit ponies in single file, as it were. Bessina took the first bundle. "Selevay," she shouted, and the string of fifteen ponies rose. She led them about the chamber while the three men prepared bundles for themselves. Three more shouts of ''Selevay,'' and they flew up the steps to the rooftop.

They rose from the building, one after another with their tethers of knit ponies streaming behind them. Hordes of soldiers thronged the citadel's ramparts and shouted oaths at them; spears, javelins, stones, and even knives flew upward. But they had so taken the force by surprise that all the missiles fell short.

The sky turned dark with arrows as hundreds of bowmen took aim. Feathered shafts sank into the knit ponies; Flin heard one sing past his head as he shook his reins to speed up the little steed.

The knit ponies obeyed the reins the same way that live horses would, except, as Bessina showed the men, the rider had to lift the reins to ask for more altitude. They rose above the great city until it lay as a brightly colored blanket far below. Catapults hurled oil and stones at them and the arrows kept coming, but all fell back on the city. The knit ponies and their riders soared above everything.

A half dozen more of the mystic toys shot from the citadel's highest tower. Experts plainly rode them; they rose like falcons and whisked after the escapees. ''Blazes,'' Flin cried. ''How do they fly so fast?''

''They are Odus' special cronies,'' she said. ''He has favored them with mystic steeds. They spend their hours for days on end by flying o'er the city. Thus, they are capable airhorsemen.''

''I can see that,'' Flin said as the six gained on them. ''Here they come.''

The six Gueltic flyers drew sabers as they pulled closer to the fleeing band. They gained on Flin and the others so fast, he hardly had time to pull his own sword before three of the men turned in formation above his knit pony and swept down on him. As the first two shot past, he cleaved one from the saddle with a single stroke. The man fell screaming toward death.

The third lagged a little behind his mates. He swept past Flin's head, lashed out with a boot, and knocked the dashing knight from his mount. Flin's heart surged into his mouth as he plummeted. He lost his sword and thrashed wildly until one hand made contact with something.

It was the leg of another knit pony, ridden by one of the first men to charge him. Flin tried to pull himself up behind the man, but the fellow's saber caused him to lose his grip once more. As he slipped downward, he made a last desperate grab at the mount's other leg and managed to pinch a loose end of enchanted yarn between two fingers.

That bit of yarn pulled with him, unraveled as he fell. He clenched it with his other hand in an impossible attempt to climb the thread—but it paid out too fast. He still plunged earthward while the unraveling process ate away the knit pony's leg, then the other hind leg, then the body. Before the rider realized the threat, he himself lost balance and fell, plunging and screaming past the knight.

To Flin's relief, his own fall slowed, then stopped. He floated through the air, supported by the enchanted yarn—even though the mount it had once formed was nearly unraveled. He looked about; the four remaining warriors still fought his partners while he floated helplessly. Then one spotted him and broke away to finish him off.

The yarn was enough to hold Flin up but the Gueltic warrior had only to slice it in half and he would plunge toward the waiting soldiers below. He had only one hope: his knit ponies still spiraled through the air like ponderous pinwheels; one end of the line would pass below and to the left of him. He let go of the yarn, waved his arms wildly, and just managed to catch one of the ponies by its woven mane.

He scrambled onto it, keeping in mind the way the other had come apart. Then he grasped its reins, dug heels into its woven flanks and brought it into a level turn. The maneuver worked perfectly; the attacking rider was unable to avoid the string of knit ponies tied together. He collided with them and fell with a cry. He tried to catch hold on a different one as it swept past, but his reflexes were not quick enough. Flin did not even watch him as he shrank, faded, then merged with the ground below.

Flin hurried to catch up with the others, but the long string of knit ponies slowed him, making him swear. He felt better when Sheldorr put a blade into one opponent; the man dropped his saber and rode away all hunched over. But Pafney still had a furious struggle on his hands, and one man hauled Bessina into his arms even as Flin stared.

Then the man's eyes bulged in surprise. He released Bessina and fell with hardly a sound, her dagger's hilt jutting out of his chest. Bessina clambered wildly and managed to haul herself astride her victim's horse. Flin blew her a kiss. What a woman!

The last opponent plainly saw that all was up with him. Though he was possibly the best rider of the lot, Flin watched with relief as he leaned in his little saddle, turned his knit pony, and swept away. He faded through the sunset sky over the ancient city. The four adventurers whistled and shouted in victory, then they regrouped. Bessina still trembled from her encounter and Pafney and Sheldorr sported wounds, but they had all survived. They and their captured knit ponies formed a strange cluster as they flew away from the city and toward the mountains to the southeast.

Chapter Twenty-one:
Sir Pallador

THE COUNCIL HALL at the Fastness of Pallas stood empty; by that late hour, the Knights, their squires, and the Fastness' hired servants and gardeners had all retired. Sir Pallador's footsteps echoed off gray granite and white marble as he strode toward the Grand Master's study.

The study's door was a richly carved panel of thick walnut, with hinges and latch of polished brass. Some boy had spent the best part of the day rubbing those fittings, Sir Pallador knew that. Every day, one lad would polish the brass with a soft cloth until it gleamed. It taught patience, steadfastness, stolid devotion to one's labors—at least that was what Sir Pallador had been told when he had done it as a youth. Now he believed it was meant to put lads in view of the most senior members of the order, to awaken aspirations in young hearts.

Sir Pallador rapped on the door and a voice echoed from within. "Enter." He pushed the panel open and found Sir Phebos seated in a far corner of the chamber, bent over his desk. The Grand Master looked over his shoulder as the younger knight entered. "Good Sir Pallador. How quickly you return. Have you performed the task I set before you?"

"Alas, the work is only half complete," Sir Pallador replied. "But matters far more pressing lift their heads: a horrible phantasm stalks the land and makes the trees and grasses dry up; even birds are dropping dead out of the sky."

Sir Phebos' brows knit. "A plague, then?"

"Worse than any plague. A crawling blot, a darkness which advances through the land and fills the atmosphere with evil.

I will swear, it's powerful enough to level kingdoms."

Sir Phebos put down his quill and looked grave. "And you abandoned your own quest to warn me of this apparition? If your warning comes to nought, I hope you see the damage you have wrought against yourself."

It was a chide; small, but a chide nonetheless. Sir Pallador went to one knee. "Master, I will swear with all my heart, this specter is a grievous threat. For it alone did I abandon my crusade—that I might warn our Knights, that we might face this challenge and so defeat it. I'm aware of risks I take against my quest; in fact, I'll take a fresh mount even now and I'll return unto the city where fair Alcyone and Krisamee await."

The Grand Master's eyebrows lifted. "You keep the company of women?" A slow smile graced his lip. "You face grave risks: the body's juices rise without regard for any vows the spirit may have made."

"Indeed, I know it," Sir Pallador replied. "But these fair women both are crucial to my quest and under my protection."

"I see," Sir Phebos said without expression.

"But I must hasten back, to see them safely from that land. For while the darkness roams, it is no place for humans. Yet I'll spare a moment to relate my first adventure." Sir Pallador told Sir Phebos of Peristeras, of how he had met the two women, and of how Lady Alcyone had turned out to be heir to Hautre and lynchpin to the young knight's plans.

The tale took only a few moments. When it ended, Sir Phebos stood. "It's ably done, then. I had feared such female graces might have turned your eyes. Now I conclude your motives are correct."

Sir Pallador turned from him and pounded fist into palm. "Ah, Sir, you gaze at me and smile and tell me all is well, when all the while you recognize my guilt as clearly as the fish which swims across a sunlit pool. Harsh forces war within me when I gaze upon her."

"On whom?"

"The maiden Krisamee."

" 'Tis well you recognize the threat. We'll conquer evils from the outside planes—it is the weaknesses which breed within that threaten to destroy us. Your own passions form the threat of which you should have told me first."

"It's true." Sir Pallador's face writhed. "I have lost control as far as she's concerned; hot blood flows through me if I even hear her name." He held forth his palms and gazed from them

to the older knight's face. "These hands which served the
Maiden, which for years fought every evil, now go forth without my counciling and nestle on her body. They feast upon the
texture of her clothing and her flesh and beg my lips to do the
same. And more. Ah, Master, how can you, with threescore
years upon you, comprehend such passions? What am I to do?"

"You love this wench?"

"How wench? How can you utter such a word? She is as
proper, pure, and maidenly as any mortal who has ever
walked."

Sir Phebos smiled; the lines of his face danced. "I must
agree the word was harsh. And yet your answer tells me of
your passion's purity—as passion goes, at least." His smile
faded, he eyed Sir Pallador gravely. "But do not come to me,
young man, and say I bear too many years to understand. Your
youth is but a weakness—every man must overcome it ere he
can attain the safety of old age. I've suffered, too; it's an
affliction known as living. I have felt those same temptations
which conspire to drag each knight from his true path. I've
seen men suffer and relinquish knighthood for a tithe of what
you have admitted."

"I must beg your pardon," Sir Pallador said. "Forgive me,
please. Absolve me from my guilt."

"You know the state of your own heart—that's all the Holy
Maiden requires, until an act takes place. Temptation is a uni-
versal demon and it festers in the soul of every man." Sir
Phebos extended a hand and lifted Sir Pallador from his knees.
" 'Arise, Sir Knight, and do thy duty.' That is what the Maiden
said unto the founder of our order. So I say to you, 'Go do
thy duty.' Only you can know just what that duty is."

"But can I act? I feel impure, too tainted for our order's
colors."

"Only you can know," Sir Phebos replied. "All men have
destinies. Some choose their own and some have fate thrust
hard upon them."

"Ah, your answer troubles me. Your council gives scant
comfort."

Sir Phebos sighed. "The truth is often troubling. Go now,
for you have your duties. I must wake our fellows, see them
armored, and ride out before the dawn comes 'round. Go to
the stables and select two quick-paced horses. See your wom-
enfolk to safety. When we reach you, we will deal with your
dark blot."

"Farewell." Sir Pallador bowed, then left the Grand Master. He returned to the stables, selected two good horses, and set out toward the Greenlands.

For all the fact that he had not slept in a great while, he rode the night out. Morning found him northeast of the city of Oron and the next night found him nearing the twisting Courbee River and the Greenlands. But his horses needed rest and there were limits past which the strongest man's endurance would not take him. When darkness came, he happened onto a rural inn. He gladly paid for a meal and to have his horses and himself put up for the night.

That same evening, a well-rested Diomedes approached the same inn. A surly mood held the burly man as he spurred his pony toward the lighted building. He had lost Palamon's trail and he would not sleep in peace until he picked it up again. He still retained what he hoped was bait for his quarry. In a bag fastened to his saddle, he carried the brass case the tall monarch had so fussed over.

Diomedes had asked careful questions over the last couple of days and he would ask more. He would find Palamon and then the king would die. Diomedes knew that as surely as he knew his own name; the fact made him smile grimly as he climbed down from his horse in front of the inn.

A boy raced past Diomedes, dodging to avoid him. But Diomedes shot out a hand and collared the child, almost jerking him from the ground. "Wait a minute," the assassin said. "Who be you?"

The boy stared at the dark man and fear showed in his face. Diomedes laughed and repeated his question. "Who be you, lad? Don't worry, I'm not going to hurt you. I wouldn't hurt a fly. Who are you, what are you doing here?"

The boy kept staring. "Innkeeper's my father," he finally managed to say. " 'Bye." He tried again to run, but Diomedes held onto his jerkin and the long step turned into a funny leap which left the lad exactly where he had started.

"Don't be in such a rush. Is this a good place to spend the night?"

"Yes, Sir."

Diomedes chuckled. "I suppose you might be biased, mightn't you, since the keeper's your old man—but all's the same for that. The place better be good; it's the only one for a half dozen leagues about. Tell me, now . . . don't jump so.

Tell me, have you seen a tall man who wears bright chain mail? He has a younger man with him, most likely.''

The boy stopped and stared. ''Why, yes. Taller than you, broad across the shoulders, but slender for all that. Armor's polished bright, the color of the setting sun shining off the Courbee. He's alone, though. Is he a friend of yours?''

''Yes, he's a particular friend of mine.''

''Shall I run and tell him you're coming?''

''Never mind, I want to surprise him.'' Diomedes put on his gentlest smile. ''What room's he in—I'd bet he'll not be sleeping tonight in the common chamber, will he?''

''I don't know, Sir. He's not in any room, he's in the stable with his animals.''

''Horses, you mean?''

''Yes, Sir.''

''Good boy,'' Diomedes said. He gave the lad a shove toward the inn's front door. ''Go tell your father to get a room ready for me. I'm as good as any other man; I won't sleep in the common space, either.'' Then he led his horses toward the stables.

Once he had escaped the light thrown out by the inn's lanterns, he dropped his horse's reins and drew his sword. This time, Palamon would not escape. He reached down and felt his sword's edge in the darkness; it was keen and sharp. A quick thrust and then he would worry about what to do next.

The stable's doors stood open and a lantern glowed within. Diomedes crept to the entrance, quiet as a spider on a wall, and peeked in. He saw no one; all was put away for the evening. A couple of stall doors stood ajar and the lantern glowed from within one. Diomedes saw where his quarry lay.

He moved closer, held his blade ready, picked his way across the straw-strewn floor. He would not stumble now, he would strike first and make excuses later. He could deal with the innkeeper and his brat.

The lantern glinted off armor and white hair as the victim stooped to brush the courser's belly. Without a sound, Diomedes brought his blade up, then swung at the exposed neck.

''Sir, your horses are standing loose in the yard.'' The boy's call was almost a scream. The head in front of Diomedes jerked back enough to make the assassin's blade miss. The steel glanced off a shoulder, leaving a bloody gash.

Diomedes hissed a curse and fought to recover his balance

as his target rolled beneath the huge horse and popped up on the far side. Worse than missing, Diomedes had struck the wrong man. The lamplight showed what the shadow had not; this man was far younger than the tall monarch, was clean shaven, and rather than being white, his hair was a sandy brown, whitened by dust from a long day on a dry road. Even as Diomedes stared, the fellow snatched up a longsword and forced the older man back.

Their blades clashed once, twice, then again. Diomedes kicked the knight's feet from beneath him and the two men rolled out the stall gate and into the center of the stable. It was an ugly fight, death waiting on the next slip, and the young knight was stronger than he had any right to be. Diomedes whirled, feinted, and brought his blade down in a mighty blow but he was too late. His opponent's longsword darted beneath his guard and he gasped as he felt the blade slide into his flesh. Numbing pain filled him, he dropped his own weapon and spun away. "By Hades' pits." One last curse, which he could hardly force out, then darkness closed his eyes and he fell against a wall, bending and breaking the weapon which had slain him.

Sir Pallador stepped back to avoid the falling sword and the writhing body, then looked up to see the stableboy standing wide-eyed at the stall door. "Coo," the lad said. "I knew he was a bad one when he asked about you and sent me in to my father. That was why I yelled—I didn't know what he might be up to. I didn't dream he had killing on his mind, though."

"But that he did." Sir Pallador winced as he touched the flap of skin the assassin's blade had lifted from the side of his neck. It was not a grievous wound, but it hurt like sin. He could feel the blood soak the quilted padding beneath his chain mail. "I thank you for your timely shout."

The innkeeper came clattering up. "What's all the commotion . . . By the gods, a killing."

" 'Twas all the dead man's fault, Father," the stableboy said. "I saw it all."

"What reason would he have to put his steel in me?" Sir Pallador said, then turned to the older man. "Your son has saved my life by timely shouting. I'll reward you once I've caught my breath."

The innkeeper looked only a little relieved. "I swear to you I never saw the man before in my life." He lifted his hands. "No one from about here had a thing to do with it, I swear.

And you're hurt, too. To your mother, boy, and bring back
linen and hot water.''

"Tut,'' Sir Pallador said. "No man accuses you. Are those
his horses?''

"They are,'' the stableboy replied as he scampered away.

"They'll pay for the burial, then,'' the innkeeper said. He
looked Sir Pallador over. "Do you object to that?''

"Not at all,'' Sir Pallador replied. "The custom is a wise
one. Still and all, I'd like to make inspection of his goods, to
ascertain his purpose in attacking.''

"It's no hard question, why he did that. You're a wealthy-
looking man. He thought to rob you; what other reason could
there be?''

"We'll know, perhaps, when we have learned of him.'' Sir
Pallador unlaced one of the dead man's saddlebags. Within,
he found a bag of gold. "So much for robbery,'' he said, lifting
out the bag. "This man had gold enough—far more than I
have. No, there's got to be another reason.'' He searched further, found nothing of interest, then went to the other bag.

Carvings and scrollwork glinted in the lantern's light as a
brass case caught his eye. He studied it, rubbed it, turned it
over. The craftsmanship was marvelous. A weathered face on
the top puffed its cheeks, blew gusts which Sir Pallador could
almost feel. He reached into his own purse and drew forth the
coin Peristeras had given him. The face was the same.

He turned toward the innkeeper. "All gold, tack, and be-
longings, I allow to you, though I'd encourage you to make
provision for your soul by giving—at the least—the customary
tenth unto the gods. But this one item interests me. I'd keep
it if you will allow.''

The innkeeper eyed the bag Sir Pallador had handed him
and all the little golden talents which lay within. He bounced
it up and down in his palm, looked up at the Knight of Pallas,
and before he even spoke, Sir Pallador knew what he would
say. Two good horses, full harness, and a bag of gold would
compensate the man for priests and burial—and a small fortune
besides. A brass box meant nothing against such a windfall.

Sir Pallador placed the brass case among his own belong-
ings, though he had no idea what he would ever do with it.
But Peristeras was an envoy from the gods—Sir Pallador knew
that—and he had presented the Knight of Pallas with a coin
of the exact same design. The strange artifact had to matter.
That decided, he walked to the dead man and his face twisted

in disgust as he pulled his longsword from the body.

The weapon came free with difficulty. It was still usable, though the bulky assassin had bent the handle badly when he had fallen against the stall. The sword was of excellent craftsmanship and still held the relic Sir Pallador had long ago set into the handle. He would keep it and have it repaired once he finished his quest. He shoved it into its scabbard as best he could.

Sunrise found the Knight of Pallas newly bandaged, remounted, and riding toward the city of Hautre. He had slept well enough during the night, considering what had happened. His horses had slept even better. They made good time; they ate the leagues up like fodder.

When he neared the abandoned city, his heart sank like a stone as he saw the dark orb resting at the center of abandoned Hautre. He had made a horrid blunder; the darkness must have shifted course and wandered into the city. His eyes misted; what could have become of Lady Alcyone and Krisamee?

He brought his palfrey to a quick halt, then climbed down, loosened his weapons in their hangers, and climbed onto his warhorse. Red haze made his head swim. His mouth clenched, moisture welled into his eyes—but he willed it not to cloud his vision. He would do all that he had to do.

He rode through the city's crumbling gate and along its main avenue, straight toward the black mound. His heart pounded, despair made him reckless. Insects buzzed all around him. Wasps, mosquitoes, and biting flies, formed a cloud about his head and plagued him, rained agony upon his cheeks and his brow. He ignored them and kept on. It took all his skill to make his horse advance into the droning, stinging maelstrom.

The black cloud loomed high and large before him, something evil and monstrous. It contained enough evil to offend the gods themselves. He rounded a turn in the dead thoroughfare, faced it, and glared at the three-dimensional shadow. It gave off tiny specks of light where insects entered it or flitted from it. He stiffened himself in his saddle, set his lance, and charged. He would destroy whatever lay within if the gods allowed him to survive long enough.

His horse surged beneath him. His lance pierced the darkness with a flash, then he himself plunged in. Dazzling light surrounded him, along with a thunderous clap, as if he had been struck by lightning. He felt himself cuffed as if by a giant hand. The force of the blow hurled him from the saddle, tore the lance from his hands, and he landed in a twisted heap at the base of a stone wall. The last thing he remembered was the buzzing of the insects and their pale, human faces grinning as they closed about him.

Chapter Twenty-two:
Two Knights

SIR PALLADOR HURT all over; he felt stiff as a fish washed up on the beach, mashed, crushed, and rumpled up. Worse, the pain of his body was nothing against the wondrous agony which clutched his face, neck, throat, and hands in an implacable grip. He would have clenched his teeth against it except the least movement brought even greater pain.

He tried to open his eyes but his eyelids were so huge and puffy he could only see through the merest slits. It was daylight; he could tell that much, but he could make out nothing solid. Shapeless light pried its way between his swollen tissues.

Something touched his forehead, hurt, made him flinch. He gasped and tried to sit but he had no strength. The pressure went away, landed on his chest, then moved to other areas. He gasped again as the pain changed in a wondrous way; someone pressed a hand against him, he realized, a healing hand. The touch turned ice cold and some kind of chill, liquid power flowed into him. Coolness and calm spread through him. The pain did not go away but it did crouch down like a vicious dog beaten by its master. The roaring in his ears went away and the haze before his eyes cleared a little.

He heard a voice in the distance, as if from the other side of some great gulf. The voice prayed to Pallas. From instinct, he tried to unite his own prayers with the voice but the hand laid itself across his lips and stopped him. An old man, white hair cascading over wrinkles and perspiration, knelt before him. Then weariness overcame him and the darkness claimed him once more.

An instant might have passed or a day or seven days. When he awoke this time, his face still felt puffed and heavy; he felt as if he were wearing a thick mask and his hands felt deadened as if he wore gloves. But the pain had gone. He tried to open his eyes; he did manage to touch one eyelid, to spread the slit wide enough to let him observe the old man.

The fellow was a Knight of Pallas by his armor, though Sir Pallador had never met him. Night had come; the man knelt with his back turned and tended a low fire against the darkness. Sir Pallador let his arm slip back to his side and the old knight must have sensed the movement because he turned.

"Ah," he said. "I see the Maiden has applied her balms and all the worst has passed."

"I feel less pain than formerly," Sir Pallador said. "Are you the one who healed me through the Maiden's wondrous powers?"

"That is correct." The older man smiled; a look of infinite warmth and kindness lay across his features, outstanding features that they were. Really, he appeared too old to campaign anymore; he looked older than Sir Phebos. Yet there was a quickness to his movements, a robust nature which almost belied his weathered skin. "I rode into the city and observed you lying crumpled, covered up by wasps and stinging, blood-devouring insects. You would not have lived if you had lain there any longer. As it is, some days will pass before I look upon your normal features. Friend, your face is swollen to a new one, not as comely as it was before, I'm sure."

Sir Pallador accepted the warm cup of spiced wine the older man placed between his palms. It had a rich taste to it. "I tried to charge the shadowed mass which squats across..." he started, then dropped his cup. Warm liquid splashed across his legs. "My Krisamee. And Alcyone. I have deserted them; what horrors might they suffer where they lie beneath that evil cloud."

"Tut-tut," the older man said. With a lightning movement, he pushed Sir Pallador back, held the younger man until he quieted, then used a cloth to mop up the spilled tonic. "You shall not aid one person through the sacrifice of your own life. You could not pierce the cloud because its monstrous evil is a barricade against the goodness of your nature. Rest and heal and pray the gods return to me the key to finishing this blight forever."

Sir Pallador felt too weak and dizzy to rise, but that did not help his despair. "I left the women hiding in the city. Pallas, please forgive me, for I've surely murdered them."

"Do not rant so," the older man answered sharply. "I'm sure you did just what you thought was best. Whoever you believe you have to save, remember this: the Maiden will defend their souls from evil, even if their bodies perish—that is in the worst event—the gods forbid that it should come to pass." He caught his breath. "But as a knight, you know that Pallas does not ask for human sacrifice—and that is what you contemplate." He studied Sir Pallador, then turned to refill the cup the younger man had spilled.

Sir Pallador stared up at the night sky. "Your words have wisdom," he said as he received the new drink. "But it is difficult to hold back while the world revolves without you—while two innocents face death."

"True. But it revolves, and that's what matters." The older man held a broken longsword out to the younger. "This, as I believe, is yours. It lay beneath you, shattered by your fall. But I retrieved the bulk of it."

"Ah." Sir Pallador gazed at the longsword sadly; he had carried it ever since he had become a tercelet—as the knights called their youngest squires. But it was broken beyond repair, now, its blade shattered by his fall and the handle, bent when he had killed the assassin in the inn, broken and mostly gone. He lifted the remnant, hoping to see somewhere imbedded the artifact he had concealed there long ago. But it was also gone; apparently, his rescuer had not noticed it among the pieces. "I thank you, Sir. Why is it that I do not know you? I know all of Pallas' Knights by face or reputation."

The older man smiled. "I am not a Knight of Pallas; that is why you do not recognize me." He extended his arm and the firelight glinted off his chain mail. "This armor, I'm afraid, was but a gift. I've never claimed to do it justice."

"You restored me from my injuries."

"No. The Holy Maiden did that wondrous deed. My name is Palamon and I am King of fair Carea."

Again, Sir Pallador sat up. "Your Grace, I've often heard of you. Men speak your name with reverence."

"I have beguiled them, then," Palamon said. "I'm just a man. And you need not refer to me by any royal title, for we're not within my palace or my hall. But you—what is your name?"

"Sir Pallador I'm called."

"A lovely name," Palamon said, and to Sir Pallador's surprise, the tall monarch reached out and caressed the young knight's swollen cheek. "But you must rest the night. When morning comes, you'll be more fit to rise. Then we will do whatever must be done. E'en now, I'm sure, my legions march to aid us. Therefore, rest."

Sir Pallador looked toward Hautre, a jumbled mass beneath the moonlit sky. He saw no clouds, few stars, only a smiling moon—and the lurking darkness barely visible beneath it. "So we must wait," he said. "Ah, curse my weakness. I should rally forth and make a war upon this darkness, for I fear it ripens and will soon attack."

"By my troth, I'm sure you're right. This is a monstrous evil—I am sure it is the menace of which the Oracle gave warning. I held an artifact which might have aided us against it. Only once I have recovered it, may we oppose the threat."

Sir Pallador listened and stared at the man. "The object—was it stolen?"

"Yes." The older man stared at the younger.

"The man who took it. Would you recognize him?"

"It was a company of priests, in fact."

"Ah," Sir Pallador said. His mind wound back to the brass case and the man who had attacked him at the inn. "I slew a man two nights gone by—I wonder if he thought that I was you."

"Say on."

"A stocky man he was, of fifty years or thereabouts. He crept upon me silently and swung a heavy blade against my unsuspecting neck. If I had not been warned, I should have been beheaded with no more *adieu* than any farmer's New Year's goose." He reached up to touch the bandage where the sword had sliced his skin. It was gone, replaced by new cloth, so he knew the older man had changed it during the day. "I am sure your eyes have shown the proof of this."

"And did this silent killer have a name?"

"I do not know; he never lived to tell, for I struck back. But he possessed a case, a box of brass so quaint that I retained it out of all the goods he carried."

"Quick," the older man cried. "Where is this artifact?"

"Inside my pack."

Palamon leaped to the horses and to the packs which lay on the ground. The tall monarch rummaged for a moment until Sir Pallador rose stiffly and went to his side. "Not that one," the younger man said, "but the other." Palamon opened the leather case the young knight had indicated and withdrew the object.

"Here it is." Palamon lifted the artifact with the same air of any other man grasping a crown. "Are you aware of what a gift I hold? Of course not, for its name is not notorious; it does not lurk in fable or in minstrel's courtly song. The *Tome of Winds* it's called, this brazen case, though what makes it a tome or how it deals with winds has not yet been revealed to me. You've done a service you cannot yet comprehend." He lowered the object and his gaze fell on the younger man's face. "Oh, I am proud of you." He threw his arms about Sir Pallador, encased him in a fierce embrace, which made the younger man wince while it perplexed him.

Then the older man stepped back. "I quite forget myself in my relief and joy," he said. "But once we learn to use this sacred tool, yon menace shall collapse before us." He glanced over his shoulder at the dark city and the unworldly blight which lay upon it.

"But wait," Sir Pallador said. "I only kept the case because it matched another curiosity—a coin of gold which I was given by . . ." he hesitated. The thunder of hoofbeats approached and made him lower his voice. "Perhaps it is too late; perhaps the force which we oppose has gained the strength to move. No, it comes not from Hautre." He clamped a lid on his tongue; he and the older man scurried toward the campfire and scattered it.

"We must away," Palamon said.

"They might be allies," Sir Pallador replied. "Sir Phebos swore to send gray Pallas' Knights at lathered pace behind me."

"I know Sir Phebos," Palamon said. "He will keep his word. But that's a different sound from heavy horse; I've heard such music many times."

A horse whinnied. The two knights snatched what goods they could and scrambled into the brush just as a hundred riders crashed out of the darkness and trampled their camp into oblivion. Horses stamped and whinnied in the dark air and the two men heard the murmur of voices. "This is the light we saw, but they have fled."

"But wait," another voice said. "They've tethered up their horses here and left some harness. Goodly animals; they both are knights, from the appearance of it."

"They're not our allies; they must be our foes," the first man said with a voice of command. "Fan out and apprehend them. Torches up; a little light will soon reveal their faces."

Palamon and Sir Pallador watched from the brush while riders put flint and steel to torches. The brands flared up and revealed stern faces, cavalry uniforms, gleaming weapons. A fierce enemy—Buerdic cavalrymen, light horse in the service of Lothar the Pale.

Chapter Twenty-three:
Riders in the Night

PALAMON AND SIR Pallador slithered through the grass like two armored snakes. "Curses," Palamon whispered as the two of them hooked themselves along on their elbows. "They are taking all our horses."

"Who would have dreamed they'd ride this distance from Buerdaunt, their base?"

"I dreamed it," Palamon replied. "Diomedes, when he still had life, informed me that King Lothar would invade the Greenlands, hurl his knights against me and my allies in a final war. I'm sure this is his vanguard."

"The Buerdic king moves at a horrid time," Sir Pallador whispered. "Dark evil threatens all the world; why must King Lothar strike just now?"

"No better time for him," Palamon said. "As always, evil spawns more evil."

"Ah." No army had marched on the Greenlands since Sir Pallador had been a babe. Though brigands now plagued those lands, that was a minor nuisance compared to the scourging blasts of war.

But there was no more time to discuss the matter; the cavalry spread through the grove, torches held high. "They cannot have gone far," an officer cried. "The fire still smokes, the grasses still lie flat about it. Seek them out, there must be two at least."

"Let's fire the thicket," another cried. "That makes a bonny torch and we will see them as they flee." He jockeyed his horse close to a patch of dead brush, then held flame beneath the driest twigs. Flames raced toward the main branches and burning brands dropped into the grass.

Sir Pallador lifted his head far enough to see the flames spread. "We must flee now," he said.

"Nay," Palamon replied. "You've not the strength to run from mounted men. Crawl toward the center of this grove; I'll help you if you falter."

"I will have no mortal aid me, for I am a Knight. I have no fear of capture. You're a king; it means your death to have the Buerdic army capture you. You must escape while I create diversion."

Palamon almost laughed. "We cannot argue thus," he said at last. "Believe me, Sir, an injury to you would wound me quite as deeply as my capture. Let us slide into the longest brush and trust in Pallas to conceal us."

More riders torched branches; flames spread in a crackling circle toward the two. A pair of dead trees caught fire, flames and heat shot throughout the grove. Wherever Palamon and Sir Pallador sought to hide, the fire lit up the grasses and they had to retreat all over. Green vegetation wilted before the flames, then lit up like oil torches and whistled and crackled as heat tortured the tissues, crumpled and wrinkled them, and set them all ablaze.

Sir Pallador's forehead, swollen as it was, grew even more puffed and sore from the glow of the conflagration. Weakness pressed him down but he kept with his older companion, scurried through tall reeds and down an embankment until he felt himself slide over mud and sand, then into cold water. "Come," he heard Palamon's voice. "Into the undercut; there's safety there."

He gasped for breath and his head rolled to one side as the two of them waded through waist-deep water, then pressed beneath an overhanging bank. The fire swept onward; Sir Pallador opened his eyes now and then to see a galloping horse and rider silhouetted against the flames. The glow danced off the dark stream's waters and made his temples throb. He nearly lost hope. But when he thought he could stand no longer, he felt the older man curl long arms about his chest and hold him against the muddy bank for support.

The fires swept past, the night grew darker, until all that was left was the crack and pop of smoldering undergrowth and the stink of scorched mud. The two men watched from their hiding place. Sir Pallador could hear the riders' voices. "They must be phantoms," one man said. "They have slipped away as if they'd never been."

"Behold this helmet," another shouted. "It came from a Knight of Pallas—nothing we would want to trifle with in any case."

"But one man's bag contained a memo from the high Carean court—the uniform of Pallas does not make a man a Knight. Send to the king: he'll want to know his enemy wears colors of the Knights of Pallas. What a low deception. Ah, I wish we had those two; I gnash my teeth that they've slipped past us."

As he spoke, the buzz of flying insects wafted through the smoky air. Sir Pallador heard cursing above him. "By all the gods, where do these wasps and biters come from? Are they spawned by smoke alone?"

Horses stamped, men cursed. "Let us ride on," the officer said. "The villains surely have expired from heat and smoke. We have no business with these nasty bugs."

The horses galloped away and the buzzing grew more fierce. Sir Pallador let out a hiss as a wasp droned up, lit on his swollen forehead, and stabbed him with its venom before he could brush it off. From Palamon's movements, he knew the older man suffered the same. The two of them ducked beneath the surface, but more attacks waited for them when they came back up for air. Palamon left Sir Pallador standing for a moment. When the older man returned, he shoved a couple of muddy reeds into the younger man's hands. "We must stay under. We will breathe through these."

It was the oldest ploy on record; Sir Pallador had heard about it in song and fairy tale from the time he had been a boy. But it saved them; the insects could not penetrate the water and an occasional outward breath kept them from crawling down the insides of the hollow reeds. Sir Pallador remembered their faces, their greedy little human faces. Doubtless, those faces scowled with frustration now.

The reeds provided a miserable way to survive, hiding in water and muck like some prehistoric fish. But at least it would let them stay alive till day rolled round. Sir Pallador closed his mind and waited for the moment to pass.

All at once, an eerie shadow, darker than darkness, fell over the water. The moon had silvered the stream's surface; now the silver turned black beneath shadow and a layer of tiny bodies. The insect horde fell and lay thick on the water, kicked, covered the stream like a blanket. Sir Pallador kept well below the surface and touched Palamon to make sure he did the same.

To his amazement, the young knight heard a voice which sounded through mud and water, hollowly but clearly like a man shouting from the other end of the cave. "Come. Come. Come along my two pets. How you do grow and prosper, as I do myself. Oh! I sense a man's near presence; he's still near, by all the forces which did breed me. Search. And bring him here, to let me have my full revenge; then rip his flesh to fragments, and devour him, make of him a meal." Unearthly laughter followed, then an explosion which caused the stream-bank to shake and tremble. "He must be near, for I sniff out the stink of his self-righteous fervor. Or am I so hot for sight of his red blood that I find him in every sound? No matter. I see someone's passed and lit a blaze."

More laughter followed, insane laughter which chilled Sir Pallador. What thing could make itself heard through earth and water? Did the evil being seek Sir Pallador himself? Had he so offended it? "Feeble men and all their small engagements," the voice cried all at once. "They've burned down a grove— the grove where I had planned my attack on yonder city. Yes, my pets, I was one time a member of that puny race, and thought myself great if I but managed then to level that same city. Ha-ha. What a manchild I was; how I've grown in my capacity. Now I shall sing when I've made black the world as have these riders blackened this small grove. Ah, they excite me; they do fill me with a lust for my true destiny. Come, now we have rested and have battoned here enough; we will begin our business. Beware, King Palamon. So hide wherever you may choose or come and charge me. 'Tis no matter; for your finish is but part of my great work." ·

More explosions followed until the streambank crumbled and mud cascaded over the two men. They did not dare lift themselves from the filth. After what seemed like forever, the shadow lifted, the insects crawled from the water, dried their wings, and flew away. The two men waited until dawn turned the waters bright, then they emerged.

It was all Sir Pallador could do to crawl onto the bank, even with Palamon's aid. With all his soul, the young knight wanted to make his way to the ruined city, to search the empty stones for Krisamee and Lady Alcyone, but there was no strength left in him. He crawled to a patch of green grass which still survived in the blasted grove, and there he collapsed.

"That's well, young Knight," he heard Palamon say.

"Your body has withstood a savage battering and will not serve you till you've rested it." The man's broad hand came to rest on Sir Pallador's forehead. "When you've restored yourself, then we shall rid the world of this abomination, for I understand it now. We've work ahead of us, so rest." Kind slumber threw its mantle over the young knight; he slept and dreamed of Krisamee.

When he awoke, he felt like a new man. The weakness had left him, the swelling had gone down on his face and hands, at least enough to let him open his eyes and flex his fingers. The sun lay on a western mountain and Sir Phebos himself spoke to Palamon in front of fifty Knights of Pallas. The Grand Master and the Carean king turned toward Sir Pallador as he stood and approached them.

"You know the way of things," Sir Phebos was saying. "The Knights are scattered all across the land; assembly poses difficulties. So this many have I brought, and four or five more times this number will arrive within the day."

"Perhaps," Palamon said gravely. "But five times five that number may not serve against Ursid, should we encounter him."

"And you are sure it's he?"

"I'm positive, though how he squeezed from evil Kruptos—that I cannot say."

"But here's Sir Pallador," Sir Phebos said. "Come hither, Sir, and show the wounds you've gained in Pallas' service."

"Not many wounds, I'm glad to say. But much embarrassment." Sir Pallador gazed at the two men. "Carea's king restored me or I would have breathed my last—defeated by my own poor judgment."

"He tried to charge Ursid," the tall monarch said. "That shows the courage of a mighty knight, and what man could have known? All people thought . . ." he stopped, then clapped Sir Pallador on the back. "Your looks show you've improved."

"I hardly could have felt the worse, so it was easy to improve," Sir Pallador said with a self-conscious smile. "But what of this Ursid of which you speak; is he the master of the insect hordes? Does he control the darkness?" Sir Pallador's eyes swept over the damage Prince Ursid's specter had wrought during the night. Craters and scorched places lay all about, trees had been uprooted, torn to pieces, and cast aside like jackstraws. The damage from the cavalry's fire was nothing beside the awful path of destruction which led from ruined

Hautre to the burned grove and on into the hills to the east. It was as if a devil cyclone—or a half dozen of them—had ripped the gods' green hills asunder. "By Pallas and the others," he breathed. "So this is what we heard last night."

"It is," Palamon said. "And it is what we have to stand against. The *Tome of Winds* has got to be the key, if we can find the key to it. But we must calm your fears about the women whom you left within the town."

"Full gladly would I do that," Sir Pallador shouted. "My soul chides me for ever leaving them." There was another reason, too, and he could see in Sir Phebos' face that the Grand Master suspected it. Krisamee, his forbidden prize. Did she live? Had Ursid destroyed her and her mother? Perhaps his love for that young woman made him unfit to be a Knight of Pallas, to bear the colors of the Maiden. But all was one for that; he had to learn his love's fate.

Palamon gazed at the Grand Master. "If you will lend two steeds, we'll ride there and investigate."

"Bring up two palfreys," Sir Phebos commanded, and a couple of tercelets leaped to obey. "We'll ride with you, good King. United faith from two and fifty knights may turn away the evil when we find it."

"Let us hope," Sir Pallador replied as young men brought the horses. Perhaps his Grand Master would see him throw his arms about Krisamee, would expel him from his order then and there, before the Carean king. It did not matter. Let the women be saved or let them have decent burials—then he would worry about consequences.

He swung himself into the saddle and heard a knight cry out. "What column travels yonder?" Dust rose from approaching riders—perhaps the same company which had burned the grove. Buerdic light horse halted at a distance and two men galloped toward the Knights of Pallas.

"What ho," the lead rider shouted as he brought his horse to a sliding halt in front of Sir Phebos. He was a hard-faced fellow; Sir Pallador recognized his voice from the night before. "What business have you Knights of Pallas in this land?"

Sir Phebos smiled. "That question might be asked of you, young man; your uniform tells who you are. We Knights of Pallas claim the passage of all lands as minions of the Maiden. But by what right does the Buerdic army pass across this land, made neutral in a treaty signed by your own king?"

The officer scowled. "You call yourself a priest and neutral, yet Carea's king sits next to you and wears your order's armor and its colors. Yield him up to us and we'll depart.''

Sir Phebos gazed at Palamon, then back at the officer. "He is a friend of mine and I shall never yield him. Were your king with me, I'd say the same.''

The officer lashed his reins against his thigh in his anger. Both Buerdic riders wheeled their horses. "Though you may claim neutrality, I see you are an ally to Carea. Therefore, you must understand your guest and you are under our attack.'' He set spurs to his horse and the two men sped back to their company.

"So,'' Sir Phebos said. "We have a fight upon our hands.''

"Nay, nay,'' Palamon replied. "They asked for me and they shall have me. I cannot ask Knights of Pallas to take risks for my sake.''

"Our bodies have no value,'' Sir Pallador replied. "We will fight in your behalf because you are alone, while they are many. In the bargain, you have saved my life; you've earned protection from the Knights.'' He gazed into the older man's eyes. "And Pallas, I will swear, looks on you fondly.''

"That is but the husk of the real truth,'' Sir Phebos muttered to himself. Then he brought his fifty lances into battle formation. The ground shook as the Buerdic cavalry set spurs to their horses. Sir Phebos turned toward Palamon. "Dear friend, our bodies grow too ancient for such sport. You're forced to ride once more with Pallas' Knights.''

Palamon glanced at the Grand Master and Sir Pallador saw a swarm of emotions play across his face. " 'Tis purest honor—I still feel as if I never left. But had I not, I never would have met this noble knight.'' He extended his right hand toward Sir Pallador and the younger man acknowledged the gesture.

"So. I find you were a Knight of Pallas,'' Sir Pallador said. "There's more to you than I may understand, but may the gods stand with us all.''

Cavalry thundered toward them, outnumbered them by two to one. The two forces met, Buerdic riders hacked at knights, knights slashed back, swung mighty maces, or circled out of the mêlée to couch their lances and charge once more. Sir Pallador slew the first cavalryman he came against, then sent a second man packing. For all that success, he missed his broken longsword. From the corner of one eye, he marveled at the Carean king's prowess; the man wielded a two-handed sword as if he would scythe his way through the enemy by himself.

It turned into even combat, a crack company of cavalrymen versus a few dozen of the finest knights on the shores of the Thlassa Mey. But many of the knights were aging men; Sir Phebos and the Carean king among them. For all their prowess, they tired and the Buerdic force began to push them back across the shattered ground and into the trees beyond.

Then a trumpet sounded from a nearby hill. All along the hill's crest, a line of gray-clad warriors prepared for battle. The bulk of the Knights of Pallas, the cream of the world's knighthood, advanced down the hillside, banners dancing, trumpeteers sounding bronze notes.

Buerdaunt's cavalry recoiled; Buerdic horsemen turned toward the south. Knights thundered after them, squires cheered, and the mass formed a striking sight as they tore across the countryside. The pursuit led both forces up through groves of trees, through a small dale, and over the brink of a long valley. The Knights of Pallas pursued the cavalry as a great hound would leap after a stag.

They topped a hill and the knights had to rein in their horses. Ahead of them, a vast army drew itself into battle formation. Line on line of dark infantry formed into companies between rows of archers, massive cadres of light cavalry and batallions of mounted knights. Off in the distance the great army's baggage train raised clouds of dust as it brought tents and victuals up from the rear.

The Knights of Pallas who had led the pursuit, Sir Pallador among them, pulled their mounts to a halt and allowed the fleeing riders to pass on down the hillside. Other knights stopped to stare at the force arrayed against them. "The mighty Buerdic army," Palamon said softly. "It's immense. How many secret treaties has King Lothar signed to gather such a force?"

"I cannot guess," Sir Phebos said. "But many."

They stared at the mass for a long time, picking out the Buerdic king astride a horse in the midst of his nobles. Sir Pallador had never seen the man but another knight pointed him out. The young knight marveled at how small a fellow Lothar was. Even at that distance and astride a horse, the Buerdic king plainly did not share the physical stature of the knights around him.

"But he is great in intellect," Palamon said grimly. "As

powerful in schemes and politics and personality as ever I have been in battle. I must ride to him. I'll lay this business all to rest.'' He gazed at Sir Phebos. ''Would you stand by me while I confer with him?''

''You cannot do it,'' the Grand Master said. ''For the high regard I bear you, I must tell you nay. I counsel you to stay here with your friends, who will defend you from some Buerdic subterfuge. I'll do the talking, for your army's not arrived. Pale Lothar shan't respect you and would snatch you up the instant you appeared.''

''Ah,'' Palamon said. ''Your counsel frets me more than any sting a wasp could carry. Still, I fear your words are true.'' He scowled and pounded his fist into his palm. ''By all the gods,'' he shouted. ''Why must men play such games? He knows as well as I do the result will be a river of bright blood a running down some hillside, guttering the earth with griefs and miseries. But go. Bring back what word he gives to you.''

''I, too, shall ride and listen,'' Sir Pallador said.

The tall monarch's gaze fell on him and Sir Pallador saw the reluctance which lay in the older man's eye. ''Young Knight,'' he finally said. ''Go if you must, for dealing with the Buerdic king's an education. Keep yourself prepared for quick escape, for, as your Master tells you, Lothar's devious. A young man's life is no more in his schemes than is the life of any bug.''

Sir Pallador accepted that advice gravely. He would keep his eyes on Sir Phebos and the Buerdic king both, would not allow himself to be surprised. He nudged his horse's flanks; he and Sir Phebos rode down to hold council with Lothar the Pale.

Chapter Twenty-four: Lothar's Legions

THREE BUERDIC KNIGHTS rode out to meet Sir Phebos and Sir Pallador, relieved them of their weapons, then escorted them to the king. Sir Pallador found the Buerdic monarch to be less tiny face-to-face than he seemed from afar. He was small, though, half a cubit shorter than Sir Pallador himself. Though clad in burnished armor and seated astride a proud courser, Lothar looked out of place among men of action, not because his nature seemed less violent, but because he seemed made of different stuff, of a more thoughtful chemical. He surveyed the hills about, eyed his guests with quick eyes. They were pale, pink orbs which seemed to gaze at a man and into him, and through him, all at once. The tiny monarch's aides kept a distance from him, looked on him with apprehension as if he were a living bolt of lightning which might strike at any moment.

"Sir Phebos," he said. "I have heard of you. Your reputation as a Knight of Pallas comes before you into my encampment. I had wished to meet you but I'd hoped for some occasion better than the present."

"I, too, regret that friendly conversation's not my aim," Sir Phebos said. "But you have brought an army into lands which are not yours. Aggression has prevented friendships ere this time, and shall not nurture ours, I fear."

"This army is a tool of policy, no more. You have no reason to oppose me, for I have no wish to fight with you."

"That well may be," Sir Phebos replied. "But we must not allow you to breed war. The gods themselves shall weep when all your troops march through these peaceful Greenlands. My stout knights do not seek battle with your puissant force, but neither shall we budge from our position. If you seek a conflict, Sir, you'll have to march through us.''

The first tracings of a scowl crossed Lothar the Pale's features. He crooked his finger at one of his nobles and the two of them exchanged whispers. Then the monarch turned back to the Grand Master. ''This army came together for a purpose,'' the Buerdic king said. ''I do not build up arms for mere enjoyment, or for men to look upon and marvel at. This army came together to make war upon the enemies of my small nation.''

''A mighty levy for those last two words,'' Sir Phebos observed.

''Perhaps,'' Lothar said. ''But then again, perhaps the gods provide large armies to those lands which cannot share the table with their wealthier relations.'' He slapped the pommel of his sword. ''But enough of this. Carea's king is there behind you; I know of your past, and that the two of you are long-time friends. That is regrettable. You cannot be an ally to my enemy and claim neutrality to me.'' He gestured toward the force which gathered behind him. ''These legions will march north into the Greenlands. If you dare remain in your position, rest assured we shall not leave an enemy behind us.''

''That is moot. You'll never be allowed past our position in the first case.''

''We outnumber you by twenty-five to one.''

''That does not matter,'' Sir Phebos said. ''For the Maiden stands with us.''

''We'll put that to a deadly test,'' Lothar said, and the glimmer in his eyes showed his anger. He fixed his eyes on the two Knights of Pallas and did not speak again until he had calmed himself. ''But you are dirty from your recent strife; the sweat clings to your brows. We're not at war, not yet, at any rate. Dismount and drink a cup of wine with me.'' He gestured and attendants ran forward with a table, campaign chairs, and a tray of libations.

''No, thank you,'' Sir Phebos replied. ''We'll be at blows and some men here shall lie dead in the dust by nightfall. That is not a drinking matter.'' The Grand Master of the Knights of Pallas turned his horse. ''Think well on what you do, pale Lothar, for the gods observe our actions. Give them no inducement to avenge themselves on you.'' Then he and Sir

Pallador put spurs to their mounts and rode back up the hill.

Sir Pallador glanced over his shoulder once or twice to assure himself that no riders pursued them. None did, a little to his surprise, and the two knights quickly reached their own lines. "Prepare yourselves to yield your lives in combat for the Holy Maiden," Sir Phebos said. "Yonder force will come against us ere the sun retreats into the west."

Sir Pallador eyed the company; each man took on a different look. For his own part, the threat did not matter; death was no grimmer a prospect than life without the maid Krisamee—or life as a disgraced Knight if Krisamee still lived and he failed to resist her charms. He would not allow himself to be captured by the Buerdic army, whatever might happen.

"We need not fight them blindly," Palamon said. "A tactical retreat would be the best. If we can hold them till support arrives, though we might lose a league or even ten in distance, we will have prevailed."

"Perhaps," Sir Phebos replied. "It is a daunting prospect."

"No more than the thought of standing fast," Palamon replied with a grim smile. "But be that as it may, I place myself at your command. What orders you may give, I'll follow."

Lothar was far too clever a general to exhaust the whole of his vast army against so small a force as the Knights of Pallas. While the bulk of his legions continued to set up a well-organized campsite, a mass of infantry formed up and advanced up the hill toward the defenders. Sir Phebos noted the advance and discussed it with Palamon and his other leaders, but the knights made no move. The infantry was not powerful enough to defeat knights on horseback; the move was plainly a ruse, some kind of bait.

The Buerdic king's plan became clear when a company of cavalry burst out of a grove to their left. They formed to meet the new threat, set their lances, and swung toward the new menace when another mounted cadre, this time of armored knights, topped the crest behind them. If they had accepted the bait and charged the infantry, the two companies would have crushed them like huge jaws.

Even as it was, they were in grave danger, with no choice but to fight their way out. Sir Phebos lifted a mailed fist and hundreds of voices shouted together: "We serve the Holy Maiden; yield or die." As one, the gray clad company thundered toward the cavalry.

They piled into the larger force like a hammer striking glass: they knocked cavalrymen from horses while shouts tore the air. The more compact body tore through the greater number and back across the ridge. The cavalry quickly regrouped and pursued the knights because of their lighter, faster horses. But having suffered the loss of nearly a hundred riders in the first clash, they did not pursue closely.

Buerdic knights thundered after the conflict but their war-horses were not as fleet as those bred at the Fastness of Pallas. The affair turned into a running battle which stretched across the hills, back toward the north, until deserted Hautre came into view. The Knights of Pallas fought with such courage and such precision that the cavalry became weary of the battle and drew away. A few Knights had fallen, a few wounded warriors straggled away. But dead Buerdic horses and riders showed the progress of the strife.

The two Buerdic companies stretched out across the hills in a ragged line. All at a moment, Sir Phebos signalled and the Knights swung about as one man and tore at the Buerdic line. Though fewer in number, the Knights kept a tighter formation. They ripped into the Buerdic warriors like a mailed hand ripping its way through a rag, then broke back toward the northwest.

For all the brilliant maneuver, for all the casualties they inflicted, each Knight of Pallas knew this was a battle they could never win. Sir Pallador's arm ached from the deadly work he had done with longsword and mace, and sweat trickled inside his armor and made his quilted gambeson sticky and itchy. His warhorse had galloped for leagues; froth flew from its mouth with every stride.

If he suffered, the older knights teetered at the brink of collapse. Sir Phebos swayed in his saddle with fatigue and blood speckled his armor. The Grand Master would not last as long as Sir Pallador's horse, by the look of him. Other Knights looked even worse. Palamon's work with his two-handed sword had been awful to behold; when slaying was needed, he slew with a fury Sir Pallador had never witnessed. But he lifted his visor and Sir Pallador stared at a wrinkled face masked by sweat, gray with fatigue. The running fray could not go on much longer.

Having underestimated his enemy at first, Lothar now showed his determination to squash the Knights of Pallas. A dark field of men advanced over the afternoon plain and another company of knights issued forth, far stronger than the first.

"Alas," Sir Phebos said between breaths. "Yon horde shall make its way across this land without respect to us. We can harass and lead a merry chase to small contingents, but the body marches on with scarce a hitch."

"You have not men to fight the endless legions of Buerdaunt," Palamon said. "You must withdraw before the pincer closes." The Carean king reached out a mailed hand toward the Grand Master of the Knights of Pallas. "Sir Phebos, I must thank you all the same, for you have shown your brilliance in the fray. These Knights, whom I would call my brothers if I could, have dueled a noble duel. But now I urge you to withdraw."

Sir Pallador frowned in frustration. The weary company turned west, into a defile which could be easily defended. There they met their support company and changed horses.

Though every man of the battered band was weary as death, they could not pause for long. They kept on through the waning hours of the afternoon, moved southwest along a smaller valley until they had left the towers of Hautre behind and neared the headwaters of the Courbee.

As they dropped down toward the river, every man's heart lifted. A huge army lay camped along the gently flowing waters, an army nearly as large as the Buerdic force. Tents and pavilions stretched along the river's edge, makeshift corrals bulged with fresh horses, endless campfires sprang up as the sun set. The waning rays bounded off fields of men and waving banners: Tranje, Oron, the Montaigne peninsula, all lands allied with Carea stood represented. Carean colors flew before many a campfire, many a pavilion.

"By Pallas, there is purpose in all this," the tall monarch breathed. "How they found us or we found them, no man can say. But I rejoice to see it."

"I, too," Sir Phebos said. "Here lies one camp where we may rest."

"Yes, camp with us this night," Palamon said. "A battle waits upon the morrow. Let us nurse your weary men until that time, at least."

Sir Phebos could smile now that the Carean camp removed the chance of instant annihilation by Buerdic knights. But he also shook his head. "You know, I stretched our canons to the utmost to impede pale Lothar. Now your army also crosses this poor, neutral land. No longer may I take your part. But know, old friend, I realize where the aggression lies; my heart will be with you.''

"Then rest with us," Palamon said. "Enjoy our hospitality.''

"I thank you, mighty King," Sir Phebos said. "And I would look once more upon your queen, for she and I had grand adventure many years gone by. But it is not to be. King Lothar is a cunning man and you must fear attack at any moment. I cannot allow my Knights to take a part in any struggle 'twixt your armies. We will make our camp a little way from yours. The best to you when battle comes.''

"Sir Phebos, you are wise; you've earned your mantle.''

"Thank you," the Grand Master said.

"But I will ask one favor: this young knight, Sir Pallador. I'd have him stay awhile with us.''

Sir Phebos gazed at the Carean king and worlds passed between them. "You know, then. My old friend, the ages pass and we see one another only at a space of years. That's far too rarely.''

"Then we will amend it—when the threat is past.''

"It's to be hoped," Sir Phebos said. "Sir Pallador, will you accompany the noble king unto his own pavilion?''

Sir Pallador felt baffled. Why should such a duty fall to him instead of one of his superiors? But his place was not to question orders. "I will, Sir. At what time should I return unto your camp?''

"Upon the pleasure of the king." Sir Phebos smiled wearily and gestured toward Palamon. "It may be a day, two days, or longer.''

Sir Pallador did not object. The Carean king intrigued him. "As you say," he replied. Then the two of them took their leave of the Knights of Pallas and rode into the Carean camp.

The army's pickets stared as their king passed them, begrimed and bloodied from battle and with a Knight of Pallas beside him. First one sentry, then another, threw up his arms in salute and passed word that the tall monarch had returned and that the Buerdic army lay just over the horizon.

Palamon's manner over the last three days had been anything but royal. Now Sir Pallador wondered at the popularity of this king among his own men. Private soldiers and nobles flocked around him, cheered him to the skies, grappled for a touch of his filthy hand. Then the Knight of Pallas saw a wondrous couple ride through the tumult to shouts of "Make way, make way."

The man was tall and thin, lean of face, lightest blond of hair, and clean shaven. Beside him rode a woman who looked even more striking, if only for the fact that she was a female in a camp of men. She appeared about forty years of age, with amber hair which streamed back over her shoulders. Both wore armor which shone like beaten gold. Sir Pallador could not settle in his mind whether the display was dazzling or vulgar, but he could not take his eyes off the two of them.

"Ah," Palamon said. "My noble Count Arcite and Berengeria." Light filled his eyes. "You have done well, to raise an army on such meager notice." He leaned from his warhorse and embraced the woman; their armor clacked together. "My sister, though it troubles me to see you risk yourself, I must admit you look the warrior—Hippolyta would glow with pride to see you cross the battlefield."

Berengeria beamed. Then she eyed Sir Pallador long and hard. "And who is this young Knight of Pallas? I beheld another knight, one time, who bore himself with just such grace and character." She turned to her brother, then glanced back at the young knight. "What's his name?"

"Sir Pallador's his name," Palamon replied.

"I see," she said. Sir Pallador could not keep from noticing the disappointment which flicked across her face. "Well. We must all have names."

"But I would see the queen," Palamon said. "Where does she hide herself?"

Berengeria smiled up at her brother. "She waits for you with aching arms." She shouted at the mob which had pressed in upon them. "Move back, all; the king would pass."

"Move back," Arcite shouted. "Move back, all."

Soldiers pressed ahead of the four of them and managed to pry a passage through the cheering mass. They passed into a wooden citadel and arrived before a pavilion of multicolored cloth, green and gold stripes which faded to black and white in the vanishing light.

The crowd was sparse here; few knights and soldiers could enter this part of the camp. Trumpets called ahead of them as they dismounted, drums rolled, and they entered. Used to the austerity of the Knights of Pallas, Sir Pallador looked about with interest tinged by distaste.

"I know the look, young Knight," Palamon said to him as

they moved along. "But you must know, these gaudy trappings aren't for me. They're for the crown I bear and that is all. Whoever wears that ornament must suffer them." He pursed his lips. "Not all men understand that; from your eyes, I see that you are one who does not. Yet I hope that someday you will see the meaning of my words."

Sir Pallador did not attempt to fathom that remark. They entered a small, cloth-walled throne room, built to be transported from place to place. It had the traditional look the young knight would have expected of such a place: severe-looking walls of canvas, rather than the more opulent cloths of other tents and chambers. Massed nobles stood ready to pay homage to their monarch and twin thrones stood on a low wooden platform.

From the smaller seat, an elegant old woman rose and approached Palamon. She was the tall monarch's age, perhaps, but her hair remained a salt-and-pepper gray while his had turned pure white. She reached out to him and tears welled at the corners of her eyes.

"At last you've come, my love," she said. "I finally see that you are hale and well, and that you be not harmed, though you have done a deadly bit of work to judge by blood and dirt which coat you."

Palamon bent to kiss the woman's forehead and smiled. Sir Pallador was surprised to see the tears also start into the tall monarch's eyes. "Ah, woman, if you swear me love in spite of stench and filth, 'tis all I'm fit to ask. I'll bathe in moments, but we first must speak of vital matters. First, though all the world may watch, I've traveled 'round the Thlassa Mey, endured long hardship—now I seek reward for all my labors. And it lies upon your lips."

Berengeria smiled and Carea's mightiest warriors stood in silence while Palamon placed his mouth on the queen's. When the kiss ended, she smiled and said, "My husband, I would have you meet the messenger who brought us to this place." A young man walked toward them, a comely youth with dark, impressive features.

"Reale," Palamon said happily. "You have done well— none could have carried such a message any better. You've a reward to claim and I will yield it on this instant. Someone fetch me up a sword."

Arcite drew a cunningly inlaid longsword and handed it to Palamon. The tall monarch accepted the weapon and bade the young man in front of him to kneel. Before Carea's highest blood, Palamon made the young man a knight, awarded him the title along with all the duties it entailed. Then the tall monarch handed the sword back to Arcite. "One final bit of business have we here," he said. "Before the Buerdic hordes embroil us in new battles, I must tend to matters which have too long lain unfinished."

He reached into a pouch he wore at his belt, fumbled for a moment, then turned to his queen. To Sir Pallador's surprise, the tall monarch's hand shook, his lip trembled, and his eyes watered. He looked as if he had suddenly taken a severe dose of ague. "My Lady, I would introduce you to your son, your missing Berethane!"

Chapter Twenty-five: Berethane

SILENCE SEIZED THE pavilion. Every eye turned to Palamon, most of all those of Sir Pallador and the queen. The tall monarch's hands wavered the least bit as he held before the woman's eyes a plain golden band. "This ring announces all," he said. "I found it spilled upon the ground beside him, broken from the handle of his sword."

He turned toward a stunned Sir Pallador. "Young Knight, my son—our son, forgive me my transgression. I picked up the ring and kept it, knowing it was yours."

Sir Pallador felt the weight of every eye in the chamber. Someone murmured something and that finally spurred him to speak. "Indeed, it is my ring—or so I thought. My parents left it to me when they died. They said it was my legacy."

"And so it is," Palamon said. "It proves your royal blood because I tied it 'round your neck when you lay dying twenty years ago. The Maiden spoke then, and you vanished. You have been apprenticed to her ever since, although you did not know it till you joined the Knights of Pallas. But I'm sure Sir Phebos knew."

"I see," Sir Pallador said. Doors opened in his mind, portals which had been shut so long he hardly dreamed they existed. "My parents often said I was their gift, their present from the gods. I never dreamt their meaning, though I'd see within the crannies of my mind, strange faces I could never recognize." His voice faltered. "Ardan and Alanna—now I find they never were my parents. . . ."

"Yes they were," Aelia said through the moisture which

215

streamed down her face. "They reared you, made you what you are. You have four parents, not just two." She paused and cleared her throat. "You're such a lovely youth in spite of all the stings which puff your features." She could say no more.

"Ah, so it is," Sir Pallador said. "Four parents, rather than just two. I need to find a seat."

Two pages hustled up with a campaign chair and slid it behind the young knight. He sagged into it, still holding the ring in one hand, wiping sweat away with the other.

Palamon eyed both him and the ring. "Did you never read the ring's engraving?"

"Of course I did, full many times: 'I Parthelon, by all the Gods' good grace, am Emperor across the Thlassa Mey.' It was a relic from the Empire Grand but never did I comprehend how it was passed to me."

"Now you do."

Sir Pallador stared at the artifact. "Yes, now I do."

"That ring is powerful," Reale broke in, excitement in his voice. "Some kind of magic gives it mystic strength. Please, let me hold it."

Eyes turned on the young man but Palamon spoke for him. "Reale, you have a gift, a knack for seeing things no other eyes discern. And if you say the ring is magical, why, so it is." He turned to Aelia. "He found the *Tome of Winds* although it was concealed most skillfully."

Sir Pallador passed the ring to Reale. "I do not doubt it," the Knight of Pallas said. "I have felt . . . felt strange sometimes when holding it."

Reale took the artifact with care, as if it were red hot. "I feel its strength," he said quietly. "It can release great power into you and make you powerful in battle." He handed it back. "I interrupted—I regret that."

Sir Pallador gripped the ring. "No matter. I am staggered; all my images are upside down. I am the son of people whom I never dreamt existed."

Palamon laid his hand on the young knight's shoulder. "The Holy Maiden swept your memory clean when she removed from you the charm which nearly took your life."

"But why did you not tell me when we first encountered one another?"

The blue of Palamon's eyes bored into the younger man's. "Would you forgive me if, with twenty years of wondering behind me, I did not believe my eyes. I held on to your ring and studied it while you recovered from your wounds. Each time you would awake, I'd put it back into its hiding place. I could not bear to speak my piece and be mistaken, don't you see?"

"And yet the proof is plain," Aelia said. She advanced and placed a hand against the young knight's cheek. "So tall, so wide of shoulder, fine of bone. I see my Palamon in you— myself as well. It is a wonder."

"That it is," Palamon said. "In two short days, I've recognized the man who lay within the little child we lost." The tall monarch's mouth formed a fine line; it was with difficulty that he held his emotions in check. "I am most proud."

"And I will make you prouder if I can." Sir Pallador stared at them, at the tent full of people. "You answer questions which I never thought to ask." The joy of the moment finally swept down upon him and he embraced the parents he had never known. "This is the happiest moment of my life," he finally said.

The Buerdic army would attack on the morrow—that was certain. Great plans had to be laid. But such sessions could wait on the glad reunion. Arcite and Berengeria embraced their new nephew, a line of nobles waited to greet their prince. As quickly as they rushed through such matters, the introductions still took time.

Sir Pallador greeted the greater portion of the House of Berevald. It was a mighty moment, yet it could not last long. Sleep was a rare prize in the Carean camp that night.

In the morning, turmoil swept through the army. Knights coated themselves in mail and plate, squires and lackeys prepared broad war horses, then struggled to load the animals with their heavy harness. Common soldiers donned clothing and what armor they had, then quarreled among themselves as they formed into companies. Pikes, spears, and hand axes bristled for the march. Bowmen limbered their long-range weapons. Officers bustled everywhere, giving orders and pushing men into position.

With the thunder of foot and hoof beneath the clatter of arms and armor, the force set off toward the southeast and took up a blocking position across the Buerdic army's line of march. Palamon still had no relish for war. Perhaps their very presence would show Lothar that his plotting had all been discovered. Perhaps he would turn from his invasion.

But hoping did no good; noon did not come before the

Buerdic army struck. Clouds of cavalry swept toward the Carean flank, a horde of infantry marched against the center but only masked the thundering fullness of the Buerdic heavy horse, which rode out of a nearby valley and hurled itself against the defenders.

The mounted spearhead hurtled through air thick with arrows, tore through the center of the Carean line, and crashed against the iron wall formed by the Carean knights. The Carean army reeled beneath the blow, gathered itself, and fought back against the assault.

Sir Pallador's horse pranced nervously as he watched the Buerdic knights break their lances at the foot of a low ridge. The king waited with him, with the Count of Tranje, Sir Reale, and Carea's finest warriors. The tall monarch gave the signal to charge and every last man threw himself into the fray.

Sir Pallador wore the Ring of Parthelon on his finger and he felt its strength surge through him. He leveled his lance at the closest Buerdic knight, the keen point struck, and the man hurtled backward like a fly swatted by a mighty hand. But after that, the surge of the battle made things too tight for lances. Sir Pallador pulled his longsword and took on the man nearest him.

Arcite and the others did the same. Reale seemed far more at home with a sword than with a lance and he fared well in the fighting. But the most noble figure of all was the old king, who unleashed his mighty *Spada Korrigaine* with such fury that men shrank from him in spite of his age. Word of the mighty weapon had spread since the day before and Buerdic knights flinched before the weapon's deadly powers. That slowed the advance of the knights behind them; the penetration tightened to a salient, to a pocket of furious fighting which the defenders pressed from every side. Finally, the assault broke and fell back.

A cheer went up along the Carean army's front and men rushed in pursuit of the retreating warriors. "Hold," Palamon shouted in a weary voice and the other nobles around him took up the cry. "Hold, hold."

A few knights and infantry were too full of battle's lust to heed the command. They chased the fleeing force on foot and by horseback, caught up with a few stragglers, hacked them down from behind, and pursued them into the trees. A cloud of arrows met the pursuit and sent half screaming to the ground. Arrows pierced neck and shoulder, and men sank from their horses and fell into pools of their own blood. A swarm of fresh infantry broke from the trees and hacked down the survivors with sword and axe. By the time the skirmish was over, only a handful remained to flee back to the safety of Carean lines.

"Alas," Sir Pallador heard Arcite say. "There always will be some who cannot heed a word of caution."

"They have paid most dearly for their haste," Palamon replied. "All men who have had dealings with pale Lothar know he will hold forces back for ambush." He sighed and the sigh carried a heavy cargo of weariness and disgust. "Why must the nations of the world manure their next year's crops with blood from gallant warriors? I've watched too many good men die; who cares to whom a peasant pays his meager tithe?"

" 'Twas always thus," Sir Pallador said. "And always shall be so."

"Much to our shame," the tall monarch said. "I grow too old for this." He sagged, slumped so far Sir Pallador feared he would actually fall from his mount.

The prince and Arcite spun their horses, reached out to hold him up. Men rushed to the tall monarch, lifted him from his saddle, and eased him to the ground. He struggled to rise but many men laid hands on him. "Lie still, lie still, my father," Sir Pallador said. The word "father" still felt odd coming from his lips, but he forced himself to use it. "You are old, too weary for more battle. Lie you down upon this bed of grass and let us younger men do battle for you."

"Lothar's not a younger man than I," Palamon said.

"Perhaps. But neither do I see him here. He leads the battle from the rear, as you should do."

"Our knights will mark my absence."

"No," Arcite said. "They need not know. Let Pallador put on your armor. No enemy shall guess that you are gone, but rather wonder at your newfound strength and deadly vigor."

"Perhaps," the tall monarch said wearily.

"His council's good," Sir Pallador said. "Remove your armor here, behind this iron curtain of your truest men." He pointed at the men who stood about them, a wall of plate and mail. "I will be proud to don your iron—thus shall we two deceive the Buerdic mass."

"It must be done," the older man said wearily. He stripped off his basinet, the camail and avantail which protected his throat and cheeks, then the rest of his gleaming armor. The chain mail itself was a wonder to Sir Pallador. He had eyed it from the first, for it was like his own, but even finer, even more cunning than the mail the Knights of Pallas wore.

Sir Pallador stripped down to his quilted underclothing, then took all that the older man handed him. " 'Tis wondrous stuff, this mail of yours," he said. " 'Tis not unlike my own. But I see in these links what seems to be a living force, a life that shimmers from the steel itself."

"There is," Palamon said. "This mail was fashioned by the gods and given to me by Pallas."

"Ah," Sir Pallador said. "The gods do not give gifts to ordinary men."

"Perhaps they do," Palamon replied. "Beware, my son. That armor fends off blows the way good thatch fends rain— but all the same, please take you care. Protect the goods within it." He gazed grimly at the younger man. Then, to Sir Pallador's surprise, threw sweat-soaked arms around him. "A thousand times more difficult it is to see your son face death than you yourself. Whatever outcome meets the end of this long day, please keep yourself in one piece—for your mother."

Sir Pallador smiled in spite of himself. "That I shall." They finished their exchange of armor; the Carean army reformed itself atop the hill and licked its wounds. Few men had any idea that their king had left them and returned to the camp.

Sir Pallador did not have long to wait before he saw a dark mass spread itself over the slope below him. He gazed down at the bulk of the Buerdic army. As it drew closer, it resolved itself into men and horses, bloodthirsty warriors in greater numbers than before.

Trumpets sounded. Buerdic knights moved forward as implacably as the plague; Sir Pallador swallowed as he counted them. They well outnumbered the Carean force. He steeled himself as he heard Arcite's words to Sir Reale: the attacking army always needs the far greater mass to overcome an entrenched opponent, or one which housed itself behind stakes pounded in the ground, as the Careans did. Besides, the force of right, for which they fought, was worth many swords.

Once more the ground shook as the Buerdic knights pounded up the rise toward them. Once more the light cavalry swept down on their flank. And once more, brutal battle surged over the hillside. Horses fell with arrows jutting from their flanks or recoiled against stakes. But the Careans held firm; from the highest noble down to lowliest knifeman, they fought back with a fury to match that of their foes.

Sir Pallador found himself locked into battle with first one Buerdic knight, then with another. He found his father's armor a wonder; it weighed no more than flannel on his arms. Three, perhaps four times in as many moments, it deflected blows which could have brought blood if he had been wearing his own mail. He needed such armor; the Buerdic knights fought like madmen and seemed willing to throw themselves upon the point of his lance or sword in return for a single chance to deliver a killing blow of their own. He did not wield the *Spada Korrigaine* and the king's colors excited his opponents as if they had imbibed some drug, some deadly liquor. Only now did he realize the great weight the king had truly borne, the invisible weight which more than made up for mystical armor.

The issue swayed at the hill's crest. Men struggled, screamed, died, and lay in mud and blood to be trampled by surging horses. Metal clashed on metal, screams of the dying and from wounded horses split the air like a prolonged thunderclap. The Buerdic army could not advance past the hill; neither could the Carean army throw them back.

Then Sir Pallador heard a man scream a different kind of scream, a scream of terror which sounded through the roar of battle like a child's cry. "By Tyche or by Typhon, what are those?" The Knight of Pallas and his opponent both jerked their heads upward and stared, but while his own heart sank down to his toes, his antagonist released a cheer and redoubled his efforts.

Strange creatures soared down at them, struck at them from above. Grown men rode little stuffed horses through the air, a sight which would have made anyone laugh, except that the riders shot down at Carean knights and struck them to the ground with weapons of real steel. In a moment, the impasse was dislodged. Men who had stood fast against lance and battle axe wavered, then broke back toward their own camp rather than face death at the hands of flying warriors. Behind them, the Buerdic horde surged up the hill in triumph.

Chapter Twenty-six:
Warriors From the Sky

THOUGH IT TOOK Flin and his men a long time, they finally made their way across the Thlassa Mey. He had talked his men into leaving Guelt without gold. He had ridden one of the knit ponies back and forth over their heads, had shown them the number he had stolen for them, but many refused the idea that flying steeds were treasure enough. Even when he had explained the plunder they could gain or the battles they could win mounted on such steeds, many of them had growled and grumbled.

But Flin was Flin and at last he talked them into it, though the grumbling kept on. Paying for the voyage homeward was no laughing matter either—and none of them cared to risk a trip across the broad waters on the backs of the mystical toys.

As they went inland, Flin saw unmistakable signs that a huge army had passed that way only days before: stables lay barren and stripped of farm animals, hayricks and granaries lay empty. Something big was afoot and he had a very good idea of what it was. "Buerdaunt's already made their move," he said to Pafney and Sheldorr. "We've got to do something about it."

"Why?" Sheldorr asked. "If they're after the Careans, that leaves the whole field open to us. We can steal anything we want, then make more cash by fighting for the highest bidder."

Flin twisted his mouth. "How small you think. Besides, the Carean king is Bessina's uncle. I can't let him down. I guarantee you, he'll pay you plenty for your help."

"Easy for you to say."

But Flin always made his point; now he led the Red Company northwest across the Greenlands. The sun shone in their faces but that did not keep him from spotting the carnage that waited for them beyond a low range of hills south of Hautre. Two great armies surged beneath them, locked in a death struggle. Though Flin and his men were still a league and a half away, he could hear the din.

The battle's tide looked as if it ran in favor of the Buerdic army. "Look," he said. "That's where old Odus and his men wound up. They crossed the sea by air and got here ahead of us. Look."

From out of the settling sun, two hundred warriors on knit ponies swooped down on the surging masses; that was why the Carean army fell back. The flying soldiers made horses and men panic; the awe they caused more than made up for small numbers. Flin led his band in a long climb which took them clear of the battle, and they hovered unnoticed above the carnage.

Flin turned to Bessina. "You can see the Carean camp in the distance. Can you fly there by yourself?"

"Of course, my darling," the beautiful woman answered. "But I would fain stay by your side."

Flin eyed her. Finally, he said, "Why not? Why should you miss the fun any more than anyone else?"

She pulled out a dagger but he only laughed. "You can do better than that."

"I have a heavier one." She pulled out another, larger dagger.

"Come on." He reached into the pack which hung behind him and hauled out a sword, a thin, saberlike affair which looked both light and deadly. "Those little knives will never do you any good. Use this; I got it especially for you."

She eyed the longer blade suspiciously, then tucked the daggers back into her sash. "All right," she finally said. "I'll use it. But if I don't like it, I shall switch to something better."

Flin laughed. "That's my woman. What any man in the world would give for you." He blew her a kiss and they led the company into a dive at Guelt's flying cavalry.

Odus of Guelt's men harried a company of Carean knights, hacked them down from above, drove them from the saddle, and broke their formation. The flying warriors enjoyed their killing so much they never saw Flin and his men until it was too late; the Red Company struck like an avenging eagle. Flin himself cut two men down before they knew what had hit them. They rolled to the ground and their knit ponies, lifeless without riders, tumbled after them.

"That was fun," he shouted as he and his men swept over the battlefield and made a broad turn. "But it's going to be more fun now that they know they have company."

The Gueltic warriors pulled up and faced the Red Company head on, but were still disorganized. A rousing battle began in the air and Flin wished he had a lance. A joust in the broad sky—that would have been sport fit for the gods. But swords and axes would have to do as he found himself in a duel with two men. They made things hot for him and took his mind away from what he would have liked to do. One fell quickly but the other flicked the end of his sword out before Flin could face him and gave the knight a nasty cut along his right arm.

"Too bad for you I can use either hand," Flin cried. He flipped his sword to his left hand, then dug his knees into his mount's flanks. He wheeled above the other man and delivered a blow which ended in the fellow's neckbone.

The Gueltic warriors regrouped and surrounded Flin's men, but had to break off their attack on the Carean army in the process. Below them, knights and soldiers regrouped in clusters and once more stood fast. The Buerdic knights had strung out over the open ground so that the defenders opposed them almost on even terms.

A few Carean officers reorganized a scattered company of bowmen and directed their fire at the mysterious riders above their heads. First a few brightly fletched arrows sang past the knit ponies, then more, then the air buzzed with feathered flights. "By Tyche's dice," Flin shouted. "They don't know their friends from their enemies."

Flying warriors went in every direction; some flew off to harass ground forces, others spun away locked in dogfights with Flin's men. The sun had settled below the horizon by this time; darkness spread its shawl across the world. Flin raced after the largest knot of Gueltic warriors and a grin worked his features as he saw among them a swarthy, bearded man: Odus of Guelt himself. "Watch your backside, old man," Flin cried with glee. "The bill collector has arrived."

Odus of Guelt rode a knit pony which was almost the size of a real horse; it was by far the largest Flin had ever seen. The evil noble shook its reins and sped away at a pace even

Flin could not hope to match. But reinforcements joined the nasty man and he circled back.

"You fool," he shouted at Flin. "To think you can defeat me in the air. The world will soon belong to us in Guelt and far Buerdaunt."

"To sneaks and thieves, you mean?" Flin grinned as he shouted his answer. "You'd better give up now; your plans have already blown up worse than a bloated carp."

The evil noble scowled and slashed the air with his saber. "Now you shall die, you interfering dog." He and three of his men shot toward Flin. He sped ahead of the rest and reached the brigand first; but though he slashed downward as he passed, Flin dodged the blow and engaged in a heated duel with the two men who reached him next.

In spite of the wound to his arm, Flin was holding his own against the two men when Odus of Guelt swept past once more. This time, the evil noble slowed his aerial steed just out of Flin's reach and twirled a device which looked like a bolo. "You had your chance at speedy death," he shouted. "Now you shall come with us and suffer what we may devise for you." He let fly; before Flin could react, metal balls and cords wrapped themselves about his arms, tangled him, and almost knocked him from his mount.

"Don't kill him yet," Odus of Guelt shouted. "Take hold of him and lead him after us; when we've returned to camp, we'll settle with him."

The two men put away their weapons and reached for Flin, but a shadow shot through the darkening sky above them. A dartlike object flicked down at Odus of Guelt. The evil ruler clutched his neck, released a cry, and slumped forward. The big knit pony slowly turned over, the Gueltic ruler's limp legs lost their hold on it, and Odus of Guelt fell without a sound. The other two riders shouted in fear and hurried away.

Flin had all he could do just to keep his balance until the dark rider swept up to him and slashed the bolo which held his arms. "There's one less scoundrel in the world," came a familiar female voice. It was Bessina; her eyes flashed in triumph. "Now he has paid for hauling me across the Thlassa Mey."

"You gem of womanhood," Flin cried as he rubbed the circulation back into his arms. "You couldn't have come at a better time; I wasn't sure how I was going to get out of that pickle."

She bumped her knit pony into his and the two of them

embraced a hundred cubits in the air. "You silly man," she said. "To tell me I need better weapons than the ones I carry. Odus lies expired upon a rock, my dagger in his neck. Do not tell me what blade works best for me."

"All right, all right. I'll never say another word." He looked about. "But darkness is breaking the battle up at last. We'd better fly down to the Carean camp and see how they fared."

Pafney caught up with his master just them. "Wait," he cried. "They'll not know us if we fly to them in darkness. Two or three of our own men already bleed from sharp Carean darts, fired by mistake."

"Rats," Flin replied. But they had to land somewhere; in moments it would be too dark to fly. Already, cooking fires sparkled in the Carean camp. He could also see the Buerdic army made camp in a valley about a league off. Either place would be dangerous for him and his men.

Then he spotted a smaller cluster of campfires north of the two great armies. "Look there," he said. "That looks promising."

"Perhaps, but we should still take care," Bessina replied.

"We will." Flin put his mystic mount into a gentle dive toward the unknown camp. To Flin's surprise, he found it to be a large company of Knights of Pallas; a dozen young sentries approached with drawn swords as the Red Company began to land just outside the circle of firelight. "I come in peace," Flin cried as he laid down his knit pony and raised his hands. "We all do."

"What sort of witchcraft can this flying be?" one squire said in wonder. Then he shouted, "Alert the Master. Rouse all Knights, for magic is at use tonight."

Flin laughed at the commotion. "He's an enthusiastic chap," he said of the squire. Then he added hastily, "But you don't have to worry about us; we're all on your side."

"Then drop your weapons," another young man ordered. "If you be honest men, you'll not be prisoners, but guests."

Flin didn't like the idea and many of his men liked it even less than he did. But he unbuckled his sword belt. "All right," he said. "All of you, do as the lad says."

"I don't like that idea," Sheldorr said.

"Me, either, but we have better enemies to fight. Drop your steel."

At that moment, a grand old man in full armor arrived, along with several other Knights of Pallas. "I am Grand Master of the noble Knights, Sir. State your name and how you came into our bivouac. If you be decent men, I guarantee you'll find our hospitality complete."

Flin glanced about. How decent could all these members of the Red Company claim to be? But he told the Grand Master how his men had come to fly the knit ponies and how they had taken part in the day's battle. He hoped that even if his tale was not too honorable, at least these lily-white knights would lend him an escort so he could reach the Carean camp.

"A noble tale, Sir Flin," Sir Phebos said. "You've done a better deed than we have on this day. For all these hours, we've waited with our arms in hand." He clapped Flin on the shoulder. "I've heard of you and though your deeds are colored by the stain of rascalry, I trow you are a decent fellow." He smiled. "I'll send messengers unto the camp of the Careans."

"Thanks," Flin said, returning the older man's handshake. "And if you have a spare bite of supper, we'd be glad to take it off your hands."

"No sooner said than done." With that, the Grand Master and his officers received Flin's company into their own tents, to eat a dinner fit for men who had fought well that day. While messengers carried his word to Palamon, Flin drank wine and hoped the tall monarch would send horses. That would be a great deal better than walking.

Later that evening, a commotion at the perimeter of the knights' camp told Flin that a return message had come. Then a young squire threw wide the flap to the Grand Master's pavilion and admitted two tall men. "Palamon," Flin shouted. As always, he addressed the Carean king by his familiar name. "What are you doing here?"

The king beamed and embraced the knight. "When word arrived that it was you who broke apart the warriors from the sky, I knew it had to be. No man but you could have arrived so timely. I greet you now in person, and have brought my son with me."

"Your son? Berethane?"

"Pallador," the proud father replied. "Sir Pallador, of Pallas' noble Knights—though he will rule Carea someday."

"If the gods should favor it," Sir Pallador shook hands with Flin.

"You worry too much," Flin replied. "Things always work out right in the end. But you're a little previous; isn't that the king's armor you have on?"

"Too long a tale for telling now," Palamon replied. "And by the way, I bring a gift for you."

Flin smiled without understanding.

Palamon led the dashing knight and his lady outside where clouds hid the stars. "Arcite and Berengeria were forced to commandeer the armor and equipment which you left in Tranje. 'Twas needed for our army."

Flin smiled ruefully. "I guess the joke was on me in the long run."

"Not really. As they marched across the Greenlands, they removed from Castle Fording this great steed. Arcite believed him stolen, so 'tis said, and thought you'd want him back."

A familiar whinny greeted Flin and he saw Velocipod's dark head tossing above two handlers. "My thanks to Arcite," he said as he rubbed the great beast's nose. "Am I glad to see you, Velocipod. You're the love of my life, you know?"

"I thought myself your only love," Bessina said in a rising voice.

Flin turned to stare at her, then back at Velocipod. Then Palamon broke the difficult moment. "Ride back to camp with us," he said. "And sleep this night within my tents. I'd have you with me when the day comes."

"I'd love to," Flin said, relieved at the escape from his last remark. He turned to Sheldorr and the other men of the Red Company. "Wouldn't you like to help Carea hack some Buerdic throats?"

Cheers answered the question, which made the knights' camp sound like a rowdy inn. The younger knights and squires looked at one another in distaste. Palamon and Sir Phebos exchanged glances and guided the rowdy leader to the edge of camp. His men followed in a stream.

But a Carean messenger burst into their midst, surrounded by shouting youths. He rushed to Palamon and threw himself before the monarch. "My King, our scouts send word the Buerdic horde is moving. Pale Lothar's legions march upon a night assault."

"Of course," Palamon shouted and clapped his fist into his palm. "I knew my foe had stratagems galore; that's why I had his army watched this night." He turned to Flin. "Prepare your men for battle. Waste no time, and concentrate your flying troops upon their airborne warriors."

"They won't have much stomach for a tussle." Flin put an arm around Bessina. She was a better partner than Velocipod when all was said and done. "My Lady here did away with their boss, who just happened to be Odus of Guelt."

"Perhaps," Palamon said. "But do not hurl yourselves against the Buerdic horse or infantry until you can be sure the skies are empty." He put his hand on the younger man's shoulder and looked him in the eye. "Be careful—nighttime battles are a horrid risk—and moreso, I imagine, when you fight above the ground. These clouds above announce the coming rain, another cause for worry."

"Don't worry. I've waited a long time for a tussle like this." Flin turned to Bessina. "Want to go along?"

"Of course." Bessina said with a smile.

"But wait," Palamon said, astounded. "She is a woman."

"So what? So's your precious Pallas." With that, Flin and his company paraded from the camp.

Palamon eyed them, then broke into a smile in spite of himself. "He knows what's best, or surely his Bessina does." Then he turned toward Sir Phebos. "Now must we leave you, Master of the Knights. I would that you could fight beside us in this fray."

"I'd have it so," Sir Phebos said. "But we have other game to follow."

At that instant, they heard a tumult from the far side of the Knights' camp. Men shouted, screamed orders, and called for horses. Frightful clacking split the air like two tree trunks being smashed together, then everyone froze as a scream tore their eardrums. Sir Phebos' mouth dropped open. "Is this some newfound stratagem from your Buerdaunt? If so, then we shall fight in self-defense."

They ran from the tent and found a monstrous insect. A mantis the size of a manor house stood poised at the edge of the camp; firelight gleamed off its green shell as it gathered itself to attack. Even as they watched, it lashed out with its sawtoothed forelegs and snatched up a horse tethered within its reach. The animal screamed; its terror and agony curdled the blood as the huge insect tore it to pieces.

Chapter Twenty-seven: Ursid

EVERY EYE STARED at the creature. It surely hailed from Tartarus' darkest depths by the way it devoured the hapless animal in its clutches. "By all my faith in Pallas' name," Sir Phebos breathed. "I do not know what monster faces us, but surely it cannot have been set loose by human hands."

"But human hands must hew it down," Palamon said.

Knights and their squires braved the creature's wrath and scuttled beneath its claws to release the other horses from their hobbles. The terrified animals bolted from the paddock but they were wonderfully trained; whistles brought most of them back. Other knights, already prepared for battle, took up lances.

Sir Pallador stared. "I feel this is a spawn of that same darkness which I saw . . ." He hesitated as he thought of Lady Alcyone and Krisamee. "Which I saw at Hautre. If so, 'twill take a mighty effort to defeat it."

Even as he spoke, a pair of knights charged the animal. The creature swept the first man off his steed before he could even touch it with his lance. The second managed to pierce the animal's thick shell; the lance stuck for an instant, then broke off and fell to the ground. That did not even faze the mantis; the hellish insect snatched up the fallen knight and crushed the poor man between its mandibles.

"Withdraw," Sir Phebos cried. "Abandon everything except your arms and armor. Mount your horses! Knights and tercelets prepare to make defense against this evil."

Knights and squires rushed about, filled with hustle and purpose. But as Palamon and Sir Pallador clambered onto their

230

horses, they heard thunderous clacking from a different direction. Another mantis even larger than the first heaved itself into view. "I must fight with my company," Sir Pallador shouted to his father. "I cannot see death dealt all my friends and mentors."

"But you must not be killed," Palamon shouted back. Anguish lay in his voice.

"E'en if that should come, I have to do what's right."

At that instant, Flin and a couple of his men buzzed by on his knit pony. "Let us take care of these two bugs," he shouted. "We'll make short work of them, for all their green armor."

"Nay," Palamon shouted. "Join your army; you and brave Arcite shall share command till I or Pallador return. I'll join my son for now; together will we face this mystic threat."

The two monsters were big as dragons. They uprooted trees, scattered animals, and killed men. They tore up tents as easily as boys ripping parchment. Flin and his Red Company flew off to the battle with Buerdaunt; Palamon and Sir Pallador joined the Knights of Pallas.

Sir Pallador couched his lance and charged, along with several other men. He aimed his lance tip at the huge creature's face, ducked an outstretched claw which whizzed past his ear, and drove the tip into one huge eye. The jolt of contact nearly struck him from his saddle and the lance shook from his grip as the insect chittered in rage and jerked its head away. Black liquid oozed out of the eye, ran the length of the weapon, and dripped toward the ground. The creature flailed madly while men and animals scattered to avoid its claws.

The armor of the insect's head cracked, faulted, fell away. Sir Pallador stared in awe. Rather than bare flesh, the falling plates revealed a huge face, pale and pasty-looking, with a moustache the size of a man's arm.

Sir Pallador stared in disbelief. The insect had a human head, the same as the stingers and biters which had almost killed him in Hautre. Then Palamon's voice reached him. "I know that face. 'Tis one long dead, an evil wizard called Navron."

"I know him not," the younger knight replied. "But I know this: the insects which flew 'round that cloud of darkness sported human faces. This foul beast is part of that same evil."

Despite its injury, the mantis continued to swat about, to fend off a Knight of Pallas here and crush one from his horse there. It bit men in half, tore them into pieces. In moments, blood and torn flesh decorated the giant face.

Since it was even larger, the other beast did even more damage. Knights fell in bold attack, no matter against which side of the beasts they pitted themselves. They managed to inflict a wound or two, but still the monsters pushed them back.

Sir Pallador, Sir Phebos, and Palamon withdrew to catch their breath. The tall monarch panted as if his breast would burst; he pulled off his helmet and his white hair lay matted with his sweat. "I swear," he said between breaths. "The years are just as much my enemy as yonder monsters." He let his lance drop and stretched to pull his *Spada Korrigaine* from its hanger. "But one more charge before I finish; I will use this light and mystic sword."

"Good King," Sir Phebos said. He was years younger than Palamon, but looked little better. "Our age makes us a futile pair of warriors. Give up your sword to youthful Pallador. You've warred two solid days; your heart will shatter from exertion. Let him bear your sword, for he is young."

"I bear my father's armor now," Sir Pallador said. "What, must I take his sword from him as well? Was I born to usurp my father's title while he lives?"

"I know my words are harsh," Sir Phebos replied. "They fall on me as well as on your father." He turned earnest eyes on the tall monarch. "Can you not see? Your lance has not gained weight; 'tis but your arms rebelling from too many years of overuse. Like me, you bear too many whitened hairs to charge these frightful beasts. Yield up your mystic sword unto a younger man and let us both retire for breath. Our strength lies in another field."

Palamon shot both of them a glare, then his gray eyes softened. "Ah, me," he said. "Is this how it's to go? Will my beloved son wrest all from me, one item at a time? Am I to be laid bare into my coffin?"

"Please forgive me," Sir Pallador said. "But I believe Sir Phebos grasps the truth. A king has more important duties than to joust with insects. Fighting is a young man's art; let me indulge in it."

Palamon gazed at Sir Pallador as if in pain but the younger man went on. "My youth's a weapon you no longer hold. But you have others—wisdom and experience. Make use of them while I make the assault."

"That's wisdom, though you are no more than a youth. You are your mother's from your top to toe."

"I think not."

"Do not argue." Palamon sighed, then released to the younger man the weapon he had carried for dozens of years. Sir Pallador felt his fingers close about the mystic handle as if his hands had cramped onto it. "It likes you well," Palamon said softly, his voice all but drowned out by the bellow and scream of the fighting. "The gods approve the transfer."

The younger man gazed into the eyes of the older. "Weapons pass from father down to son, but wisdom must repose where it was born. So use your wisdom, Father. We'll prevail against these enemies."

Palamon nodded. "I shall. Before you charge, give back to me that brazen case you carry in your pack. The Oracle puts mighty faith in it. I'll toy with it awhile and seek the answers which it holds."

Sir Pallador agreed and sent a squire to fetch the box from his palfrey. Then he turned his attention to the mantis which fought as if it would hack the Knights of Pallas to pieces. He wore mystic armor, an enchanted ring, and carried a weapon crafted by the gods themselves. Surely, if his heart were pure, he would slay any beast which Hades might spew forth. If only his heart were pure—that was a hard question. He tried not to think about it; he would live a hero or die a victim of his own weakness.

Rain came. He raised the sword and cantered through the falling drops toward the larger creature. Its bulging eyes gleamed in the torchlight; perhaps a second face lay behind those eyes, but the creature did not show that there might be anything human within it. It sprawled toward him, lifted its razor-ridged forelegs, and swatted at him the way a man might swat at a meddling fly.

Sir Pallador ducked the blow, but felt the breeze as the member went by. Rain pattered through his visor and glistened off his face as he swung a mighty stroke. It, too, missed by a hair's breadth. The creature understood the weapon, he could tell. It turned wary, the plates which covered it rasped softly against one another as the two of them circled for advantage.

A blow from behind knocked the wind out of him, bowled him off his mount and head over heels. The second mantis had attacked him from behind; even as he hit the ground, pincers closed over him, made sparks against his mystic armor, squeezed the breath from him. The huge face glared a few cubits from his own. He brought the *Spada Korrigaine* up and struck the joint in the center of the leg. The creature shrieked in rage and pain and the member fell away with a crash.

Sir Pallador fell with it, badly shaken. He rolled to his feet and dodged the other foreleg. The two creatures closed on him; he ducked another blow, rolled, found himself beneath a mammoth belly. He gripped the mystic sword in both hands and thrust upward with all his might. The blade hissed and pierced heavy plate, the animal above him shrieked, and then he grimaced as he found himself inundated by hot, sticky fluid which bubbled, boiled, and stank like Hades' pits. It gargled from the wound and swept him off his feet once more.

He gagged, fought for breath, and fought to regain his feet as the dark flood washed him out from beneath the beast. He managed to catch hold of a tree stump and steady himself. The monster collapsed; its legs sagged, the puffy abdomen thudded onto the ground, and sticky fluid splashed everywhere.

Legs waved feebly, the head drooped, the mighty jaws tore at the soil. Sir Pallador waded through black slime to strike at the elm-thick neck. The blade screamed again and the head toppled, fell like the top of an oak, struck the ground and bounced once. The shell of the head cracked away and showed this monster's hidden human face, a visage even more awful than the first one. It was an old man's face, bearded, wrinkled, a travesty of human features which looked more monstrous than even the insect face which had concealed it.

"Alyubol," he heard several voices cry. Then the monster fell apart. Plates teetered from the body, revealing glistening black muscle and pale sinew. Quaking flesh steamed in the rain and black ichor ran everywhere.

Alyubol. Sir Pallador had no time to ponder that name, vanished into lore a generation old. He had to face the first monster, which bore down on him like an avenging demon. He dodged the deadly forelegs, worked closer, and tried to slip beneath the creature as he had done with the other. But it had learned from its brother's demise; it was quick and the sticky fluid which seeped into the ground slowed the young knight. He managed to strike at a moving foot but could get no closer.

He gathered himself to parry, dodge a blow, and strike again, but the air grew thick with flying insects which hindered him. Wasps, mosquitoes, and biting flies dived at him with malevolent intent. Each bore a tiny human face. He threw up his arm and tried to fend them away, tried to swat at them, but there were too many and they were too quick. Where they flew against the blade of his holy sword or against his mystic armor, they disappeared in little flashes of light; he sparkled all over. But they lit on his helmet and before he could knock them away, a few managed to crawl through the eye slits and sting him.

He writhed his head inside his helmet, tried to squash evil little bodies. Then he felt the thunderous blow as his huge foe struck him. Once again, he flew through the air and lit with a thud that drove the breath from him.

"Ah, Pallador, my son." The young knight heard the voice and swung his head about to see Palamon's face. Though heaped years kept the older man from the fray, they plainly could not deaden the pain the younger man's suffering caused.

"Beware," Sir Pallador cried. "Don't let the beast come on you from behind." He heard the monster's crushing approach but Knights of Pallas hauled him to a stretcher.

"I am not hurt," he protested. "Please, let me go. I'll finish this great business."

"No," Palamon said. "The beast is slow enough to outmaneuver for a while. You've done all things that could be asked of you."

"The darkness comes," another voice cried. "The evil cloud blots out the very torchlight."

Sir Pallador tried to rise. "Then that is what I must oppose. The evil cloud, the orb which rules these ghastly beasts, which took my . . ."

"Nay, nay," the older man cried. "The *Tome of Winds* was given by the gods to free us from the blackness. The Oracle proclaimed it."

"But can you use it yet?"

"Not yet," Palamon cried. "But I will find the answer, just as surely as the sun twirls 'bout this world."

Sir Phebos held a small object before Sir Pallador. "This coin fell from your armor," he said to the young knight.

Palamon eyed his son. "Who gave you this?"

"A man . . . a being known as Peristeras." Sir Pallador replied. He stared at the coin, then at his father. "I think he spoke for the almighty gods."

"And this face on the obverse matches that engraved on the *Tome of Winds*. This has to be the key."

"Then, Father, solve the mystery. I'll fight once more

against the mystic forces. I will enter the foul darkness and attack what lies within its center.''

"You're not protected," Palamon said. "When you tried before, it almost killed you."

"But I have your armor now, your sword as well. This time I'll pierce the darkness and destroy the evil at its core."

Sir Phebos cautioned him with a touch. "Remember, though, your helmet and your gauntlets are not blessed with mystic powers as your hauberk is."

"Then bless them," Sir Pallador cried. "The power of a hundred Knights at prayer—that must have some effect. Come, bless me, bless my armor and my fittings so that I might face this evil."

Palamon's shout interrupted him. "It fits. This coin fits on this brazen circle. I will set it here and we shall see . . ." He placed the talisman on the *Tome of Winds*. The case shimmered, glowed a hundred different colors, then faded from existence. Left in Palamon's lap was a thick volume, bound in vellum. He lifted the cover, then let it fall back. "Enchantments to forestall the evil—this is our great weapon."

"Bless you both, then," Sir Phebos cried. "Together, you will wage the battle. All you Knights of Pallas—come to us. Lay loving hands upon these men, give blessings to them for the duty which they must perform."

While the rain fell, scores of knights surrounded the three men, laid their hands on Palamon, on Sir Pallador, and on their armor. All bowed their heads. The king and his son joined the knights; every man shut his eyes and blocked out the clash of night battle which echoed from distant hills, the pelting of the rain, and the screams of the approaching monster. Massed prayer filled the air with soft music and Sir Pallador felt holy strength flood into him. So powerful was its effect, even the devilish insects held back, as if blocked by the wall of goodness the knights threw up.

Hands lifted and the knights rose, threw themselves back into the fray against the monster. Even in their numbers, they could not hold it for long. Their horses slipped in deepening mud; the mantis did the same. But it managed to sweep men off animals and tear them with its claws.

The smaller insects bored in once more but they could not harm Sir Pallador now. They sparked against his armor, against his helmet, and fluttered to the ground as if they had flown into a lantern's flame. For all the torment they dealt to the rest of the company, he did not even mind them. He lifted the *Spada Korrigaine* and approached the monster through the mud.

It turned toward him, and the hellish face writhed into a sneer of hate and fear. But a voice like tinny thunder rolled out of the black shadows and said, "Wait there, my pet. The battle which is coming is not yours, but is mine. Now I've found you, Palamon; now you shall die."

Sir Pallador turned toward the sound just as the dark hemisphere of shadow enveloped him. To his surprise and relief, the shadow did not fling him away this time; his armor sizzled and flashed for an instant, then returned to normal. The *Spada Korrigaine* flickered longer; beads of light sparked and danced along the blade. Then it, too, went silent.

Laughter rumbled from some point a hundred cubits away. "Ha-ha. You have mastered this fell shadow. And yet you wear armor; 'tis most curious. No one may enter this, my sphere, unless he's helpless, yet now you are here. Is it because you're helpless here before me, Palamon?" Again, laughter shook the ground.

Sir Pallador could see nothing except the ground and the hordes of placid insects which now covered every stone, every stick of wood. Even the rain did not penetrate the blackness. But he had listened to his father and he knew the voice belonged to a dead prince named Ursid. "I am not King Palamon," he shouted. He understood Ursid's error, though, and the reason the orb of darkness had moved so aimlessly across the land. As priests and poets recorded, the souls of the dead knew the past and the future—but they did not know or understand the present. Ursid's soul was dead, as dead and corrupt as Kruptos itself. That was why Ursid had taken such a jagged course to Hautre; that was why he was so easily fooled into thinking Sir Pallador was, in fact, Palamon.

"Don't deny your own name," Ursid thundered. "I remember well your armor and your crest. In thousands of the nights I spent deep crushed beneath the sea in those dead vaults of Kruptos, there I dreamed of you, my Palamon. Now is my time for vengeance. Shall I kill you now with lightning?" A bolt of lightning struck in front of Sir Pallador; the explosion deafened him and hurled him from his feet. "Shall my winds tear you asunder?" The young knight tried to rise but wind tore at him and pushed him back down. Fingers of atmosphere tugged at him and he really wondered if he would be torn apart.

He curled himself into a ball, fought to keep his grip on his father's mystic sword. Of course that was the reason this demon from Kruptos thought Sir Pallador was the Carean king. The young knight wore the tall monarch's armor, he carried his weapon. What could be more natural? "I am not the man you think I am," Sir Pallador shouted. "But by the mighty gods, I'll vanquish you."

"Silence." The cry thundered out of the darkness, almost burst Sir Pallador's eardrums. Another bolt of lightning drove him farther back; he landed atop a swarming heap of insects, which crawled out from under him and lowered him to the ground like a rack dissolving. They surrounded him in mounds and leered at him with greedy human eyes. "My pets there all desire you, you see? Should I leave you to them? They are the souls of those most evil dead that this harsh world can form and they are covetous of your soft flesh and your rich blood. But I don't let them eat yet; only my two mantid pets may touch your sustenance. Thus they grew large with life as in life they grew large with evil."

"You are mad," Sir Pallador shouted, only to be knocked down again by more gales and laughter.

"Where I come from, no madness does exist. There's only evil, hatred, and my vengeance." More laughter came before he resumed. "My little friends do lust to taste of you. Still, I say, you are not theirs while you're alive. I shall break your bones and tear your skin to ribbons. Then, perhaps, I'll leave your dying flesh to them."

Moisture masked Sir Pallador's face inside his armor. Was the rain able to pierce the darkness after all? No, of course not. His own sweat drenched him. "Show yourself," he said.

"I'll confront you when it's time. And there is time; oh, there is time—in the darkest Kruptos, there I learned of time the most of all. Oh, there is time. And you will savor death as I, for twenty long and bitter years in all the torments of that evil place, have learned to savor my revenge." More laughter came and the insects slithered forward. But as they touched the young knight's armor, they sparkled, flamed, and died the same as they had before.

"So. Your armor's strong and it protects you well. Your mighty sword, too—you'd be nothing but for them. Then die by my bare hand." The darkness parted a little and Sir Pallador saw a human figure. The thing glowed like a firefly but the radiance cast a greenish tint. The man—if man it could be called—exuded evil.

The figure advanced across the black ground, a man no older than Sir Pallador. The spectral face was crosshatched by scars and he wore the armor and trappings of an earlier generation. He laughed again, then extended a finger. Lightning leaped from the end of it and struck at Sir Pallador's feet. Once more, he felt himself hurled through the air.

This time he had the presence of mind to writhe about and land upright. He sprang at the spectral figure with all his strength and brought the *Spada Korrigaine* down on top of it. An explosion blinded him, he felt himself thrown backward again. He picked himself up to see the brilliant form still advancing—and half again as large as it had been before.

Ursid laughed again. "You're a fool, my puny Palamon. I now have strength you cannot comprehend. So strike again, and then prepare for death."

Sir Pallador leaped forward and struck again, was blown backward the same as before. For all the powers of his wondrous equipment, for all the strength he gained from his mystic ring, for all the fact that he could vanquish Ursid's minions, he could not harm the specter itself. The glowing form advanced against him, larger than it had been after the first blow.

"Strike again," the voice screamed. "All your weaponry still fails you." Again, the pointed finger; again, the bolt of power from the fingertip. It struck Sir Pallador on the shin this time. When he picked himself up, he stared dumbly at his foot. The plating had been torn away; he could see bare, bleeding flesh.

He struck the ground before Ursid with the *Spada Korrigaine*. The blade sizzled into earth and stone, rumbled like an earthquake. The terrain split open and Ursid tumbled into the gap.

Sir Pallador crawled to the edge and peered down, but what he saw filled him with awe. The specter lit at the bottom a great way down—but even as the young knight watched, it began to climb up. It walked up the vertical stone as if it were level ground.

Sir Pallador jerked away from the opening but he was too late. A blast struck the earth in front of him, hurled him away, knocked his helmet spinning. Before Sir Pallador could snatch it back, Ursid reappeared and another blast turned the young knight about and tore his gauntlet from his right hand; the metal glove and the *Spada Korrigaine* landed several paces from him. He scrambled after the mystic sword, then cried out as he put pressure on the heel of his hand; the blow had broken bone. Fear crept into him for the first time, but he shoved it back. What had his father told him: call the weapon by name.

"Spada Korrigaine," he shouted, and the blade shot back to him, though he cried out again as his broken hand clamped onto the handle. With all the strength he had left, he struck the ground in front of him once more—but this time he could not catch Ursid by surprise. The spectral villain stepped across the opening as nimbly as an acrobat twirling on a trapeze.

"Prepare for death, my puny Palamon," Ursid roared. He lifted his hand to hurl another bolt, then hesitated as he saw Sir Pallador without a helmet. "You are not . . . you are not the enemy."

"I told you I was not your Palamon," Sir Pallador cried. "But slay me if you wish; I shall not cringe. I know a better death awaits me than the life or pseudolife you seem to live."

"Then die, as you do wish," Ursid replied.

"Nay, nay, Ursid. He's not your Palamon. But I am, and as I have done before, I'll end your violence." Human and spectral eyes swept toward this new voice. To Sir Pallador's amazement, Palamon himself stood on a low stone, his white hair flying about his wrinkled face, the *Tome of Winds* open in his broad hands.

Chapter Twenty-eight:
The Final Battle

THE *TOME OF WINDS* rested like a sacred relic—which it was—in Palamon's hands. Bands of vapory light rose from the volume, pierced the darkness, and swirled about the tall monarch like a protective mist. On the ground, legions of white-faced insects shrank from him as if they knew—though Ursid plainly did not—the nature of his weapon. "For years, Ursid, you burdened me with blame for all the hate which festered in your soul. You never tried to staunch its flow and now, e'en after death, you burst from this unholy city's bonds and vex mankind with your lust for vengeance. Have done; if your soul's not lost already, save it now by overcoming your own evil—go back to death's eternal pouch."

"Nay, Father, for his soul's as vanished as your childhood's blush."

"I shall have your death," Ursid howled. "That for sure, and then all of the world as my playtoy." He extended his hand to blot Palamon from existence.

"The gods have warned me well against your evil," Palamon cried, "that mankind might be defended. Behold the *Tome of Winds.*" But Ursid drowned Palamon's voice; he loosed a blast of lightning against the old man's chest, a bolt powerful enough to knock down a wall. It struck the mystic volume in Palamon's hands and its energy faded as harmlessly as fog on a sunny morning.

The specter sent another bolt against the tall monarch, and another, but his evil was harmless against the holy book. Palamon smoothed the parchment pages and intoned note after

241

mystical note. His voice rose and he stood impervious against bolt and beast.

Ursid sent blasts of wind and vapor, stirred the evil insects from the ground, hurled them against the tall monarch like giants' fists. But Palamon ignored the danger. The darkness above them opened, and a counter gust of immense proportions swooshed down. Streamers of cloud and vapor hurled themselves through the shadow and tore it into evil ribbons. The earth trembled, the sky itself seemed to pour down through the rift in Ursid's shield.

Clean wind tore at Ursid, stripped armor and clothing from him, stripped away his unearthly glow until he stood dark and glowering against its blasts. He had nothing left to defend himself except his hatred and his evil, and these he now used. He grimaced in foul fury, extended both arms, and released from his fingertips a black eddy of unearthly current. The blackness tore at Palamon, burst against the holy protection about him, sundered it and cast the tall monarch backward.

Sir Pallador cried out. Ursid had the power of the dark gods behind him; even the *Tome of Winds* seemed too little to bring him down. The young knight raised the *Spada Korrigaine* once more, ignored the pain and the tumult, and brought it down in front of the evil specter. The black stream struck the blade, glanced off, deflected, and Sir Pallador felt himself crushed as if by a giant hammer. He shrieked in pain as he felt his tissues rend.

But a tortured glance at Palamon told Sir Pallador what he had to know; the respite gained the older man the precious instant needed for the last word of the incantation. The faded lips moved, the voice boomed, a stream of pale ectoplasm shot from the volume itself, struck the specter that was Ursid, and blew it asunder. The stream became a whirlwind, whipped about them all, tightened like a corkscrew, and shot heavenward. It drew all after it.

Dead insects followed the suction, the mantis Sir Pallador had killed and its brother, all struggled and rose helplessly. Sir Pallador felt his hair stand on end and did not know whether it was from fright or lightning or the pull of the wind. Last of all, the cosmic cyclone sucked up the scattered pieces of what had been Ursid, or at least of what had been the specter of Ursid. Upward and upward the mass shot, then vanished into a brilliant opening where the firmament had parted. The sky closed, the clouds closed, and the two men found themselves alone, sitting in the rain.

"So," Palamon said with a mask of a smile. "That is that." He looked very weary.

Sir Pallador rose stiffly. It was a struggle; the younger man's leg was lacerated and bleeding, his hand was broken. He hurt in every joint and every pore. But he managed to stagger through the muck and drop down next to the older man. "Ah, Father," he said. "A mighty battle have we waged this night."

"Yes, greater than was ever fought." The tall monarch cocked his head and listed to the tumult and crash from afar, from the two armies which fought to the death beneath the black clouds. "Whatever happens in the lesser war, whichever side may win, men will still rule themselves. That much we've gained." He listened again. "Methinks I hear the noises of a rout—one army flees with empty hands. If gods take part in earthly battles, then I pray the victory is ours."

"Perhaps we should prepare to flee, in the event the Buerdic power won."

"Perhaps," Palamon said. "For my part, I care not. But you are young, your legacy must be maintained." He stood and Sir Pallador smiled, for all his aches and pains. "I had no kingdom last week," the young knight said. "If I have none now, the loss is not extreme." He thought about Alcyone and Krisamee. Ah, Krisamee. That was the great loss, not some throne he had never sought. "But still, let's go seek out the news."

The moon rose, the clouds split, and Sir Pallador felt surprise that the conflict with Ursid had taken them within sight of Hautre's dark ruins. Downhill, he could see the shadows of great armies moving away from the city, but could not make out which force was which. As Palamon had foreseen, one force pursued the other.

A sound behind him made him turn; it was Sir Phebos and a cluster of Knights of Pallas. "By my faith," the Grand Master said. "We had a devil of a time to find you. We are but a ragged company, but we survive and evil meets an end. Thereby, the Maiden's served."

"Thereby the Maiden's served," Palamon repeated. "What word have you of battle, and about my precious queen."

"No word," Sir Phebos said sadly. "So mighty was this battle with the evil beings, we know nothing of the human fray."

Trumpets split the darkness, then horses thundered toward the band. Out of the night rode a posse of warriors. Sir Pallador could not stand quickly; pain so filled his wounded body that it rebelled against movement. But he sagged in relief as he saw Sir Flin and Arcite climb down from their mounts.

"A mighty victory," Arcite cried. "We fought them through the darkness, to the very gates of Hautre. We thought our cause was lost, but then a mighty wind swept down on us from this direction, carried leaves and dust and foul debris into our foemen's faces, gave us the advantage. That led to our glorious triumph."

Palamon managed a smile and clasped the younger man's hand. "It seems too wonderful to contemplate."

"We even have Buerdaunt's albino king here to prove it," Flin said happily. "He didn't plan on being caught but that freak storm caused his horses to panic. They stampeded right over the top of him and his highest nobles; all we had to do was pick up the pieces."

"Ah." Palamon knelt. "I thank the glorious gods," he said. "The wind which swept away our evil and unearthly foes, has also turned the tide of battle. Thus it is that goodness triumphs over all. The love of pure hearts conquers evil, though that evil comes in many forms."

"You make it sound too easy," Flin said indignantly. "You should have tried flying one of those knit toys in all that wind, with bugs and sticks and pieces of dirt hitting us in the faces. It was hellish, I can tell you; half of my men are going to have aches and pains and arms in slings for a long time."

Palamon almost laughed. "Ah, Flin," he said. "You never change—and may the gods preserve you. But I must go and speak to Lothar." His nobles showed him the way to the fallen monarch.

Sir Pallador allowed a physician to clean and bind his broken hand and his leg. Then he slipped his arms about the shoulders of two squires and hobbled after the rest of the party. He found them a short way off, kneeling over a dark form in a litter.

Sir Pallador recognized Lothar, though the man now bore little resemblance to the haughty king who had confronted him before. Lothar the Pale was physically broken, bruised, smashed, streaked with mud. Only the lingering fire of his pale eyes showed what he had once been. "So you have won, Carean King," he said to Palamon through swollen lips.

"No nation wins a war," Palamon replied. "The best that

can be hoped is that we trade old threats and problems for some new ones. I have seen it all before." He smiled bitterly. "No, I've not won."

"You have not lost, which my Buerdaunt has done. Your ships still ply the Narrow Strait." Lothar grimaced in pain; Sir Pallador saw signs of broken bones, of internal injuries. "By all the gods, I hope this punishment is satisfactory. If I allied myself with evil wizards and with darkness, then what choice had I? My land was at a disadvantage—I employed the means which lay within my grasp."

A real look of pity entered Palamon's eyes as he reached out his hand and gently swept the rain from the broken monarch's forehead. "Poor man. With all that's passed, with all the lives and livelihoods you've sacrificed, how can you still not understand? No matter what your nation's needs, when you use evil means for policy, for earthly goals, the gods and all good men oppose you. Thus, your strategy was doomed from its beginning. With the genius you possess for ruling, I must wonder that you never learned that fact. It's known to men much simpler than yourself. I mourn for you, I truly do."

"Have done. What's passed is passed, so let me die in peace."

"That shall we do," Palamon said. He stood and physicians pressed about the litter. "Now that you lie defeated, that would be the greatest kindness we could give you, by my troth." He turned away from his longtime enemy and placed a hand on Sir Pallador's shoulder. "And so it ends."

"Ah, what a world it is: all ripped asunder, no man's hopes fulfilled. The best and happiest of us have only our survival to rejoice at." The young knight thought of Krisamee, he thought of the future he had pictured for himself as a Knight of Pallas. "What shall become of me?"

"You'll be the prince of our great land and take the robe of office from my shoulders when I die."

Sir Pallador sighed. "That's not the rôle I would have chosen for myself."

"It is the one the gods selected for you, as I've known since first the Priests of Pallas left you with your foster parents," Sir Phebos said gently. "Duty is not often pleasant, but we cannot live without it." He patted the younger man on the shoulder. "There will be some pleasures with it, I am sure, and you will grow into the office."

"So I hope."

"Is anyone here named Pallador?" Flin's voice cut through the rain like a breath of sunshine. Sir Pallador jerked his head toward the sound. Torches lit the night and he saw the knight approach at the head of a large party. Flin and his wife escorted two blanket-wrapped figures at the head of the column. "Bessina and I found these two ladies at the center of that deserted city. They say they know you, Pallador."

Sir Pallador stared at the faces beneath the hooded blankets. The breath went from him; he tried to cry out but could only whisper. "My Krisamee. And Lady Alcyone; I thought you dead, devoured by beasts of foul Ursid or swallowed up by writhing insects. Bless the gods." He fell to his knees before the younger woman. "Ah, what a wonder."

"A wonder in true fact," Bessina said. "When harsh winds struck, a dozen of us flew down to the shelter of yon city's walls. All crumbled up, destroyed, and blackened was that ruined town. But 'mid the fallen stones, we found these two in an undamaged chamber, all surrounded by high stacks of human bones."

Lady Alcyone came forward. " 'Twas awful, what transpired these last few days. Ursid had two enormous mantids, which he kept beside him as his servants."

"Yes, we know them well," Palamon said grimly.

"But they were smaller when he first arrived. They fattened on the forest's animals, and on the thieves which forage through these woods. They'd hunt them down for dinner while Ursid would laugh and cheer them on, then bring them back to Hautre and eat them up before our eyes."

"Indeed, 'twas horrible," Krisamee said. Her shudder caused Sir Pallador to put an arm about her. " 'Twas awful—and he always threatened we would make the next day's meal."

"But I knew better," Lady Alcyone said sadly. "For I knew that some spark of good burned in him still, that he would ne'er allow the death of me or of my daughter. That one faith sustained me through the hours."

"Mother, you're incredibly romantic," Krisamee said with a shake of the head and a sound that was almost a laugh. "We survived because we hid amid the bones and tattered clothing." She turned to Sir Pallador. "But my love, the fact is that we did survive. And now I come to you again."

" 'My love'—what words those are," he replied. "So many things have changed since last I saw you—but one fact remains. I love you, Krisamee. My love grows with each day, and how it pained me all the time I thought that you were lost." He pressed her hand to his cheek. For all his vows, he would have kissed her then, had no one been watching.

Then he looked about and smiled at himself. Every face smiled back at him; he had no secrets before these people. Flin slapped him on the back. "Well, well," the knight said. "A Knight of Pallas with a lady friend—now there's a lad who has spunk."

"My troth," Sir Pallador said. "Had I suspected that my . . ." he held back another instant. "My love for this young maiden would be joyfully received as this, my mind would never have rebelled against it."

"So it should not have," Palamon said. "For all the fact your life was dedicated to high Pallas' Knights, both gods and men had other plans for you. And so rejoice: this maid shall be your bride; that shall be your reward for the great weight you'll carry."

"A good plan," Flin said. He gave Sir Pallador a sly wink. "If you marry her, I'll give you a the best wedding present you'll ever get. I've a warhorse so fine he even makes my wife jealous. I can live without him for her sake and I think you'd look good on him."

Sir Pallador had to laugh. "I thank you," he said.

"Flin, you are a generous man," Palamon said, also with a laugh. Then he put an arm each about Sir Pallador and Krisamee. "And so it is that evil lies defeated—for the nonce— and good men travel to their firesides once again."

Sir Pallador turned to Krisamee, gazed into her moist eyes. "You've heard the king and noble Flin," he said. "If you will have me, I will take you as my bride."

"So shall it be," she whispered. The words almost died, she spoke them so softly. Thus emboldened, Sir Pallador took her in his arms. Then their lips met, to delighted murmurs from all who watched.

"Ah, children," Lady Alcyone said. She wept tears of joy. "How can the world be bad when such a sweet love blossoms on it?"

With that, noblemen and soldiers of the great army gathered themselves and made their way homeward. Palamon and his newfound son returned to the queen's side, husbands returned to wives, and for one night at least, men would sleep soundly on the shores of the Thlassa Mey.

ABOUT THE AUTHOR

DENNIS MCCARTY was born on June 17, 1950, in Grand Junction, a small town in western Colorado. His family traveled a great deal because of his father's work. By the time he had graduated from high school, Dennis had attended eight different public schools, most of them before he was twelve.

He graduated in English from the University of Utah and served four years in the United States Coast Guard. Over the years, his hobbies have included fishing, hunting, photography, and automobile racing.

His greatest love has always been reading and writing fiction, however. He made his first attempt at a novel of science fiction when he was seven. He began writing seriously at the age of twenty; *Flight to Thlassa Mey* was his first published novel.